Praise for Zoë Marriott:

"Zoë Marriott's writing is fabulous."
Children's Books Ireland

"Zoë Marriott has a high level of literary
intelligence and is terrific at rebooting fairy
tales with wonderful descriptions of the natural
world… [She is] a rising star of fantasy fiction."
The Times

"Richly imagined yet sharply topical.
You'll fall in love with Zhi."
L. A. Weatherly, author of the Angel trilogy

"Zoë Marriott has mastered the art of the
retelling. She combines cultural touchstones
with carefully researched historical setting
to create something truly special."
Lauren James, author of
The Loneliest Girl in the Universe

THE HAND, THE EYE & THE HEART

Zoë Marriott

WALKER
BOOKS

First published 2019 by Walker Books Ltd
87 Vauxhall Walk, London SE11 5HJ

2 4 6 8 10 9 7 5 3 1

Text © 2019 Zoë Marriott
Cover illustration © 2019 Kate Forrester

This book has been typeset in Berkeley and Caslon

Printed and bound by CPI Group (UK) Ltd, Croydon CR0 4YY

British Library Cataloguing in Publication Data:
a catalogue record for this book
is available from the British Library

ISBN 978-1-4063-8354-6

www.walker.co.uk

*To all those who generously offered up their
time, experience, expertise and brilliance
to help bring this story into the world.
With deepest love and gratitude.*

Author's note

This book was inspired by several versions of the traditional Chinese story of Mulan. But while the fictional "Red Empire" depicted within its pages is inspired by Chinese history and culture (in much the same way that Tolkien's Middle Earth draws on Celtic and Anglo-Saxon Europe), *The Hand, the Eye and the Heart* is not intended to offer an accurate portrayal of real world China or its people during any point in that country's long, noble history. The Red Empire is a fairy-tale land that never was – except perhaps in dreams. Likewise, though some of the poetry depicted here owes a debt to the work of legendary poet Li Bai, it makes no claim to his genius.

The author would like to thank Alice Fanchiang, Kuo Fanchiang, Kao-Han Fan, Jenni Nock, Si Jialing, Joy Chuah and Dr Pauline Park for their support and invaluable advice. A special thank you is due to Randolf M. for his brilliant personal insights. Particular gratitude is owed to my dear friends Fox Benwell and Dr Susan Ang, and to the talented and wonderful Jay Hulme, for being willing to read this huge manuscript, and for helping me to improve it in a thousand ways, large and small. Any mistakes or any liberties taken in service of the story are my own responsibility.

And finally, thank you to Arts Council England and the Royal Literary Fund for believing in this project and buying me the time and space to deliver it.

CONTENT WARNING: the author would like readers to be aware that this book contains depictions of deadnaming and misgendering. Please use your own best judgement as to whether you will find this content triggering. The book also contains depictions of chest-binding which, while inspired by real practices within certain periods of Chinese history, are entirely unsafe and should not be adopted by any reader under any circumstances.

*"All warfare is based on deception …
Know yourself as you know your enemy …
and you need not fear a hundred battles."*
Sun Tzu, *The Art of War*

One

I should have died when I was seven. Any ordinary child would have. But it was many years before I would realize how far from ordinary I truly was. You've heard the saying that no one is entirely what they seem, yes?

What few people ever have the courage to admit is that this includes ourselves.

To begin with, it was the brilliance of the full moon that saved me. Or, to be more accurate, gave me a chance to save us all.

When I stirred from my sleep that night, surfacing reluctantly from dreams of soaring through ragged clouds above the mountaintop that sheltered our small town, I found pale, bright light shining in my eyes and the pillow hot and damp under my cheek. It was enough to bring me fully awake.

And so I heard the assassin speak.

"Leave Hua Zhou for last."

The unfamiliar voice was close enough to make the pink and gold embroidered peonies of the silk window screen shiver. I jumped, then blinked sleepily. Who was that? What … what had he said? There was only silence now. Had it been another dream? It must have been a dream…

I closed my eyes again.

Then another voice came – not speaking, only a muffled, questioning sound. And in answer, the first man spoke once more: "Old Zhangsun wants him to see his family dead first. Then we can finish him off."

My eyelids snapped wide, my entire body going stiff and heavy with shock. I opened my mouth to cry out – and on a sharply indrawn breath, clenched my teeth together instead. I *couldn't* scream for help. I wasn't safe. They would hear me.

The intruders passed between my window and the moonlight, their shadows trailing stealthily across the silk: one, two, three, four. My breathing was ragged, deafening in my own ears. Too loud. I trapped the panicked wheeze behind my closed teeth, holding my breath. Another shadow passed silently by. Mother and Father would never hear them coming.

My chest ached as if my ribs would crack, but I did not dare to make a sound. Not yet. My eyes followed the assassins' shapes like the deer at bay watches the tiger. One man came close to the window … and paused. The shadow's head tilted as if listening.

He had heard me; sensed me.

He would draw his blade, slice through the thin silk screen and then—

The man's shadow seemed to shake its head before slithering swiftly from sight.

I waited, but no more shadows passed.

And then, then, when I could finally breathe, finally move … I found that I could not.

Fear had seized hold of me, turning my limbs dense and numb, like rock. My familiar moonlit room swam and blurred before my eyes, and then disappeared as I squeezed the burning lids shut so hard that white sparks bloomed across my sight. I wanted to go back to sleep, to pretend I hadn't heard any of it. I wanted this to be a dream. A nightmare.

Father's voice seemed to speak in my mind, calm and yet challenging: *Are you a coward, daughter?*

The first breath seemed to claw my throat as I forced it in.

No, I told my father. *I am of the House of Hua.*

My knuckles popped with strain as they unclamped from the bed covers. I knew I should spring up from the bed, strong and swift – but my fumbling hands could hardly find the strength to push the covers back. I wobbled as I stood, the soft rugs next to my bed seeming to dip and sway beneath my weight, as if the floor had become the deck of a boat.

I swallowed, a dry and painful gulp, and then squared my shoulders.

My journey through the narrow black corridors was clumsy and halting. Every tiny night sound echoing through the house froze me in place with dread. The squeaking of my own feet on the floorboards terrified me. The men might already be inside. They would hear. They might be lurking in the shadows, ahead, right now, waiting for me. What if they caught me – got me before I reached my parents?

By the time I stumbled to a halt outside my father's chambers, I was crying, soft whimpers escaping despite my best efforts. I did not know what I would find in my father's rooms. What if I was too late – what if – what if—

The carved wooden screen that separated Father's bedchamber from the corridor was still closed. No sounds came from within. Torn between fear and overwhelming desperation to know, I shoved the screen back too swiftly, cringing from the squeak of wood sliding against wood.

There was a soft snort from within and then my mother's voice: "Zhilan? What are you doing out of bed?"

Not too late.

Tingling all over with relief, I rushed into the room. "Mother, wake up! There are men in the house!"

I heard her sigh. The moonlight did not reach as far as their bed, and so I only just made out her shape, the pale smudge of her face, as she began to sit up. "Child, it was only a bad dream—"

My father's voice broke in, intent and alert, even though moments before he must have been asleep: "Speak again, daughter."

"They were in the courtyard, Father! They said Zhangsun wanted us dead, but they were to save you for last."

And then, from the other side of the compound, the

frantic jangle of a bell and the sound of Xu Guo Liang –
my father's oldest and most faithful retainer – shouting:
"'Ware! 'Ware! Thieves! Murderers! Raise the house! Wake
the master!"

There was a flurry of movement which I could not
follow in the shadows. My father stepped into the pale
shaft of light from the open screen door, his face grim and
composed. In his hand was a sheathed sword – a bright,
glittering thing that I had never seen before. A quicksilver
flash of moonlight almost blinded me as he drew it from
the scabbard. He stretched, the movements halting and
awkward at first, slowly loosening. His stance changed,
settled, became more balanced somehow, became …
dangerous.

"It's already too late to get you out," he said quietly, not
looking back at us. "They most likely have men waiting
outside for anyone who tries to flee; it's what I would have
done. How many men did you see, Zhilan? Think carefully."

I swallowed. "Six, Father."

"Good girl."

"Zhilan, come to me," my mother said, her voice
urgent. "Come here."

I darted towards her on eager feet and flung myself
into her arms where she sat on the edge of the bed. The
swollen roundness of her belly kept me from pressing as
close as I wanted, but I was still able to bury my face in
her sweet-smelling, tumbled hair. I felt the trapped-bee
hum of her heartbeat against my cheek and the rough,
quick rasp of her breath washing over my neck.

There was a terrible sound outside – a panicked wailing

that I recognized as coming from one of the young serving girls, but which sounded like the screams of a trapped rabbit in a snare. Xu Guo Liang shouted my father's name again, and then there were thuds and crashes. Windows and doors flying open, or being slammed shut? Running footsteps moved closer and closer. The men were coming.

"I can't risk leaving you alone. I must meet them here. Jia Mei, get down in the corner. As low as you can. Don't move, don't make a sound." Father seemed to hesitate. "Don't ... let her see."

Wordlessly, my mother obeyed, rising with a groan of discomfort and urging me into the furthest and darkest cranny of the room. She pushed me down to the floor, following with another pained noise as she drew her legs up, and then embraced me again, clutching me painfully tight.

"Father will look after us," she whispered. "All will be well. Father will keep us safe. Nothing bad is going to happen."

For the first time in my life, I knew that my mother was lying to me. I trembled, hiding my face in her hair again.

There was a thunder of hasty footsteps right outside the open door. Father's blade flashed up – and then lowered as Xu Guo Liang stumbled into view. There was a large knife, a kitchen knife, clutched awkwardly in the old man's fist. His lined face was chalky-grey behind his white beard, and his clothes were rucked and dishevelled, but his eyes were alight with fury.

"I am here, Master," he said breathlessly.

"Get behind me," Father ordered with a jerk of his head in our direction. "Protect them."

The elderly servant slipped past him, bowed to my mother with his usual grave politeness, and then took up a position before us with both hands – visibly trembling – clenched around the long handle of the knife. My eyes were drawn irresistibly to the white, skinny ankles that poked out of the bottom of his rumpled robes. His bare feet were as thin and fragile as a bird's.

"Zhou..." my mother spoke Father's name hastily, her voice cracking on the word.

"I'm sorry," my father said, glancing back over his shoulder. His voice did not tremble, but I felt as if a wave of sorrow had washed over me at the sound of it. "I am so sorry, my love."

A flicker in the darkness. Some change in the quality of the shadows. My mother stiffened. Father's sword lifted once more.

The first assassin entered the room. Without hesitation, he attacked my father.

These men knew who Hua Zhou was. They knew that the wounds he had taken had almost killed him, and had ended his military career. They believed he would be easy prey.

But the assassins had not reckoned with Hua Zhou's iron will. My father might be unable to run any more – but he could stand, and that meant he could fight. And when a man fought as he did, what need was there to run?

One by one, the would-be killers seemed to fling themselves on to his blade, eager to meet death at his hands. Mother tried to press my face into her shoulder and cover my eyes, but her hands were shaking too hard to hold me against my struggles. And I did struggle. Somehow I knew that I had to see.

In moments, Father single-handedly slew four of our attackers. They fell before him, and their blood was black in the half-light. But as he battled with the fifth – faster or more cunning than the others, perhaps – the last one slipped past him. Slipped past him, and came for us.

Xu Guo Liang let out a cry of defiance, slashing wildly at the air with the cook's knife. His great spirit was like a flame in the darkness. With a high-pitched squeal of metal, he caught the assassin's blade on his own, trying to force him back.

There was a meaty sound, followed by a wet, bubbling gasp. I saw the kitchen knife fall, unbloodied, from the servant's grip, and Xu Guo Liang crumpled to the floor before us. His outstretched hand slapped limply against my bare foot. I jerked backwards with a choked cry. There was nowhere to go – my mother was behind me. Long pale fingers twitched against my skin, but his open eyes stared past me. He wasn't moving. His chest did not rise or fall. He … he…

Mother screamed as the assassin carelessly kicked the old man's body away. A droplet of blood landed on the side of my face. I still remember how warm it was.

Fast as a striking snake, my father wrenched his sword from the fifth assassin's chest, whirled towards the threat that loomed above us – and faltered, his bad leg going out from under him. With a yell of anguish, he fell. He fell.

It was like watching a mountain topple.

Everything up to that moment is as clear as the slow,

serene drift of clouds moving over still water. But what happened next, I barely recall. I can only believe it happened because my father gravely described it to me, so that I could understand what I had done, and accept it. My mother always refused to speak of it.

The assassin stooped over me and my mother. His shadow enveloped us, blocking Father from sight. The blade in his hand was black and wet – it slashed through the air towards my mother's throat.

And I, the seven-year-old daughter of the house, with arms as small and thin as twigs, who had never even seen a weapon before, let alone held one, ripped free of my mother's desperate grasp and seized the fallen kitchen knife from the floor.

I stabbed the murderer with it.

You might question how my tiny hands had the strength – how I even knew where to aim the blade – but somehow I managed to drive the knife into the assassin's gut hard enough that it wrenched from my fingers as he flailed back. He fell with a howl of surprise and fury, and landed in range of my father's sword.

It only took a single stroke of that great blade to finish him. Panting, Father staggered to his feet and turned to stare at me in disbelief.

"Don't you dare go near my mother!" I snarled, my bloodstained hands curled into fists – shaking not with fear, my father swore later, but with fury. "I hope it hurts, you coward!"

Two

A single lantern lit my parents' faces with wavering orange light. The servants huddled in the other half of the kitchen, warming themselves by the vast, smoking cavern of the hearth fire, whispering and casting us worried looks. The doors of the dim, low-roofed chamber were barred and barricaded, the windows shuttered and bolted; we were waiting for dawn, and for our hastily dispatched groom to return with the town guard.

In the meantime, with patient, steady hands, and a piece of rag, Father cleaned the drying blood from my small fingers.

"Why now?" my mother asked, hushed. "After all these years... I thought the empress had forgotten us. How can anyone carry a grudge for so long?"

"It doesn't matter. Whatever her reasons for acting, she is finished. I found a note – written in her own hand – ordering our deaths! The emperor will never forgive her for this. She won't have the power to hurt us again. What matters is…" He lowered his voice, whispering above my head. "What matters is Zhilan. No ordinary girl could have done what she did. No ordinary child. This can only be a sign."

"A sign of what?" my mother demanded sharply. Her tone made me flinch. She had never spoken to him in such a way before, not in my hearing. "A sign that she was born under a death curse? That she should never have been born at all?"

I bowed my head, tears prickling at my eyes. The fear and twisted excitement of the night's events were swiftly transmuting into that vague, terrible child's guilt of having transgressed without knowing precisely how. Kind old Xu Guo Liang, who had gravely guided my first steps and called me "young mistress", was … gone. I had made my mother sorrowful and disappointed. I wanted to take it back. Even if I didn't really understand what "it" was. I was certain I had protected my mother – so surely that must be all right. But I could not … exactly … remember how. Lingering over it too much made me feel rather sick, with swooping feelings in my stomach and cold, clammy sweat springing up on the back of my neck.

Mother reached out as if to touch my hair, and I yearned towards the contact – but her fingers clenched, and her hand fell to cup her swollen stomach protectively instead. "No *normal* little girl *could* act as she did."

Father's fingers did not stop their gentle work. He dipped the cloth into the red-stained water in the chipped dish and turned over my left hand to scrub at my palm. "Zhilan is better than normal. She must have a great destiny. The heavens themselves intervened to spare her."

"What *destiny* could require a girl to kill a man before she has even bled herself? I—" She cut herself off with a gasp, and the silence stung like vinegar in a fresh cut.

I huddled in upon myself, waiting. But whatever she might have said next remained unuttered. She ended their argument by going into labour nearly a month early.

A day later, she was delivered of a small, rather delicate, but ferociously healthy baby. A boy. A brother. An heir. They called him Da Xiong.

I do not think Mother marked or even remembered her strange conversation with Father. I certainly forgot it at the time.

But Father did not forget.

Mother often liked to say: *All great men make enemies.*

My father was a very great man.

Twenty years before my birth, raiders from the Land of Clouds attacked the borders of the empire – and Father, not yet sixteen years old, received the red-sealed scroll, calling him to fight. To represent the honour of the House of Hua on the battlefield. And that he did. By the age of thirty, he rose to the rank of Iron General of the Southern Provinces, and became the late Emperor Gao Zi's favourite. When the emperor's half-brother marched on the City of Endless Serenity to try to depose Gao Zi, Father's armies confronted them at the Heavenly Gate of a Thousand Steps that lead to the Imperial Palace.

Even though the usurper's army outnumbered them four to one, my father's soldiers drove the traitors back, back, down the thousand steps one by one, until they had nowhere to go but into the great Gold Dust River. There, the Imperial Army drowned them.

But it was in this moment of triumph that Father himself was undone. Taking a spear thrust to his leg that shattered the bone and shredded its tendon, he fell into the same waters that had swallowed his enemies. Hidden amongst tall reeds, he lay undiscovered for four days. By the time he was found, the emperor's best doctors declared him beyond any mortal aid.

I was less than a month old, and my birth had been a hard one that nearly ended my mother's life. But that did not stop her.

She packed up household and baby and drove us halfway across the country to the capital city in under two weeks. When she arrived, she took over my father's care and, defying all the naysayers, brought him back from the brink of death.

Overjoyed, the late emperor offered my father a title, lands, the income from a hundred towns and a post as his close advisor. But Father had been changed by his four endless days lying in the shadow of death, and the following weeks of sickness. He would never be fit to run into battle again.

With polite reverence, he refused the emperor's honours and begged only to be allowed to go into peaceful retirement, to raise sons who would fight for the emperor's sons one day.

It was a risky choice. Had his Imperial Highness been offended, our family might have paid a heavy price. But though Gao Zi was a stern ruler, he was also known for his wisdom. He granted my father's wish and sent him home with trunks loaded with gifts of books, precious relics and only a reasonable amount of gold. More than any of these, though, my father treasured the emperor's sincere blessing.

"Hua Zhou," the emperor is said to have declared, "is the most honourable, dutiful and humble servant I have ever had. Let him be praised, and let others seek to emulate his example! If only the heavens had given me a son such as him."

Others were … not so pleased with my father.

Empress Zhangsun had borne the emperor two sons. One had been banished for plotting against the emperor, and the other died falling out of a window whilst drunk. Perhaps unsurprisingly, she was said to have taken her husband's words as a personal slight upon her and her offspring. The empress could hardly revenge herself upon the emperor for the humiliation, but my father and mother were another matter.

Zhangsun bided her time. It took over seven years, but at last, she acted to take her revenge. And just as my father's bravery had led to his downfall, Empress Zhangsun's resentment led to hers. Implicated by the assassins' accomplices, she was disgraced, deposed and exiled.

We were lucky, of course. If she had been the mother of a son who stood in the line of succession, perhaps it would have saved her and sealed our family's fate. But her only surviving children were girls. And so the emperor took a new empress – his Most Pure, Fragrant and Virtuous Concubine Wu Fen, a lady who had long been his favourite, and who had just been delivered of a healthy boy, Li Xian. And when Gao Zi died, it was Wu Fen who was at his side. And it is Wu Fen who reigns now, not as regent – but as Daughter of Heaven. Our first female emperor.

While these cataclysmic changes shook our nation like earth tremors shake the distant mountains, equally astonishing changes were happening within the House of Hua. For, as the weeks passed, and things settled down again into the normal pattern of day-to-day life, Father carefully, methodically – stealthily – began to test me.

At first he must have been disappointed. Despite the seemingly impossible feat I had accomplished, I showed no signs of supernatural speed, enhanced reflexes or unusual strength. After some thought, he offered me a variety of weapons, in case my gift was that of inborn aptitude, but he desisted after I dropped his dagger and nearly pierced his foot with it.

Still, he could not get the memory of that night out of his head. His daughter, standing in the darkness, bloodied and unafraid, victorious at only seven years old. If I had been a boy, he would have known I was meant to be a general, a commander of great armies, and scourge of the enemies of the empire. All a son would have needed to be worthy of this great destiny was training.

But girls could not be trained in the martial arts.

Yet, against all odds, against all the teachings of sages and scholars and the rules of common decency and common sense, a little girl had saved his wife and unborn son.

What if one day she was called on to do so again?

What if that was her fate?

How could he leave her, leave his family, unprepared for that day?

His answer came the afternoon when he attempted one final test. He had noticed that I tended to have a somewhat reckless bent – skipping happily along the tops of the tall, meandering walls of our home compound (before my mother scolded me down), attempting to climb scraggly vines to reach the peak of a large rock (before the servants caught me), and teasing the legendarily savage guard dog that resided on the steps of the mayor's house (before making a friend of it). Was it possible, he wondered, that my gift was a lack of fear?

He had one of the servants call me from the women's quarters to his study, knowing that I would have to cross the large, open central courtyard to do so. Then he took his blunt practice sword and concealed himself behind the squat, dark trunk of the venerable magnolia tree that dominated the centre of the courtyard with its clouds of pink, wine-cup-shaped blooms.

As I passed beneath the magnolia tree – reaching up on tiptoe to brush the very ends of my fingers through the golden pollen of the sweet-smelling flowers, as I always did – Father lunged at me from his hidden position, sword raised.

My shrill shriek banished any suspicion that I was a fearless child. But even as the cry broke from my throat, I felt something shift within me, some odd, yet utterly natural twist of my inner self that happened without conscious thought, without any movement of my physical body at all.

As a tiny fish swiftly darts and manoeuvres among the stones and currents of a river, so I slipped sideways through the light to what I felt, without really knowing how or why, was a place of safety.

That is how it felt to me. To my father's eyes, though, something extraordinary occurred.

I vanished.

Later, as I sat in the calm quiet of my father's study, clutching the last crumbs of a piece of honeycomb – a rare treat – and still trembling a little, he explained to me what I had done. What I was.

There were many names. Some of them I had even heard before, in the stories my mother or my nursemaid told me before bed. Light-shaper. Mask-maker. Shadow-weaver. Child-of-a-phoenix.

Banner-breaker.

Once there had been hundreds like me, my father said. They had been the pride of the great Red Emperor, the founder of our nation. Their name came from a trick they had famously deployed against the barbarian invaders from the west, who had sought to take the empire for their own. If the tide of battle seemed about to turn against the Red Emperor, they would hide him with shadows, and create a perfect illusion of the imperial banner elsewhere on the field. When the enemies swarmed that new location to try to capture the emperor, they would instead find themselves surrounded and cut off, while the prize they had sacrificed themselves to seize melted away like smoke in their hands.

But the number of such illusionists had dwindled as the empire grew. My father guessed that it was because, while at first banner-breakers were respected – and trained – regardless of gender, once the empire was established it became seen as undesirable, even unnatural, for a girl to possess the ability. Females who could use *qi* this way were taught that their gifts were shameful, or taught nothing at all.

Now only a handful of people – boys – in each generation would be born with the gift, and they were highly prized, regardless of rank or family status, and earmarked for high military service.

"My commanders saw me as a gift from heaven and welcomed me into their ranks – but they always insisted my ability was kept a closely guarded secret. One should never freely give away useful information, unless in doing so some more useful information can be gleaned. The only ones alive who know it are the emperor himself, your mother … and now you."

As I watched, spellbound, he lifted the familiar green-brown head of his walking stick – and the handle was a carved dragon no more, but a live one, curling around his broad, scarred hand. Its scales glinted as it stretched, sinuous and catlike, a tiny puff of smoke escaping the be-fanged jaws. I gasped, expecting to smell the magical scent of a dragon's vapour, but the only smells were honey, sweat-dampened silk and the warm, waxy wood that panelled Father's study. With the next blink, the dragon was frozen in stone again, stiff and unmoving.

"It makes sense now," my father said, a gleam of feverish excitement lighting his eyes. "Your ability to shape illusions is what saved you and your mother from the assassin. Not extraordinary speed or strength. He simply didn't see you. He drove *himself* forward on to your blade."

For an instant, I felt the smooth wooden grip of the kitchen knife against my palm – smelled the wet gush of iron-stinking blood drenching my hands. I still did not remember much of what I had done. I did not want to. But sometimes ... sometimes I imagined how it must have felt when the knife went into that man's stomach. And my imaginings felt like memory.

I swallowed hard, the taste of honey turning sickly on my tongue. "Why do *I* have this gift? What use can I make of it?" I imagined what Mother would say – how she would purse her lips and how her eyes would dart away from me – and whispered, "Will ... will any man wish to marry a girl with such a power?"

My father's face changed then, and he leaned forward, grasping my forearm. "Any man worth marrying will treasure you for all your unique beauties and abilities, just as anyone with a discerning eye values the natural patterns in a unique piece of jade. You have a great destiny, my daughter. The heavens have granted you this power for a reason, just as they did me. Perhaps, like the great lady hero Dou Xianniang, you will undertake a legendary quest of honour for the gods. Or perhaps, like the wife of the Red Emperor, one day you will ride into battle at your husband and sons' sides. Many stories call the Red Empress a banner-breaker, you know."

None of the stories Mother or the servants had told me said that. None of them mentioned the Red Empress ever being in battle at all, let alone taking the role of banner-breaker. And Dou Xianniang was supposed to be a fallen woman, an outlaw, who had come to a sticky end. As must all women who failed to respect their rightful place.

Perhaps they tell different stories to daughters than sons…

Unaware of my thoughts, Father squeezed my arm and pressed a dry, whiskery kiss to my forehead. But he looked away as he added, "Besides, there is no reason for anyone but you and I to know of this."

Three

Ten years later…

The war horn's low, melancholy voice rang out as I threaded a strand of scarlet silk on to the shuttle of my loom. Strung tight on the warp, thousands of coloured threads – a half-formed picture of red-crested herons in flight – seemed to tremble.

There was a sharp clatter. Mother, half-hidden from me behind her own loom on the opposite side of the sunny room, had dropped her bamboo shuttle. Her deft fingers were frozen on the silk pattern of pink peonies taking shape on her long, narrow *kesi* tapestry. The single dark eye that I could see flashed with startled fright.

"It is not the call to battle," I spoke into the sudden silence hastily. "It – it is only the call to gather. We're not under attack."

Yet.

For months we had listened in increasing disbelief to the stories of the rebellion across the five rivers. Stories of the rogue general – Feng Shi Chong, nicknamed the Leopard – who had betrayed Emperor Wu Fen, and the terrible crimes he and his army of murderers, rapists and thieves had carried out. And now – now the war horn. The army was calling the men of our region, our *town*, to gather.

They were looking for conscripts.

Mother gave a long, shaky exhalation of breath. "They have come for him."

The great horn bellowed again.

As the sound faded, I heard the distinctive squeal of the stiff screen door that lead to Father's study on the other side of the courtyard. Then the *crunch, drag, crunch, drag* of his steps as he passed by the weaving room on his way to the great gates that guarded our home.

Mother's hands lifted slowly from the tapestry on her loom and pressed over her face, concealing her expression from me. I didn't need to see it. I knew. I stared blankly at my own weaving, telling myself comforting lies: *They can't call him up. Not again. They wouldn't. He's too sick, too weak. He already gave up his health and his youth for the empire. There's nothing else left.*

Nothing, said a cold voice at the back of my mind, *except his life.*

My own hands, still clutching at the shuttle and thread, did not seem to belong to me. They looked white and frail, like bird bones. A memory clutched at my heart – an old man's skinny, pale ankles, and his thin fingers twitching against my skin. In the corners of my vision, shadows swarmed, running up the walls wherever the light failed to reach. Against my will, I jerked around to look.

There was nothing there.

I laid the shuttle down with a soft click. There was a rising babble of men's voices outside. The village gathering place was only a few paces beyond the copper handles of our jade-and-vermillion-painted gates. The sight of those gates was barred from me by the tapestries and heavy, carved wood screens that divided the women's quarters from the courtyard. But if I were to step into the hallway, or better yet stand in the reception room in the southern wing of the house, I would be able to hear properly. Hear what the men were saying.

Hear which names were called.

I rose to my feet in a graceful, unhurried movement, allowing the emerald-and-russet silk of my *shanqun* gown to fall into place around my slippers with a soft whisper as I rearranged my shawl over my elbows.

"Where are you going?" Mother asked, voice sharpened with a razor-edge of panic. "You cannot go out!"

"I know, Mother," I said calmly. "Of course I won't go out. I just need to use the water closet."

"Zhilan! Please, don't—"

Don't leave me alone, don't act so strangely, don't disappoint me by failing to act like a proper daughter again...

I cut her off gently. "I will be back in a moment, I promise."

And it wasn't a lie. I had no intention of going out. And would use the water closet. Eventually.

I left the room before she could say any more, pulling the screen door gently shut behind me. Then I hooked my shawl messily over my shoulders, seized great crumpled handfuls of my skirts in both hands and darted down the narrow, wood-panelled passageway, soft slippers skidding over the floorboards. A lightning-fast glance out of the wooden lattice that separated the women's wing from the reception room showed me a view of shadowy banners, hanging still in the air above the top of our outer wall, dark against a pale sky. The imperial banners? I scurried on, hoping to avoid any servants on the way—

"Sister?"

I stopped in place, squeezing my eyes shut. "Yes, Xiao Xia? Shouldn't you be with our brother in the schoolroom?"

"I heard a big noise – a strange noise – and there is shouting outside. What does it mean? Are – are the bad men coming? The ones who eat little girls?" Her voice wobbled on the last words.

My shoulders slumped involuntarily.

Letting go of my dress, I crouched down to hold out my hand. Xiao Xia's plump, dimpled fingers grasped mine, and I realized that she was shaking, though I no longer was. My hand looked strong, weathered and capable around her tiny one – like my own familiar hand again.

Gazing into Xiao Xia's wide, worried eyes under her thick fringe, I reminded myself that I was sixteen, nearly seventeen. An adult. I had stopped cutting my hair and begun pinning it up into a tall conch-binding two years ago. Xiao Xia was only eight.

I permitted myself a short, resigned sigh.

"There's no need to be afraid. The bad men are miles and miles away! They're just having a public meeting, and Father has gone out to deal with it. Why don't you come and sit with Mother and me? I'll let you sort my threads."

"The pretty silk ones?" she squeaked, her face lighting up.

"If you like," I said, my smile coming a little more naturally as I straightened to my full height.

"Can … can Da Xiong come, too?" She leaned in to whisper. "He was more frightened than me."

I blinked, looked around, and saw another pair of bright, dark eyes – the twin of our mother's and my own – peering around the corner at me. He startled as our gazes met, making as if to dart back out of sight. At ten, he was old enough to understand exactly what "the big noise" was. And, if I knew him, perceptive enough to be afraid of exactly the same thing I was.

I reached out a hand towards him. "Come out then, Da Xiong Mao."

Da Xiong emerged and ran forward, though he stopped short of grasping my other hand. His dimple winked shyly. "I'm not a panda," he told me seriously. "I'm a boy."

I silently congratulated myself on the use of the old nickname.

"Oh? Let me check." He didn't attempt to dodge when I prodded at his round cheek, squinting at him in feigned concentration. The dimple deepened when I finally shook my head and pronounced: "No. Definitely panda."

Xiao Xia giggled.

The deep, rattling call of the war horn sounded once more, and both the children flinched.

"Come along. Don't step on my hems," I scolded, raising my voice above the noise as I led them quickly back towards the weaving room. "Watch where you put your feet. Now, what has Ai Bo been teaching you today?"

"Songs!" Xiao Xia said eagerly. "Would you like to hear?"

"Ah – not just now, dear one! I'm sure Mother would *love* to hear. Later." Xiao Xia had a face as delicate and lovely as a hummingbird's wing, and a voice as shrill and discordant as a wailing cat. Ai Bo would have done much better to focus on teaching my sister to play a *dizi* flute so that no one asked her to sing, ever. "And what about you, Da Xiong Mao?"

"Maps," he said, voice soft. "Geography, terrain, provinces and territories, names of rivers … things I'll need to know to be a soldier. When I'm old enough."

I swallowed hard. "You must tell Father about that when he returns."

"Where did Father go?" Xiao Xia asked. "He never goes anywhere!"

"Well, today he went to the town square." I released Xiao Xia's hand and pushed back the screen of the weaving room, forestalling any further questions.

"Look who I found," I said brightly, nudging my sister in ahead of me and squeezing Da Xiong's shoulder before releasing him. "Visitors for us, Mother. Aren't we lucky? Ai Bo seems to have let them go early today. I can't think why."

"Oh! How … nice. You must have worked very hard for your teacher to release you so quickly! I shall talk to her later." Mother cast me a withering look. She knew that Ai Bo would be in the servants' quarters gossiping, half in glee and half in terror, about the latest stories of the rogue general's terrible deeds – just as Mother knew that my abandonment of her had not been motivated by duty to my siblings. Her hand, as she reached out to draw Da Xiong to her, was shaking.

I couldn't leave her again. I would have to wait with them. This time I managed to hold my sigh behind my teeth.

We sat. We waited. Xiao Xia sang for us, and made a tangled mess of my threads. Da Xiong explained in a soft, grave voice the lessons he was learning. The war horn did not ring out again.

But Father did not return.

The time when Mother would normally have gone bustling away to chivvy the servants about the evening meal came and went. None of us stirred. Even Xiao Xia didn't complain about being hungry: the nervous atmosphere taking its toll upon her. Night was beginning to draw in by the time we heard the familiar steps – uneven, with the faint drag on the left – carrying Father slowly but unhesitatingly to the weaving room.

"Father!" Xiao Xia crowed with uncomplicated relief as he pushed back the screen. "You're back at last!"

I rose slowly to my feet. Across the room, Mother did the same. My gaze alighted upon Father's worn, handsome face, with its long, noble bones and grey streaked beard – upon the expression of grave solemnity that

Xiao Xia's delightful enthusiasm would usually have lightened – and then his hands. One clasped the smooth jade head of his ebony walking stick, as it always did. The other … the other…

"You have the scroll," Da Xiong said blankly. "The red-sealed scroll. They called you up."

"Yes, my son," Father said. The words were kind but very, very tired. "It is my honour to serve."

Blinking rapidly, I looked into his face again. But Father's sad, grey-brown eyes were not on Da Xiong or on me. They were focused beyond us, in the now dim weaving room. On Mother.

Behind me I heard the tiniest possible sound, so quiet that it was almost inaudible, so quiet that it was impossible to know what it had been – perhaps a soft intake of breath, or a gasp of pain. It was enough. I whipped around, the silken layers of my gown billowing around me like the sails of a ship, and reached out just in time to catch Mother before she fainted.

"You are sure you are well enough to be up?" Father asked gently as Mother knelt opposite him at the end of the low dining table. The servants glided silently around us, casting long, flickering shadows on the red silk walls, arranging platters of steamed rice, stewed meat and stir-fried greens, soft steamed buns and soup. "I can have the maid bring you a tray in your room."

"Of course! I am not ill – it was only standing up so suddenly," she said, as bright as shards of broken glass. I could almost see their glint in the soft lantern-light. The servants finished laying the table and departed, the last one drawing the screen door shut behind him with a soft click.

My heart was laden in my chest. *She isn't going to tell him.*

Mother had not confided in me. She hadn't told anyone. But though I may not understand my mother, or she me, I did know her. The fearful hope I glimpsed on her face was as obvious to me as a declaration, even if I had not observed the telltale signs of sickness in the mornings, the slight puffiness in her face, the way she had been eating pickled plums by the jar...

Looking conscious of the awkward pause, she reached for her cup. "I should have been more careful. Leaping around that way was foolish. A woman of my years knows better—" She cut herself off with a tiny choke.

Yes, I knew her, and I knew the thoughts behind that expression.

I can do it this time. That was what she was thinking. *I can do it.* No longer would the townsmen look at my father with confusion and pity, wondering why he refused to take a second, more fruitful wife. She knew he would never do it while she lived, that he would view it as a betrayal even if no one else judged it so. He had never blamed her. But their eyes did. Only one boy in the house! Only one boy for the war hero! The waste of it!

She had never once said it to me, but I had seen her think it many times: *You should have been a son. Why couldn't you have been a son?*

"I am glad that you are well," Father said. "Now, what of you children? You are all very quiet today. What have you been up to?" His cheer was less brittle than Mother's, but no less feigned.

He wasn't going to say anything either. We would sit here and eat, and pretend everything was normal. That the red-sealed scroll was not tucked neatly into his belt pouch. That he had not just received the equivalent of a death sentence from the army.

The Leopard's men did not fight with honour. They did not take prisoners or negotiate. They were butchers, and if my father went to fight them he would die. That was reality.

I heard the dry swallowing noise as Da Xiong, beside me, visibly struggled to speak, then shook his head, bowing his shoulders over his bowl. Xiao Xia frowned at him, finished chewing a dumpling, and said, "What was that big noise today, Father? Zhilan said you were going to a meeting! Who with?"

"Xiao Xia—" Mother began.

"Is that bad Leopard man coming here? I think you should fight him. Then he would run away." My little sister nodded wisely and slurped her soup.

"That's enough," Mother said, too late.

Xiao Xia's face crumpled in confusion. "Why—"

Da Xiong finally looked up. "I'm sorry, Father."

"For what?" Father asked calmly. His refusal to comprehend was like a stone wall, and Da Xiong quailed before its blankness. His head bowed further and he said no more, although the words were splattered before us for all to see. *I'm sorry I'm not big enough. I'm sorry I'm not old enough. I'm sorry I can't take your place.*

And Da Xiong didn't know the worst thing. He didn't know what Mother might do if this pregnancy ended, like so many others, in miscarriage, or a heartbreaking still-birth. What she might do if she failed for the last time and Father was … gone.

She had nearly done it once before.

The doctors said she had not been in her right mind, that the loss of two late-term pregnancies within a year had unbalanced her humours and temporarily stolen her reason. But I would never forget the sight of her face, calm and determined, hair and clothes perfectly neat, as my panicked father wrestled the cup of poison from her hand.

It had taken all his strength to do it.

"Father," I said, making sure that my voice was utterly calm, that my face was composed and my gaze even. "I realize that you do not know the new emperor well—"

"That unnatural woman," Mother muttered, apparently from habit. She kept her voice just low enough that Father could pretend not to hear it, just as he always did.

I cleared my throat and went on, hands clenching into an icy knot under the table. "But surely your exceptional service under her husband would win you some recognition. If you were to write to her, or visit court perhaps, and explain your state of health – I have heard of exemptions being granted in some cases. Just for a few years. Until Da Xiong is old enough to carry the family honour."

My father gave me a long, serious look. My lead-weight heart seemed to plummet through my ribs to the pit of my stomach. "Drink your soup."

The rebuff was kind, but unmistakable. Da Xiong's small hand found mine under the table and squeezed for an instant before it darted away again.

We sat. We ate. We did not talk any more.

After dinner we scattered like dry seeds in an autumn wind. My father went to his study. I followed him there.

"I am tired tonight, daughter. I do not wish to talk." He sighed, leaning heavily on his walking stick, already about to turn away.

I interrupted using the only weapon I had. "Mother is with child again."

He rocked back as if from a blow, desperate sadness, anxiety and the faintest hint of joy flickering across his face. For a moment, I thought he would fall. Then his shoulders sagged, and he drew one hand across his eyes.

The quiet drew out between us, trembling with unsaid things.

"Thank you for telling me," he said at last.

I had never heard his voice so dull. It was as if he were already defeated. I couldn't bear it. "Won't you at least write to the emperor?" I pleaded.

He took his hand from his face. "I spoke to the censor today. The war is going badly – they are desperate for men. No exemptions will be granted."

No, it can't be. I can't let it be. Ancestors help me, I should have been a son…

"Father … Father, listen. Any one of us would be willing to surrender our life for the good of the empire. That is our privilege and our honour." I tried to keep my voice level, tried to express myself with logic and intelligence instead of emotion. Yet as the words poured forth, I could feel tears welling in my eyes and my hands reached out to beseech him. "But if *you* go, and – and something happens. To you. Or to the baby. You know what Mother will try to do. What will happen to the House of Hua then? To our family? If both of you are gone? Da Xiong is not old enough to be the head of our household! And for what? What good will it do the emperor? Your courage burns brighter than anything, but your lungs are ruined and your leg is weak. You are *vital* to us, vital to Mother and Xiao Xia and Da Xiong – but to the army you … you would only be a burden."

His sagging shoulders straightened until he looked into my eyes. His face had become still and stern, deep lines carving out a mask that showed no emotion. "Zhilan. Your intentions are good, but you seek the impossible: a way out. There is no way out. Not with honour. The Leopard is a perversion of everything we hold dear and he must be stopped. *Someone* must fight for the empire, *someone* must fight for the House of Hua. This is the world. What is, is."

"I should have been a son…" The words slipped out, and I felt myself blanch.

For the first time since he had returned to the house with the red-sealed scroll, a faint smile moved his pale lips. "You would have made me very proud, I think." The smile died. "I will begin preparing to leave tomorrow. Do not increase my burdens by interfering, my daughter. This is not women's business."

I let myself be pushed, tenderly yet inexorably, from the room. The soft sound of the door closing made me flinch.

Not women's business.

I should have been a son.

Someone must fight for the House of Hua.

A son…

Four

Many things changed after the night the assassins came. My relationship with my mother never quite recovered from what she had seen me do. And my father's reputation, already a fearsome thing, became the kind of story that young men whisper around a campfire at night to give themselves bravery.

Hua Zhou, the Wild Tiger, who retired a hero and killed six assassins – or perhaps it was ten, or even twenty – single-handedly to protect his home.

Hua Zhou, the greatest general the Red Empire ever had, the greatest swordsman ever to walk from the field of battle alive.

Hua Zhou, the living legend.

It was after the night of assassins that the boys began to come. Throughout the long dry summers of my childhood, every trade caravan brought at least one challenger for my father.

Some were brash and cocky, seeking to make their own names by throwing my father's legacy down. Others were reverent and wished to become his students. Many had the names of great houses. A few had no name at all.

But despite their many differences, all the boys had two things in common...

I thought of that now, as I crept through the darkened house. My sleeping robe drifted around my ankles and wrists like white mist as I walked soundlessly past my father's bedchamber and his study to the furthest room of the men's wing. I hesitated outside for one moment, fighting the instincts that cried out at me to turn back. Then I slid open the dark, carved wood screen and stepped over the threshold, before closing myself within.

Merely by standing there, I was breaking my father's sternest and most long-standing prohibition for me. For this room, still and dim and seemingly empty, the walls lined with cedar cabinets, the floor with simple woven rush mats, was the *wu kwan* – the place where Father stored all his weapons and his armour and uniforms from his army days. Where he had trained me in wushu and banner-breaking since I was seven.

From the first day of those lessons, I had been forbidden to enter this room or touch anything in it without his presence and permission. Tonight, I entered with every intention of touching Father's things. In fact, I was going to steal them.

I pressed one hand flat over my heart and willed its rapid pace to slow, counting my breaths. *He who is victorious knows when to fight,* I reminded myself, quoting from the books on warfare that Father had let me read. *The quality of swift decision in a soldier is like the swoop of a falcon that allows it to capture its prey.*

There was no turning back.

The first thing all the challengers had in common was that none stood a chance of defeating my father in battle. From various hiding places around the compound, I would press my eye to a crack in the window screen or door, listening out warily for the footsteps of my mother, and stare, shivering, at my father's face in these moments. I hardly knew if what I felt was fear or excitement.

It never took him more than a few movements to disarm any of his challengers. Sometimes, with the best, he would draw them out, allowing them to attempt some of their favourite tricks. But, usually before my count had reached a full minute, the hopeful duellists would see their sword go flying and feel Father's blade pressed to a vital point on their body while they sprawled, dazed, on the gravel.

I got into the habit of assessing them. Their weaknesses, their flaws, their failings.

This one was not strong enough for the sword he wielded. This one favoured his left leg – an old injury. This one was too sure of himself, and this one too tentative. After a while I could guess, almost as soon as they began to move, how they would fail...

Swiftly, I stripped off the light, gauzy fabric of my robe and bundled it into the back of one of the cabinets where it would not be seen. Tugging harshly in my haste and causing tears to spring to my eyes, I pulled my hair from its long sleeping plait – the tip of which reached past my waist – and instead coiled it tightly into a mannish topknot. Securing the hair with two long bronze pins and a strip of rawhide from a ceramic pin dish on the shelf of the closet, I inspected myself in the round, polished bronze mirror that stood there for the purpose. The unaccustomed style did make me look more masculine, my face more angular and less soft. That would help with my mask of illusion later.

I lingered over the reflection for a moment, and then another, studying the blurred lines intently. A shiver of something, something cold and hot at the same time – fear? Delight? – made the skin on my back prickle with gooseflesh.

Tearing my eyes away from the mirror, I opened another cabinet and drew forth breeches of soft, supple leather and a tunic of heavy undyed cotton, and pulled them on. Originally they had been Father's. He had ordered a confused servant to alter them years ago – to fit me, for training. It hadn't required much: he had a slight, whipcord frame, while I was tall and broad for a girl, taking after my well-built mother. The garments were always kept here, hanging next to Father's things, and so, even when freshly laundered, they always smelled of him.

I do this for my family and for my country, I told my trembling hands. *It is my duty, and by embracing duty, all actions become correct.*

My hands didn't stop shaking. Why were they shaking so much? I had expected to be afraid. I just hadn't expected to feel so strange, so … so *excited.*

Concentrate, Zhilan. Concentrate on what you must do.

There was a second thing all the challengers had in common. Whether they were awed and astonished by his skill, or chagrined and bitter, none of them ever realized what Father was hiding. They knew the legend. None of them knew the truth.

While his limp added a sort of weathered, menacing majesty to his stride, the injury it betrayed would not allow more than a few of the swift, graceful movements needed for sword-work without collapsing beneath him. Nor could his damaged lungs handle the demands of extended battle. If he was forced to fight on, he would begin to wheeze, and then, more frightening still, his lips would turn grey.

Once he began to cough, he was finished.

Outside the room, dawn birds were starting to stir and chirp in the trees on the hillside. The sun was beginning its steady creep over the mountains.

Faster now, I pulled the lightest and least elaborate of Father's suits of armour from the cabinet. A long red, felt coat that fell to below my knees, a pair of heavy boots that could be strapped up to just above them. Then a plain steel helm – Father's first, standard army issue, from before he was awarded the white horsehair plume of a general – and a long vest formed of panels of square, boiled leather scales, reinforced by metal studs, with similar scale panels at the shoulder that tied under the armpit to offer protection to the arms. I struggled to tie them, and gave up only half-satisfied, hoping they wouldn't flap around too badly. Next, a pair of leather gauntlets. A wide leather belt to strap the armoured vest down firmly on to the red coat. And finally…

The sword.

My fingers hesitated a butterfly's breath from the gilded pommel of Father's blade, laid reverently at rest on its ebony stand. It was a two-handed *shuangshou jian,* nearly five and a half feet long, a straight, double-edged blade with a golden pommel and golden winged guard, each chased with flowers in honour of our family name "Hua". The hilt and scabbard were inlaid with rough, pearly sharkskin, dyed a vivid emerald green. The sword had been awarded to my father by Emperor Gao Zi himself.

I had never touched it, and I could not bring myself to do so now.

Sighing, I turned aside and chose a basic steel sword with a bronzed, rounded pommel and heavy guard in the old style, and a plain leather grip and scabbard. I had used it to practise many times and knew there were countless others like it scattered throughout the empire. Nothing about it would invite interest or recognition, and, therefore, I would not need to expend any extra effort to shift the shadows over it into an illusion of another sword.

It would be hard enough to keep myself disguised in the midst of battle.

I secured the sword to the leather belt that I had tightly cinched at my waist, tucked the helm under my arm, and walked – a little heavily, as I accustomed myself to the weight of the full armour, which I had never worn before – across the room to the screens that divided it from the courtyard beyond.

Fumbling the screen open, I peered out. It was still mostly dark – the coming day was a milky ripple of pale grey-blue above the rooftops. There was no sign of bent-backed old Yong Chou shuffling across the courtyard to unbar the great gates, and I could smell no smoke drifting from the kitchen building. I stepped down into the court-yard, carefully. In the stillness of such a clear morning even small noises might start my father awake. If he, or anyone, came to investigate now, all would be lost.

The magnolia tree was in bloom, the thick swathes of wine-cup-shaped flowers providing deep, shifting shadows that would conceal my presence until the right moment. I made sure both feet were solidly planted and that I had the support of the twisted trunk to help me stay still, and carefully placed the helm on my head. Then I closed my eyes and focused on my *qi* as Father had taught me.

I saw my *qi* in my mind's eye as light suffusing my veins, liquid gold that ran within my blood from the tips of my fingers to the top of my head and the soles of my feet. As my state of inner contemplation centred me, I examined the *qi*, seeing it swirl in mildly agitated patterns – a response to my anxiety – over my cardinal points and the major acupressure areas. A few moments' concentration drew thin threads of it up and outwards so that it tingled on the surface of my skin, and then, with a slow exhale, I pushed it up, out, beyond my skin, until it hovered around me like the corona that blazes around the sun in a lunar eclipse. I felt the illusion form. It was a face. A new face.

A boy's face.

The energy settled. I opened my eyes. Now I must wait for the sun to rise, the servants to stir, and Yong Chou to unbar the gates. Despite my attempts at discipline, my hand slowly crept to the hilt of the sword and clenched there.

At last, sunlight warmed the courtyard. I heard the rattle and grinding of a door as it slowly opened, out of sight, on the other side of the tree, and felt my nerves vibrate with tension and anticipation. Equally slow footsteps moved past me and towards the entrance to the compound. Iron grated against iron, and wood thunked.

The house gate was open.

Yong Chou passed me again, moving in the other direction.

It was time.

I slipped out from under the tree. As I had hoped, the servant had propped the gate open to allow bad dreams to flow out. He was already reaching for the door to my father's bedchamber, his back to me.

"Respected servant!" I bellowed, nerves making my voice hoarse and aggressive despite using the most polite language possible. "Wake your master! I have come to challenge the legendary Hua Zhou to a duel of honour!"

My father defeated his opponents quickly because he had no choice. That was his greatest secret – and I knew it. I knew all his weaknesses. He taught them to me, day by day, for ten years.

He taught me how to do what no one had ever done.

He taught me how to beat him.

Five

I faced my father across the worn paving stones of the courtyard.

The magnolia's shadows danced gently as the sun rose behind it, a faint, warm breeze stirring its leaves and blossoms. Father was hastily dressed and his topknot was not as perfectly smooth as it was wont to be, but he exuded that familiar, unfamiliar sense of menace and purpose, his grip on Gao Zi's priceless sword relaxed and ready, a sort of fearsome suppleness in his stance.

His eyes had never looked on me this way before. Coldly, assessing, as a stranger. It was … not exactly pleasant. Yet it also carried a strange thrill. A bead of lukewarm sweat trickled gently down the side of my face beneath the steel helm.

"What is your name, boy?" he asked casually. "Where is your family from?"

No one has ever called me "boy" before...

I shook the thought away. There was no illusion that could disguise my voice, and so I shook my head, refusing to answer his question.

His eyebrows quirked, but I thought that something at the back of his eyes softened. "There is more than one path out of this courtyard, you know," he said. "Perhaps you have travelled a long way, prepared for many days … but that does not mean you must go through with this fight."

He was thinking of Da Xiong, I realized – how when my younger brother was scared, his nerves overcame him and struck him dumb.

Father went on, "A good soldier knows the wisdom of retreat. If you have changed your mind, you may walk away now with no shame."

No, no, don't feel sorry for me, I begged silently. Another moment and he would refuse to fight and send me away. All would be lost. I could feel my chance slipping from my grasp, and there was no way to stop it, except one: force him to see me as a threat, a target.

Slowly, infusing my own movements with as much prowling menace as I could muster, I began to circle him. My overly large boots made tiny scuffing sounds on the flagstones. I was used to practising in my bare feet on wooden boards. I ignored the noise as best I could and shifted my blade from a one-handed to a two-handed grip, positioning it defensively across my body in the Dancing Crane form.

Father's face went blank as he quickly reassessed me.

I had given away both training and some measure of skill. The softness vanished from his gaze and his eyes narrowed again. He began to turn to keep me in sight. "Very well. Let us begin."

I nodded, prowling on. Father circled his wrist slowly, loosening the muscles of his hand and arm, still absently turning to keep his silent challenger in view. I waited until the sun was behind me, and he was halfway through shifting his weight off his bad leg … and suddenly changed direction, darting to the right.

He faltered, minutely off balance. The hesitation would barely be perceptible to any ordinary observer. It was exactly what I had been waiting for. I lunged into his space.

His sword was a flash of lightning. Our blades met with a clash that made my heart leap in fear and exultation. He twisted his blade, trying to unbalance me and steal my sword from my gloved fingers, but I shifted, shadowing his movement and keeping my grip on the hilt. His superior strength bore down on me. The muscles in my arm screamed in protest. With a fluid sideways motion, I disengaged our blades and ducked away.

To my astonishment, I saw the faintest hint of a smile pulling at one corner of his lips as I fell back. He looked … impressed.

"You are one of Sifu Jiao's, aren't you? I didn't know he was still taking on students, but your form is unmistakable. Did he send you here to face me?"

Sifu Jiao had been his own master.

I shook my head again, moving restlessly into the shade of the magnolia tree, trying to keep my movements unpredictable, as he had taught me. My head was buzzing as if a swarm of hornets had nested under my helm. *You are fighting Father, Father's sword is raised against you, you are fighting your own father.* But it was working. I just had to keep it going, keep him curious and distracted.

"How old are—" he began.

Before he could finish the thought, I spun out of the shadows and came at him once more. Our blades clashed at the height of my waist, disengaged, clashed again before my face. The point of his sword slipped under my guard and grazed the shoulder of my armour, sending a handful of leather scales flying. I turned the movement against him and my elbow thudded solidly into his gut. I heard the hard cough of his breath and the soft wheeze beginning beneath it.

He was already beginning to tire. He would seek to end the fight quickly. I must prolong it.

This time when I tried to glide out of range, Father pursued me, sword a whirlwind of metal that I could only barely fend off. I felt pride and reverence bloom warmly inside me even as I ducked, dodged, feinted. He was a marvel, a master; any student of sword-work would have wept tears of joy to see such a display of finely honed skill.

I could not hope to match his speed or strength. My greater agility was my most valuable weapon. Swiftly, I leapt back into the shadows of the tree and then changed my path, drawing Father off the paving stones on to the uneven surface of the raked gravel where I would have the advantage.

"Who are you?" he asked, voice a little hoarse now as he followed me: "I must know your name."

Not yet.

I sought to spin again, to force him off balance – and the toe of one of the too large boots caught on the very surface I had sought to use against him. I stumbled. Before I even had time to register dismay, he was upon me.

Now the fight was in earnest. He treated me as he would have an enemy on the field – no mercy, no hesitation, no quarter. It was all I could do to meet his sword blow for blow, to keep to my feet as he drove me back towards the side of the building. The harsh sawing of my own breath rattled me from within. Sweat poured down my forehead and my back.

But even above my own discomfort, I could watch it happening. Father's face was turning pale. His breaths had become gasps, shallow and painful. He was reaching the end of his endurance and now he would be getting desperate.

When a man is desperate, he had always told me, *he will all too often bring about the very destruction he has sought to avoid.*

Wait, I told myself, bringing my blade up and wincing from the shrill scream of metal as I clumsily parried Father's powerful slice. *Wait. It will come soon...*

In the next instant there it was. He was shifting, preparing to deploy the Striking Snake attack against me. A thrill made my hairs stand up even while my stomach lurched. He had only used this form once in a duel before, against a young man whom he had almost agreed to train. I had done more than impressed him.

I had won his respect.

As he began the characteristic short, chopping movements of his sword, I felt my own body go liquid, flowing instinctively, easily into the risky counterattack. I matched his movements, forcing him on to the defensive, driving him back now as he had done to me a moment before. His mouth gaped in disbelief and then his icy eyes flashed with sudden fury as he realized he could lose his own sword instead of taking mine.

With a painful sideways wrench, he managed to disengage his blade and foil my attempt to steal it. But his retreat became a painful stagger; his bad leg was giving out.

I saw my chance.

Slipping forward, I brought my knee up and hit him hard in the upper thigh, swiping his shaky leg out from under him. He twisted away, already falling – and his sword hand flew up. I dropped my own sword, grasped his wrist with one hand and jerked the hilt of his blade from his fingers.

He hit the ground with a soft grunt and rolled, both hands slapping down to break his fall. The next second he was up again, wavering on his feet, his eyes fixed on the shadows under my helm in an expression of stark, almost comedic disbelief.

I stood motionless before him, dazed and panting. The bright emerald-and-gold of the emperor's blade glittered in my hands. If he could have seen my face in that moment, I have no doubt my expression would have mirrored his exactly.

It worked. It worked. It actually...

I won.

With a sharp crack that made both Father and me jump, the screen veiling the great room on the southern side of the compound flew back. Da Xiong and Xiao Xia stood in the opening, their faces pale blurs with wide, dark gaps for eyes and mouths. Behind them, Ai Bo and Yong Chou stood frozen in similar attitudes of shock and dismay.

White-eyed fool, I cursed myself. I should have realized they would spy. After all, I always had. Now it was too late, and they would have to see, which meant the news would fly to Mother like an arrow.

"Who are you?" Father demanded, keeping steady in his stance with what I could tell was an effort.

I let out a slow, shuddering breath. Then I sank down on to one knee and held up Father's sword in both hands, reverently offering it back to him. He hesitated for a moment, as if suspicious of a trick, then reached out and, when I made no attempt to hold the sword or draw it back, took the unsheathed blade from my fingers.

With my hands free, I reached up and pulled the helm from my head, letting the shadow of illusion I had cast over my face dissipate as I did so. I placed the helm neatly on the ground before me. Long strands of hair fell from my topknot to brush my cheeks. I forced myself to look up.

"Zhilan." Father breathed the word, nearly soundless.

Xiao Xia let out an aborted shriek. Without looking I could guess that Da Xiong had slapped his hand over her mouth.

"Most beloved and virtuous Father," I said formally. "I beg a thousand pardons for my deception and will accept any punishment that you think just."

"*Why*, daughter? Why have you done this?"

"To prove I could. To prove that you have trained me for a reason, just as you promised all those years ago. And to prove that I am your equal, any man's equal, in battle. The emperor demands the Hua family send a soldier to fight for the army. Very well. Let that soldier be me."

Six

A high-pitched, warbling trill cut through my dreams, scattering the hazy fragments of sleep as wind scatters the early morning mist from the mountain. I blinked reluctant eyes open to see a pair of small, vivid blue-and-gold robins fighting among the interlaced branches of the sapling that swayed over my head. The sky beyond them was soft grey, lightening to yellow. Dawn, but only just.

In the next blink, I remembered where I was – and why.

Before letting out my next breath, I found the warm light of *qi* within myself, unravelled it through my pores as fine threads that formed an increasingly familiar shape, and let go, feeling it gently drape into place as the air whistled gently between my lips.

I eased myself cautiously into a sitting position, groaning, then let out a yawn that cracked my jaw. I squashed the urge to politely cover my mouth, as my mother had many times chided me to do. Boys did not have to cover their mouths. Instead I stretched out stiff back and shoulders that were unused, as yet, to sleeping on the ground, rose to my feet and dutifully began the *qigong*.

The slow, precise, almost-dancing exercises did not only warm up my aching muscles and soothe my cracking back. They helped stimulate the flow of my *qi* to its highest potential, and maintained those energy levels day by day. The most important part was *neigong*, the internal movements, the deep, conscious breathing and invisible tensing and releasing of muscle and tendon; these made each external movement twice as difficult – and twice as potent.

You do not have qi. *You are* qi. That was what my father taught me in my very first banner-breaking lesson. I remembered staring up at him, wide-eyed, not wanting to admit that I was already lost.

"It is the energy that binds together your tiniest fibres and fragments, warms your blood, animates your consciousness. It is in all things. It is the essential building material of the universe. And aside from being made up of *qi*, every person, animal and object also generates new *qi* … and that is where the ability of banner-breakers originates.

"Banner-breakers," he said, "had the ability to sense *qi* and to manipulate it in order to create illusions. These illusions, also called seemings, masks or shadows were woven from the fabric of our own energy, just as an ordinary weaver used silk or cotton to create new cloth. The thin energy constructions warped perception, causing people who looked upon them to see, or not see, what the banner-breaker wished."

"But only what they see?" I had asked. "Not what they hear, or feel, or taste?"

He nodded, pleased, and I felt a flare of pride. "Very good! Yes. But vision is usually enough. My teachers told me: people believe their eyes, but often they see what they wish to see or what they believe they should see – not what is truly there. There are a few exceptions. Other banner-breakers or those skilled at the manipulation of *qi*. Children can sometimes be impervious to illusions, because they don't yet take the nature of reality for granted. And, occasionally, those whose minds have been stretched or unbalanced through great trials in life, or desperation or illness. Those whom the world might call mad. When using illusion, beware such people above all else."

They called the Leopard mad. But it was foolish to call men "mad" simply because they were brutal. Some might have called my mother mad, for what she had tried to do – and yet she was the gentlest creature alive, and had never tried to hurt anyone in the world but herself...

A muffled thud from the other side of the clearing brought my arms down from their final pose and my eyes open.

"Patience, Yulong," I called, then stopped, noticing the lightness of my voice. The tincture was wearing off. I must apply it again before I broke camp today. I swallowed reflexively.

My father's horse responded to my words with a high toss of his dark mane and a blustery snort, kicking his back hoof against the tree trunk where I had tethered him the night before.

"Spoiled, is what you are, my fine warhorse." I stepped over the cold remains of last night's campfire towards him. Grasping the halter with one hand and gently smoothing the other over the snowy white blaze on his forehead, I murmured, "No oats this morning." He flicked his ear at me. "Bear up, friend. You want to make your father proud, don't you?"

Yulong's father, Tianma, had been my father's last great warhorse. He had survived the Battle of the Thousand Steps by simple luck: Father had been forced to leave his mount at the top of the steps in order to lead his troops down on foot. In his retirement, Tianma had gone on to sire many fine sons for the Hua family stables. Yulong was his very last progeny, and my father's favourite mount. He was as well trained as any young, untried stallion could possibly be – and, like me, he had grown up in the shadow of a parent who had achieved the status of legend. I loved him dearly.

He whuffled at my hair. I allowed it, but jerked back when he attempted to playfully nibble on my ear. "Man-eater! You can't be that hungry!"

I patted him on the shoulder, pulled off his blanket and untethered the short rein that had held him overnight, leaving him on a long halter rope. He brushed by me eagerly on his way to the little rill that crossed by the far end of the clearing, and I left him to forage for his own breakfast. The sounds of his splashing and whinnying kept me company while I swiftly washed, refolded my belongings and stuffed them into the saddlebags. Then I had a choice to make. Tincture before or after breakfast? On the morning I set out I had chosen after – and nearly vomited.

Before, then.

There was a hidden pocket in my left saddlebag. It contained a carved ivory flask filled with murky brown fluid – a mixture of dried herbs extracted in alcohol. Most of these herbs were easily gathered in the countryside, and the alcohol could be any kind, in a pinch. My father made sure I knew the recipe, but he'd had this generous flask made up for me by the herbalist in town before I left. It was traditionally added to boiling water to create a steam that, although noxious, helped to clear congested lungs. It had saved my father's life on at least three occasions. But it took a toll. After using it his throat was left raw, and his already deep voice became a husky rasp.

I poured a tiny drop of the liquid into a cup of water, nerved myself up with a deep breath, and then tipped it into my mouth, gargling it for a bare second.

It was enough. The tissues of my mouth, tongue and throat caught fire, and as I spat the tainted water out, I retched and then coughed uncontrollably, gasping for air. My stomach clenched and churned, abdominal muscles quivering.

It was several minutes before I got my breath back. My throat still burned and my breath still whistled, but when I swallowed I did not choke. I rinsed my mouth and was able to take a small gulp of water.

"Yulong," I said, experimentally. It felt like I had tried to drink boiling vinegar, but my normally light, feminine voice emerged in a low, manly sounding growl that seemed to vibrate through the top of my chest and lungs. It was a novel sensation. If not for the suffering required to achieve it, I might even have found it pleasant.

Thank the heavens I only have to do that once every three days...

The handful of dried venison meat, dried apricots and nuts that were earmarked for my breakfast stayed in their wrappings. Maybe later. Or ... maybe not. That was all I'd eaten for three days, after all. Thoughts of warm, soft, steamed rice, soup dumplings and sweet bean-paste buns drifted through my head, and I sighed.

The sky was yellow and blue now. I called a damp and smelly Yulong out of the stream and rubbed him down with handfuls of grass, then heaved my saddle on to his back and loaded up, pleased to see that my hands hardly shook at all, even if my guts did writhe.

According to the map appended to the red-sealed scroll, I should reach the army's training camp before midday today.

I ran light mental fingers over my shadow mask. Unless I focused on it, I couldn't feel it there any more; I had been wearing it during all my waking hours for the last three days of travel and for the two days of preparation before that. At this stage, it took less effort to hold it in place than to walk in the dainty silk slippers that were part of my usual attire.

There was nothing I could do about the sleeping hours,

though. A banner-breaker must be conscious to shape their *qi* into the form of an illusion: it was an exercise of will, not a spell from a storybook. But real shadows and uncertain firelight would help to hide me during the nights. Anyway, in manly clothes, with my hair in a topknot and any hint of cosmetics scrubbed away, there was little to mark my appearance as strikingly different from those of the young men I would be surrounded by. No one would be looking out for signs of deception. Slim, round-faced young men were hardly an unknown sight. There was no reason to expect any trouble. No reason. None at all.

I stepped away from Yulong and slumped gracelessly on to a mossy rock.

My hands clutched at each other, tightening and releasing as if they had minds of their own. They were shaking now, all right.

There must be a saying from Father's books that would help to calm me. I searched my mind frantically and found only emptiness, a frightening white void, filled with incoherent What Ifs. What if someone recognized me, the real me, somehow? What if someone checked the records and found the discrepancy in birth dates and became suspicious? What if I made some terrible error – something only a real man would know about? What if someone spied on me and told all the rest, what if, what if, what if…

What if I'm not good enough to make this work?

I didn't have my father's knowledge, his experience or his skill. Yes, there was some natural, base proclivity within me for disguise and concealment. But larger illusions of the kind that an army banner-breaker would be called upon to produce remained beyond me. As soon as I attempted to manipulate the *qi* outside myself, something went wrong. I became uncertain and even frightened. My attempts at large-scale illusion, halfway formed, would suddenly darken and shrink, and my father would turn to discover that I had once again vanished, no more than a patch of shadow against the wall of the *wu kwan*.

It was as if the very strength of my affinity for self-concealment prevented me from doing anything else. As if my ability knew my secret: that somewhere within, I was still just a child, frozen with fear in the dark.

I fumbled in my pocket and withdrew a small bronze hand mirror. It was about the size of my palm and etched finely on the back with graceful flowers – peonies, orchids and hydrangeas. It had been mine since I was small, a rare and treasured gift from my mother, who had been given it by her grandmother. I had not yet managed to come up with a plausible reason why a male, let alone a trainee soldier, would carry such a thing on his person – everyone knew that men did not indulge in vanity – but I had been unable to force myself to leave it behind, or even to hide it at the bottom of my saddlebags.

I needed it.

Angling the reflective surface just so, I gazed into my face. My new face.

I forced my lips into a small, reassuring smile. The mask echoed the movement. Perfectly. There was no delay in my reactions now, no expression that was stiff or unnatural, no artificiality perceptible to a human eye. This face looking back at me seemed every bit as real as my own.

In fact, the strangest thing of all was how little difference I found between illusion and reality. I had expected a male version of my face to strongly resemble my father or Da Xiong. Instead I looked ... like myself. Like my mother, more than anyone. Her warm, hazel- and gold-flecked eyes, expressive, strongly marked brows, wide cheekbones, slightly short nose and long upper lip.

True, this nose was a little broader than the one I was born with. The chin was rather squarer. The skin was a tad more tanned and coarse. There was the hint of a bulge in the line of my neck, and a shadow both there and on the lower jaw that might have been dirt or an inexperienced young man's imperfect attempt at shaving. These changes were undeniable, almost overwhelming to my eye.

It was still, undeniably, me.

I shivered, breathing out slowly. What was it about this boy version of me? Something in his eyes, the way he returned my gaze so straitly. I felt as if he knew something. Something I didn't.

You're being ridiculous.

Of course my own face, subtly altered, still resembled me. There were practical reasons for it to be so. If my mask slipped or I was caught for a moment without it, it would be next to impossible for anyone to consciously mark the difference in the few seconds that it would take me to weave it anew. And a less radical disguise meant less overall effort to create and hold it in place.

But.

But.

But looking at this face calmed me. Every time. Leached away my doubts and fear and replaced them with this new feeling that I could not quantify. As if I were on the verge, not of danger and possibly death and dishonour, but of some wonderful adventure. As if I *were* good enough.

This face looked *right*.

Yulong's velvety nose dropped gently on to my shoulder – and deposited a long, foamy streak of half-chewed grass over the boiled leather scales of my brand-new armour. With an indignant yelp, I shoved his face away and began trying to clean up.

The mirror went back into my pocket, and soon we were on our way.

"Help!"

I stiffened in the saddle. Yulong flicked his ears as he drew up short, dancing in place.

"You heard it, too?" I muttered, turning my head this way and that in an effort to pick up the distant voice's direction. There was nothing. My ears captured only the shifting music of leaves and birdsong that filled the golden morning.

My father had advised me to avoid the main roads; they were dangerous for everyone with the Leopard at large, and since the conscription of this region could not be a secret, the rogue general might have set ambushes along the route specifically to take young soldiers unawares. But that didn't mean the woods were necessarily safe either.

Best to keep moving quickly and get to the camp.

I tapped my heels to Yulong's sides to urge him back into a canter. He tossed his head sideways and scraped insistently at the packed dirt path with his hoof.

"Yu—" I began between gritted teeth.

Before I could finish the word, a gust of wind from the west carried the voice to me again, this time with startling clarity. "Help! Someone, please – down here! Help!" Male and young – cracked, hoarse with strain or fear or exhaustion.

Yulong let out a quiet whinny.

I bit my lip. *Oh, curse it.* I dismounted, pulling the reins over the horse's head to lead him off the path into the trees. "If this *is* an ambush," I muttered, "I hope you know you'll never taste oats again."

The trees were tall and ancient, closing overhead like the living roof of a green-gold temple as we brushed through the sparse undergrowth, both of us – if Yulong's swivelling ears were any indication – listening intently.

"Down here!" the voice cried out, nearer now. It didn't sound like the voice of a bandit.

"That could just be good acting," I whispered to Yulong.

The young man shouted for help twice more before we broke through into a wide clearing of tall meadow grasses. I made to step forward; Yulong baulked again, jerking me back so hard that my shoulder popped in protest and I let out a cry of pain. My riding crop, clutched in my left hand, flew from my grasp.

It fell into the tall grass a foot or so from the tips of my boots. There was a metallic clang – and then a sharp *SNAP* that made the hairs all over my body stand up straight. A circle of grass gently slipped down, as if scythed.

Comprehension rushed over my skin in a tide of hot and cold prickles, and my heart surged painfully against my sternum. *Great Dragon and Phoenix. One more step – one more – and—*

"Look out for the traps!" the voice yelled, frantic. "If anyone is there, *look out for the traps!*"

I breathed in deeply and patted Yulong fervently in thanks. My hand shook. So did my voice when I shouted back: "I heard you! I can't see where you are! Are you hurt?"

There was a moment of silence, then a raw sound like a cough or a laugh or a sob. Maybe it was all three. "I – I'm in the ground – there's a pit, with spikes. But there are traps up there, bear traps, they're all around. I was trying to avoid them, that's how I fell in. Be careful!"

Spikes? I swore under my breath. A sunny, inviting-looking meadow like this, pocked with bear traps and pits... There could only be one explanation. Oh, the Leopard was clever. Horribly clever. He knew that cautious travellers would avoid the roads. So he made the woods and meadows close to the camp into death traps for them instead.

It could have been me in that pit, or another like it further on. If I'd kept travelling, oblivious, it probably would have been.

"Are you still there?" the boy called.

That made me start guiltily. "I'm here!" I shouted, trying to make my voice firm and reassuring. "I'm – I'm trying to think how to get to you. Hold on!"

My hands were still shaking, but there was no time to dwell on What Ifs now. I must only think: what would Father do? And I knew the answer. Someone needed my help, and I must give it. I rubbed my hands hard over my face, wiping away the panicked sweat on my brow and upper lip and making my mask buzz under my touch.

I could do this.

Yes. I would do this.

After backing Yulong up a few paces, I tied him to a sturdy tree branch. There was a coil of rope in my saddlebags. I pulled it out and tied it in a loop around my waist. Then I took my father's – no, *my* – knife from my belt, hacked a slim tree sapling off near the root and stripped the small shoots and leaves from its sides.

"I'm still here!" I called out. "Don't worry. I'm coming for you!"

Another small silence. Then a ragged: "Thank you."

What else might be needed? I couldn't think of anything. All right.

I sheathed the knife, took a firm hold on the end of the sapling, which had now become a stout staff, and carefully moved forward into the meadow. My first step brought me to the trap that my riding crop had set off. The crop was a mangled ruin, snapped in two by the vicious, rusted teeth of the trap's mechanism. If those teeth closed over a man's leg, he would lose the leg, and almost certainly his life, too.

Tightening my grip on the staff, I bent my knees and swept it in a wide arc through the grass. At the very edge of the arc, there was another metallic clang as the tip of the staff hit a new trap. But this time the trap did not snap closed. Not enough pressure. I used the staff to shove the trap sideways out of my path, tipping it on to its side – and now it did snap shut with that same terrible sound. I flinched, drew in a slow breath and straightened.

"That's one more trap out of the way!" I called, hoping I seemed cheerful rather than manic.

"Good?" the boy called back, not sounding entirely sure. "Please be careful!"

I knew he was probably mainly worried about his potential rescuer dying before they could reach him, but still – the concern was warming. "I'll be there soon."

Stepping gingerly into the slightly flattened grass I had cleared, I swept the stick again. Nothing. Another step. Another sweep. A *SNAP* that sang up my arm. I jerked back, nearly falling, and dragged the trap with me – fixed around the end of my staff. Planting my boot against the brutal curve of corroded metal, I wrenched the stick sideways. With a crunch, it came free, leaving the last four inches of wood still caught in the metal teeth, oozing green sap.

"Still safe?" the boy asked. He was closer now, more speaking than shouting.

"Still safe," I confirmed, taking a moment to brush back the stray strands of hair that had plastered themselves to my damp forehead. "You? Are you all right down there?"

"Oh, fine," he said, dry as dust. "Enjoying the shade."

I let out a snorting laugh and heard him echo it shakily.

I swept the next section of grass more cautiously. No trap. Stepped, then swept again. Clear.

"Nearly there," I muttered, mostly to myself.

"Watch out!" He sounded worried again. "I – I can hear you. You're nearly on top of me. Don't fall in!"

He sounded like he was speaking from under my feet. But I couldn't see him, or any trace of a pit. Frowning, I planted my feet and jabbed the stick firmly down at the ground. Solid. Here? No, solid. Here? No. Here—

The staff plunged into the ground with no resistance. A mound of dry-looking, tussocky grass collapsed in on itself with a gentle rustle, revealing a deep crevice, cunningly camouflaged. As the grass fell, a waft of fetid, stinking air drifted up into my face and I gagged. It was the smell of decay, of spoiled meat. I coughed, and my mouth and nose watered.

"You're down *there*?" I asked, my voice coming out higher than I'd intended. Without waiting for an answer, I went down on my knees, shoving away more of the dried grass to reveal slender bamboo sticks, woven into a lattice. These were what made the ground above the pit appear solid – until weight was placed on them. I squinted down into the darkness, shielding my nose from the stink with my free hand. The pit was deep. Very deep. More than eight feet, maybe ten. But in the dappled light falling through the bamboo rods, I could make out the glint of what looked like … armour at the bottom. A metal helm, still brightly polished. The distinctive shape of a sword hilt.

And under that…

In the moist darkness, tangled amid leaves and the very tips of savage-looking wooden spikes, there were bones. New bones. White and glaring, as if picked clean by insects or scavengers.

No way to tell what kind of bones. They could have belonged to any animal. Any … *large* animal. But these woods were full of deer – far more deer than people. There was no *real* reason to believe I was looking at a human leg bone. It was so dark down there, I could hardly see it anyway.

Swallowing hard, I demanded, "Talk to me. I can't see you."

"This way," he said, a little muffled. "I – I think you're on my left? Does that help?"

He didn't sound as if he'd been pierced by spikes. *Please, ancestors, don't let him be impaled on the spikes…*

"Just – just hang on. I'll work my way to you."

The edge of the pit seemed to be straight, but I prodded and swept with the stick anyway, testing for more traps, gingerly making my way forward, expecting at any moment to see a sign of the boy. The pit wasn't just deep. It was long. I walked several feet along its edge before I reached a surprisingly small hole in the grass and bamboo cover. This must be it. I opened my mouth to call out, leaning a little way over the edge.

Before I could say or glimpse anything, a bird – reddish brown and about the length of my hand – shot up out of the darkness almost directly into my face. I flinched back as its fanlike tail brushed my cheek. The bird fluttered around my head, letting out a mixture of harsh, rasping sounds and sweet trills, and then darted away into the trees. My last, fleeting glimpse of it showed me the distinctive white streaks around the eyes that marked a *hwamei*, a laughing thrush, often kept as caged songbirds.

I closed my gaping mouth and bent down on to one knee again, leaning more fully over the edge of the pit. "Hello?"

"I'm here!" the young man replied. "Thank the heavens. Thank you for..." The words cracked and trailed off.

"Are you hurt?" I squinted down into the pit, trying not to block the light as I struggled to make him out. A quick, tentative movement caught my eye, and suddenly what I had taken for a bulge of earth on one of the sheer walls resolved itself into a person. He was spreadeagled, body plastered flat against the side of the pit. Both hands were grasping at the white, tangled roots that peppered the dark reddish earth, and one leg seemed to be wedged at the knee on to a tiny chunk of rock or natural ledge that protruded from the dirt. He was almost at the bottom of the pit, only a few feet above the deadly spikes. If he fell – if he let go – he would land directly on them.

"I don't dare try to climb out," he explained, answering my question before I could voice it. His voice was rasping and dry. "Every time I move at all the earth starts to crumble and the roots loosen."

"How long...?" I began, disbelieving. That position must be excruciating.

"Since just after dawn."

At least three hours. My arms would never have held me up that long. And the smell! It wasn't as bad at this end, but it was still enough to make me feel dizzy and sick. *Dear ancestors, he's strong.*

"I've got a good length of rope," I said. "I just have to anchor it somewhere and – and we'll have you out in no time."

"We? Is there someone else up there?" he asked hopefully.

"Only me and my horse. But don't worry! I know what to do."

I twisted around, looking for – ah, I knew it.

A few more moments of hastily sweeping and poking at the ground – it had now occurred to me that any square of ground not marked with a trap might easily have another pit instead – brought me to a nearby thorn tree. It was shorter than I, black and twisted and dead-looking, but such trees had deep, iron-hard roots. The gardener at home had often complained to Father that it took three of his workers half a day to heave such plants out of the ground. I pulled on my riding gloves to protect my hands, grabbed hold of one spiny branch and dragged with all my might. As I'd hoped, the tree barely rustled. It would be strong enough to hold a person's weight.

I ducked under the thorns and tied one end of the rope around the twisted trunk, securing it with two knots. After a couple of testing tugs assured me the knots would hold, I headed back to the pit at a run, following the path of flattened grass I'd made on the way out.

"Still here," I said. "Not much longer."

"No rush," the boy joked weakly. "I've no pressing appointments this morning."

I pressed my lips together to hold in what would probably have been a shrill giggle and uncoiled the long loops of the rope from my arm as I knelt above the boy in the pit again. "What's your name?"

"Ah. How rude of me. Yang Jie, at your service," he answered without moving. His face was still squashed against the mud wall of the pit.

"Nice to meet you. I'm Hua Zhi—" I broke off with a choke of incredulous, self-directed rage. *No!* How could I have made such a stupid, such a foolish, basic mistake already?

"Hua Zhi?" he repeated, a little doubtful.

I ground my teeth. Too late to correct myself now – Da Xiong and Zhi sounded nothing alike.

"Yes, sorry – bug in my throat!" *Bug in my brain, more like.* "I've tied the rope off. I'm going to lower it in. You just need to get a good, solid hold on it."

"All right," he replied, voice firming with resolution. "I can do that."

I lowered the end of the rope carefully over the side, aiming it to hang by his hands so that he wouldn't have to stretch for it. But as I let the last coil fall, I realized with a sinking feeling that the gap between his closest hand and the end of the rope was nearly two feet. He wouldn't be able to push himself up, not if the wall crumbled whenever he moved.

The rope was too short.

"Any time," the boy prompted, still not looking up.

I blew out a long, slow breath and pulled the rope back up. "Change of plan. I'm going to have to come down there."

"What – *what*?" His utter stillness against the wall of the pit made the sudden horror in his voice stand out all the more starkly. "You can't! Why?"

"The rope isn't going to reach you," I said flatly, hoping my uncertainty wasn't obvious. "But if I tie myself to the end of it, *I* can. You'll have to climb over me, and then pull me up."

A moment's silence. "You're sure the rope will hold both of us?"

I hesitated.

He swore loudly and I rushed into speech. "I think it will. But I also can't think of any other way to get you out. We have to risk it."

"*We* don't. I … I shouldn't let you do this."

Suddenly I felt a smile pulling at the corners of my lips. "Well, I don't really see how you can stop me."

He made that rough, cough-laugh-sob sound again. Then he moved minutely – a nod.

Good enough. I circled my waist with the end of the rope and knotted it in place. Unfortunately, that shortened the length considerably – but I should still be able to reach him. *I hope.* I pulled my knife back out of my belt, took a deep, fortifying breath of the clean air above ground, and then leaned over the edge again.

Slowly, accompanied by the strangely ominous pattering of small bits of soil and grass crumbling from the edge, I let myself down into the pit. With one hand braced against the mud, I stretched out the other – the one holding the knife – as far as I could. My feet dug into the tussocky grass at the top. The rope tightened uncomfortably around my waist. A little further. Just a little further. My fingers inched downward towards the place where the boy clung to the wall. Closer. Closer. Almost – not quite...

I plunged the knife into the mud wall to the left of the boy's hand, as hard as I could, and wrapped my fingers around the hilt. It was the only grip I was going to have. With a quick prayer to my ancestors, I took my other hand off the mud, lurched downward another inch, and let my fingers dangle by the boy's head.

"I'm ready," I gasped out, lungs compressed with my feet over my head and the rope biting into my stomach. "Let go."

The boy didn't move.

Now it was my turn to swear. "Come on! Grab my hand!"

"I ... I don't think I can let go," he mumbled. "I can't. I'll fall."

Nononono...

"If you don't try, then both of us are going to be stuck in here! I can't get out on my own now!" I heard my own voice beginning to crack with panic. "Look at me! Yang Jie – *look at me!*"

We were only inches apart in the gloom. Slowly, the tousled head of dark hair below me shifted, tilting back to reveal the pale oval of the boy's face. He was streaked with mud, his eyes squeezed nearly shut with pain and shame, lips a thin, trembling line. "I'm sorry. I can't."

Of course. Of course he couldn't.

He didn't know me. He didn't trust me. I should have spent more time talking to him, reassuring him. I should have known this would happen. He'd been clinging to this wall, alone, for hours, knowing that if his grip loosened for a second, he'd fall – fall on to the spikes and suffer a slow, horrific death among the rotted things at the bottom. Willing himself to hold on. Willing his fingers not to let go. *Of course* he was terrified by the idea of letting go now.

For a heartbeat, the white void of panic surged at the edges of my consciousness. *I'm going to die here. I'm going to die hanging head-down in this pit. There's nothing I can do. I can't get out. I can't get out…*

And then, as if he had whispered in my ear: *Are you a coward, daughter?*

I forced the roaring white blankness away. *No, Father. I am of the House of Hua.*

From somewhere, words came, soft and steely. "Yang Jie. There's something dead in the bottom of this pit. You can smell it, can't you?"

He nodded again, a tiny movement. His eyes were fixed on mine, but I didn't think he was seeing me.

"It might be a man. It might be an animal. It's been down there a while. But there was no hole in the layer of grass where it fell in. Was there? Or you'd have seen that this was a trap and not fallen in yourself."

A tiny frown crimped Yang Jie's dark brows. "What does that mean?"

"It means someone covered the pit back up again. The same people who filled this meadow with traps and dug this hole in the first place. The Leopard's men. And if they came back here once, they'll do it again, to reset the traps. All the traps. They could come at any time. If we're still here … do you know what the Leopard does to people he captures, Yang Jie?"

He stared up at me, eyes growing wider and wider until they were like black holes in the white blur of his face. Now he was really looking at me. "Yes," he whispered.

"Do you want to be here when they come? Helpless and weak but still alive? Do you want them to pull us out? Do you?"

"No."

"Then. Grab. My. *Hand*."

For another long moment, he was motionless. Then one of his hands slowly uncurled from its death grip on the vines. It shook visibly as he flexed his fingers – and then reached out and clamped on to mine. I let out a grunt of effort as his weight pulled my sore shoulder and made the rope cut into me even more. My fingers tightened on the hilt of the knife until they cracked.

"Catch my belt with your other hand." I squeezed the words out between my teeth. "Pull yourself up."

If Yang Jie made any reply, I couldn't hear it over the white-water roar of blood in my ears. But he shifted, released my hand, and surged upward. His body pressed into my back. The rope at my waist was too tight now, it was unbearable, I couldn't breathe at all, and Yang Jie's shadow blinded me so that I could no longer tell what was going on as he squirmed and wriggled against me. Was he actually going anywhere? Was he climbing up, or dragging me down?

The knife was moving. Our combined weight was pushing it down in a long slide through the mud. And I was sliding, too, crushed flat into the wall, my other hand scrabbling uselessly at the roots as Yang Jie clawed at my legs.

"Almost there. Almost … nearly there now…" Yang Jie was muttering. "Hold on."

Was *he* trying to reassure *me* now?

One of his hands closed around my ankle, crushing as a vice. His flailing boot clipped my knife hand and I let out a pained croak, vision swimming from lack of air.

There was a sudden flurry of upwards motion. The weight on me eased suddenly enough to make me gasp, and then I was jolted, yanked. My hand – still clutching the knife – was wrenched away from the wall of the pit, and the world upturned itself in a nauseating whirl.

I … was lying on my back amongst fragrant, swaying meadow grasses, a cloudless blue sky above me, Yang Jie sprawled at my side.

Seven

"We got out. We actually got out. I can't believe it. I thought we were both dead," I rambled mindlessly, staring at the sky. "Dead for sure."

Yang Jie made a noise like a startled horse. "You did? You – you said – why did you – *what is wrong with you*?"

"Whatever is wrong with me, you owe me your life – so what does that say about you?" I turned my head to meet the boy's gaze properly for the first time, and started when I found him unexpectedly close. His nose almost brushed mine.

He blinked ridiculously long lashes at me. "Are you a girl?"

"No!" I yelped, a lightning-fast check of my mask assuring me that it was still in place. "Are you? You – you're prettier than I am!"

I managed not to add *so there!* but only just. And it

was true, even if I hadn't been wearing this seeming of a boy, and even if he was pale and mud-streaked. His face was heart-shaped, fine-browed and delicate, with huge, amber-brown eyes. Even the hair had a distinctive and beautiful mahogany gleam. He looked about fourteen, although I thought his voice too deep for that.

"No!" he growled, lip pouting in a thunderous scowl that reminded me irresistibly of Da Xiong Mao.

I hastily clapped one hand over my mouth, but couldn't quite keep the snort in. Yang Jie's face twitched. He fell on to his back again, letting out a low, rumbling chuckle. Before I knew it, I was clutching my bruised stomach, helpless with laughter, Yang Jie's shaking shoulder pressed against mine.

We had just been through an exhausting ordeal. Yang Jie had been close to death, and for me, the war and our enemy's ruthlessness had been made abruptly and horrifyingly real. We were still in this awful place, inches from a pit which might be the grave of at least one murdered man. But how could either of us find the words to discuss any of that, even if we wanted to? What could we say? Instead, we lay side by side in the grass, sniggering and hiccupping like children until Yulong – feeling he had been neglected quite long enough, no doubt – let out a high-pitched, imperious whinny from the edge of the clearing.

"All right, all right!" I called out. "I'm coming."

As I began untying the rope from around my waist, Yang Jie jolted upright and hit his forehead with the flat of his palm. "Bingbing! I forgot all about her!"

"Bingbing?" I suddenly remembered the little song-bird that had nearly flown into my face as I approached the canyon. "That was your pet? How did she get in the pit with you? Why was she out of her cage?"

"She doesn't need a cage. After I fell, she flew in and perched on my shoulder. She sang to me the whole time – kept me steady." His face was tragic as he gazed at the trees.

That was why the bird's song had been harsh and rasping. I picked up the makeshift staff again and led the way back to where I'd left Yulong, the other boy trailing behind me listlessly. I felt doubly glad to have my animal companion safe, and I gave Yulong a gentle rub on the nose as I reached him. He lipped at my fingers, kindly not biting. Awkward in the face of the other's distress, I said, "I'm sorry, Yang Jie."

"She's never left me before – she might just have been hungry, I suppose. She has to come back."

Personally, I wasn't sure the chances were high. But I nodded anyway. "How did you train her to be so faithful?"

"Oh – it wasn't me. She was – a gift." He cleared his throat, avoiding my eyes. He wasn't blushing, but he might as well have been. So the bird was a gift from a lady friend. "Can you whistle? She's trained to come back to a whistle, but … er … I can't."

I decided, given the circumstances, not to mock him for that. *Everyone* could whistle, even girls – although we weren't supposed to. "What kind of whistle?"

"Three high, long notes, going up and down. Like the sound the bird makes."

I nodded, wet my lips, and stepped back from Yulong a little before letting out my best version of a *hwamei's* call. I repeated it twice, and we both looked around, fruitlessly searching the sky for a sign of the little bird.

Just as Yang Jie's shoulders began to sag, there was a sweet, liquid trill, and a reddish-brown flash zipped past my face and landed on his shoulder. He stroked the *hwamei's* head tenderly with one finger. "Good girl, Bingbing. I'm glad you're all right." The look he gave me was glowing. "Thank you!" he said, sounding almost more grateful to have the little song thrush restored to him than he had to be rescued.

I cleared my throat and scratched Yulong's poll absently. "My horse needs rubbing down – will you help?"

By the time we had attended to Yulong and shared a canteen of water and a small packet of preserved lemon peel that Yang Jie had in his pocket, we were well on the way to becoming friends.

"So you're headed to the army camp, too?" I asked, trying not to wince as I swallowed the last lukewarm mouthful of water. My throat was still horribly sore from the tincture. "How long have you been travelling?"

"Only a day. Our lands are just over that last hill, see? My father wouldn't even give me a horse for the journey – he said the army ruins them, and it would be a shame." Yang Jie cast a frankly envious look at Yulong's gleaming lines.

"So you fell in a hole on your very first night away from home?"

"Don't say it like that!" he protested with a sheepish

laugh. "I've crossed this part of the forest a dozen times before. There was no sign anything had changed until it was already too late. It could have happened to anyone. I'm really not helpless."

I eyed him doubtfully. I was slim for a boy my age, and a little below average height. But not remarkably so. Yang Jie was nearly two inches shorter, and even slighter than I was. His perfect complexion told me that he hadn't yet attempted to shave. Of course he, unlike me, would probably grow taller and fill out as he aged ... but still...

"How old are you?" I asked casually.

"Sixteen," he said candidly, showing no evidence of a lie. "You?"

I cleared my throat. "The same. I'm the oldest boy in my family – what about you?"

"I have two older brothers. But they're both married, and busy running things for my father. Mother thought I was too young to go, but Father said I was the one who could most easily be spared. He says the army will toughen me up, ancestors willing." He spoke without any resentment – or any particular emotion at all – but I felt my jaw tighten.

"Did you have a camp somewhere?" I asked him. When he looked at me blankly, I added. "You don't have a pack or a sword or ... anything with you."

He stared at me for a second in dawning horror. "I was carrying my pack when I fell into the pit. It ... it must be at the bottom."

I smacked him lightly on the shoulder in a mannerism

I had seen local boys use with their friends. "Don't panic. We can go back and fish it out."

He blinked, one eyebrow creeping up. "We?"

I nodded firmly. "We."

We crested the hill above the camp and stopped by unspoken agreement, staring. I barely managed to stifle my instinctive noise of disgust and took comfort that Yang Jie didn't bother to hide his own horrified expression.

"Not ... much like the ballads, is it?" Yang Jie said faintly, leaning around Yulong's shoulder to get a better look. Bingbing fluttered up and perched on the horse's head. Yulong flicked his tail, but didn't try to shake her off.

The delay of helping Yang Jie, followed by our need to test the ground ahead for traps until we hit the main road, had brought us to the camp in the late afternoon rather than before the midday meal, as I had planned. I had spent the time observing Yang Jie's subtly swaggering walk and trying to learn to make my own movements a little more masculine. I'd thought I was doing rather well.

Staring down into the valley, I felt that sense of optimism drain away.

Crimson tents with gold insignias were neatly pitched in military formation, interspaced here and there by rough wooden buildings flying the emperor's flag. In between was a churning mass of barely organized chaos: grim-faced men and foam-flecked horses stamping, bellowing, marching, running. Even from the top of the hill, the stench was overwhelming: the eye-watering tang of urine and dung and a musty fug of sweat, wood ash and burned food. It hadn't rained in three days, but the floor of the valley was thick, black mud. I could feel the damp of it, moisture hanging in the air like an invisible fog.

"Where are we supposed to go?" Yang Jie asked. "It's so…"

"I'm sure we – we'll get used to it" – *if I'm not discovered and killed within the day* – "soon enough." I tried to pull myself together. "For now, I need to stable Yulong, and then we should report to the censor. Someone ought to be able to direct us."

The stables, logically enough, were situated close to a narrow stream, upwind from most of the camp but still protected by the bulk of the valley's north ridge. After all, most generals would freely admit that a trained warhorse was worth the same to them as about half a dozen green, untrained recruits. Bringing a mount of Yulong's calibre would increase my status as a conscript, but I would be expected to care for him myself, unlike the recruits who were assigned army mounts, and that would add to my workload.

Handing Yulong over to the brusque and competent grooms was the work of a few moments. I retrieved my sword and fumbled through fastening it at my side. Yang Jie, to my surprise, managed it twice as quickly. I noticed with a pang that his sword was brand-new … and of questionable quality.

The weight of my blade made me very conscious of the way I moved as I said a temporary goodbye to Yulong. No one so much as glanced at us as we headed out into the camp, dodging other men, the sucking mud and steaming piles of horse dung – after all, new young men would have been flooding in from all directions for weeks now. But I felt as if my skin were ill-fitting, prickling and chafing, a size too small. My walk was all wrong. My arms were awkward as they swayed uselessly at my sides – I was used to clasping my hands before me, inside my sleeves. I checked my shadow mask three times before I could force myself to stop.

Yang Jie also became quieter and quieter as we approached the centre of the camp. There, where the stable boys had pointed us, was a large, grand tent, with a wooden sign painted with the censor's name, governmental rank and noble titles. It seemed like bad strategy to give away such good information to potential spies or assassins. But, well, no one wanted my opinion.

"Do you have your scroll?" I asked Yang Jie, gesturing with the slightly crumpled roll of paper that my father had entrusted to me.

"Yes, here," he mumbled, pale-faced, pulling it – pristine – from a stiff leather pouch on his belt.

The tent's front flaps were drawn back to create a wide entrance, and scented smoke and the steady light of good oil lanterns warmed me as we stepped inside. I stopped to allow a trio of other young men – as dishevelled and travel-stained as I felt – to pass by on their way out, and then took a place one polite step behind Yang Jie, who had already reached the great wooden desk that dominated the tent.

The censor was a small man huddled in a grand sweep of crimson-gold-and-black silk, wearing the black hat of a government official. His desk was covered with neat piles of ledgers, and a fine writing brush was poised in one hand, ready to leap into action. He lifted his head, revealing a snowy white moustache and brows, and a face that was as brown and wizened as a walnut.

"Brothers?" he asked, eyeing us.

"Er – no, sir, sorry," Yang Jie stammered, clearly thrown. So was I, a little. The two of us looked nothing alike.

"No need to apologize," the censor said, with a hint of amusement. "Name and scroll."

Yang Jie looked at the paper in his hand as if he'd never seen it before, then dropped it before the censor. "Oh – I – I'm Yang Jie, third son of Yang Wei, of the village of Nine Rivers in the prefecture of…" And then he was off, listing every fact and figure down to what seemed like his great uncle's birthdate, and finally finishing with: "And this is Bingbing!"

As if she had been waiting for her cue, the little bird let out a soft trill and ruffled up her wings. I hoped, for Yang Jie's sake, that birds were allowed in the camp.

"That is … quite an introduction, thank you," the censor said. He flipped a page in his ledger and made a brief note, setting Yang Jie's scroll to one side, then turned bright eyes on me. "And this is?"

Before I could think how to stop him, or even damn myself for forgetting until this second the confusion over my name, Yang Jie leapt in to proudly announce, "This is my friend Hua Zhi."

The censor's brow wrinkled a little. "Hua? Of which prefecture and town?"

I told him, swallowing dryly as I stepped forward to hand over my own paper.

"But that would make you – we were expecting your father. There is no record of a son of fighting age." He had laid his brush down to examine my scroll carefully, thin fingers massaging out the creases. Apparently satisfied with it, he began to page distractedly through the ledger, the wrinkles on his face deepening. "Zhi, you say? There is a *girl* here, sixteen last year—"

Why did I think this would work? Why? I had a plan, didn't I? Dear ancestors, what was my plan?

"Sir," I interrupted as politely as possible, "I – I believe that is … my … twin sister. Zhilan?"

"That might be, but *your* birth was never noted." He gave me a searching look – not yet suspicious, but … uncomprehending. As if an unregistered person were an impossible, mythical creature. It wouldn't be long before he decided that if the record showed only a girl, then it must be a girl who stood before him as well. "Surely your father would have ensured his son and heir was correctly entered into the records!"

That … was an excellent point. Now what did I say? My mind spun madly, and then, like the sun breaking through storm clouds, an answer came to me. It was shameful. Wicked. Cynical.

It was perfect.

"My birth was a time of great sorrow and upheaval," I said, lowering my tone gravely. "My sister died at birth. My mother nearly lost her life also. And my father…"

"Yes?" the man urged.

"If you will examine the date of my birth, I think things will perhaps become clear."

His head bent. There was a long moment of silence. Then he breathed, "The Battle of the Thousand Steps! Yes, yes – I see. I remember – I met your father once, you know, when I was a junior censor. A remarkable man. We all prayed for him in his convalescence. I believe he was unable to return home for many months, and why then check the records? A very understandable mistake, with the similarity in names, and with one child living…"

He picked up his brush, rewetted it, and made a note in tiny, meticulous characters. When he raised his head, his eyes were bright and clear again. "And so, the great Hua Zhou sends us his son! You have – I notice it now – something of the look of him. He was a little taller, perhaps, but you still have growing years ahead of you. The son of the Wild Tiger, in our regiment! It is an honour to have you, young man."

Yang Jie was staring at me, wide-eyed. Reeling with the knowledge of what I had done, I clasped my hands behind my back to hide the tremors. "Thank you, sir." My voice cracked and broke on the words, just as the voice of any boy my age might do.

The censor cleared his throat, drawing his professionalism around him along with a handful of his heavy silk robe. "You're among the last to arrive. Training will start tomorrow – the great gong will wake you. Report to the east barracks now with your friend."

"Sir?" Yang Jie piped up unexpectedly. "Hua Zhi and I need to report a hazard we encountered on the way to the camp. So it can be marked on any maps and passed on to army intelligence."

I quickly nodded in agreement, trying to conceal my flash of chagrin. I had forgotten about the trap field.

"A hazard? Very well, but you'll need to talk to one of the captains about – ah, here is Captain Lu! Captain!" I turned to see a man who had apparently been passing by the tent stop and then shoulder his way through the entrance. He was in his late twenties, very fit, handsomely moustached. His expression was one of barely concealed impatience.

With his nose already back in his papers, the censor was apparently oblivious to the other man's mood. "These young men have to report something to army intelligence. Take them away, would you, and see that they find their way to the barracks. Good man."

The captain's face darkened even more as he took in the pair of muddy, undistinguished young recruits he had been assigned to babysit.

Yang Jie let out a tiny, almost soundless noise of dismay.

"Of course, honoured sir," the captain said quietly, voice containing no hint of the resentment in his eyes. He jerked his head at us and stalked from the tent.

Yang Jie and I scrambled after him.

He strode a few feet away from us, then turned and crossed his arms. "Well?"

Yang Jie's face had gone grey with nerves. He cast me a helpless look, and I gulped. All right then.

"Sir, on the way to the camp this morning my friend

and I were travelling through the forest in order to avoid the main roads—"

"How fascinating," the captain said with a sigh.

I cleared my throat. "Sir, we found traps in the wood. In at least two different locations. Bear traps and bear pits with spikes. We think the Leopard is trying to thin the ranks of conscripted soldiers arriving here – he knows most of them will avoid the roads. And his men must return to them frequently because none of the traps had been sprung when we found them, and the pits were newly covered up so they couldn't be detected."

I ran out of breath and snapped my mouth shut.

The captain stared at us both for a moment, impatience fading into something more difficult to read. "And you two … you avoided these traps successfully and arrived here unscathed."

Best not to go into Yang Jie's adventure in too much detail. "We had some trouble. We were able to help each other out of it."

"Oh, were you?" Now his lips twisted into a smirk, and I was sure I wasn't imagining the innuendo in his voice. "Thank you for this … intelligence. However, if the Leopard had any such organized campaign, we would have had word of it by now. Nor do I believe that two such … unseasoned boys could have navigated a trap set by the Leopard's men. It's more likely that some locals have fallen on hard times and are over-hunting the forest."

I unclenched my teeth with an effort. "There was imperial armour at the bottom of one of the pits, and what looked like a human skeleton."

"Unfortunate," Lu said without blinking. "In any case, you can be assured that I will treat your intelligence with the attention it deserves. Dismissed."

"But—" I blurted, helpless to prevent myself.

Fast as a snake, the captain unfolded his arms and took a step forward. "But *what*, recruit?"

Yang Jie took hold of my arm in an iron grip and bowed humbly, keeping his face firmly aimed at the ground even as he began to back away. "Nothing at all, Captain – thank you so much for your time, sorry to bother you!"

The captain bared his teeth. Before he could say anything else, Yang Jie clucked his tongue, and Bingbing shot up from his shoulder, fluttering directly past the older man's face and momentarily distracting him with a flurry of wings. He fell back a step.

Before he could recover, Yang Jie was off at a near-running pace, hustling me out of sight behind the censor's tent and then away. A few breaths later, Bingbing landed back on Yang Jie's shoulder, chirping smugly.

When Yang Jie's grip on my arm finally loosened, I stumbled to a halt, looking around in some surprise to find us just where we ought to be: by the eastern barracks. He'd dragged me half the length of camp and found the place unassisted.

"Thanks…" I began sheepishly.

"Hua Zhou is your *father*? Why didn't you *tell* me?" Yang Jie demanded.

I looked at him in some surprise, taking in his heaving chest and tight lips. "I told you my name. I don't usually introduce myself by bragging about my father. Why does it matter?"

"Because it's going to get out! Everyone will know who you are, and everyone will be watching you, and if I'm near you then they'll be watching me, too, and that's exactly what I didn't want! It's going to be hard enough here for someone like me!" He gestured down at his slim form. "Most of the men here are going to assume they could snap me in half with one hand! And that's without – without the sort of thing Lu was implying just then, too!"

I wasn't imagining that, then. I took in a deep breath, then let it out as a sigh, feeling my shoulders sag. I hadn't really thought of how this would look from someone else's perspective. I'd just been glad to have found someone to … to blend in with so quickly. Another form of disguise. But not only that. A friend. It was selfish of me. He didn't even know how selfish – how much of the wrong kind of attention I could attract.

I should have known better.

I rubbed both hands tiredly over my face. The thin skin of *qi* that concealed my real skin thrummed warmly under my fingers. "You're right," I admitted. "I – I really – don't know what I was thinking. You don't owe me anything, Yang Jie. If I could swap my name with someone else's, I would. I can't. So if you want to find other friends, I'll understand."

There was a taut pause, during which I waited with painful certainty to hear Yang Jie's departing footsteps. Then his hand returned to rest – gently now – on my shoulder.

"I don't want to. I like you. I just wish you'd thought this through and *told* me." He pulled a wry face. "Though if you had stopped and thought things through before you came to rescue me from that pit, then perhaps you'd have left me there... So maybe I like your reckless streak. Just a little."

There was a pause as my thoughts turned back to the death traps we'd found on the way here. To Captain Lu's reaction – or lack of. "Lu's not going to take any action about what we told him, is he?"

It wasn't really a question. I asked to distract myself from my other pressing thought: what would a man like Captain Lu do to me if he ever realized the truth about who I was?

Father had given me some cryptic-sounding warnings about the consequences of what I wanted to do. Mother had cried and refused to meet my eyes. By my count, I was already guilty of several crimes: lying to the censor and making fraudulent changes to official records. Soon I would be training with the men while deceiving everyone about my real identity...

If I was lucky, the officers would have me dragged away to rot in some jail for the rest of my life. My family name would be disgraced. And Father would be forced to fight anyway.

If I wasn't lucky...

I didn't want to think about it.

"I don't know. But I think we've done everything we can." Yang Jie seemed to shrug off his grave mood, squeezing my shoulder before letting go. "Now we need to attend to our own business. And find something to eat! I'm starving. Come on."

I made an effort to put my own worries and misgivings aside as we headed to the barracks together. But even as I chatted companionably to him and went through the motions of settling into the camp, a sense of deep foreboding descended over me. I had succeeded in convincing my family to let me come here and succeeded in convincing the camp officials to accept me into the ranks of the army. At home, when I planned this, those had seemed the biggest obstacles.

But this morning the enemy had been close to killing me without coming anywhere near me. I had made my first and only friend and then almost lost them again, because of who my father was. And nearly incurred the wrath of the first senior officer I spoke to without even trying.

With a sensation like falling, I realized that, despite all my preparations to come here, I wasn't prepared for this. I hadn't been prepared for anything that happened today. I wasn't prepared for tomorrow, or the next day, or the one after that. I had no idea what challenges were coming next.

Eight

I passed a restless and chilly night in the bed closest to the badly cut, draughty door of the barrack building – all the warmer beds having been claimed by recruits who had arrived earlier. In the dark, with the whispering of strange men's breath and the stink of their sweat, unwashed hair and night gasses all around me, the white emptiness of fear screamed at the edges of my mind.

What was I doing there?

I wanted to go home. I wanted to know my place and exactly what I was supposed to do, even if I could never quite do it well enough to please everyone. I wanted my quiet brother and cheerful sister, my solid father and my mother, my mother who always seemed so far away from me, but at the same time was always there.

They were mine and they were safe and I had never realized, until now, how much I needed them.

But they … did not need me. They never had.

This was the only thing I was good at, good for, the only good thing I had been able to offer them since the night of assassins.

I had to see it through.

Waking from a light doze before dawn, I shifted uncomfortably in the creaky bed as I pulled my male mask across my face, aware of a low, grinding ache in my abdomen and an uncomfortable, sticky sensation in my loincloth.

My eyes snapped open on a wave of realization. I barely prevented myself from bolting upright in the bed and waking everyone around me. My monthly bleeding!

Shaking with tension, I scrambled out of bed, grabbed one of my saddlebags and fled to the river. I had always been taught to avoid getting cold during what my mother referred to as "heavenly waters", in case I fell ill, but I had no choice now. With fumbling hands, I undressed the minimum possible amount and hastily cleaned myself up, thanking my ancestors when I saw that the blood had not soaked all the way through my clothes.

The ruined loincloth I flung into the river. Bloody scraps of cloth would hardly cause any remark downstream from an army camp. I padded the new one thickly with bandages – the same soft cloth bandages any soldier might carry with him – wrapped around a wad of cotton batting – still easy enough to explain away if anyone found them in my pack. My bleeding was usually light, and this would suffice for most of the day, but I would have to sneak off to take care of it before bed tonight.

I rinsed my stained hands in the icy water, scrubbing feverishly to try to get the red crescents from beneath my nails. My ribs shuddered with a combination of cold and suppressed, self-directed fury. I knew the bleeding was coming today, I had planned for it. How could I have forgotten? Just *forgotten*? Something so vital to my charade, something so simple to prepare for?

I knelt at the edge of the river and tried to calm myself. Deep breaths, following the flow of *qi* through my body, allowing the bad feelings to drain away. It was all right. I had made a mistake, a stupid, stupid mistake, but it hadn't cost me anything, and I wouldn't allow it to happen again. It was all right. All right.

The sky was beginning to lighten, and muffled noises told me that some in the camp were already stirring. There was no chance of more sleep for me, not after that. I might as well take advantage of the extra time.

Creeping stealthily back into the barracks, I made my bed, put on my new uniform and left to fulfil my first duty of the day: caring for Yulong. By the time the great gong forced my fellows to begin thrashing and groaning among their threadbare blankets, I had slipped back into the barracks and seated myself cross-legged on the floor beside my bed, beginning the process of transferring possessions from my saddlebags to the wooden trunk I had been issued, so that I would be able to find what I needed more easily.

Then the senior officers made a surprise inspection of the barracks.

"On your feet," an officer bellowed from the doorway.

Cold air gusted in around him in misty tendrils. "Your commander is present!"

The other recruits – caught in the process of ever-so-slowly inching their way out of warmish beds into freezing air – exploded into panicked activity. I saw one boy flail so hard that he flung his bedclothes halfway across the room. Another hit the floor still tangled up in his. Yang Jie, who had been yawning hugely in the bed next to mine, stared at my neatly bound hair and smoothed-down blankets with an expression of deepest betrayal.

"At ease, men, at ease!" a genial voice rang out. "This is my first time meeting most of you: welcome! Welcome to the Glorious Brotherhood of the Imperial Army!"

I glanced up furtively to see a man about my height, though of much more powerful build, in a suit of splendid gilded armour. The helm of a banner commander, with its crest of crimson horsehair, was tucked casually under one arm. His hair was thinning, but he had a magnificent dark-brown beard, and steely eyes that belied the informality of his tone.

I managed to get my gaze back on the floor before he caught me looking, noticing that Yang Jie, like me, had shrewdly chosen to stay at attention.

"These are Captains Lu Buwei and Sigong Qi, my right-hand men," the commander went on. "They will be assessing your skills and fitness, starting this morning. I am Commander Diao Tian Ning. I hope to have cause to be proud of you all in the coming weeks and months, during your training and in the fight against the vicious traitors who threaten our empire."

Despite the encouraging nature of his words, the silence that fell as Commander Diao paced up and down the central corridor that separated the rows of beds was anything but relaxed. He took a moment to stare at each bed and each recruit. His genial expression never changed.

"Captain Lu," the commander spoke again at last, voice still mild, "perhaps I am mistaken. The morning gong. Did it not ring a full five minutes ago?"

"You are not mistaken, Commander," Lu Buwei said. I risked a fleeting glance at him. He was fairly radiating smug satisfaction. "In fact, it rang nearly six minutes ago."

The commander paused in the exact centre of the building, rotating slowly on the spot. "Can anyone tell me, then – why, five minutes after the morning gong summoned you to training, are you all still dressed in sleeping clothes, unwashed and undressed, with your beds unmade?"

His answer was a silence that squirmed like a nest of slugs.

"You. Are. Soldiers," he said, words thudding into our ears hard enough to make several people flinch. "And this is a war. Three months ago, I finished training the last crop of conscripts to this army and sent them into battle. Over half those young men are already dead. This is not a game. It is life and death, and if you want to survive, *you will toughen up*.

"From now on, you will rise, make your beds, make yourself presentable and ready to fight before that gong has finished shaking. Am I understood?"

More silence.

"AM I UNDERSTOOD?" the commander roared.

"Yes, sir!" the pathetic chorus of voices squeaked, cracked and shook – mine amongst them.

"If I visit again at this hour and find you and your quarters in such a state of disgusting disarray, each and every one of you will get five stripes on your back. Captain Lu! Make a note. The east barracks is on probation! Half rations for a week!"

An audible gasp went through the barracks. This was a severe blow.

"Sir!" the captain acknowledged, smiling through his moustache. This seemed like a script which had most likely been acted out between them, word for word, many times before. That didn't make it any less effective.

The commander paced back towards the door and, incidentally, towards Yang Jie and myself. He took a deep breath – most likely in preparation for bellowing again. I braced myself. Then he paused.

Right in front of my bed.

Right in front of *me*.

I prodded so hard at my shadow mask that I almost tore it off. No, it was perfect. What had I done now? Was I standing like a girl? *Ancestors help me!*

"Who is this young man, Captain?"

"Er…" Captain Lu stared at me with a faint hint of recognition that slowly turned to frustration as he realized he had no idea. He had never bothered to ask my name. "I am … not quite sure, sir."

"Captain Sigong?"

The second officer spoke up for the first time, voice quiet and non-committal. "I believe that is Hua Zhi of the House of Hua."

"Well, well, well," Commander Diao murmured. "Hua Zhi. At ease."

I took him at his word this time, forcing my shoulders to unsquare a little as I raised my head and offered my first – probably awful – salute. "Sir."

The commander stared through me. "I never had the privilege of meeting the Iron General. Of course, I have heard of him and his exploits. But what I see here today speaks better of him than any ballad or battle report. It is your first day of training, and while your fellows lazed in bed, you are washed, neat to a fault and fully armoured, with your bed made. And made well."

One of his hands shot out. I couldn't restrain my flinch – but his fingers merely plucked a tiny fragment of hay from between the scale plates of my left gauntlet. I hadn't even noticed it there.

"Saw to your horse first thing, did you?" he asked.

I gulped. "Yes, sir."

What seemed like a genuine smile broke across his weathered face, transforming it. "You are a credit to the House of Hua. Watch out, Captain Lu! This one is after your job."

The captain's expression congealed into one of bitter resentment. "Indeed, sir."

Commander Diao nodded at me. "I will be watching you closely, Hua Zhi. Continue to perform at your best, and take care not to disappoint me."

With that, the man swept from the building, Captain Lu at his heels. Captain Sigong lingered at the door, quiet voice carrying beautifully in the fragile stillness left behind: "Make sure this place is neatened up and get yourselves to the mess in the next ten minutes, East Barracks."

The door closed behind him softly.

The tall, stringy youth across from me let out an explosive noise, as if he hadn't drawn breath the entire time Commander Diao was in the building. "Heavenly Phoenix! Hua Zhi, I don't know whether I ought to envy or pity you."

"Pity," I said with feeling, collapsing on to the edge of my bed. "Definitely pity."

"Come on, we've only got ten minutes!" Yang Jie interrupted, pouncing on one of his boots. Bingbing, perched at the roughly hewn head of his bed, made a rude noise, then tucked her beak under her wing and went back to sleep.

We did make it to the mess, and with a minute to spare. By the time our bowls were filled with their meagre half-portion of breakfast – rice porridge – the skinny boy had introduced himself as Ma Wen, nineteen, of the House of Fong.

"So, what is it like, then?" he asked eagerly as we sat, already cramming rice into his mouth. The next words came out muffled and I looked away. "Having Hua Zhou for a father?"

My teeth clamped together. *Maybe I should move seats...*
Yang Jie nudged me gently with his elbow.

I sighed. "What's *your* father like?"

Ma Wen swallowed with an effort and shrugged. "I don't know. Normal. Like any father, I suppose."

"Well, there you are, then." I picked up some dried meat and tore off a healthy bite. "The reason I was up early is that my bed is next to the door and it's too cold to sleep well. That's all. If Commander Diao does watch me, he's going to be very bored."

Ma Wen nodded slowly, looking equal parts relieved and let down.

Yang Jie gave me a sidelong look. Under his breath, he mumbled, "My bed's right next to yours. I slept fine."

"Shut up," I muttered back from the corner of my mouth.

He gave me a sunny grin and I couldn't help but smile back.

Don't relax, spoke a voice from the screaming white void of fear. *You don't really know him. He doesn't know who you truly are. What you truly are.*

And you need to make sure it stays that way.

Nine

After breakfast we, along with the other men of east and south barracks, gathered on the muddy field at the east end of the valley. Captain Lu awaited there for us, an unimpressed sneer firmly fixed on his face.

"You know," Yang Jie said softly, "I could easily learn to dislike that man."

My monthly bleeding was giving me cramps again, and I wasn't in the mood to chat – even if I agreed with Yang Jie. "He's our commanding officer," I said sternly, hoping to shut him up.

"I envy Captain Sigong," our new officer said silkily, pacing lazily up and down at the head of the field as we formed into slightly ragged lines. "North and west barracks show at least some promise. I'm stuck with you. May my ancestors have mercy on me."

His gaze seemed to narrow on me as I attempted to

make myself inconspicuous behind Ma Wen.

"Here are the rules. You won't be warned again. You will care for your sword, and keep it clean and in good condition. If you have a horse, you will do the same. You are also responsible for the care and maintenance of your clothes and armour. If anything you've brought is of unsuitable quality, report to the ironsmith or quartermaster for a replacement, or mend it. Anyone caught with dirty, broken-down swords or armour will get ten stripes from my whip. Understood?"

"Yes, sir!" we shouted dutifully.

"You will receive training in swordsmanship, pikework, archery and fighting on horseback. You will also learn how to operate a basic four-man cannon, a fire lance, and how to safely handle gunpowder explosives. If you show talent in any of these fields, we will give you extra training. Don't expect it to happen, though. I'm the best swordsman and horseman in this camp and I'm not easily impressed."

I wondered if the commander and Captain Sigong had heard this speech and what they thought of being relegated to – presumably – second and third place.

"You're expected in this training field, armoured and ready to learn, twenty minutes after the gong rings each morning. You will wash and make your beds and ensure that the barracks are tidy and clean before you leave them every day. They will be subject to surprise inspection." Again, his gaze seemed to seek me out. "I don't like whiners, so don't come complaining to me about fights or hurt feelings – I don't care who your fathers are or what house you come from. But if you're *caught* fighting any-where other than this practice field? You will be whipped. Twenty lashes. Stealing from the officers or stores? Twenty lashes. Trying to smuggle a woman into camp? Twenty lashes – and the rest of the men will share the woman. What's left of her after I'm done, anyway." He smirked. "If you attempt to desert? It'll be a sword to your neck and a letter of apology to your mother. And you'd better hope that Commander Diao has Sigong do the killing – because I won't make it quick. Any questions?"

A cold sweat had sprung up on my upper lip and brow, and my stomach was churning. I swallowed fran-tically as bile crept into my throat. I didn't dare look at Yang Jie, although I could feel him nearly vibrating with tension behind me.

"Good." The captain nodded in satisfaction. "Everyone take a practice sword from the bins on either side of the field, then form up into pairs. I'll demonstrate a basic sword form. You will imitate me and I will assess you. Go!"

I broke quickly for the left side of the field, sure that anyone who was tardy in getting back into their line would end up facing some form of awful punishment. With a quick glance, Yang Jie and I paired, taking positions opposite each other. I already knew the form, but I forced myself to watch Lu carefully anyway, in case there was some small variation I might miss. I breathed slowly and deeply through the familiar movements, trying to centre myself and expel my anxiety … and ignore my throbbing abdomen. Yang Jie's movements were a little hesitant, but surprisingly smooth and graceful.

I spared a quick smile for him, and he grinned back.

"All right, enough," Captain Lu bellowed, waving the recruit who had been working with him back into place amongst the ranks. "Congratulations, men! Despite first appearances, you're not totally hopeless. Time for something a little more advanced." He smiled, working his sword idly in figure-of-eights in the air. "Let's have a new volunteer, shall we?"

The clammy cold breath of inevitability chilled my spine. *No. Please.*

Lu's eyes fixed on me. "Ah, Hua Zhi. I'm sure you must be dying to share your skills with your fellows. Come up here. The rest of you, break ranks and gather around – you'll want to see this."

Yang Jie bit his lip, looking faintly grey again, but he tapped me bracingly on the shoulder as I passed, working my way through the other recruits. I tried to slow my breathing. *Don't panic.*

Clearly I was about to receive some form of payback for having inadvertently made Lu look unprepared in front of his senior officer, and probably for having talked back to him yesterday, too.

But it couldn't be anything too extreme, could it? Not with all these witnesses. I hadn't actually done anything wrong. Lu didn't … he didn't know. He couldn't have guessed. No, I just had to play along with it. Take it with grace and a laugh, if I could, and…

And don't give yourself away.

I stepped into place before the captain and bowed deeply, trying not to wince at the pull in my belly.

Lu's answering bow was perfunctory, little more than a head nod. It shouldn't have grated on me, but it did. My father gave even the youngest and most feeble of his challengers a proper bow.

"This is a slightly more difficult form," Lu said, addressing the gathered men. "Still easy enough for a beginner, though. Its name is Typhoon Water. Do you know it, boy?"

Typhoon Water was one of the most advanced and showy forms for disarming an opponent.

"No, sir," I said, allowing my – genuine – nerves to colour my voice. Depending on how far he took it, this might be about to hurt a *lot*. Practice swords were blunt, but they were heavy.

"Just follow my movements and we'll soon have you up to speed, then," he said soothingly. "First I will move into your space like this, bringing my sword across your guard like so. Try to block me – no, faster, keep up!"

I allowed him to lead me through the opening movements of the form, arranging my expression into one of tense concentration, even though he wasn't actually teaching me either the defensive or offensive movements. In fact, he was merely using the inexperienced, fumbling responses of a novice to starkly display his own practised ease.

He hadn't lied. He was a good swordsman. It took some skill to keep my own movements halting and hesitant without seeming too clownish. But the hardest part was to hide how much I was braced to take a painful hit at any moment. It had to be coming.

"No, no – keep your shoulder extended. Up!" Lu

snapped, hitting my elbow from beneath with the heel of his palm. The blow drove the soft flesh of my inner arm against the scale plates of my shoulder armour. This time I let the wince show, and Lu raised his eyebrows.

"Bruise easily? Well, we'll soon beat that out of you!"

There was a tentative gurgle of laughter from the other trainees, and I aimed a quick grin at them, letting them see that I didn't mind being the butt of the joke. The laughter became a little more enthusiastic.

I caught the sudden movement from the corner of my eye and whipped back around instinctively, registering the angle and speed of Lu's blunt blade in the flash of an instant. He was going for my shoulder – the weak place where the two sections of scale armour were laced together – and the full weight of his body was behind the thrust—

If the blow connected, then my shoulder could be dislocated.

I didn't think. With a yell, I dropped my blunt, useless sword. A flex of the knees and a twist spun me beneath the jab of Lu's blade.

My right hand flew up as I surged upright with my back to Lu's chest. My fingers clamped on to his wrist, twisting it outwards in a movement that made him snarl with pain – and allowed me to scoop the sword from his suddenly loosened grasp with my other hand. I twisted the arm that I still held to me with all my might, wrenching it across my body and using the captain's own instinctive, off-balance movement to throw him over my shoulder to the ground.

He landed with a soft, winded gasp. His sword fell beside him into the mud.

Wary and breathing hard with reaction, I backed away.

There was a silence that seemed very, very long.

Somewhere in the far distance, I could hear briskly raised voices shouting orders, the wind as it moved across the hills above camp, and a songbird warbling. I wondered faintly if it was Bingbing.

The recruits stared as Captain Lu slowly rolled up to his knees, gained his feet, and turned. His face was as pale as wax. He looked at where his practice sword was sinking into the wet dirt. Then he raised his gaze to mine. His eyes flared with rage.

One hand snapped down to his belt, where a whip with a sharp metal tip was coiled. He pulled it free and snapped it out with a sharp crack that made everyone watching leap back.

I alone was frozen, unable to move, to think or even breathe as he took a step forward.

The sound of applause broke the tension like a bamboo pick shattering ice.

"Well done," Commander Diao boomed, striding forward. "A fine demonstration, Captain! Really very fine! And this is Hua Zhi again, I see. All becomes clear."

The fury disappeared from Lu Buwei's eyes instantly, replaced by a bland smile. He swiftly recoiled the whip, and answered with a small laugh. "Yes, sir! Hua Zhi is a promising young soldier."

"And a good thing, too, from what I saw." Diao's face

was immobile, steely eyes glinting opaquely in that expression of fearsome geniality which I was convinced was every bit as fake as my shadow mask. "But perhaps Typhoon Water is a little advanced for the first day, Lu Buwei?"

"I took the liberty of assessing Hua Zhi for the advanced training," the captain said confidently. There was no trace of his former loss of control. *I* almost believed him. "With Captain Sigong."

Diao turned his hard eyes on me. "Well. A rare recommendation from Captain Lu! And as it happens, I agree. Tomorrow after the first gong you'll report to the west field, Hua Zhi. I'll let Sigong know at dinner. But in the meantime, Captain, perhaps you could finish the morning's basic training as scheduled. Less disruption that way."

"Of course, sir. Back to ranks, men!" The captain saluted Diao sharply. His other hand made an equally sharp cutting motion at me, which I interpreted as, *Get out of my sight*. I almost ran back to the rapidly reforming lines of men, pathetically grateful that Ma Wen was so tall as I darted behind him. He gave me a look of pained sympathy as I passed, but kept his face pointed at the front.

"Are you all right?" Yang Jie murmured behind me.

Was I? I had been one blink, one moment away from disaster. Maybe even from death.

Yang Jie's hand appeared before me, holding my abandoned sword. The blade and grip were smeared with dirt. I took the practice weapon, letting it droop from my fingers without bothering to wipe it. My hand was shaking so badly I could barely hold on anyway. Belatedly, I nodded. "I'm fine."

"You don't sound fine. I wouldn't be fine. He'd really have done it. Broken your arm. Or whipped you for not letting him." He sounded grim. "Bastard."

"Did your father teach you to fight like that?" Ma Wen asked out of the corner of his mouth.

I let out a shuddering sigh that changed midway into something shamefully close to a sob. "Yes. Yes, he did."

"Lucky for you. I wish my father had taught me things like that," Ma Wen said, sounding a little queasy.

I was beginning to think mine hadn't taught me nearly enough.

Ten

Almost three months later…

Diao had Lu carry out the whipping under the midday sun in the centre of camp, with all trainees in attendance.

Purple-black stripes bloomed on the recruit's back. After the tenth blow, the skin broke open, spilling crimson, and flies began to buzz around the red drips on the parched earth. At the twelfth blow, the man broke under the punishment and screamed: hoarse, broken sobs and cries for mercy. At the fifteenth, he passed out, sagging limply from the cords that held him to his post while Lu continued with his task, face gleaming with sweat, teeth bared in a grin of what I hoped was effort.

Next to me, Yang Jie's hands were clenched, yellow and red with strain, around the buckle of his sword belt.

He didn't flinch. Didn't look away from the flogging. I wasn't even sure he was breathing.

Diao had called the recruit an attempted deserter. A man who had lost his honour. After this he might very easily lose his life. Yet the punishment was still considered merciful. Diao could have had him executed outright for such a serious offence.

Lu paused for a moment. He dragged his forearm over his face, resettled his feet. His eyes were fixed on the bleeding welts, and his tongue came out to moisten his bottom lip. As the whipping restarted, I closed my eyes, clenched my teeth, and tried to be somewhere else in my head.

When it was over and the surgeons had carried the unconscious soldier away, Diao gave the order for us to disperse. It was time for the midday meal but, although my stomach was empty and rumbling, I was sure if I tried to eat anything right now, it wouldn't stay down long. As the other trainees began to shuffle off – Ma Wen loping past with a wave, in search of extra rations as always – I looked at Yang Jie.

He forced a stiff smile, cleared his throat and said, "You should get the surgeons to look at that black eye before pike training this afternoon."

"What?"

"It's swelling. Much more and you won't see a pike coming, and you'll have a matching bruise on the other side."

I snorted out a sound that might have been a laugh. "Mother? Is that you?" The forgotten bruise on my face – gained during advanced sword-work training with Captain Sigong that morning – throbbed.

Yang Jie gave me a withering look, much more natural than the ghastly smile, and shoved me with that surprising strength of his. "Never mind. Go drown yourself instead, fat head."

"All right, all right – I'll go!" I said, relief making my smile wide. "This is me going, see?"

But I didn't.

Even if my eye had been much worse than it was, I wouldn't have dared to visit one of the doctors here. Military doctors were the best, and that meant they were experts in *qi*. My father had warned me before I left home that while these men wouldn't be able to see through my shadow mask, if one of them touched me, they would probably feel that it was there. I really would rather drown myself – in the valley's stream, now flooded and fast with melt-water from the mountains upriver – than risk that.

If I was discovered, would I be whipped like that poor man? He had begged at first. Begged for mercy, for the pain to stop...

I hurried to the barracks, finding them deserted as they normally were at this time. Grateful that I'd taken to carrying my little hand mirror with me everywhere, I checked on my shadow face, ensuring that the bruise on my skin had transferred perfectly to the illusion. The reflections I could glean at the river weren't good for that kind of detailed work, although I was getting better with practice. But it would have been far too conspicuous if the bruise hadn't shown up; at least six other people had seen

Sigong nail me right in the cheekbone with his sword hilt.

These were the sorts of details that could ruin me, if I wasn't careful.

Like that jagged new scar by my right eye, still red and glaring though the wound had been healed for weeks. Lu's work. I had, according to him, failed to salute promptly enough, and he had shoved me face first into the barracks door.

The sharper cheekbones, those were important. We'd all grown thinner and more hungry-looking, with how often our rations were halved for infractions. My skin was two shades browner now, from training all day in the sun. And I needed to make sure my mask reflected smudges of dirt, a speckle of gunpowder, and stubble. Looking too clean would be a real giveaway, especially since I stank just as much as everyone else.

Spring had long passed into deep summer, and the heat pressed down on our little valley from dawn until after dusk, baking the mud solid. Mountain snow-melt had poured into our stream, turning it into a fast-moving river that was the only place to reliably cool down. But as the sun rose earlier and earlier, it became much harder for me to wash in private. I had endured some ribald remarks and teasing for being so weirdly shy about stripping off … until Yang Jie told everyone that assassins had tried to murder my family when I was a little boy, and I was covered in hideous scars.

When the other men stared at me for confirmation, I stared back, unblinking, until they retreated, mumbling apologies.

"How did you know about that?" I asked him later, wondering if it had ended up in a history book somewhere, or if it was just common knowledge.

He gaped at me. "I – I didn't? Hua Zhi, I made that up! You mean it's true?"

I could have corrected him on the hideous scars, but it was a very convenient explanation, so instead I told him a carefully edited account of what had happened, and left his imagination to fill in the rest.

"No wonder your father taught you to fight," he mumbled. "Argh, just bury me in a hole. I'm so sorry."

"I'd only have to dig you out again," I said cheerfully. "And now people will leave me to wash in peace. Come on, don't pull that face. Everyone here has their own tale of woe. Even … even you?"

He pulled his lower lip between his teeth. "Maybe."

Tentatively, I made to touch his shoulder, as he often did mine. He flinched. I realized with a queasy lurch that Yang Jie never seemed particularly keen to strip off entirely at the river either.

I never brought it up again.

Over the past weeks I had watched my friends and fellow recruits calm and settle, toughening up into competent young soldiers. If I could have seen myself from the outside, I wondered if I would have been able to observe the same process taking place – or if my shadow mask would have hidden it from me, as it hid my real self from everyone else. I didn't feel any different. And I had already been very physically strong, well-trained, used to getting by on less sleep than most people. But now I could run for longer, and faster, fight all-out without getting winded, and I'd had to adjust my armour to accommodate new muscles in my shoulders and upper arms. I walked differently, too. I saw it in the square shoulders of the long black shadow that preceded me as I strode purposefully across camp, and the way that people unthinkingly made room for me when I arrived.

There were still close calls. My monthly bleeding continued to cause me varying levels of anguish and inconvenience each time it came, and once, in sword training, another boy had accidentally ripped a great hole in my shirt, forcing me to hold an illusion over the bandages around my chest for the rest of the afternoon. The drain on my energy and resulting lack of focus had resulted in a sprained knee for me and a bloody lip for him. But despite this, despite all my anxiety and care, sometimes … I forgot I was not Hua Zhi.

I forgot I was different from anyone else in the camp, that I had lived a vastly different life. I forgot I wasn't born a boy. It ought to have been impossible. But it wasn't. That was the trouble. It was *easy*.

Don't. Just … don't think about that now.

I tucked the mirror back into my pocket, blew out a deep, slow breath – forcing the memory of those stripes of bruised flesh and oozing blood from my mind – and pushed open the barracks door. Outside, a group of the older recruits were pissing up against the wall, boasting, laughing and gibing. I stopped for a second, going hot with the realization that they had been so near, and I hadn't heard. One of them might have decided to fling open the barracks door at any time and seen me adjusting my face. I had let myself become too focused.

I was so busy chastising myself that at first I didn't notice what they were saying.

"… gave her a good slap and she yelped like a goat in season! So then I bent her over and—"

"Tell us another one, Cheng Yi! You'd have been finished after the first go," another one jeered, laughing.

"What would you know about it, silk sleeve?" the first one snapped. "You probably can't tell a woman's arse from a little boy's—"

With a yell they flew at each other. Neither bothered to fasten their pants first. I slipped past, holding my breath against more than the stink of their urine.

This was the army and, as far as the army was concerned, it was just a day like any other.

My hastily consumed midday meal gurgled queasily in my stomach. Sweat oozed everywhere, trickling down the back of my neck and between my shoulder blades. I gritted my teeth and thrust the long, octagon-shaped shield – formed of a heavy metal plate laminated with leather – forward into the red, annoyed faces of the other team.

The dozen men who had been assigned to the shields on my side of the field grunted and jostled around me. Many had gained the sergeant's permission to strip down to their bare chests, and their shoulders gleamed in various deepening shades of bronze under the afternoon sun.

Clad in only a thin linen shirt, with a small additional illusion woven atop the firm binding of my chest, I felt intensely vulnerable as we grappled and slid together in such close quarters. It would only take a little slip and... But surely, even if someone did feel something, they wouldn't believe it?

Pikes and swords thudded against the barrier formed of our shields as the opposing team attempted to force their way through. One of the men next to me skidded half a pace backwards as a trainee on the opposing side threw themselves violently at the shield wall. A long pike, headed with a blunt blade, found the narrow gap in the defence and jabbed through – heading straight for my face.

I couldn't duck without jerking my shield out of position and giving up ground to the other side. I gritted my teeth, bracing for the impact—

Yang Jie appeared next to me in a graceful swoop. One strong, small hand snapped up to seize the shaft of the practice pike, forcing it away from my face. With his dominant hand, he jabbed a blunt sword back through the gap into the opposing trainee's ... gut, by the sound of the stunned *Ooof.* My shield suddenly met no resistance. I surged forward, the trainees next to me following with whoops of triumph. The pike rattled over our shields to the dusty dirt at our feet.

Yang Jie – mood seemingly back to its normal buoyancy, despite the morning's events – winked at me, scooped up the fallen pike, and braced himself against the back of the man next to me. With a chorus of animal grunts and snarls, we pushed the other side back. I heard their leader cry out, "No! Hold your ground!"

A savage grin split my lips. We were going to win.

Then, above the familiar cacophony of shuffling feet, panting breaths and clattering weapons, there came a high, clarion call – the bright and unmistakable notes of a sentry's horn, carried on the hot summer wind that flowed above our heads.

Someone was approaching the camp.

As one, both sides fell back, dropping practice weapons and reaching for real ones, turning to face the western hills where the horn had blown.

"Wait!" the sergeant bellowed, voice tense. "It was an alert, not the call to arms."

Nevertheless, we scrambled into formation and stood tense and prepared. My heart was drumming with readiness, and I wished I had my armour. Who was coming here and why? There had been nothing but regularly scheduled supply caravans in the months since training began.

"Alert from the west?" Yang Jie muttered. "No one ever comes here from the west…"

The horn sang out again: three long, wavering notes that reminded me of Bingbing's welcome song. The sergeant sagged for an instant, then straightened, his hand falling from the hilt of his sword. "All clear!"

He might have said something else, but I heard nothing more than that.

There, on the crest of the hill above the valley, the crimson banner of the Imperial Army rose into view, held on a long silver pole by a military outrider on a dark horse. Another reined in beside him, this one with a dappled mount, holding a flag of rich, deep blue, picked out in gold with a personal emblem that I did not know.

And finally, followed by a small gaggle of servants, spare mounts, a wagon and pack mules, a towering war-horse appeared. Its heaving sides were the colour of blood, its legs, mane and tail black as night. The animal would have dwarfed Yulong, just as its rider dwarfed me and almost every man in the training field with me. Silhouetted against the bleached-blue sky, he appeared the size of a giant.

The sun flashed on the plates of his armour, setting fire to the flying white horsehair plume of his helmet. His red horse reared – and the rider lifted a burning sword, seeming to salute us. Around him the banners snapped and rippled in a sudden hot wave of air that washed over us, gritty gold with dust and summer grass pollen. High overhead, a hawk dived, its haunting shriek echoing through the valley.

I sensed the indrawn breath of my fellows, the feeling of unreality. This was a scene from a tapestry or ballad, an image from a legend. It couldn't be real.

The horse's front hooves hit the ground again with a puff of dirt. Then the rider and his followers turned and began a sedate descent down the hill.

"General Wu," Yang Jie whispered, eyes wide.

"Who?" I asked, only to startle when everyone turned on me with expressions of disbelief and annoyance.

"Wu Jiang!"

"The emperor's favourite nephew!"

"He's the youngest general in the history of the Imperial Army! Only twenty-one years old!"

"They call him the Young General," Yang Jie said more quietly. "The hero of Black Gorge. It's said he's the best the emperor has. The best since your father."

There was a weighted pause while everyone stared at me. "Oh, him," I said feebly.

I had *heard* of Wu Jiang. From my father, in passing. Not with this froth of hero-worship bubbling around his name.

Even before the Leopard's uprising, before the war, the emperor had paid a heavy price for the throne. Many of her family had died in the earlier conflicts which had sealed her reputation. After her oldest brother lost his wife to poison meant for the emperor herself, Wu Fen had taken his only child, his son, into her own household and raised him as a sort-of big brother to her child, the crown prince.

And that was all I knew of Wu Jiang.

Perhaps they tell different stories to daughters than sons…

"Men!" the sergeant shouted, making us all jump. "Did I declare a holiday and forget it? Did I ask you to stand around gossiping like women in the middle of doing the laundry?" His face was like a thundercloud as we all scrambled back into place. But hardly had the opposition hefted their shields again when his own head whipped around.

Commander Diao was approaching the training field. Captain Lu walked on his left, and they were trailed by the censor, the camp's priest and the novice priest, Diao's aide-de-camp Sergeant Yun, and every other person of any importance in the valley.

Towering over Diao on the right was an astonishing physical specimen, as broad across and nearly as tall as half a barn door. His glossy hair gleamed a true blue-black, drawn up from a severe widow's peak into a simple knot. His jaw was square and stubborn, adorned by a beautifully trimmed dark beard which framed a wide, full-lipped mouth. The beard was probably an attempt to make himself appear older, because his face, though bronzed, was young. He wore the gilded, bejewelled armour of a general, and bristled with weapons, but walked as if the weight of metal plate, scale and steel was nothing to him, even in this blistering heat.

Once again I felt the interest and awe ripple through my fellow recruits and, once again, their emotions were mine as well. This could only be the Young General. The man was the pinnacle of masculine beauty and power. At a single glance I knew he was everything that every man aspired to be.

How must it feel to be him? It must be something like paradise, to be a man like that.

"Form up, recruits!" our sergeant ordered. His second order came in an undertone that was still perfectly audible to the back ranks. *"Hold your tongues and look sharp."*

I skidded into position, still examining the Young General avidly. He turned his head, and I caught my breath as I glimpsed the dark fire of his eyes, alight with fierce intelligence and ambition.

"Some of our most promising young recruits," Diao was telling Wu. "And Sergeant Sui, who is invaluable in helping whip them into shape."

Our sergeant bowed deeply. "An honour, General."

"Indeed it is!" Diao agreed heartily. His expression was even more fixed than usual. "I only wish that we had been offered some small warning as to the general's planned inspection—"

"Oh, not an inspection, Commander," Wu Jiang protested. His voice was deep but surprisingly soft, and he drew his words out almost sleepily. "A friendly visit."

"Regardless, I fear you'll find our ability to entertain you lacking," the commander finished. "We are a mere humble training facility. Luxury is not to be expected here."

Yang Jie made a small, pained sound. I agreed silently. For some unfathomable reason Diao seemed to dislike the Young General, or resent his presence, and he was taking little trouble to hide it.

Captain Lu, on the other hand, was oozing around to the Young General's right side with a smile that positively beamed. If he had been a cat, I would have been checking the ground for feathers. "I'm certain that a decorated military hero like Wu Jiang expects nothing that our camp cannot provide, sir."

Was that ... a subtle dig at the commander for implying that Wu Jiang was a soft nobleman?

"I'll wager we can offer the finest martial entertainment in the empire. Perhaps even fine enough to present the general with a real challenge. I, myself, would be happy to engage in a friendly sparring match before dinner—"

Diao cut Lu off ruthlessly. "The general has ridden several thousand miles to grace us with his presence. I'm sure that what he would like most is to bathe, eat and rest. Is that not so, General Wu?"

"Whatever you say, Commander Diao. Very kind of you," the general said amiably, giving the impression that he'd barely heard anything either of them had said. His eyes were scanning our ranks with interest, and he murmured a question to our sergeant, who looked almost as star-struck as we all felt at speaking to such an august personage.

Lu wilted, while the commander's face hardened even further into a smile that was painful to see. Diao led the general away, and everyone else scurried to follow.

The sergeant turned back to us, ran his gaze over our ranks, and sighed. "Go on, then – clean yourselves up and get your chattering and dreaming done," he ordered wearily. "You stink and I'm sick of the sight of you."

The east barracks were filled with jubilation. Not only had we been blessed with a glimpse of the famous General Wu, but we had somehow gained an hour's free time before dinner without incurring any punishments for it. After the morning's grim events, it really was like a holiday.

The others chattered eagerly, turning over every detail they had observed – the height and colour of General Wu's horse, the way he shaved his beard, the possible maker of his sword – as if it were a precious gem. I alone seemed troubled by the murky undercurrents which had swirled around the commanding officers and their royal visitor.

"Your problem is that you use all your brain power up worrying about things that are none of your concern," Yang Jie told me. He was reclining on his bed eating a few precious slivers of his favourite lemon peel, the picture of ease, with Bingbing perched on his updrawn knee. "Then, when you actually need the use of your brain, you find that it's given up, exhausted, and you're on your own."

I threw a smelly sock at his head. He batted it out of the air with a moue of disgust, and I snorted out a laugh.

"Lucky I've got you around then, isn't it, Oh Wise One," I said. "I suppose you spent your time in that pit contemplating the mysteries of the universe, and if it wasn't for me interrupting you, you'd be penning a book of philosophical poetry right now."

He finished his lemon peel, folded his arms behind his head, and softly recited:

"Fires on the horizon.
Wars never end.
We fight and fall,
And the dark birds pick at our flesh
Perching on dead trees surrounded by the dead,
Where we have painted the grasses red."

The words made the air resound, vibrating like the iron strings of a zither. I swallowed. "That's…"

He arched a fine brow at me. "You're not the only one that can read, you know. Come on. We might as well get to the mess early. I'm still making up for last week's half rations."

But we hadn't been eating long before a wave of excitement and surprise washed through the recruits.

Captain Lu himself had entered the mess – ushering the Young General before him.

Both men had changed from their armour into more casual loose robes, but the fineness of the garments, the neatness of their hair and the pristine cleanliness of their skin – the kind of cleanliness that could only be achieved with the application of copious amounts of hot water, foaming soap, and access to a mirror – made them look glaringly out of place in the mess among the scruffy, barely washed, unranked men. I had never even glimpsed an officer in this building before; the sergeants and officers ate in their own smaller mess, and the two captains dined with Commander Diao in his large, opulent tent each night.

What was Captain Lu thinking?

General Wu looked around with a hint of reticence, clearly aware of all the eyes on him. Captain Lu simply walked up to a table by the tent wall and cleared it of its occupants with an excoriating glance. Two of the men hurriedly tidied away all the plates, cups, trays and chopsticks, while another departed at a run and came back with a new, heaping tray of food which he humbly presented to the senior officer. The Young General and Captain Lu seated themselves. Lu wrinkled his nose at the food and pushed it aside. General Wu began to eat.

It seemed prudent at this point to at least pretend we weren't gawping at the two senior officers, so we all turned back to our food, and a subdued hum of conversation slowly built around us. I couldn't help observing the officers from the corner of my eye, though.

"Do you think Lu's angling for a promotion?" I asked softly. "Does he hope Wu Jiang might take him on as part of his personal staff? It's no secret that he hates being here."

"Promotion doesn't work like that, does it?" Ma Wen asked. "Aren't there … rules and … proper channels?"

"If you're as well connected as Wu Jiang, the proper channel is probably a wave of your hand," Yang Jie said dryly. "But he doesn't look all that impressed by Lu to me."

The Young General had propped himself up on one elbow, visibly bored, while Lu talked at him.

Before I could reply, Commander Diao stormed into the tent. He was smiling so hard and so terrifyingly that several nearby trainees cowered in their seats.

"Oh dear," said Yang Jie, with what I felt was admirable understatement.

"Ah! There you are!" Diao boomed pleasantly as he strode across the room. I imagined lightning bolts crackling in his thick beard and bristling eyebrows, and found my back bowing down of its own accord, as if to get further out of range.

The commander's next words, as he arrived at the general's table, were too quiet for us to hear. Lu spoke and was seemingly crushed by a single retort from Diao, subsiding into his seat with a frustrated expression. General Wu appeared placatory, lifting his hands as if in apology and shaking his head. Diao kept on smiling.

"What in the world is going on over there?" Yang Jie mumbled, giving voice to the flame of curiosity which burned in every breast.

Then, with the feeling of inescapable doom that you might expect when observing the first tiny rolling rocks that signal a coming landslide, I saw Diao turn his head, as if searching for someone that he expected to see in the mess.

"No. Please no," I whispered, causing my tablemates to look at me askance. I wiped a bead of sweat from my forehead and slumped down as low as possible over my half-eaten dinner. Diao's eyes lit upon me. "Not again, *not again*," I moaned.

Diao made a peremptory gesture of command. *Come here.*

"It's been nice knowing you, Hua Zhi," Ma Wen said gravely. "Make your ancestors proud."

Yang Jie just stared, open-mouthed – along with the rest of my barracks – as I reluctantly pushed to my feet and walked slowly over to the table by the wall.

Eleven

"**G**eneral, this is Hua Zhi of the House of Hua – Hua Zhou's son," Diao was saying as I arrived. My jaw clenched so hard that pain zigzagged into my teeth. Why was Diao talking to *General Wu* about *me*?

I saluted.

The general nodded in my direction, eyes assessing me keenly. "I didn't know the Wild Tiger had a son."

Oh, ancestors. I cleared my throat, praying I could get through this without ruining everything. "In fact, he has two, sir. Myself and my younger brother."

The general accepted it without apparent doubt. "Well, this is a pleasant surprise indeed. I met your father when I was very young, and always remembered it. He is an excellent man. I hope he is well? And your mother, too?"

The man's presence – the heat of his interest – was overwhelming. I tried my hardest not to melt into the floor. "I – left them well, sir. I have not heard from them recently."

"The soldier's life," he said wryly, as if speaking to a man of similar rank.

Against my will, my gaze slid sideways to see what Captain Lu thought of this. The captain's expression was hard, but as his eyes met mine he smiled: a humourless baring of teeth. A chill slithered down my spine. *He'd murder me if he could.*

Diao clapped my shoulder with a friendly if heavy hand. "Hua Zhi is, as expected, a very skilled young fighter. And he will truly benefit from a match – facing up to such a superior opponent will allow him to polish and refine his already impressive skills. But you must promise me to take account of his youth and inexperience, and treat him kindly."

A sparring match. That was what this was about? I almost wilted with the relief. Lu had tried to get the general to spar with him earlier, probably hoping to impress him with his abilities. Diao had blocked that, and was doing the same again – only using me, this time – probably out of spite. Lu's sycophantism towards a man Diao disliked must really have rankled.

"I really have no need of any entertainment," the general protested. "This is not a state visit. I don't want to cause any disruption."

"Oh no, how could I be such a bad host?" The commander clapped me on the shoulder again. I resisted the effort to rub the feeling back into it. "And we cannot dash this fine young man's hopes now, either, can we, Hua Zhi?"

"Of – of course, sir," I stuttered, slightly late.

"No time like the present then, gentlemen!" Commander Diao gestured at the general in much the same imperious manner he had used with me. Wu Jiang – who I felt had every right to be losing patience at this point – only let out a faint sigh as he pushed away from the table. To my dismay, Captain Lu followed as Diao steered General Wu and me towards the entrance.

As our group of four left the mess, there was a sudden rush of frenzied motion behind us. I knew without looking that every man in the place had leapt to his feet, rapidly emptying the building as they scrambled to follow us and get the best view of the coming "duel". Diao noticed the sounds – I could tell – and I fleetingly hoped that he would turn back and order everyone to return to their dinners, but his only reaction was a slight crinkling around his iron-hard eyes.

We reached the small, oval-shaped practice field that sat near the centre of the camp. I'd never trained here. It was reserved for the officers only. Accordingly, the ground had been packed with gravel to keep it dry and free of mud, tall posts at either end flew the imperial standard, and at the base of each pole there was a rough wooden bench to rest on and a trough of fresh wash to drink or to splash a hot face and hands.

This was where Lu had flogged the deserter this morning, on Diao's orders. My stomach lurched. I struggled to keep my shadow face neutral.

Diao's aide-de-camp, Sergeant Yun, appeared beside us. After a quickly murmured conversation with the commander about practice weapons, he hurried off again, pushing through the rapidly growing crowd that hovered a few feet back from the edges of the duelling ring.

"Blunt blades?" Lu said challengingly, bringing my attention back to the ring. "What if the general objects?"

My stomach turned over again, this time with a surge of loathing towards Lu. I kept my teeth firmly gritted on the hasty and insubordinate words that wanted to jump out. Diao, who was not similarly constrained, opened his mouth – but before he could speak the Young General himself turned an incredulous face on Lu. "I am not armoured, Captain."

Oh. I looked down at myself. I wasn't in full battle armour, but I had shrugged my light scale-mail coat back on over my shirt after washing. It was hot, but I liked the extra protection it offered, the break from holding an illusion over my chest. My boots also had shin guards buckled to their fronts.

I unbuckled my sword belt from around my waist and laid it and the scabbard on the bench close by. Then I reached under my left arm and began to unlace the leather ties which held the armour in place. Diao realized what I was doing and, to my astonishment, went to my right side to help, his thick, gnarled fingers picking deftly at the laces there. I took a deep breath and centred myself, quickly spinning out threads of *qi* into a robust seeming over my chest area – flat planes of muscle and lightly tanned skin, no telltale bandages, no soft curves… If Diao did notice something, his eyes would reassure him that he had been wrong. The effort left me dizzy for a moment. I stood as still as possible, waiting for the unsteadiness to pass.

General Wu had moved to the other side of the ring and was removing the fine silk of his outer robes. Lu took them reverently and folded them over the back of the wooden bench. Clad only in snug leggings and a thin shirt – like my own, though considerably crisper and whiter – the general began to gently stretch out.

"Listen, Hua Zhi," Diao murmured, as he helped me pull the armour up over my head. "Wu Jiang isn't a bad fighter. His aunt paid for the very finest tutors. But he is used to winning because his opponents fear her, not because of his own skill. I've watched you train with Sigong. You are the better swordsman, and you are entirely capable of beating him. I'll undertake to ensure that there are no consequences for you, although I fancy your father's name would be protection enough regardless. In return, you are to fight full-out, do you understand?"

Why? I wanted to ask. *We're all supposed to be on the same side!* But of course I didn't. My commander had ordered: my lot was to obey without question.

"I – I can try, sir," I whispered. Regardless of what Diao said, it was obvious to anyone who had eyes to look at General Wu that I didn't stand a chance. He was built like three of me. He was a war hero.

But I could try.

"Good man." He knelt at my feet to unbuckle the shin guard from my left boot as I bent over the right one. A moment later, Sergeant Yun returned and handed me a practice blade. It was high quality, much better than the battered old ones we recruits used day-to-day. Stepping away from the bench, I circled it in the air, testing the weight and balance as I moved slowly into a series of very basic sword forms, warming my muscles and working out any stiffness while gaining familiarity with the sword. I chose the basic forms because the Young General would almost certainly be keeping his eye on me, just as I was keeping mine on him, gauging what kind of threat he would be.

I needed to give away as little as possible.

Opposite me, Wu Jiang had his own blunt blade in hand, and was doing a different series of forms. More advanced than mine but still undemanding, standard enough to reveal little. Except that, to me, with my habit of analysing and homing in on the weaknesses of others – a habit formed through years and years of observing my father's duels – the movements revealed a surprising amount.

Despite his height, he was light on his feet, with that natural nimbleness some very large men seemed to possess. His movements weren't showy, but they were confident and graceful. In the light garments, I could see that his size was more than mere bulk – shoulders, arms and legs displayed hard muscle, the kind that took work to maintain.

"Court duelling rules, I think, General?" Diao said, stepping into the middle of the duelling ring. His tone made it clear that while this might be phrased as a suggestion, it was in fact a command. I watched Wu Jiang's face carefully. It betrayed no annoyance – only resignation and a faint gleam of what I thought was amusement. "Three bouts, each to a disarming or a standstill – or until I call 'break'. No hand-to-hand moves will be permitted. Sword-work only."

Diao's rules favoured me in this instance. I couldn't hope to punch or kick with a fraction of the power of such a weighty man as General Wu – the use of hand-to-hand moves would have given him a considerable advantage over me. He still had a greater reach and more power than I did, but in the generous space of the ring I might be able to put my speed and agility to good use and make a respectable showing. I hoped.

"Ready?" When Diao received two head nods, he backed out of the circle, leaving me face to face with Wu Jiang for the first time. We bowed formally. His bow, I noted, was just as deep as mine.

"May the best man win!" Diao boomed from the edge of the duelling ring. There was a muted cheer from the onlookers.

I eyed Wu Jiang warily as we began to circle each other. I made a slight movement to my left and tracked the minute tensing of Wu Jiang's muscles as he began to respond – but instead of lifting his blade, he backed off. Taking my measure? *Clever.*

Beginning a standard offensive form – Floating Lilies – I quickly closed in on him. Our blades clashed for the first time. He blocked me easily, shifting into the offensive posture to force me on to the defensive. The movement seemed aggressive. And yet...

His shoulders had relaxed. Why?

Switching to a different, more advanced form, I came at him in a barrage of quick, darting cuts, trying to get him off-balance. He parried, blocked and deflected, matching my speed as if by rote – but never exceeding it. He wasn't pushing me. I wasn't even breathing hard. From outside the ring, it doubtless looked very impressive, but it felt *wrong*. Like duelling with a mirror.

I switched forms again, reversing my blade's sweep into a complex corkscrewing twist that would break through his guard—

Faster than thought, he blocked me.

A flicker of a grimace crossed his face. In the next moment he disengaged, backing away hastily as if to get out of trouble. But he hadn't been in trouble. He had blocked me – easily, effortlessly – and could have countered to attempt to take my sword. *Why didn't he?*

A formless suspicion was beginning to niggle at the back of my mind.

I engaged him again, falling back into the familiar patterns of Floating Lilies once more and allowing him to do the same. Slash, block, turn – more like a dance than a fight – every move predictable and choreographed until...

There. The minute relaxation in his shoulders. I switched forms again and dived beneath his blade in the Striking Mantis attack.

His blade flashed down. It caught mine on its guard. Metal screeched shrilly as his superior strength bore down on my sword. My arms trembled as I fought to keep his sword engaged – the twin blades shook and grated between our faces. His brows had drawn together with effort. I felt his weight shift and knew he was about to twist, so he could use my own momentum against me and turn my attack back. I braced myself to fall and roll up, to counter—

Our eyes met. His widened, then narrowed. His brow smoothed out.

He fumbled his sword.

Without thinking, I surged into the opening. The blade popped out of his hand and landed on the gravel with a hollow clatter. He swore – loudly, but just an eye-blink too late to convince me – and stepped back, lifting his hands in surrender.

The roar of the crowd was triumphant. "Bout one goes to Hua Zhi!" Commander Diao announced.

I didn't take my eyes off Wu Jiang as we bowed to each other. His gaze was averted, and he sucked in deep breaths as he turned away, as if he was winded. But I had been close enough to hear his breathing a moment before, and he had not been out of breath then. He was faking.

I knew it.

I barely noticed Commander Diao guiding me back to my bench, although I gratefully accepted Sergeant Yun's offer of a cup of water. My throat felt as if it was packed with sand. I saw my friends in the ring of watchers and nodded to them, but they stayed back and I was grateful for that, too. My head was spinning. General Wu was not slow, or an average, complaisant swordsman.

He was something else.

Absent-mindedly, I splashed my sweaty, dust-smudged face with water from the trough, smoothing back stray strands of hair that had fallen into my eyes with damp hands. Then I knelt and took a handful of dirt, rubbing it into my palms to improve my grip. I was still thirsty, but I knew better than to gulp down more water. In this heat and with the exertion, it might make me sick.

Diao was leaning on the bench beside me. "Excellent work. Excellent," he murmured. Whether he spoke to me, or to himself, I couldn't tell.

Suddenly I felt very tired of him. His dislike of the Young General might be well-founded for all I knew, but I no longer cared to puzzle over it. What I cared about was this: I had the opportunity to duel with a swordsman who might match the skill of my father, but instead of fighting me with honour, he apparently intended to treat the whole thing as some kind of joke.

It was... I searched within myself for the right word. Troubling? Baffling? *Annoying.* It made no sense at all to feel slighted, but I did. I didn't seek this out. The situation was not of my making. I had been forced into this position by this dispute between Wu Jiang and Diao – pushed into the limelight again against my will. By the heavens, I at least deserved the respect of being treated as an equal in the ring.

A resolution formed. I had to draw him out somehow. If I was to win against the Young General here today, it would be for real. And if I lost, let that be real, too. Whatever happened, at least it would not be another lie.

I caught Yang Jie's worried look and dared a jaunty

wink, enjoying his expression of surprise. Energy surged through me and I felt a smile pulling at the corners of my lips.

I moved back to the centre of the duelling ring, tossing the hilt of my sword idly between my hands, flipping it over and over until I felt it settle naturally into my palm, until it belonged there.

"Ready?" Diao confirmed as Wu Jiang took his position opposite me. "Begin!"

Diao stepped out of the way and, as before, we bowed in unison.

As I straightened, I deliberately stared full into Wu Jiang's face until his gaze, as if irresistibly drawn, met mine. But this time I didn't bother with a manly, challenging glare.

I raised one eyebrow and gave him a conspiratorial grin. *Let's have some fun!*

His eyes – so dark as to appear almost black – went wide with surprise. And then, like a nugget of gold gleaming in the shadowy water of a river, I saw the wink of a dimple almost hidden in his thick, dark beard.

I raised my blade and this time he surged forward to meet me. No basics now. I recognized the Drifting Clouds form and instinctively responded with the most technically challenging defence, Scattered Clouds.

Exhilaration made my skin tingle, my cheeks flame. We were dancing again – but this time it felt right. Two swordsmen, equals, duelling not for pride or anger but for love. Love of the sword. Our swords met and parted, clashed and parted again. He pressed into my space and

I darted back. I took the advantage and he spun out of reach.

I could feel a manic grin splitting my face in two, and though his lips were firmly pressed together, the dimple in his cheek was as obvious a tell, to me, as a laugh.

Suddenly Wu Jiang broke away, stepping back and settling into the familiar stance from Floating Lilies once more. I felt a moment of confusion and then a flash of joyous realization. It was an invitation. Floating Lilies could be used to transition into Tiger Lilies – one of the most difficult and beautiful forms my father had ever taught me. I'd only practised it a few times, but at that moment in the ring with Wu Jiang, I knew I could do it. I had to.

I flowed into the movements and he flowed to meet me.

The settling sun bathed the duelling field with eerie amber light that flickered and sparked from Wu Jiang's blade like lightning. Behind the general's shoulder, the hills were black, and fire-edged blue clouds lay across the sky like banners. The shouts and awed murmuring of the watchers faded into silence. Dust seemed to hang motionless in the air around us, as if time herself had drawn in a breath, and we two were the only things that moved in the world.

Arms trembled.

Legs burned.

Breath rasped.

I was fighting full-out and still Wu Jiang matched me. Surpassed me. It was a struggle to keep up with him now. I could hardly follow the movements of his blunt practice sword, hardly gauge the minute tensing of his muscles that allowed me to meet and counter his attacks.

In a split second, I knew the truth: the Young General was a better swordsman than me. He was a better swordsman even than my father. To have attained this level of skill and yet conceal it so convincingly, from everyone... Wu Jiang was the greatest sword master I had never heard of.

And then his eyes met mine again, and he saw that I knew. The hidden, dimpled smile disappeared, like a light going out. In the next movement he slowed. Just a fraction – just enough: a masterly exercise in control. My blade, which he could easily have deflected with his own, pierced his defence and thudded solidly home against his right pectoral muscle. The impact shuddered through my arm.

Like an actor in a play, he staggered in place, one hand clasped over his chest. Suddenly his sword hand was in the path of mine, perfectly placed. The two blunt blades clashed.

His sword slipped from his loosened grip and skittered across the gravel to lie at Diao's feet.

"What – why..." The words tumbled from my numb lips as I stepped back.

The Young General bent over at the waist, one hand braced on his knee, the other still dramatically clutched over the "wound" on his breast – probably a nasty bruise. He threw his head back as if gasping for air and I heard the soft words: "Well fought, Hua Zhi."

The crowd were yelling, stamping, jumping, filling the air with the victorious sound of my name.

I felt hollow and shaky and distraught, as if I had lost something before I even realized its value.

The sun slipped below the hill as Diao charged into the ring to clasp my shoulders and congratulate me. I couldn't even look at him. I barely noticed Lu's poisonous glare.

My eyes followed the general instead, as he slipped silently off into the deepening shadows.

At some point Yang Jie arrived by my side. He slung a seemingly companionable arm around me – but his hand clasped my shoulder, squeezing as if in support. "Are you all right?" he asked, his voice buzzing in my ear.

"He let me win," I mumbled distractedly. "He just … let me win."

Yang Jie's brows drew together. "What? Are you sure?"

His doubt pressed down on a raw nerve. I shrugged his arm off. "Never mind. You wouldn't understand."

Twelve

I crouched behind the stables, coughing and gasping as I spat again and again, swirling lukewarm water from my canteen around my mouth. I had forgotten to shake the flask of tincture thoroughly before taking it, and the drop I had gargled had been painfully potent. Every time I spat I expected to see blood. Dear ancestors, it hurt. Both my nose and my tongue were numb. I couldn't even smell the stink of the horses.

A high-pitched, frenzied warbling noise brought my head up. "Bingbing?" I rasped.

The little bird shot into view as if she had been searching for me. Her wings beat a frantic tattoo around my shoulders, so close that I didn't dare to move in case I knocked her out of the air. She continued to scream. Her cries sounded almost human. Human – and afraid.

Yang Jie.

I had no memory, later, of the run that must have followed. The next thing I knew, my hands were shoving open the rough wooden door of the barracks, searching for Yang Jie – but finding only the sober, pale face of Ma Wen. He jumped to his feet as I careened in. "Hua Zhi! I was looking all over for you."

"Where is he?" The words emerged as a hastily, garbled croak. "Where is Yang Jie?"

Ma Wen's hands lifted in a helpless gesture. "We found him in the river – just now. The surgeons took him away. He's in the infirmary."

"Why? What *happened*?"

"I don't – Hua Zhi, I don't know for certain but … I think someone tried to kill him."

The great gong would ring out soon. I would be expected to leave and go about my morning's work: food, training, caring for my armour and weapons.

But I could not bring myself to leave.

Not yet.

Yang Jie made a faint snuffling sound, familiar to me from the many nights he had slept in the bed beside mine. Then he groaned.

"Shh," I whispered, although the bustle of the healer's tent continued undisturbed, noisy and businesslike, all around us. After a moment's hesitation, I leaned over him to lay one hand on his shoulder. "Stay still. You're all right, Yang Jie, you're all right. Just be still."

"Mother?" he muttered. "Is that you?"

I was so taken aback that I choked on my own breath.

Was it worse than I thought? Was he delirious? Then I heard the tiny, pained snort of his laughter, and panic dissolved into annoyance and amusement. "You ass!"

"Insulting me when I'm down, Hua Zhi? I'm shocked at you."

I sat back, scrubbing the heels of both hands into my eyes. When I lowered them, he had managed to roll his head sideways on the thin infirmary mat where they had laid him out, and he was looking up at me. His eyes looked huge in the dim interior of the building. The white of the left one was marred by an ugly red bleed around the iris, and the delicate skin of his left eyelid was painfully swollen, blotched black and purple.

"Shouldn't you be at training?" he asked.

"Not yet." I took a deep breath. "Yang Jie, you have a head injury, bruised ribs, a possible chip to your eye socket, a badly sprained wrist—"

"And a chill from lying in the river unconscious for my ancestors know how long before Ma Wen found me and dragged me out," he completed acerbically. "Yes, I know all that, thank you. The doctor told me when I woke up the last time. Any particular reason for *reminding* me?"

"They said that you didn't see who attacked you." I leaned in again, lowering my voice again. "Is that true?"

"They got me from behind – I only felt the first blow. Then I was out." But his eyes flicked away from mine as he said it, and I knew. He might not have seen the person who attacked him, but just like me, he had worked it out.

I couldn't even tell if it was rage or terror I felt, or some mixture of both. When Ma Wen found him, Yang Jie had been almost fully submerged, only a buried tree stump just under the surface keeping his head partially out of the fast-moving water. His attacker had tipped him into the river without caring if he drowned – or worse, had intended for him to die.

"Hua Zhi?" Yang Jie's voice was suddenly nearly as hushed as mine had been. "Your face is doing that – that scary blank thing. You know I hate that."

My shadow mask had not been designed to reflect such emotions. My real face, I had no doubt, would have scared Yang Jie far more.

"It was Lu, wasn't it?"

Yang Jie said nothing.

"There's no one else who would want to hurt you. You weren't even worth robbing. Your money purse was still in the barracks. It's punishment for yesterday – for me sparring with the Young General instead of him. For showing off. He couldn't go after me directly, so he punished you instead." I closed my eyes as my tumbling words slowed to a halt, leaving only the fatal ones left to be spoken. "It's my fault."

"Oh, don't start," he said wearily. "It's just as likely he did it because he despises me for being a weakling and, anyway, you're not my bodyguard—"

"Yang Jie!" His name came out as a shout. A nearby doctor and two of his assistants looked up from grinding mysterious powders to stare at me curiously. I fought the urge to cringe away. They couldn't find me out just by looking.

Yang Jie was staring at me in concern. "What?"

"You almost died." The words hung in the air between us and Yang Jie's face went still. "Lu tried to kill you because he hates me. I caused this. What do I do?"

Yang Jie's fingers twitched. Gingerly, he slid his hand up to clasp mine where it rested on his shoulder. His hand was very warm.

"You realize I'm the one lying here in my sickbed," he said dryly. "Aren't you supposed to be comforting me, instead of the other way around?"

Stricken, I started to pull my hand away. "I'm sorry—"

"*Listen.*" His fingers tightened around my hand. "This may come as a shock, but the fact is: not everything is about you. You didn't do this to me. He did. Him. You can't take responsibility for whatever warped thoughts make him act this way. People like Lu … you can't appease them. I know that because I tried for years with – with my father and brothers. It never, ever worked." His words slowed, and he took in a short, gasping breath.

"You don't have to tell me this," I said, alarmed at the sudden welling of moisture in his eyes.

"Shut up, will you? Let me speak. It's hard enough."

I clamped my lips closed.

"My family. They hated me. My whole life. Just because I was the youngest, the smallest, just because I was…" He waved his free hand to indicate his delicate face, his slim form. "The way I am. I followed their rules, I tried to be what they said they wanted me to be, but I think that just made them despise me more. My mother would comfort me, but it was always the same questions. What had

I done to deserve it? Had I spoken too loudly? Spoken at all? Breathed in their presence? Why couldn't I just … not do whatever it was I had done? I had to have done something. It had to be my fault. For a long time that defined me. They made me feel there was nothing about me that was worthy of love, or kindness or respect. But I couldn't live like that, hating myself the way they hated me. I would have … broken. Become just as bad as them, or worse. Eventually I had to accept that it wasn't my fault. It was hard – hard to admit to myself there was no hope, that they would never love or accept me. That there was no perfect way I could conduct myself, no better version of the person I was that would deserve not to be hurt and scorned and despised. But it was freeing, too. Because if nothing I did could change them, then I could stop trying to please them, and just survive them. I could finally accept that there was nothing wrong with me."

Without realizing it, my other hand had moved to cradle his, holding it gently as if I could protect it. "You volunteered. Didn't you? When your family received the red-sealed scroll. You wanted to go."

He blinked at me for a second, light still glittering wetly in the corners of his eyes. Then he snorted out a feeble laugh. "Good guess. Hua Zhi, I'm not telling you this to make you sorry for me. I'm telling you this to try to make you see the truth. This is the kind of man Lu is. He will always find someone to hate and torment. This sort of thing has been going on in this camp since long before we arrived and he will keep on this way after we're gone, too. It's not our fault."

"But…" *There must have been something I could do to prevent this. Don't you see? I'm an imposter. I'm not even supposed to be here. I'm a – a…*

A girl.

I wanted to spill that pain out, to confess everything to him. In that moment I wanted to trust him, so much. He had opened his heart to me – I ought to have the courage to do the same in return.

But how could I bear it if he turned from me? He was the first, the only real friend I'd ever had. What if he was disgusted and hated me for what I had done? What if he told everyone? I couldn't bear it if he was the one to bring me down.

I just couldn't.

He waited for me to finish, and when I didn't, he cleared his throat. "Last night, when you fought the general, I was … I was shocked. I don't think I've ever seen you that way before."

I frowned, baffled. "What way?"

He sighed. "Happy. When you were fighting him, you looked happy. You're always so careful, so locked down, as if you expect the world to collapse on you if you stop worrying for five minutes. I know you have your own troubles; that you came here under a weight of expectation I can't even imagine. But last night I felt as if I glimpsed someone else – someone inside you that I barely even know. The real you. You were extraordinary, and I feel privileged to have witnessed that. You didn't do anything wrong. There's nothing wrong with you."

The words plucked some deeply hidden chord inside

me, and rang true, like a clear, high note of music ringing through my whole body.

On the other side of the valley, the great gong rang out.

"Time for these girlish confessions to come to an end," Yang Jie said, straight-faced.

I nodded, hid my face in the bend of my elbow, blinking away the telltale moisture hidden by my shadow mask. If I stayed here much longer, I would collapse and weep all over Yang Jie's thin, bruised chest. "I – I'd better go, I haven't eaten and Sigong will have my hide if I'm late." I climbed unsteadily to my feet, then stopped, worried I'd been too abrupt. "Thank you, Yang Jie. Thank you for … everything."

He gave me his usual sunny, guileless grin – only now, of course, I knew him well enough to see the sly intelligence and humour hiding behind those wide eyes. "All part of the service. Bring me my money purse from the barracks next time you visit, will you? I have to pay some people here."

"What? Why?" I asked, momentarily distracted from the confusing whirl of thoughts in my skull.

"Bribing them to keep my secrets, of course," he said, deadpan. "And for a better grade of slop than the rest of the patients have to choke down. The food in here makes our rations look like a banquet at the Imperial Palace. Blerk."

I laughed, a real laugh this time, if a bit watery. "I'll remember. Rest and get well quickly. We'll miss you." *I'll miss you.*

As I left the infirmary, I saw Bingbing perched on the lintel of the doorway. I whistled at her and she chirped back, but didn't leave her post. Yang Jie's words were still echoing in my head. Such simple words.

There's nothing wrong with you.

The great gong had rung. I was going to be late. But instead of running for the mess or to the field for training, I stepped back into the narrow, dusty gap between the surgeon's tent and the one next door, grasping at the dry wood of a tent pole for support as my thoughts surged and whirled in my head.

I had won the right to be here, hadn't I? Fought for it, not just by defeating my father, but day by day, down in the mud and dust. Learning and bruising and bleeding and laughing and sweating alongside all the other men and boys of this camp. What they had gone through, I had gone through. What they had endured, so had I.

A mere imposter would not do any of those things. A deception couldn't learn and bruise and bleed and sweat. Or laugh. A lie couldn't love his friends so very much.

I had been living in a state of constant fear since I arrived here. Fear of getting things wrong, of exposing my deception, of dishonouring myself and my family. But I hadn't.

I wasn't fooling anyone. There was no deception. There was no Hua Zhi and Hua Zhilan. My soul didn't separate neatly into dutiful daughter and mirror-image fake son. I wasn't lying about who I was. There was only me. All the fractured, uncertain, masculine and feminine aspects of me – and whatever those added up to, it was enough. I was a good soldier. A good man. I had risen to every challenge this place and these people threw at me. I was Hua Zhi *and* Hua Zhilan, both and neither, always and never, and there was nothing wrong with that. There was nothing wrong with me.

The thought was as beautiful as the still silence that falls when a storm dies. The white, roaring void that had clawed and screamed at the edges of my consciousness the whole time since I left home was gone. I could think and see – see myself – clearly for the first time in months.

It was in this moment that I saw Captain Lu rounding the corner of the tent in front of me.

My shadow mask flared, stretching out across my entire body, cloaking me first in threads of *qi* and then in the rough, faded red fibres of the tent wall behind me. In an instant, I was nothing more than a shadow, a fold in the cloth. I cowered back behind the shelter of the tent pole, trying to breathe silently, and Lu brushed by so near that I could have reached out and touched his sleeve if I had wished it.

Then, almost directly opposite my hiding place … he stopped.

For a moment, I feared he had somehow seen me, sensed me, after all. But his glittering eyes passed over the tent wall without any visible reaction. He was breathing fast. His fists were clenched and his brow damp. He was angry all right, but more than that – afraid. His expression was distant and his eyes, I realized, were focused inward.

My gift's response to seeing him had been born of unthinking panic. But now I felt my focus on the captain sharpen. Here he stood, Yang Jie's attacker: bully and tormentor of those weaker than himself. If I had chosen to, I could have pulled my knife from my belt and struck him down – struck at him without honour, as he had struck down my friend. I almost wished I could be that kind of man. Yet even as the thought came, I allowed it to dissolve. Such a man could not be Hua Zhou's son.

Such a man would not be Yang Jie's friend.

I had crammed myself into this dark gap between tents because I was overcome and needed a moment alone. The more I looked at Lu, the more I realized it was the same for him. He was taking deep, slow breaths, trying to calm himself. Trying to nerve himself up for something.

We were probably only a few feet away from where Yang Jie rested.

My own hands knotted slowly into fists. If Lu thought he was going to sneak into that tent to finish the job – but no. He couldn't try to murder one of the patients in front of the medical staff. Did he intend to question Yang Jie on what he remembered? Threaten him to ensure his silence?

Before I could begin to make my mind up, Lu lifted his chin, squared his shoulders and turned back the way he had come, slipping out between the tents. Driven by an instinct that overbore everything else, I drew my cloak of shadows close and followed.

If Lu had marched out into the bright daylight, I would have had a hard time keeping up. Such illusions as mine were more effective in the shadows, and ensuring that the flicker of my movement went unobserved would have taken a great deal of energy and effort, the kind that would have been difficult – near impossible – while also moving at a trot and avoiding bumping into other soldiers in the busy camp.

But Lu was sticking to the shadows, darting almost soundlessly from tent to building to tent. It was easy to keep track of him without being seen because he clearly didn't want to be seen himself. What under the heavens was he up to? He definitely wasn't heading to the medical tent, to Yang Jie. But he couldn't possibly be planning anything good, either, not when he was acting so furtively.

He stopped by the wall of a large tent, cocking his head as if listening for sounds from within. All was quiet. I heard him take another deep, slow breath. Then he fell to his knees, seized the bottom of the crimson fabric and swiftly ducked beneath it, into the tent. I stared at the place where he had stood, jaw slack in astonishment, not daring to follow. What was he doing in there?

I crouched and put my eye to the coarse fabric, squinting through the holes in the weave. The tent beyond was not brightly lit, but I could see the dark blocks of camp furniture and the shape of Lu himself. He was standing by a tall, thin cabinet of some sort. I saw light gleam on a pale, curving shape as he lifted it. A wine gourd?

There was a small, metallic clink … a pause. The clink again, and then a sloshing sound. He had uncorked the gourd? And now he was shaking it…?

I stiffened, my blood turning cold.

He had put something in the wine.

Captain Lu was trying to poison someone.

I drew back, thinking frantically. Whose tent was this?

Not Commander Diao's – we all knew that one by sight. It was too big to belong to one of the other captains… Perhaps the censor? Maybe one of the other officials?

But why? Why would Lu do this unless…

My chilled blood seemed to freeze in my veins. I couldn't move. Only my mind was still alive, still working, finishing the thought.

Unless Lu was a traitor.

Unless he worked for the Leopard.

I crouched unmoving as Lu replaced the gourd in the cabinet and then ducked out of the tent again. He actually did brush against me this time as he passed, but he didn't seem to notice anything. He probably thought he'd touched a rock. I felt as solid as one, paralysed.

The captain paused above me for a minute, still sheltering in the shadow of the tent. He closed his eyes, nodded to himself. Then a tiny smile curved his lips and he strode away in the opposite direction.

I watched him go, still struggling to come to terms with what I had seen. A traitor, one of the Mad General's agents, right here in our camp, all along.

I had to report this.

It didn't matter that it would be my word against Lu's, or that Diao might not believe me at first. It didn't matter that if I couldn't convince anyone I spoke the truth, I would probably be flogged – maybe even by Lu's own hands – and exposed, and killed.

I had to try. If I kept silent, someone was going to die.

Shaking, I made to scramble up and nearly fell, letting out a tiny sound of exasperation at the weak, numb sensation in my limbs. My *qi* was low. I was out of practice at larger scale illusions like this, and I hadn't eaten or drunk anything today, in addition to having my dinner interrupted the night before. But I had to know which tent – whose tent – Lu had visited, or my information would be worse than useless.

I let the draining expanse of my shadow cloak disperse back into my skin, retaining only the light mask of my face that was second nature to me now. Immediately, I felt my energy levels stabilize. Before anyone could spot me, I hastily pushed up the fabric wall and ducked inside, looking around me for evidence of who made their home here.

Details spun before my eyes. A beautiful and probably priceless rug in shades of red and gold and cream underfoot. The largest bed I had ever seen in a tent anywhere, so finely wrought that one could hardly tell it was designed to fold up and be carried. An equally large desk with maps, papers and books neatly piled on it. Dark wood trunks and cabinets, inlaid with mother of pearl. A finely worked bronze shield, a spear and several swords, hanging on thin iron chains between the tent poles: decoration. There was a smell of expensive grooming oils and fresh soap. The wood shone with polish and the bed linens were spotless and uncreased. I had never been inside the commander's tent, but this was how I would have imagined it – warlike luxury. So who on earth could this place belong to?

Maybe I should just find the gourd of poisoned wine and take it with me to show Diao. Surely the surgeons would be able to test it and prove my story – and that way no one could drink it before I could convince someone, anyone, to believe in Lu's perfidy.

Yes, that was what I would do.

I sprang towards the tall wine cabinet and flung open the doors, only to be confronted with over a dozen gourds and bottles. Which was the right one? This? Or … this?

I was so busy panicking that I didn't hear anything – not approaching footsteps, not the rustle of tent fabric – until the sharp intake of breath brought my head around.

The Young General stood frozen mid-step, halfway inside the entrance of the tent. He was fully armoured, his helm under one arm. On his right and just behind him was Commander Diao. They stared at me. The silence rumbled like the quiet before a lightning strike, while Diao's face slowly darkened to a thunderous purple, hand tightening on his sword hilt.

"Hua Zhi?" General Wu said, in tones of disbelief.

"Sirs," I croaked. "I promise I can explain."

Thirteen

The stockade was really more of a glorified barn. It was most often used to house the horses and pack animals of army supply caravans, and one end of the large, draughty space was stuffed with bales of feed, barrels, coiled ropes, extra harnesses and other spare pieces of equipment.

But the six wooden cells which occupied the other end were sturdy and practical.

I was the only occupant.

Rain battered the wooden shingle roof. It was leaking on to the rest of the stockade, but the cells had their own low roofs, probably to keep prisoners from trying to climb out, and mine seemed waterproof for now. Not that it mattered. The heavens had opened as I was being dragged across the camp, and I was soaked by the time they flung me into the cell. The downpour had been warm, but after being stuck here in my heavy, sodden clothes for nearly two hours, I had begun to shiver. My muscles had tightened up and my bones were stiff and aching. I had worked through three sets of *qigong* exercises. Each one warmed me and boosted my *qi* levels for a time, but I was too tired and thirsty now to keep it up any longer. I had no idea how long I was going to be waiting here.

I sat as my father had taught me. Back straight, legs folded neatly, hands resting upon my knees with palms upward. I breathed deeply and slowly, and reminded myself that the damp, unpleasant feeling of shivers crawling over my skin was a mere inconvenience – a trick played on my mind by my feeble flesh – and if I could do nothing about it then it must be ignored.

I needed my mind to attend fully to more important matters.

No charges had been levelled against me yet. I wasn't sure if I was here because they thought I'd been trying to steal, or if they suspected me of being a traitor. Either way I was in huge trouble. But worst of all was that they hadn't let me speak. That poisoned wine was still in what turned out to be the Young General's tent, lurking in the cabinet, waiting to be drunk. Just as Lu was lurking somewhere out there, no doubt laughing into his sleeve at my arrest and waiting to betray and murder us all in the Leopard's name.

I had to get someone to listen. If Diao or Sigong came through that door to interrogate me, I had to find the right words to make them believe my story, that we were all in danger.

If Lu was the one who came through the door … I'd

most likely be dead before anyone realized I was telling the truth.

I eyed the crude lock on the cell door. Among my other martial lessons, my father had taught me a peculiar skill he had some pride in: lock-picking. I was no genius at it, but a simple latch lock like this one wouldn't require any finesse, and I had three good iron pins holding my hair in its topknot under the rawhide wrapping.

But breaking out wasn't going to help my case. If I escaped, I'd be labelled as a traitor and deserter for sure. And Lu would be free to keep plotting until it was too late. So I had to stay here obediently and wait. *Wait.*

I took another deep, slow breath, feeling my ribs expand. Held it. Gently released it through my chapped lips, tensing my stomach muscles to properly empty my lungs.

If I got out of this with my skin intact, Yang Jie was going to *kill* me.

If I didn't get out with my skin intact…

I tried to imagine myself maintaining a good enough illusion to fool a camp full of soldiers while being stripped to the waist and flogged twenty or even fifty times. If I failed, then what would happen next would probably make death from internal injuries or infected whip wounds look merciful by comparison.

What would Lu do if he realized the thorn in his side, the boy who had dared to knock the sword from his hand, had a body that he saw as female? No matter what I knew about myself and who I was, that was how they would see me. All of them.

What would any of them do if they realized there was

someone like me among them? How would they react if they felt a "girl" had tricked them, bested them, maybe laughed at them?

I flinched away from the thought of my own barracks, men who had trained by my side, turning on me, hurting me...

My teeth had started to chatter. I broke my meditation pose and rummaged through my pocket for the tiny hand mirror I still carried there. The light in the stockade was bad, especially since it was still pouring outside, but I could make out my own eyes and the vague pale blur of my face.

I had dropped my mask after they locked me in here. Small as the expenditure of *qi* was, it still seemed foolish when I was starved and shivering, and no one could see me. It ought to have been a shock to see myself – my ordinary face – again for the first time in so long. Instead, as before, I was only startled at how little difference there really was between the face everyone else knew as Zhi's, and the face I had been raised to call Zhilan.

Either way, it was just me.

I felt my heartbeat and breathing begin to calm and even out in a way that the two hours of meditation had not achieved. *There's nothing wrong with me.*

This was the beginning of my story. Not the end.

With a squeal of protest, one of the large double doors of the stockade began to open. My heart hiccupped.

Hastily, I fumbled the mirror back into my pocket, centred myself and then, with an ease born of all those many long hours of practice, pulled my mask of illusion back out of my skin. It only took a few seconds. When I was certain the fine threads of *qi* were settled firmly in place, I rose creakily to my feet and stepped towards the bars at the front of my cell.

Watery silver light spilled into the dim interior of the building from the entrance, illuminating specks of dust and powdery straw floating in the air. I squinted, trying to make out who had entered – Diao? No. The person who dragged the stockade door closed and latched it was far too tall, too wide in the shoulder, to be any of the senior officers. One of the servants – perhaps with food or water? I frowned, pressing my face to the bars as the figure swept off a drenched cloak to reveal...

The Young General, still in full battle armour.

I bit my lip to hold in a gasp of shock and stepped back quickly, falling into parade rest.

Purposeful steps echoed on the packed dirt. General Wu appeared at the barred cell door, eyeing me impassively. I saluted but forced myself to remain silent.

"Well?" he barked. The deep voice was anything but sleepy now, and his eyes glared, hawk-like, through the bars. "What have you to say for yourself?"

He didn't exactly appear in a listening mood, but the invitation to explain was more than I had dared expect – more than I had prepared for. I fumbled for the words I'd been rehearsing in my head, but they made no sense to me any more. I opened my mouth, felt my breath hitch with emotion, and closed it again hastily.

Wu Jiang's already forbidding expression was hardening.

You have one chance. Speak!

"There's a traitor in the camp!" The words came out fast and garbled. I sucked in a harsh breath and hurried on before the general could interrupt. "It's Captain Lu. He poisoned at least one of your wine gourds. I think he works for the Leopard."

One dark brow lifted, conveying mild contempt and vast disbelief. He made a soft huffing noise that might almost have been a laugh. "That – that's your story? Honestly, I had hoped for something better than pure nonsense." He was already starting to turn away. "I should have let Diao in here first."

I tossed aside all thoughts of reverence for his position and reputation. "Sir, I have no reason to lie!"

That brought him back around sharply. "Do you think me a fool?" he demanded. "Of course you have every reason to lie! You were caught, red-handed, trespassing in my tent!"

"Yes, and if I were a thief, the best I could hope for would be to confess and receive fifty lashes," I said urgently. "Trying to implicate my own captain as a traitor would only worsen my lot. *I'd* have to be a fool to try that."

He cocked his head. "Maybe you are a fool."

"Current situation aside, sir – I promise you I am not." I looked him straight in the eye, trying to force him to remember our sparring match, and the dual of wits between us it had become. My father always said you could learn more about a man in a single fight than in ten years of close acquaintance. I prayed that Wu Jiang believed that, too.

The Young General's gaze narrowed. "All right. You're not a fool. Maybe you're the traitor. That's what Lu is telling Diao right now. He's not convinced you're even the real Hua Zhi."

My teeth ground together. "Then have the wine tested. If the surgeons find poison, then you'll know I'm telling the truth."

"No. All that would prove is that you're a clever traitor. You were caught with your head in the wine cabinet – we might have tested the contents anyway." He crossed his arms and leaned against the cell door, sceptical but willing to be entertained.

I lifted my chin. "If I were that cunning, then I'd grovel at your feet and pretend to be a thief after all, knowing that the punishment would be lesser and that, in the absence of any reason to test the wine, my plan to assassinate you with poison would still bear fruit."

The words seemed to hit home. He frowned, blinked and straightened. "That actually makes sense."

"That's because it is the truth. Sir, I'm not asking you to spare me punishment. Leave me in here to rot for ever if you wish. But I do beg you: do not drink any wine from that cabinet. Do not trust Captain Lu."

He turned away from me, paced a few steps, and then paced back. "Lu is an imperial captain with more than a decade of faithful service to the emperor. His identity is beyond question. His record is … nearly faultless."

I was getting through to him. "And I'm a raw recruit with no record at all, and Lu's making everyone question if I'm even who I say I am. I understand that you have no reason at all to believe what I'm saying, but, sir, I swear to you on – on anything you like, on my ancestors, on my father's honour—"

"Swear on your mother's life." He stepped closer to the cell door, staring at me as if he wanted to dissect my soul. "Swear to me on your mother's life."

For some reason, this brought me up short. I had tried, very hard, not to think of my mother since I had arrived here. Not her, and not the baby she carried, the baby that might kill her, one way or another. Recruits were not permitted to send letters home or receive them. For all I knew, this baby could be making her ill, as so many had before. For all I knew, the child was already lost. And Mother … she could be…

I had no way of knowing. Even if I made it through all this, I might never see her again.

Swallowing made my throat burn. "General Wu, I swear to you on my mother's life…" My voice trembled a little. I cleared my throat. "On my mother's life. I am no traitor. What I have said is the truth."

Wu Jiang kept staring at me, wordless. I made myself hold that gaze. Slowly, slowly, something shifted in his eyes. He released his breath. "I can't believe I'm entertaining this."

"But you do believe me?" I ventured hopefully.

"Provisionally," he said, with a faint quirk at the corner of his lips. "At the least, I believe that you believe what you're saying. But I'm not letting you out of there, so don't think it."

I let my head fall back, relief making my whole body

shudder. "No, sir. Just … don't drink the wine. And don't let Lu get you alone."

The general's gaze turned distant. "Now that I consider it, he *is* always trying to get me alone. A private sparring match. A special wine we could drink together. A quiet game of *Go*. He even offered to let me use his bath, since he was sure he had the largest one in camp. I thought he was angling to join my staff. Or that he was in love with me. No such luck."

I pulled a face – I would rather have my throat slit than have Lu in love with me – and the expression was so heartfelt that it twisted my mask before I could prevent it. General Wu's distant expression changed into a quick, sardonic grin that made his dimple flash.

"All right, I'm going back to talk to Diao – and Lu. Try not to cause any more uproars while I'm—"

The brassy, unmistakable tones of the alert cut through Wu Jiang's voice, making us both stiffen like hunting dogs, our heads lifting to listen.

"Visitors? Diao will not be pleased," he muttered.

"The supply caravan isn't due for another four days," I told him. My hand closed uselessly at the air by my belt, where my sword hilt should have been. I'd been stripped of my weapons, of course, before I was put in the cell. From here I could see my sword belt tossed casually over the top of a barrel on the other side of the stockade, far out of reach.

"Don't panic, soldier," Wu Jiang said, eyes on my clenching fist. "It's only an alert, not the—"

The urgent notes of the call to arms brought goose-pimples to my skin. The distinctive call rang out again

– and fell silent mid-note, as if the player had dropped his horn. Or been dropped himself. Through the sound of the rain on the stockade roof, I could hear horses and men screaming. Weapons clashing. The sudden, shocking boom of one of the small cannons.

We were under attack.

Yang Jie. Ma Wen. Yulong.

"This can't be a coincidence," the Young General said, softly.

He drew his sword with a barely audible whisper of finely sharpened steel. He turned away, and I expected him to make for the exit, but to my surprise, he hesitated.

"Sir? It's – you must go, they need you…" *Yang Jie. Ma Wen. Yulong…*

He shook his head sharply, frustration stamped on his features. "Damn it! I can't leave you locked up in here, unarmed. I might as well kill you myself. But you're still officially a prisoner, so stay close to me. If I see you trying to sneak away, I'll assume you're deserting and act accordingly."

He grabbed a key from a pouch on his belt and unlocked the latch on the outside of my cell, wrestling the stiff iron bar up, then allowing the door to swing open.

"May I arm myself?" I asked, already moving away to the barrel beside the door, where my sword rested.

"You won't stand much chance out there if you don't," General Wu tossed back at me over his shoulder as he ran to the heavy stockade door and began to open it. Beyond him I saw fine plumes of blue-grey smoke drifting and shadows of men, moving fast through the rain. I seized my sword belt and began the now-familiar process of slinging it around my waist and buckling it into place.

I'd just pulled the leather taut when there was a crash, a surprised yell and a heavy thud. The stockade door flew violently back on its hinges, heading straight for my face. I jerked out of the way, tripped over my own feet, and ended up pressed against the wall. The door hit the barrel next to me hard enough to send chips of wood flying. If the barrel had been a couple of inches further back, the wooden planks would have hit me instead.

As the door swung away, I caught a glimpse of the scene beyond. Instinctively, I grabbed the iron handle, keeping the door between me and what was happening in the stockade so that I wouldn't be seen.

Captain Lu stood over the unmoving, crumpled form of General Wu, a bloodied sword in his right hand. The captain's left held the general's sword. The blade was still clean.

Honoured ancestors, holy Celestial Animals – he's – he's killed *him. He's murdered the emperor's nephew—*

Then the Young General let out a faint groan. He stirred on the ground, touching his forehead. Blood dripped through his fingers. Not a sword-thrust then. A head wound. I clutched at the edge of the door in relief and realized there was more sticky crimson under my fingers. Lu must have charged the door as the Young General opened it and managed to catch him in the temple as he forced it back, stunning him. He was still alive.

But not for long. Captain Lu was already lifting his sword.

My feet were nearly silent, but the faint metallic noise as I drew my weapon was enough to alert Lu. He whipped around and struck my sword away from its target – his throat – with contemptuous ease.

"Oh, look who's out of his cage," he sneered. "I was going to save you for last, you little worm, but I don't mind getting it over with now."

As Lu shifted to face me, I saw movement behind his right leg. The Young General's bloodstained hand – reaching down furtively. Reaching for his belt. Did he have another weapon?

I backed up. General Wu wasn't out of the game yet, but the captain was a skilled swordsman. Ruthless and without compunction. A would-be murderer and an agent of the Leopard. And he was between me and General Wu right now. I needed to distract him – force him to focus on me instead of the vulnerable, wounded man at his feet. Give the general time to do … whatever heroes did.

I sucked in a trembling breath and attempted a snarl. "You're lower than a worm, you traitor!"

Lu laughed through a wide, deranged grin. He darted forward, bringing both swords up in a cross designed to slice me open from gut to sternum.

I dodged, blocking wildly.

Keep him distracted. Keep him away from the general. Just keep him busy…

The general surged up off the floor, a short knife glinting in his hand. He lunged at the captain's unguarded back. Lu somehow caught the movement from the corner of his eye. Shock crossed his face and he whirled to meet the Young General's attack.

I darted into the gap in his defences and drove my blade into his right side. The sword hit his lower ribs. I twisted the blade upward as my father had taught me, forcing it under the cage of bone into his chest cavity. There was a telltale, sickening *pop* as the tip of my sword pierced his heart; a shudder in my blade as the muscle tried to beat around it.

Lu let out a tiny, choked gasp, face twisting into an absurd expression of betrayal.

Then he toppled sideways, ripping my sword from my grasp as he fell. Blood spurted out of the wound, coating my hands and gauntlets. It steamed in the chill air: hot and iron-stinking. The captain hit the ground, twitching and kicking in his death throes.

The overpowering metallic stench of blood and waste, the impact I could still feel in my arms … it was too much.

Without even stopping to check if the man was dead, I turned away. My head was filled with distant whooshing sounds and my stomach flipped and shuddered like a landed fish under my ribs. I was going to faint. I was going to be sick.

I braced one bloody hand against the stockade door, gulping air and desperately trying to swallow back the bile that wanted to rise in my throat. Water trickled from my eyes, almost burning my damp, cold cheeks. I coughed, spat, unthinkingly swiped at my face with my spare hand, and realized I'd only covered myself with more blood.

"Steady." Wu Jiang's voice made me jump violently, and he kept me in place with one big hand braced firmly against my back. "Steady now, you're all right."

"Apologies," I managed to whisper.

"First time?" he asked with rough kindness.

It wasn't. It wasn't. I shouldn't be reacting like this. But I had only been a child before, and the man I had stabbed had been a stranger whose face I had never seen. This was the first time I had really known what it was to take another's life. That *pop* and the way the blade had moved my hand… I didn't have the words. I jerked one shoulder in a shrug.

"I was sick my first time." He thrust a square of cloth – silk, embroidered with gold and red peonies – at me. "Wipe your face. Take a deep breath, blink and swallow. You'll stop shaking in a moment."

I stifled my protest about the cloth being too good to ruin – really, if he didn't care, why should I? He probably had five hundred more like it – and hid my face in it, scrubbing it roughly as I obeyed his instructions, forcing myself to breathe as if I was meditating. I blinked my gritty eyes twice, and swallowed three times.

It worked. I felt the shaking ease from my hands. My stomach still felt raw, but it stopped churning. I cleared my throat, clenched my teeth and straightened up, pulling my other hand away from its scarlet imprint on the wall. "Sorry," I repeated, more loudly this time.

"No apologies – you saved my life. Now, are you with me? We need to get out there."

I nodded jerkily. Of course. The attack. Captain Lu and the truth of who he was, how this had happened – it would all have to wait. We were needed.

Fourteen

General Wu handed me my sword. He must have pulled it from Captain Lu's side – and, I noted gratefully, he had wiped it clean as best as he could. The grip was still sticky and uncomfortable in my hands. Blood was already browning under my fingernails. It would take a lot of scrubbing to make either my weapon or myself entirely clean again.

Blood clung to everything it touched. I'd found that nothing more than a nuisance during my monthly bleeding. Now it seemed more like a judgement...

"Your head, sir," I said abruptly. "You – you were injured..."

"Nothing serious. He just stunned me," he said, turning businesslike now that I seemed to be pulling myself together. "You stopped him before he did any real damage."

I peered up at him, seeing that, despite the gory smears decorating the right side of his face, the cut had already stopped bleeding. It was hard to make out in the dim light, but I thought that the colour in his cheeks looked healthy enough, and his eyes met mine evenly, without any sign of pain. That was as far as my limited knowledge of healing took me. I would have to accept his word.

"Do we have a plan?" I asked, hoping that if I acted unshaken and competent, it would force me to *be* unshaken and competent.

"Our first duty is to find the commander and seek orders from him. We must suppress any resistance we encounter and render help anywhere it's required along the way."

"Understood." I hefted my sword and followed him in a generous circle that took us away from … from the mess, back to the door. I left a trail of wet, crimson footprints as I went.

Perhaps my pretence was working, or maybe it was an effect of too many shocks in one day, too little food, the cold … or some combination of all those. Either way, a strange feeling enfolded me, a kind of numbness. I felt as if I was watching everything from the outside, at a slight remove from my own body and actions. It was nothing like my father's descriptions of mindless, hot, battle fury. I was vaguely grateful that Wu Jiang was there to give me orders. Otherwise, I might have sat down on the floor and stared at the wall until someone came along and kicked me.

The scene outside was one of total chaos. Trampled

tents in ankle-deep mud; thick, drifting fog – a combination of mist and smoke from the fires I could see in the distance and the cannons I could still hear booming erratically somewhere nearby; men running back and forth so quickly that my eyes could not distinguish friend from foe before they had already passed. The corpse of a shaggy, palomino pony lay half-buried in the mud, nearly blocking the exit to the stockade. Its back and neck bristled with arrows. The battle had already swept through here and moved on to a different part of the valley. This was its graveyard.

A frenzied scream on my left. A man clad in dark armour that had been clumsily painted with golden spots – leopard spots – charged us, sword bared. Before I could even shift my grip on my weapon, the Young General was there. His sword flicked twice, deceptively leisurely, and the enemy fell.

The general looked back at me as if to say something – and I reacted to a flash in my peripheral vision, leaping at Wu and dragging him down to his knees. The arrow whistled over our heads and embedded itself in the stockade door, still vibrating.

"That's twice," the general said, staring up at the arrow. He gave me a slightly sick smile. "Slow down a little, would you? It's starting to look like showing off now."

Another cannon blast shook the air, closer, almost deafening. A wild cheer of triumph went up somewhere on the other side of the stockade. Two men – no – three … four men in the dark, gold-spotted armour of the enemy fled past in the other direction, not even noticing us.

Wu Jiang grabbed my forearm and heaved me out of the sucking mud, then took off running in the direction of the cannon fire. I laboured after him, tripped over a body lying face down in the dirt – a man I thought I had known slightly, from south barracks – scrambled to my feet again and caught up just as he reached the centre of camp.

At the officers' practice field, the place where I had sparred with the general, someone had made a rough but effective barricade from two overturned wagons. Who? The enemy or our people? The ground before the barrier was littered with fallen from both sides.

The general did not stop to check. He charged around the closest wagon and stopped dead. A spear-point glinted at his neck. I dived past him with a cry of defiance, already bringing my sword into position, and was confronted with a hundred or so imperial soldiers. It was Captain Sigong who held the weapon to the general's throat.

He let the weapon fall. "Praise the heavens it's you, sir," Sigong said fervently.

The others let out a ragged cheer. As if that had taken the last energy they had, some of them slumped down to sit in the mud, exhausted. I wished I could join them. I let my sword point fall but forced myself to remain upright.

"Situation?" Wu Jiang barked.

"We've sent them packing. They weren't expecting us to be so good with the new fire lances, I don't think. We've taken losses, but at this point I believe not as many as might have been expected. A few of my men went to harry the last stragglers from the camp, but only a handful of them escaped us. We've already started treating the wounded and gathering the dead."

"Where's Diao?"

"I haven't seen him since the battle started," Sigong admitted. "I was forced to take command."

"And a very good thing you did, from what I can see," Wu Jiang said sincerely. "But we must find out where the commander is."

"You think he may have been taken?"

"Unlikely. If the rebels had intended kidnap, either for ransom or leverage, I would have been the best possible target for them," he said matter-of-factly. "But instead, as soon as battle began, a Leopard spy attempted to murder me outright."

"A spy? Here?"

"I'm afraid so. Captain Lu."

Sigong's eyes bulged. "Captain – *our* Captain Lu?"

The general pointed to his blood-streaked temple. "Gave me this, and would have run me through without Hua Zhi's timely intervention."

Sigong's eyes flew to me as if noticing my presence for the first time. He gave me a nod. I saluted, for want of anything better to do – then sucked in a sharp breath, a sudden horrible thought bringing me out of my half-stupor.

"Something to add?" Wu Jiang asked, eyes intent.

"You said you'd left Lu with Diao … trying to convince Diao – about me…"

General Wu unsheathed his sword. "They were in my tent. Hua Zhi, Sigong, come on."

Slightly bewildered as to why I was required, I followed.

The general's tent was still standing, as were most in the central region of the camp. Sigong reached the entrance first and flung back the tent flap, then cursed: a single, short word under his breath. I'd never heard him swear before, not in all my advanced training sessions. As soon as I stepped inside, I realized why.

Diao and his aide-de-camp Sergeant Yun were still there.

I clamped my jaw shut against another surge of nausea at the stench of death in the small, enclosed space. Diao's body was slumped in a camp chair, a dark wound gaping horribly at his neck. It was a clean, skilful cut. He would have been dead before he even had time to gain his feet. I guessed that he had been the first to die. Sergeant Yun had managed to get up, tipping his own chair over in the process, and his sword was half-drawn. He lay on the beautiful, ruined rug near Diao's feet. He had been stabbed in the chest.

Sigong crouched beside Yun. "They're warm, not beginning to stiffen yet. The blood's going tacky, though." He gently closed the dead man's eyes.

General Wu nodded grimly. "So they were killed at the start of the attack."

"Or their deaths immediately preceded it," I put in, surprising myself. I had not intended to speak – but once I had started, I found it impossible to stop. "Lu was a traitor and he had a contingency plan, in case he was ever discovered. Kill anyone in his way and signal somehow to this raiding party so that he could escape in the confusion of the battle. This happened because I let myself be caught in here. Lu realized what I'd seen and panicked. I panicked him. I caused this."

"Did you also cause Lu to sneak into my tent and try to poison me?" the Young General retorted. His voice was flat, but there was understanding in his eyes. "Don't be ludicrous. The fact that you caught him at it and prevented my assassination merely accelerated his timeline. By forcing Lu's hand and causing him to act before he was prepared, when only a small party of the enemy were near by to assist him, you may have prevented a much worse slaughter later on. And – I cannot emphasize this enough – saved me from a highly unpleasant death from whatever he'd dosed my wine with. That's three times now, in fact." His dimple flashed. "Didn't I tell you to slow down? You're making everyone else look bad."

I looked down, blinking hastily, even though a careful check reassured me that my illusion was hiding the wet gleam in my eyes. As if anyone in the whole world had a chance of making General Wu look bad.

"Sir, I don't know if this has occurred to you yet," Sigong said, after a moment, "but Commander Diao's death makes you our ranking officer. You're in command here now."

I glanced up again to see Wu Jiang regarding Sigong with almost no expression on his face. "Surely, as Diao's remaining second in command, it would be more fitting for you to step into his place," Wu Jiang said slowly. "My visit here was entirely informal and though I still hold the rank of general, I do not currently have command of any active troops."

"With respect, General, you now have command of what amounts to a battalion. Nearly a thousand men." Sigong paused. "Depending on our losses here, of course. It would fly in the face of protocol for a mere captain to lead them when we have a general present."

General Wu bowed his head. When he straightened again it was with tense shoulders, as a man who is forced to stand under the weight of some great burden. "Very well. Then if I am to be commander-general, my first act will be to clear Hua Zhi of any suspicion of wrongdoing – and promote him to corporal."

I felt my jaw drop, and quickly closed my mouth again before anything foolish could fall out. That was an unprecedented promotion – a leap up three ranks, since I hadn't even attained private status officially yet. I allowed my illusory face to glow with happiness and gratification. That this man, this astonishing officer, should rate my skills so highly! I saluted, swallowed and said merely, "Thank you, sir."

"Oh, don't thank me. There's a price: with Yun dead I'll need an aide-de-camp – secretary, servant and general dogsbody – and you're the unlucky man I've chosen. It's the worst job in the army. By this time tomorrow, you'll wish I'd had you flogged instead." He sounded remarkably cheerful all of a sudden.

Sigong's weathered face creased into a rare smile and he gave me a nod, which I took to be approval. "Very fitting, if I may say so, General. What are your orders for me?"

Wu frowned, eyes going distant. "The Leopard knows we're here. He held off from attacking because he had a spy in place who was presumably feeding him valuable intelligence. But now the spy's gone and I'm still here, like a sitting duck just waiting to be plucked and roasted. Our recruits have proved themselves in battle and need no further testing – we'll pack up and leave this valley with all possible speed, and put as much distance between us and it as fast as we can. Once we're clear of the area, we'll march to the City of Endless Serenity to reinforce my aunt's standing army there for the time being." He nodded decisively. "Every recruit who survived the battle will receive the rank of private, effective immediately. Training is over."

And despite myself, despite everything that had happened … I felt a thrill of excitement.

My first act as a newly struck corporal was to locate the commander's large tent – half-trampled into the dirt, but otherwise undamaged – and hunt out a group of able-bodied men to quickly clean and re-erect it. We carried out the broken furniture, rearranged what was left, and transported over General Wu's own things from the guest tent where he had been sleeping. Luckily, General Wu's chief body servant, a crisply efficient imperial eunuch named Shu Yuen, had survived the attack. After appraising him of the changed situation, he bustled into action, chivvying the rest of the general's entourage along and quickly taking over the task of ensuring Wu Jiang's comfort on his first night as commander-general.

"Fast work," Wu Jiang said as he appeared at the entrance to the tent, surveying the sparse but cosy interior. Lamps were lit, a hip bath of steaming water was waiting, and Shu Yuen was in the process of laying out dinner on the desk. Wu's shining armour had become plastered in mud since I last saw him. There was even a dripping white mark – bird mess? – on his left shoulder.

General Wu was still talking. "I won't need you again this evening, I don't think. Go and get something to eat and get cleaned up, Hua Zhi. You've worked hard today, and I want us up an hour before dawn tomorrow."

"Yes, sir. Good evening." I saluted and backed out, barely noticing the friendly clap on my arm as I passed.

Outside, I allowed the tent flap to fall shut. I stood for a moment, blinking dazedly and barely aware of the hostile and appraising stares of General Wu's two bodyguard-outriders, who flanked the tent entrance.

Yang Jie. Ma Wen. Yulong.

I spun on my heel and bolted.

The strange sense of distance which had taken over me in the stockade fell apart like paper in the rain. They had been under attack – fighting for all our lives – and I hadn't been there with them, hadn't even had the chance to try to help any of them. Yang Jie was injured, isolated in the infirmary without even his sword. So many awful things could have happened to him, to any of them. Fear and desperation burned in my chest like an ember, physically painful. I was surprised smoke didn't belch from my mouth.

I sprinted past the stables on my way to the east

barracks building, almost choking with relief when I saw they were intact – untouched by fire or any sign of attack. Yulong would be fine, then.

East barracks had escaped the raid unscathed, too, with no visible damage. Surely it must be a good sign? I hit the door with a bruising thud and flung it wide.

The room beyond was filled with smoke-stained, blood-spattered faces – exhausted, but familiar and alive. Many of them jolted at the thoughtless violence of my entrance. I mentally cursed myself. On a nearby bed, a young man I knew quite well was sitting slumped over his knees. He came to his feet in a rush and ran to me, grabbing me by the shoulders for a hearty shake.

"You're alive!" He was surveying my gory appearance with a mixture of awe and concern. "Someone said they saw you marched into the stockade right before we were attacked – what happened, Hua Zhi?"

"Oh, that's – never mind that, I'm fine," I said. "Is – is everyone else all right?"

He drooped. "Ma Wen is dead."

The breath whistled out of my lungs as if I had suffered a blow. "How?"

"He … he was right next to me. A spear went through his throat. There was nothing…"

"I'm sorry. I'm so sorry." I went to pat his shoulders, but thought better of it at the sight of my filthy hands, streaked with dried blood.

"Two others are in the infirmary for now. The new infirmary, I mean – the motherless bastards set the old one alight. It lost half its roof. They've set up in the sergeants' mess for now. Zhang Yong will be all right, but Li Wei – it's his leg. They'll probably have to send him home."

I stared up at him, my sense of dread almost suffocating me. The infirmary had been on fire? "What about—"

"Me?" a familiar voice interrupted. I jumped like a nervous cat and spun round to see Yang Jie behind me. His face was still mottled red and purple with bruises from the beating, just as it had been the last time I saw him – but he also sported a vicious-looking new cut through his left eyebrow and a bandage around his head. With his hair hidden he looked so young I could almost have taken him for a child.

"You walked right past me," he said with a tired grin. "Losing your eyesight, Mother?" On his shoulder Bingbing gave a subdued chirp.

I couldn't help myself this time. I reached out and pulled him into a desperate hug, clinging too tightly and for too long, but unable to let go. I felt his hands clutch at my back, dragging the layers of my armour and clothes taut. A shudder rocked me. Was that me shaking? Or him? Or both of us together?

Thank you thank you thank you…

One breath, then two. On the third, he sighed and pulled away. The other boy nodded at us, smiling, and left us in – relative – privacy.

"Don't think you can 'never mind' me," he said, coughing a little as his voice broke. He dragged one forearm roughly over his eyes. "Where were you all this time? I heard you'd been *arrested*."

"It's a long story. Very long," I hedged.

"Tell the short version, then," he said, shoving me gently down to sit on a random bed, and then almost collapsing next to me. "I thought you were dead!"

I let out a short groan, more weary than exasperated. "It was Lu. Captain Lu. He was … was working for the Leopard. He tried to kill General Wu. Twice. First with poison, but he tried to blame me – that's why I was in the stockade – and then again after the call to arms. I … sort of … saved Wu Jiang's life?"

"How?"

"I…" I swallowed hard. "I killed Lu."

Yang Jie's face was completely still. "You did?"

I nodded. "So now I'm a corporal. And General Wu's aide-de-camp."

Yang Jie kept staring at me. His mouth opened. Then closed. Finally he stuttered, "C–congratulations?"

"Thanks," I said with a weak smile. "I don't deserve it. I don't even know if I can do it."

"You can," he said after a moment. "And if anyone deserves it, you do."

"But?" I prompted.

He pulled his lower lip between his teeth, thinking deeply.

I waited in expectant silence.

"I'm glad for you," he said at last. "Working for him could bring you a lot of good things. But you should be cautious, too. He's a prince. He's used to getting whatever he wants when he wants it. He might not be safe to trust. And people who get too close to Wu Jiang, or to any member of the Imperial Family… Well, just look what happened to Wu Jiang's mother. It could be dangerous."

Recent events flickered through my mind: the devastation of the camp, the smoke and mud and piled-up bodies. Yun and Diao slowly cooling where they had died, discarded like rubbish in the wake of a traitor. Lu's blood gushing over my hands. I shuddered at the visceral sense of the memory, and knew abruptly that these were experiences which I would never forget. They would affect me for the rest of my life, in ways I probably could not yet fathom.

Yet to General Wu those things had been ... not nothing, but business as usual. He had dealt with them and moved on. What must his life have been like, to make that possible for him?

I didn't know if I would ever possess that kind of strength. If I even wanted it.

I swallowed. "I know. But you don't have to worry. Wu Jiang's a good man – and he's miles above me. The closest I imagine I'll ever get will be washing his socks."

Yang Jie snorted and knocked me on the shoulder with his fist. But I couldn't help noticing that he still looked worried.

Fifteen

Just as he had promised, General Wu was up before dawn, sending Shu Yuen to rouse me from my uneasy sleep in the barracks. We had a lot of work to do.

The first job was to line up the bodies of our fallen soldiers and double check their identities with their sergeants and friends – also called from their beds for the grim task. Peering down at the cold, distorted or disfigured faces in the merciless glare of lantern-light shook all of us of any lingering desire for sleep.

At least it had stopped raining.

Each death needed to be marked by the censor on the official record, and each man must have a notice drafted to his family. Officially, the camp's commander should pen each of the death notices, but in practice he was far too busy writing official, coded communications. The task, therefore, fell to me, with General Wu's involvement limited to his official seal affixed to each one.

I wrote Ma Wen's notice first. Then Commander Diao and Sergeant Yun. After that, the distant phrases of confirmation and condolence, copied from a book which Wu Jiang had wordlessly handed to me, became rote. My hand moved the brush unthinkingly, tracing black lines on creamy paper while barely noticing the meaning of the words. That only freed my imagination to dwell on the shock and grief that each of these hastily penned notes would garner from the houses of the lost boys and men. I felt I was firing arrows into the darkness, knowing each one would find its target but with no real idea of the specific devastation they would cause.

It was a melancholy task.

From the way that General Wu sighed and shifted in his seat across from me at the desk, his letters also brought him little joy.

He broke at dawn to attend the mass funeral. The imperial soldiers were buried with necessary haste, but with all due honour and ceremony, just as their families would hope.

The enemy fighters, along with the body of Captain Lu Buwei, were tumbled into a shallow pit on the other side of the valley, a location that lay mostly in shadow. Forty-eight bodies went into that grave, but not a single prayer was said for them, and no offerings of rice or wine made. Given the rumours about the vile murderers and rapists that had flocked to join the rogue general's forces, I was not troubled with thoughts of their possible grieving loved ones.

By the time the Young General returned from overseeing the burials, I'd finished my writing. He sealed each letter with gold wax and a jade seal that he carried on a chain around his neck, then hauled me off across camp to badger the medical staff into working faster. It had already been decided that the wounded troops should be loaded on to wagons and make a speedy departure – along with the death notices and other official letters and reports – to the nearest large town, five days away. They would report to the City of Endless Serenity to rejoin their fellows when they had been deemed fully recovered.

I was relieved beyond measure that Yang Jie had not been deemed badly injured enough to go. It was selfish, but I did not know how I would manage without my friend.

Having attended to the most pressing matters, Wu Jiang drove us hard, convinced that the Leopard would be mobilizing his forces to capture us with twice the speed with which we could prepare to escape. My own mental calculations, undertaken the night before as I struggled to find rest, had estimated that the earliest we could possibly be ready to move out would be the next day. Wu Jiang defied not only my private doubts but any protests by his officers, and had us mobilizing directly after the midday meal.

As we rode out of the valley that day, our lumbering caravan of wagons, infantry and cavalry – with the Young General on his giant blood-red mount at its head – slowly climbing up to meet the sun in the shallow bowl of tall summer grasses on the other side, I had every intention of heeding Yang Jie's warnings. I liked and admired Wu Jiang, and was intrigued by his decision to hide his true skill as a fighter, just as my father had hidden his ability as a banner-breaker and I hid ... other things. I saw the same look of respect on the face of every officer and soldier in our newly formed battalion. We all thanked the heavens that General Wu had been in the camp to take command after the fall of Diao.

But Wu Jiang's sharp, dark eyes missed very little.

So I needed to be very careful.

The rank of corporal – and more importantly, the post of aide-de-camp to a general – came with certain privileges. A small tent next to General Wu's, rather than a place huddled in one of the cramped five-man tents that the new privates shared. I was not expected to take part in the mandatory mass training drills that brought the privates groaning from their bedrolls in the early hours of each morning. Nor was I given sentry or scout duties. I did not have to dig waste trenches, or help to pitch any tents except the general's and my own. I didn't have to elbow and shove for a place to scrub myself hastily – and furtively, half-dressed, desperately holding illusions in place – at whatever freezing river or lake was available for washing: Shu Yuen brought me cans of heated water and soft cloths. He even offered to clean my armour, and brushed off my demurrals by pointing out that since my appearance reflected on his master, it also reflected on him.

I was still expected to care for Yulong myself, since

the general's personal groom was occupied with his two war horses and two riding mounts. But in all other ways my life, overnight, had become immeasurably easier.

And immeasurably lonelier.

I had been so glad when I heard that Yang Jie was deemed fit enough to accompany the battalion to the city that it never occurred to me how little he, as a new private, and I, as a formidably busy administrative corporal, would ever have opportunity to cross paths.

When Yang Jie and the others were eating, training, at watch or marching, I was with the Young General. During the day I rode by his side. When we made camp I was running around after him on foot, wishing for longer legs as he forced me to trot to keep up with him.

Despite this, I made an effort to seek out and socialise with my fellows. Of course they couldn't be expected to come looking for me in the commander-general's tent – they'd get into trouble. The overtures had to come from me. Each day I looked up their schedule and, if I could, arrived in time to sit with them when they ate, or to share their sentry fire for an hour.

Sometimes, if a few days had passed, things were a little stiff at first – but a few gently embellished stories of the general's more outrageous demands, in which I figured as a hapless clown, usually had everyone laughing again. And they always seemed as glad to see me as I was them, especially Yang Jie. Still, I worried about it.

"Does it look odd to people that I just ... arrive, without an invitation?" I asked Yang Jie from my place holding the head of a lieutenant's horse. Yang Jie had been assigned to help the grooms this evening, and this particular horse didn't like having his tail brushed, so it seemed only fair to pitch in. There was a rolled cloth of sweet red bean buns – a present from Shu Yuen, the one member of General Wu's staff who seemed to have taken a liking to me – waiting for us to share when we were done. "Am I acting wrong somehow?"

I couldn't see Yang Jie at that moment – he was brushing furiously, knowing that if I let the horse's head slip for a second it would either rear up or whip around and attempt to bite. But I heard the eye roll in his voice as he replied: "You're more concerned with how things look and acting 'correctly' than anyone I know. Is there some great, juicy scandal in your past that you're attempting to atone for or something?"

I flinched. "What, me?" I forced a laugh. "O–of course not."

Unless you counted stabbing a man in the guts at seven years old.

Or being born a female banner-breaker when no one had heard of one for hundreds of years – most probably because their families hid them away in shame.

Or secretly going against all the precepts of proper womanly behaviour by training in martial arts totally forbidden for my birth gender – and keeping it a secret from my own mother and siblings.

Or becoming, in every meaningful sense, a boy, in order to illegally join the Imperial Army and fight in my father's place...

Quite a lot for which to atone, if you looked at things

that way. I had transgressed many rules that my people held dear.

But all my actions had been driven by the highest and most treasured values of the Red Empire: love for family, for country, respect for duty. *Should* I feel guilty about saving either of my parents, about serving my emperor, because I had been born a girl? Was there … something wrong with me, if I didn't?

"You don't sound very certain," he said, suddenly at my side, the horse brush still in his hand.

I could see the shadows cast by his long, thick lashes over cheeks flushed pink by exertion, skin glowing in the light of the sun as it set behind us. He smelled of horses and sweat and of his own personal Yang Jie smell that I was sure, by now, I would recognize anywhere. Always.

I cleared my throat and let go of the horse's head, swiftly stepping away.

"Hua Zhi?"

Now he sounded really concerned. I groped for something to say – anything – to distract him from whatever suspicions might be crowding into his quick, clever mind.

"No. You know how lucky I am. My family … I've been so lucky. I have nothing to complain about. Especially not compared to – I mean – nothing."

"Nothing?" he repeated cautiously, as though feeling his way. "Not even … what you told me before? About the assassins?"

I wished I'd never confided in him about that. As if by rote, I spouted my mother's favourite platitude: "Great men make enemies. My father is a very great man."

He blinked at me, biting his lip. His fingers were white around the horse-brush, and his other hand was extended towards me, as if he was on the verge of trying to snatch me back from some invisible precipice. He cared. He was my friend. And he was Yang Jie. Of all people, of all the people in the world, he might be the only one who would understand what I'd done. What I was doing.

Tell him. Tell him. Tell him.

But the person he cared for was Hua Zhi. A boy. How could I possibly explain that even though my body was different from those of other men, even though the name I had been given at birth was Zhilan … I was still that person? The one he knew? Wouldn't he think I was sick, twisted inside, insane – or all three? I let out a long, slow breath.

I can't.

"Being the oldest child of a great man isn't always … easy. No matter what you do, you're never quite enough. They love me. I even think, sometimes, that my father might understand me. But then I realize that he's just … just sorry for me. Because I try so hard, but I can never be what he was. And my mother looks at me, and sees the person I could have been – the person I should have been. And she's disappointed. Every time. No matter how much she loves me, that disappointment is always there."

And, ancestors – that was a lot more honest than I had meant it to be, even if it couldn't possibly make any sense to Yang Jie.

He was still chewing at his bottom lip, making it disturbingly plumb and red as he worked through my words.

Finally, he dropped the horse-brush and came towards me, silent despite the dry crunchy grass underfoot.

He was too close. That was all I could think. He stood there, no closer than he ever stood, but somehow, now, it felt entirely too close. *Or maybe* – a jolt of giddy realization – *not close enough.*

"I don't know your parents. I'm sure they're just as wonderful as you say. But if I've learned anything from my life so far, it's that sometimes you grow up believing things that, outside the family, just make no sense."

I nodded, blankly, unable to tear my eyes from his lips.

"And the idea that anyone could possibly be sorry for you, or disappointed with you, Hua Zhi," he went on softly. "That makes no sense to me. No sense at all."

He was looking at me. I could feel his gaze on my face, my shadow face, like ... like a kiss. Involuntarily, my eyes lifted from his lips to his eyes. *Such beautiful eyes...*

For just a breath, a blink, we stared at each other. All was still. Waiting. Waiting for one of us to move. This was what he had been implying before. That his family hated him because he was "the way he was". Yang Jie was attracted to other men. He was attracted to me. And I ... I wanted him back. So much ... so much that it was terrifying.

Tell him.

Yang Jie's hand, that strong, small hand, lifted tentatively towards me again.

I can't.

With a graceless jerk, I turned away, hiding my face by

pretending to scratch my nose. "Oh! I – I forgot I have … the general needs me. I'd better go. I'll – um – come to the dice game at your tent tomorrow night. I can win my coins back. See you!"

Are you a coward, daughter? my father's voice asked in my mind as I ran away.

Yes. I told him. *Yes, Father. I am.*

I didn't go to the dice game.

I didn't go to east company's evening meal. I didn't turn up to keep anyone company on watch, and I didn't help Yang Jie with the horses.

I couldn't face him. I couldn't even *risk* facing him by spending time with any of my other friends. I knew it made me the worst kind of coward, and each day when I woke I resolved to do better, to seek him out, to tell him…

What? What was I going to say? How would that conversation unfold – how could it end in anything but heartbreak and disaster? I had woven myself into a tangle that my fingers did not have the ability to unpick. Yang Jie wanted to know me, the real me – and that was impossibly dangerous. Too frightening even to contemplate. Because even if, through some wild fortune, Yang Jie accepted me, understood what I had done…

How could the two of us ever hope to be together?

This world would not accept either of us. It would tear us apart from each other, and then from ourselves. We would both be destroyed.

And so each night, I didn't go to the dice game.

I didn't go to the evening meal, or turn up to keep a friend company at their sentry fire … or help Yang Jie with the horses.

With shocking abruptness, and entirely through my own actions, I was alone.

When, early one morning, the battalion passed through the forested foothills of the Blue Heron Mountains, where the leaves were just starting to take on rich tinges of gold, and tiny white-and-grey snub-nosed monkeys cavorted high among shreds of mist in the bright treetops, Yang Jie was the one I longed to turn to in wonder. The one with whom I wished to share a look and a smile, so that the memory of this would be impressed on my mind for ever. It would be more beautiful reflected in his eyes.

But Yang Jie was nearly half a mile back with the other troops, still helping our overloaded wagons to rumble and splash their way across the wide, icy froth of the Gold Dust River. I hadn't seen him, hadn't even glimpsed the back of his head in passing, in nearly a week.

So the one beside me that morning was General Wu.

His eyes met mine, gleaming with pleasure, and the dimple flashed in his bearded cheek. It was an uncomplicated moment of kinship – shared appreciation of our beautiful country.

I couldn't smile back. My mask did, but it was a pale effort. I reigned Yulong in, turned my face down as if to check the ground, and pretended I didn't see the smile die on Wu Jiang's face.

He wasn't the one I wanted. He wasn't my friend. And he couldn't ever be.

The weight of my self-imposed exile from family and friends, the burden of my new identity – for I could no longer bear to call it a "deception", even in my own head – bore down on me then as never before. I began to suffer with the worst bouts of homesickness I had experienced for weeks. Great waves of churning, all-encompassing *need* to return to where I was known and loved left me queasy and almost shaking in their wake.

I wanted my own things around me, my loom, my books, my bed. I wanted the smell of my mother's rose-water perfume, so familiar that I hadn't even noticed until its ever-present comfort wasn't there any more. I wanted the walls I had grown up within, the sounds of the servants' footsteps and the click of distant screens rolling open and shut, my siblings' voices raised in the distance with laughter, my father's gentle rumbling voice, too.

But I discovered a curious thing. When I imagined myself back there among my family, I did not see myself as I had been. The vision was of me *now*.

Hair free of ornaments, face bare of cosmetics, dressed not in layers of flowing silk but in my boots and army uniform. I did not see myself sitting quietly with my mother as she sewed, gently brushing my sister's hair, or secretly training with my father – even though those were all things that I had loved, that I still missed.

I saw myself striding through the halls without care for dainty, ladylike steps, laughing without reserve, riding home at the end of a day's hunting, flushed and overloud and cocky about my kill, as I had seen the sons of other families act.

I saw Zhi. A boy whose skills at combat and horsemanship were proudly acknowledged by my father. A boy whose banner-breaking was a source of public celebration and joy, not a guilty secret. A boy whose mother, having provided her husband with a healthy heir on the first try, had never looked upon him with puzzlement, confusion, or guilty disappointment. A boy whose mother had never sought to end her own life right in front of him.

I was sick for something – a place in the world, a role within my family – that was not mine to inhabit. That, apart from this moment, could never be mine. Not to keep.

My original goal had been to serve the empire in my father's place without being discovered, and then return neatly to the life and the person I had been before, just as if none of this had ever happened. It was what I must do. And I would do it, because there was nothing else, no other option, no second choice to be made.

I dreamed of Zhi, loved and accepted just as he was.

But it was only a dream.

Sixteen

After eighteen days of hard travel, one of our rear scouts returned from his duties with the news that he had spotted fires – a lot of fires – burning in the same foothills of the Blue Heron Mountains, which we had left behind us three days ago.

With a curse, Wu Jiang snatched up his spyglass and went to look for himself. On a tall ridge that sat just above the treeline, I crouched down beside him. Captain Sigong and one of the Young General's bodyguard-outriders, who he had on this occasion failed to scrape off, were on my other side.

Wu Jiang cursed again, even more fiercely, after a long look through the glass. When he passed it to me, I saw why. The scout had been right. Those were no ghostly blue forest spirits, nor the torches of some trader's caravan in the distance. Campfires. Over a hundred at my count, on the other side of the Gold Dust River. It was a sizable force. Maybe larger than our own.

I passed the leather-wrapped glass to Sigong. He pursed his lips thoughtfully in the twilight as he squinted through it. "Reinforcements from the emperor?"

I sensed more than saw the general shake his head. "My letter can only just have reached her, even on the empire's fastest horse. It's the rebels. We're going to have to divert through the Stone Forest."

Sigong made an unhappy grumbling noise. "The men won't like that. Most of them are convinced it's haunted or cursed, or both."

"They'll like facing down a thousand or more of the Leopard's worst considerably less," the general retorted dryly. "It'll buy us at least an extra day's lead. Give the order, Captain."

Directly after dawn the following day, we diverted from our original route and, with fifty men following on foot to obscure as many traces of our passing as they could, are headed into the strange landscape known as the Stone Forest – or, to the more superstitious, the Graveyard of the Lost.

The shifting stone shards underfoot made the passing of so many men and horses sound like fine plates shattering – or bones crunching – with every step. The wagons rocked and lurched over the ground, their contents at times threatening to spill over the sides. At several points, everyone on horseback was forced to dismount and lead their horses, as the way was too treacherous. But apart from the noise of our progress, the gulley was almost eerily silent.

A wide, deep gorge that descended sharply from the level of the grassland that preceded it, the Stone Forest appeared alien and discordant to the eye. The "forest" itself was composed of jagged spires of grey stone – hundreds upon hundreds of them – that arrowed up from the uneven shale floor to points at least fifty or more feet overhead. But it was impossible to say how high they went for certain. The tops of the spires were wreathed in thick mist that closed out the sky, making for a muffling, claustrophobic roof.

The walls of the gulley and the spires had strange bulges, hollows, twists. As we passed them, the formations often seemed to shift, suggesting faces – one moment laughing, the next sneering – or mythical creatures, savage and poised to leap. As if that wasn't disturbing enough, every now and again great carrion birds would drift silently overhead, dark wings casting shadows through the clouds of mist.

From the corner of my eye, I caught Sigong making a sign that I had often watched our cook at home perform – warding off bad spirits with a triple-flicking of the fingers – and found I didn't blame him in the least.

There were myths about this place: that the stone spires were the grave markers of women who had died unmourned, discarded by their husbands, abandoned by their children. It was said their spirits still dwelled restlessly within the rocks, and at night they would be drawn to the living warmth of travellers, and might seek to lie down with them in their bedrolls to console the endless chill of death…

Even Wu Jiang seemed a little quieter than was usual. He didn't give himself away with any of the twitching or muttering or anxious looks of the other men, but his horse – a golden palomino today, with tail and mane like spun silver – betrayed its rider's tension. It snorted, jumped at shadows, shook its head restlessly ... even reared once. The sudden sharp whinny brought my head around in time to get a perfect view as the violent movement of the stallion nearly unhorsed the general.

He clung on grimly, wrestling the animal back on to its front hooves with a display of horsemanship that brought on a helpless surge of admiration in my breast. *Ancestors, he's strong...*

Yulong flicked one glossy ear and stood as still as the stone spires next to him until the palomino had been brought under its rider's control. I had drawn him to a halt and backed him quickly into a narrow space between two spires when I saw what was happening – I wanted us well out of range of the other stallion's lashing front hooves. Sigong had halted behind us, too, but seeing after a moment that all was well with his commander, nodded to me and signalled to the column of men behind him to carry on, giving Wu Jiang a little space and time to fully calm his mount. And himself.

The men adjusted their course and streamed around us quickly, leaving us alone for a moment.

Taking advantage of the privacy, Wu Jiang threw back his head for a deep gulp of the dank air. Sweat shone on his face, emphasising its strong, masculine lines and making his bronzed skin gleam. I averted my eyes, and saw that the two bodyguard-outriders were making their way back towards us – too late to be of any use. Again. The Young General waved them off brusquely. Then, as if reading my mind, he turned dark, piercing eyes on me.

"Your horsemanship is impressive." He was faintly winded – and faintly annoyed, if I was any judge.

"Mine?" I cleared my throat when my voice squeaked on the word. I wasn't flustered, oh no – it was … it was that stupid tincture. That was it. "Ah – no, sir, it is Yulong's training which is truly excellent. He is my father's favourite mount." Warmed by a sudden happy memory, I smiled, and didn't prevent it from showing on my mask. "My mother always says Father must have been a stallion himself in a former life, he understands them so well."

"'The best trained mount can only be as good as his rider,'" Wu Jiang quoted good-naturedly. "Which means my current difficulties are a reflection on me, not poor Eagle, here." He leaned down to pat his horse's neck, and my smile broadened.

Then some instinct prickled the back of my neck. I turned my head to see Yang Jie, framed between two rock spires a little way ahead of us. His face, as he took in this tableau – my smile, the Young General's smile – was stricken.

I felt my own expression turn instantly to one of helpless guilt. I opened my mouth, though I don't know if I would have had the courage to call out. But before I could make a sound, all the emotion drained from Yang Jie's eyes, leaving him white and expressionless. He turned away, stooping to pick up a fallen pack – probably why he had returned – and departed at a run. He didn't look back.

I became conscious, after what felt like a small eternity, that the Young General was looking at me, still waiting for an answer.

"Surely not, sir," I said dully.

General Wu frowned at me. Then he snorted through his nostrils, rather like a horse himself, and shook his head.

That night, as we huddled down in various miserable poses along the damp gulley wall, none of us as close to our campfires as we really wished to be, I was man enough to admit to myself that I was grateful for the reassuring bulk of the Young General looming between me and the sinister shadows of the Stone Forest. If any cold, desolate spirits were looking for the consolation of human warmth in the dark, he'd be a more tempting target than I.

I expected to stay awake late into that night, worrying and missing Yang Jie and feeling sorry for myself. But riding on such treacherous terrain all day long seemed to have left me more tired than was usual. I could feel my eyes drooping even as I shifted on to my side, searching for a more comfortable position on the uneven ground.

General Wu's horse, hobbled near by, stomped his hoof – once, twice. Yulong, who stood nose to nose with him, whickered softly as if in reassurance. The other horse quieted.

When I woke, I wasn't sure how much time had passed. With the mist blocking any sight of stars – or the dawn, if it was coming – all I could see was that it was still as dark as ink in the gulley. But I knew instantly what had woken me. The wind had risen. It was whistling – no, *singing*, singing around the tops of the stone spires. Playing over the unusual formations in the rock. The resulting noise was like nothing I'd ever heard before, seeming both low and high at once, almost like … like a chorus of voices. Human voices.

It was beautiful. It was chilling. The humming notes blended together into a peculiar, haunting music that made the Stone Forest itself vibrate. The more I listened, the more the wind rose, the colder I felt. All around me, small campfires, which had been burning merrily away in the darkness, were beginning to dim and sink down. The increasing wind should have whipped them up. Instead it seemed to suck the air away from them – and from me – as the darkness grew deeper.

Nonsense, I told myself fiercely. *It's just the wind, just these odd rocks. That's all. Don't let your imagination run away with you.*

But the men were stirring restlessly in their sleep. One of General Wu's bodyguards thrashed in his bedroll, and as he turned over I saw his face in the light of our dying fire. It was twisted, still sleeping, into a rictus of horror or despair. Near by, someone let out a wavering moan, nearly drowned by the eerie moaning of the wind.

The walls of the gulley were shaking now. I could hear … I could hear the voices in the wind. I could hear them. They cried out for help, for release – tormented by the most terrible grief and pain – and their music rumbled through the ground and through my bones, louder and louder. The campfires were nearly out now. I lay frozen, gripped by fear, the same fear that had held me still on a night long ago when I heard assassins creep into my father's house, the same fear which had paralysed me for that vital moment when I saw Lu standing over General Wu with blood on his hand. Only this time I couldn't break free. I couldn't move.

One voice rose above the others. A voice as familiar to me as my own. More familiar. One I had listened to before I even had a voice: my mother's.

She was screaming.

Screaming … for me.

The edges of reality cracked. The cold and the dark were eating through me, damaging me, like a hard frost turns soft fruit black. This was going to drive me out of my mind, I realized dimly. This would kill me. Every man in the gulley would be dead before morning.

Yang Jie is in this gulley.

With a kind of wrenching, ripping effort that made me cry out in pain – I broke free.

I was crouching in the tangle of my damp bedroll, staring into our substantial campfire, which had died down a little, but was by no means near to going out. The other campfires flickered and danced: pockets of light in the darkness around me. The men lay still and peaceful in their places. There was no singing. No wind. No ghosts.

On the other side of the campfire, someone let out a choked gasp. Furs and blankets flew back as they clawed their way out of their bed and on to their knees, panting harshly. It was General Wu.

His face, even bathed in the rosy glow from the fire, was set and white. I opened my mouth – but the look in his eyes, half savage, half lost, stilled my tongue. It didn't matter. I didn't need to ask what had woken him. I knew. I knew.

Instead, after a moment, he was the one to speak. His voice was almost a growl. "Who? Who did you hear?"

I swallowed. "My mother."

He closed his eyes, nodded wearily. "Me, too."

Swiftly, he turned away and lay down again, pulling one of the heavy, fur-lined blankets up over his shoulder so that his profile was hidden.

Little by little, my marrow aching like that of an old man, I shuffled back into my own bedroll. The mist that had hung above the Stone Forest all day and all night was beginning to break up, and stars were winking gently overhead. I lay stiff and unmoving among my blankets for some time, listening to the unrestful quiet of the dark, before I remembered something. Something I should have remembered before.

Wu Jiang's mother had been murdered when he was a little boy.

The Young General had just heard his dead mother's voice for the first time in over a decade, and she … she had been screaming in agony. I felt a warm tear track down my cheek and scrubbed it away impatiently. He wouldn't thank me for my pity.

It was a long time before I was able to sleep again that night.

Seventeen

ven by Wu Jiang's standards, he pushed us hard the next day. Before mid-afternoon we had reached the steep and treacherous rock slope that lead upwards out of the gulley into the warm, green-gold light of the bamboo forest beyond.

It took a good three hours to push and drag all the men, horses and wagons up that horrid slope, but the relief of being out of the Stone Forest, away from the waiting silence and the steadily thickening cover of mist, was euphoric enough to make everyone count the sweat, sore muscles and bruises well worth it. All around me, I saw the men turn their faces up to the sun, breathe in the earthy forest smell, and smile.

Never would I laugh at ghost stories again.

General Wu signalled to Sigong. "We've a lot of ground to cover today, Captain. Let's set a fast clip, please!"

The bamboo forest that bounded the Stone Forest was a farmed one, maintained over the steeply sloping ground by villagers who also, luckily for us, ensured the roads were in good condition. We achieved a pace that put a satisfied look even on the Young General's face, moving through the soothing green ranks of trees with a speed borne, I thought, of both relief and a strong desire to put the day before behind us. A mood of good cheer hung over the columns of soldiers, and Sigong wisely encouraged it.

Tall tales of heroic adventure, battle prowess or romantic conquest began to circulate among the senior officers. Sigong enraptured the company by relating the time when, he claimed, he had glimpsed Dou Xianniang herself in the flesh, despite the fact that if she still lived she would have been over a hundred years old. And that was if one conceded that she had ever really existed at all.

According to Sigong, everything in the stories was true. The honourable lady outlaw was a wild beauty with flying raven hair, scarlet-lacquered armour and a sword that flashed quick as lightning.

"I swear to you I'm not lying!" the normally laconic man protested, laughing at his own vehemence. "On the life of my favourite wife, I swear it! It was her. She ran those rebels through as if their bodies were paper, and dragged the children from the burning house with her own hands! I was as close to her as you are to me now."

"And did she give you a kiss – or more – for good luck, too?" someone mocked good-naturedly.

"No," Sigong admitted through a chorus of hoots and

catcalls. "Although I would have been in fear for my life if she had. She had eyes like a wild creature – like a tigress at bay. Feral! She'd have taken a bite out of me."

"Coward!" General Wu chided affably. His eyes had lit up like a boy's when Sigong began the story. "It would be worth it to die at the hands of such a woman."

"Yes, you'd have died smiling!" another officer shouted, making an obscene gesture.

By mid-morning we were all joining in when some of the men broke out in a very old and very bawdy marching song.

"Helps them keep time," Wu Jiang told me with a faintly sheepish grin.

I smiled back, glad to see him in better spirits, even if the song did make my cheeks burn.

Ahead of us, the front ranks of infantry broke through the last of the trees, sunlight flashing from their helms and the rims of their shields. Almost at once, their light-hearted singing dissolved into shocked cries. I heard the sergeant in charge call out a halt and then shout for Captain Sigong and General Wu.

Sigong quickly turned back to pass the order for a full stop to the columns behind us. Wu Jiang was already kicking his bay mount forward into a trot. I followed, stomach cramping with apprehension.

What I saw as I left the shady green cave of trees was both better and worse than I had feared.

No company of Leopard fighters aimed cannon at us from the forest, and the pale road that wound around the hillside ahead was clear.

Instead, at the base of the terraced green valley below, surrounded by the glimmer of rice fields, I beheld a small farming settlement. A few dozen families, perhaps. Almost certainly the same farmers who had planted and harvested this forest, and maintained this road.

They would do so no longer. There was nothing left but blackened ruins.

The Leopard had been here before us.

Wu Jiang drew in a deep breath through his nose. His jaw worked as he turned in his saddle to look at Sigong, who had reined his horse in beside ours.

"No smoke still rising, no taste of ash on the air," Sigong commented, matter-of-fact. "Those fires have gone cold. This is a few days old at least. Just an unhappy coincidence."

"More a sign of how bad things are becoming," General Wu said heavily. "If we hadn't happened on this road, it might have been days more, even weeks, before anyone realized what happened here. And there are most likely dozens more the same, scattered up and down the empire."

"Orders, sir?" I prompted when he fell silent, and seemed disinclined to say more.

The bay horse jinked restlessly beneath him – the only sign of his internal disquiet. "We must investigate. The war office and the emperor will expect reports. And we owe it to these people to bury their remains, make the proper offerings."

It was quickly arranged for the main body of the battalion to break on the road, and keep watch. The last thing any of us wanted after the ambush on the camp was to be caught off-guard again. Wu Jiang picked out nine men – plus his two bodyguards, me and, strangely, one of our precious doctors – to enter the ruins. It wasn't usual to bring a surgeon along unless…

"Nothing is moving down there, sir," I said tentatively. "Do you really think we'll find survivors?"

Wu pressed his lips into a remarkably humourless smile. "Unlikely. But having a doctor present is often useful. Besides, it's not beyond the realm of possibility that someone could have escaped. They may emerge when they see the empire's colours."

Soon we were ready to leave the battalion and the road behind, descending on to a narrower, but still dry and well looked-after trail down to the base of the hill. The sight of the blackened, gaping buildings was disturbing, but as we came closer, I found the worst thing was the quiet. I compared the stillness to what I should have heard: dogs barking to announce intruders, the lowing of cattle and the clucking of fowl, followed by screaming, excited children running out to pet the horses, and their parents yelling at them in turn…

Insects chirruped in the wild grasses of the verge, and in the rice fields, frogs croaked. Somewhere above, a carrion bird coughed.

I shivered. This felt as haunted a place, in its own way, as the Stone Forest.

"We'll split into three groups," Wu Jiang said. "Check each building carefully and note the number of bodies or the possibility of survivors. Hua Zhi, you're with me."

We left our horses tethered to a miraculously intact rail at the edge of the village. General Wu's two bodyguard-outriders took on the task of entering the burned ruins and reporting what they had seen. The Young General opted to appease them by staying away from the possible danger of collapsing floors and walls, and I perforce remained with him, pressing notes on to a wax tablet.

The small houses here had been wood-walled and grass-roofed. The fire had devoured the humble dwellings hungrily, leaving many so gutted that only a few beams and the odd wall still stood. It was necessary to poke through piles of ash and debris to look for human remains. The devastation was stark. But ... there were no bodies.

"Where are they?" I murmured, hardly aware that I spoke aloud. In the distance, back at the centre of the village, I could see one of the other groups – the one with the doctor – still scratching through the wreckage. "Even if we assume some escaped, or that the Leopard took some as slaves, this fire was out of control. Most of these people must have died here. Where are their bodies?"

"Maybe the Leopard took them all for slaves, and only then burned the place," one of Wu Jiang's guards suggested. Since they never acknowledged my existence if they could help it, I took this as proof that they found the lack of remains as unsettling as I did.

Wu Jiang said nothing.

"General." The doctor was approaching, the soldiers from his group behind him. All of them were a little out of breath. "We found evidence in the town square that the rebels stayed here for several days after the attack. We believe they were … feasting."

There was a sick significance to that word. My stomach cramped again, and the feeling only intensified when the doctor offered some slender, yellowed sticks to the Young General. He took them without hesitation, but his shoulders were tense, his head drawn down towards his chest.

"So small," he muttered.

"No more than three years old, I would have said." The doctor's usually impassive face twitched. "You can see the teeth marks."

My stomach heaved and I breathed out, slowly, through my mouth. The sticks were a baby's bones. And they had been gnawed on. Not by fangs – not by animals. But by humans.

"There are also signs that they corralled the cattle, pigs and so on, and took them when they left."

"To sell or eat later," Wu Jiang said, utterly blank. "Easier to transport than human livestock."

"Sir," one of the bodyguards broke in, ashen-faced. "Are – are you saying that they kept the cattle alive – and – and ate the people?"

"That's how he came to be called the Leopard," the doctor said, when Wu Jiang failed to respond. "It's said leopards hunt men sometimes, in the mountains. Once the beasts have tasted human flesh, they become man-eaters for life."

The guard took two hasty steps away and went down on his knees, dry-heaving. The other guard averted his gaze, as if ashamed at his fellow's weakness. Personally,

I was entirely in sympathy with the man. I might have joined him – except that just then General Wu's large hands tightened around the small bundle of bones. One cracked in his hand, a dry, pathetic little noise. With a look of sudden horror, he dropped them.

"General Wu?" I approached cautiously, stowing my papers and writing equipment in the canvas sack slung around my chest. "Sir, are you well?"

"What a waste," he said softly, staring down at the fragile, broken little bones lying in the dust at his feet. "This – this should never have happened. What a stupid, damned waste."

He blinked, swallowed – the same trick he had taught me in the stockade – then jerked his head. "You're dismissed."

It took me a couple of puzzled seconds to work out that he meant not just me, but all of us. I opened my mouth to protest. It wasn't safe for him to be alone, not in unsecured territory. The guard who had been sick got in first, stumbling back to his feet.

"General Wu, no – our orders—"

"I don't care," Wu Jiang said through gritted teeth. "Leave me. Now."

Still, we hesitated, thrown by the disregard for protocol or, in my case, his uncharacteristic display of emotion. The doctor moved closer and began in soothing tones, "Now, now, sir—"

Wu Jiang snarled, furious. "I said *leave me!*"

Well. That was quite clear. I saluted sharply, then turned away. Behind me, I heard the others reluctantly following suit. I felt a little guilty for being the first to give in, but I was equally anxious that my own stomach might revolt at any time – a cold sweat had broken out on my brow and upper lip and my vision had gone a little blurry at the edges. *Shock,* I thought distantly. I'd really … rather be alone, just now. Wu Jiang deserved the same courtesy.

I wandered away from the others aimlessly. General Wu might have ordered us from his presence but he hadn't sent us off duty, which meant I needed to stay within hearing distance of his bellow. I left Yulong where he was, after a quick check on his comfort, and then decided to head downhill, following the road to the rice fields. A small stream ran almost alongside it, most likely artificial, dug to water those same fields, and my canteen was nearly empty.

I scrambled down the shallow, grassy bank and crouched by the water, listening to the peaceful splash and ripple of its movements with relief. It was a sound which I had always associated with tranquillity and wellness. I closed my eyes and breathed in the green, earthy smells, appreciating the warmth of the sun on the backs of my hands and scalp, the fact that I was alive and well and still able to enjoy such things.

My *qi* gradually calmed. My stomach stopped trying to heave. I sighed. A general, or even his fancy hand-picked bodyguard from the city, might be allowed some show of great emotion at such destruction as this. They had nothing to prove. But the rest of us, unless we wished to be labelled cowards, or worse, girls – *How I despise that stupid insult!* – needed to at least attempt to remain stoic.

Who were these ... these monsters that we were fighting? Could they really be mere mortal men, like the rest of us, if they were capable of such acts? This place had held no strategic importance, contained no great wealth or influential people. It had simply been here. And they had destroyed it, and everyone within it, and consumed them.

Just because.

The Leopard must truly be as depraved as the stories said. Nothing else could explain this. And yet he was ... not *winning*, surely not – but holding his own against the very best our empire had to offer. Three years after he first reappeared, he was still running unchecked through the countryside enacting such obscene violence. No one could catch him. No one could stop him.

What if such a man were to win? What if he were to take the Dragon Throne?

What would become of us then?

Slowly and deliberately, I refilled my canteen, marvelling at the crystal purity of the water, the slow-moving silver flashes of the carp, and the jewel-like smoothness of the river stones that made up the water's bed. It was safer to think of such simple, lovely things just now. Tormenting myself was a waste of time, a waste of this, the first snatch of true privacy I'd had in weeks.

No sooner had the thought crossed my mind than I saw the house.

It lay on the other side of the stream, set a good way back from the road and the water, in the shadow of the hill, and sheltered by a thick bank of trees. From here it appeared undisturbed – a small but surprisingly gracious dwelling, with expensive green clay tiles on the roof and what appeared to be a pocket-sized ornamental garden flourishing outside the front door.

The home of a local official or dignitary, perhaps a poet or a scholar, a person of some little wealth who had chosen this idyllic, isolated spot to hide away.

As I leapt across the narrow waterway, I felt a faint glimmer of hope. The little house was untouched by fire, secluded from the rest of the village. Perhaps the Leopard's men had missed it. Perhaps the people were hiding. Perhaps, perhaps, perhaps here I would find that single precious survivor of this massacre that the Young General had dared to imagine.

But when I reached the end of the short, paved pathway to the red-painted door, I found it unlocked. A bad sign. Inside, the receiving hall showed evidence of disturbance: a teacup knocked over, the now cold beverage allowed to drip from the table to the faded but lovely rug beneath.

A little deeper inside, and I saw scuffmarks on the polished wooden floor, as if someone or something had been dragged. There was a small splash of blood, dried to black. And there was a smell, growing with each step. An unmistakable smell.

I breathed through my mouth, and pressed on.

In a small room that reminded me irresistibly of my father's study – dim, book-lined and comfortably shabby – I found the people who had lived there.

Eighteen

I slammed the screen closed, gagging on the cloying, fetid stench of death. I staggered away, only realizing as I collided with the wall that my eyes had snapped shut. But it was no use. What I had seen was in my head now. I could still see it. I would always see it.

A man, middle-aged and dressed in clothes that were of fine quality, but well worn. A woman of around the same age. Probably his wife. A boy, lanky and only half grown – in his mid-teens. Their son, most likely. And a man in spotted armour. All dead. All dead, together, and already beginning, *oh ancestors*, beginning to bloat…

The middle-aged man's throat had been cut. His blood had spilled over his desk as his body slumped over his papers. His wife – maybe she had tried to help her husband, or get away, but the Leopard's man caught her. The bruises on her throat and wrists, her thighs, the

way her fine gown had been ripped and left rucked up...
There in the same room where her husband lay dead...

Perhaps her son had been somewhere else in the house
and heard the screams? Something had brought him into
the room. But he was only a boy. Only a boy.

I thought the mother had tried to fight, to protect him.
There ... there had been a bloodied paper knife clutched
in her hand. But in the end it didn't matter. They all died
there. Murdered and murderer. Rotting together.

I raged for them, as I stumbled from that room of
death. I raged for her. This woman, this mother, this
stranger. For all she had been forced to do and see, and
endure, and at the useless, meaningless way it had ended.
We would have helped them. We should have helped
them. Now they were all beyond anyone's help.

I heard the echo of my mother's voice crying out to
me in the Stone Forest last night, and shuddered. *Too late.*

Light fell across my face. I opened my eyes, and found
myself at the open doorway of another room. A weaving
room. Smaller than the one in my home, but in every way
familiar and ordinary and reassuring. Two looms, both
strung with *kesi* tapestries – one complete, one unfinished –
occupied the majority of the space. A beautiful thread box,
inlaid with peonies in mother-of-pearl and shell, lay open
as if in invitation, skeins of coloured silk neatly arranged
and ready to be used.

A screen door to the ornamental garden outside was
slightly open, and there were large, dusty boot prints on
the otherwise carefully swept floor. This was how the
murderer had crept in. The room was untouched by the

chaos and violence beyond. The only trace of what had happened to its owner was the dust.

The rage inside me stilled – not dissipated but suddenly contained. As if in a trance I entered and sat before the larger loom. The incomplete tapestry was beautiful. A round panel with three vivid blue-and-copper flycatcher birds picking red berries from a branch. The edges featured bamboo leaves and peach blossoms, symbolizing long life and an upright character. Flycatcher birds might refer to an administrative rank in the court that could be obtained with favourable civil service examination results.

My breath caught in my throat. She had been making this for her son. A piece of art that symbolized all a mother's hopes for her child and his future...

Only a few places remained to be completed on the tapestry – mostly on the decorative edge.

I should have got up and left right then. Such a thing was not for me. I was a soldier, and this was women's work, utterly and irrefutably. No one remained to appreciate this piece and what it meant, to care whether or not the tapestry was ever finished. It was a meaningless gesture.

But already my fingers were reaching for the first leaf-shaped shuttle, with the dark green of the bamboo leaves threaded on to it, and the comb.

It had been months since I had touched a loom, and any tiny flaw in a piece like this was irreversible, ruining the whole. Yet the delicate, skilful movements came back to me in exactly the same way that fighting did when I needed it – muscle memory, engrained in the very fibres of my body.

Weaving was always one of my chief womanly accomplishments. One of the few things I could share with my mother. Something that made me feel connected with her, even if at other times we struggled to understand one another.

The churning centre of fury inside me slowly flowed away as I threaded, cut and combed, following the pattern that the dead woman had laid out on the horizontal raw-silk warp threads strung into the frame. My mind emptied of thoughts, of worry and mourning. Peace flowed into their place. I simply existed: a pair of hands that allowed the silk to find its proper place and nothing more.

I guided the final weft of green into place. It was done.

I'm sorry. Whoever you were, wherever you are now… I'm sorry we didn't get here in time. I'm sorry I can't do more for you than this.

Behind me, there was a soft indrawn breath.

For a frozen instant I stared at the tapestry, motionless. *No. No, please.*

Slowly – so slowly that I could feel each muscle shift under my skin, name each bone as it moved – I turned.

There in the doorway of the room stood the Young General. Our gazes locked.

I waited. Waited for his expression to twist, his cheeks to flush with rage, his teeth to bare, for a shout of fury. I wouldn't have been surprised if he had rushed at me with knotted fists or even drawn his sword. With this action I had given myself away as surely as if I had walked into his tent in my best silk gown and slippers, with my hair in a conch binding. Weaving was an art exclusively for women. No man should have been able to do what I had just done.

He smiled, dimple flashing. "It's a beautiful piece. I'm glad you were able to finish it."

His expression held nothing of fury or betrayal – only wry understanding. It invited commiseration, and asked me to smile in return. I felt myself crumple in the face of his friendliness as I would not his anger.

"Wh–what?" I stammered, shameful tears springing to my eyes.

In a rush, he crouched before me and grasped one of my hands in both of his. "Shh. Don't. From the very first I sensed that there was something different about you. When we fought, there was something there, an aware-ness, a sort of knowing. But I dismissed it. I had to. Every time I felt it, I dismissed it, because it seemed outlandish and impossible. Then last night, when we looked at each other over that fire … your face seemed different. And I was sure."

I realized with a jolt of sick, lurching horror that when I had woken from the nightmare last night, my mask had been off. Of course it had been off – I couldn't maintain it in sleep.

"I'm sorry, sir." It was a feeble, incomplete admis-sion – but he clearly needed no more than that. His hand tightened on mine: "What are you going to do to me?"

His face became serious. "Tell me this. Why did you perpetrate such a deception?"

It's not a deception. It's who I am. I tugged at my hand

restlessly, but he held it. Eventually I gave the only answer I could: "To save my family."

"Your family? Are you really from the House of Hua, then?"

"Yes, I swear – I'm not a spy or an imposter."

"But then why come here in your brother's place?"

I let out a weak laugh. "My brother is ten years old and my father … my father is the best of men, the greatest of warriors, but … he is crippled. He has given our country all he has to give. To fight again would kill him. And that would kill my mother." I paused, then in a low voice confessed, "And I wanted to serve the empire. I wanted to prove my worth. To show that I could bring my family honour." That was as close as I could come to the full truth.

"I knew it," he said warmly, nodding. "Hua … Hua – what is your name? Your real name, I mean?"

Hua Zhi is my real name! I struggled against the dart of red-hot rage and forced it back. My life hung in the balance. "Hua Zhilan," I said, forcing the words out.

"Very pretty. It suits you. Hua Zhilan, you are … something I never thought existed. At least, not in real life. A woman like Dou Xianniang, or like the Red Empress. A myth, come to life. To have met you by chance … it is like stumbling over a diamond in the grass, unnoticed by anyone."

A frown wrinkled my brow. In what way was I like a mythical female outlaw who had stolen from the wealthy and corrupt to feed the virtuous and poor? Or like the famous battle-empress, first wife of the founder of our empire? My father had said a similar thing once.

It had rung false then – especially after I sought out and read the true stories of these women, not the morality-tale versions that my mother had thought suitable for me – and it rang false now. I had not earned such legendary comparisons merely because of the sex with which I had been born.

And it still brought me no closer to knowing the consequences of Wu Jiang's discovery.

"Please be plain. What are you saying?" I stared into his face. "Aren't you angry? Disgusted? Are you going to have me arrested? Killed?"

"Do you want me to?" he asked, half bewildered, half amused.

His smile was like salt water in a cut. "No! But I know that no one else can be expected to understand the choices I've made. I always knew that. I always knew that if anyone ever found out—"

"You're wrong. I know what it is to pretend to be something you are not. To seek to protect family, even when it means going against every rule you've been taught – against honesty, and perhaps even decency. If anyone in this world can understand you, Hua Zhilan, it is me."

"Because you hide your true skill as a warrior. You pretend to be a decent swordsman, powerful but unimaginative, a little slow. You fight badly on purpose. I was right."

"Yes." He looked down soberly – and then up again, smiling once more. "And you saw through it. You alone."

"Why did you perpetrate such a deception?" I asked, carefully using his own words.

He answered almost eagerly, as if he had only been waiting for a chance to explain. "Because I have seen what happens to those who stand out at court. My mother stood out. She was brave and kind, and good. So good. And because some at court could not stand to see such uncorrupted brightness there, she was poisoned. I still have a father and a stepmother, and siblings – and my position, the role in which my aunt has placed me, puts all of them in constant danger. The only way to mitigate that is to make the most powerful figures at court believe that I am complacent. Average. No threat to them or their schemes. Only my closest intimates know that I am a decorated general not because of my aunt's fondness for me, but because I have earned that rank five times over."

I realized with some astonishment that I had allowed myself to be sidetracked. "General Wu, please tell me. What is going to happen to me now?"

"Nothing. Nothing that you don't want."

I gaped at him, made truly speechless for perhaps the first time in my life.

He squeezed my hand. "Continue to do your job as well as you have been, and I will do mine. And when this damned war is over and peace is finally secured ... then you and I shall have a long talk. I will have a long talk with your parents, too. I think I shall enjoy meeting your father. Your whole family. The House of Hua is a truly remarkable one. Is this acceptable to you?"

His eyes seemed to be expecting me to understand something – something important – but whatever it was, it was lost on me. He had discovered me. That was all

I could think. No matter what he wanted, I had no room to fight back, to refuse. He wasn't angry now, and I had to keep it that way.

After an awkward wait, I nodded hesitantly.

Wu Jiang grinned a wild, dimple-flashing grin. Then he stood and pulled me to my feet in a brisk and comradely fashion. "Come on. Let's leave this cursed place behind."

I went with him, numb and wordless. My great secret had been discovered and the result was … nothing? I should just continue with my work and he would talk to my father when it was all over? Talk to him about what? Possible punishments for me, or our house? But he had said he looked forward to meeting my family…

I was so taken aback, so utterly unable to fit his response into any of the disaster scenarios that I had mentally constructed that it took several hours for everything he had said to really soak into my brain.

By then we had returned to the battalion, marched down the road for several more miles to a better sheltered spot, off the road, and made camp. I had carried out my usual tasks in my usual way, without anyone appearing to sense anything different at all, but in truth I was in a daze, going over the meeting in that sad, bloody little house again and again. What had he meant? What on earth had he been trying to say? Surely there must be some consequences, some terrible sequel to this?

As always in the evening I was sitting across from him at his camp desk, working on my own reports and waiting on the servants to bring us some dinner, when it dawned on me. In fact, it was completely obvious. But at the same time it was so impossible that I couldn't blame myself for not realizing it until then.

General Wu Jiang, his Imperial Highness, Prince of the Red Empire and nephew of Emperor Wu, had proposed to me.

And I had utterly failed to say no.

Nineteen

My brush trembled in my hand. I stilled it with a furtive glance at Wu Jiang and pretended to bend my head over my papers again.

What could have possessed him? Anyone who knew him would be horrified at the idea of such a connection! I was no one's ideal wife! He had compared me to Dou Xianniang and the Red Empress, but that was nonsense. For a start, they were both supposed to be raving beauties. I could happily and easily live as a boy for the rest of my life.

Besides, he was a royal prince. He was young, but he should already have had a couple of princesses lined up to be first and second wives by now, even if they weren't officially married yet.

Is he saying he wants me to be an official concubine? Perhaps the prestige of being Hua Zhou's daughter outweighs the fact that I come from what, to the nephew of the emperor, must seem like complete penury. But surely not the small matter of me running around the country dressed as a soldier...

Can he be serious?

Is he trying to trick me?

Seduce me?

That seemed much more likely than any honourable offer. I was so far beneath him in rank and position that it was laughable. And anyone who heard that an unmarried girl had been living with hundreds of soldiers for months would probably assume she had no virtue left anyway.

But then why all that talk of waiting until the war is over, of speaking to my father? He could just demand that I lie down with him now, on pain of reporting me. Why hide his true motives?

Shu Yuen entered the tent with a smile for me, placing a simple yet hearty supper on the desk. The Young General sat back from his papers, and nodded to me politely.

"We'll eat and work, Corporal. We should pass the town of Honourable Prosperity tomorrow and I want to ensure these reports are complete and ready to be sent to the proper offices by then."

"O–of course, sir." I made a production of rewetting my brush. It spoke worlds for my frame of mind that I was actually glad to immerse myself in these notes again. As I forced myself to apply my attention to the gruesome details of what we had found in the bamboo village, I shivered a little.

"Add some more fuel to the brazier before you go, would you?" Wu Jiang said to one of the servants.

After over two hours of intense scribbling, both Wu

Jiang and I were flexing cramped, ink-stained fingers, and the Young General declared our work done for the night. It was late, and very quiet, and for the first time I really noticed that the two of us were entirely alone together.

Instantly, I felt my hackles rise, wary of some attempt at flirtation – or worse. But Wu Jiang didn't even look up as I rose to my feet and began to move towards the exit. Relieved, I reached the tent flap and grasped the material in my hand.

He called that name. My other name.

I failed to control my flinch. My heart began to thump against my ribs like a lead weight.

"Yes, sir?" *No, please.*

"Today was ... difficult," he said. I heard the rustle of cloth and the creak of his chair, and pictured him standing behind his desk. There were no footsteps on the rug, though. He was not – yet – approaching. "I'm grateful for your good work. I couldn't have done this without you."

I stood frozen, grinding my teeth together as I waited for him to go on. But he said nothing more, only waited in expectant silence for a response. A quick check of my mask ensured it was composed. Turning to look over my shoulder – not as polite as I should be, but my fingers had spasmed into a death grip on the tent flap – I saw him bathed in golden light from the last dregs of oil in the work lamps.

"I'm ... honoured to have been able to serve you, General." Apprehension made my voice even huskier than usual. The servile phrase had never felt less comfortable on my tongue.

A slow, gentle smile played across his mouth, causing that incongruous dimple to wink. "Sleep well."

"And you, sir."

I turned to face the entrance again, his gaze a sort of shivery heat on the back of my neck.

Please don't stop me. Please don't. Please don't call me back. Please let me go…

I drew the heavy canvas aside, and stepped through. The flap fell shut behind me with a soft whisper.

Chilly night air burned my throat and came out in a long, trembling plume of white. On either side of the tent entrance, General Wu's bodyguards studiously ignored me as always, and I was grateful, although I knew they would have ignored other things, too, like my screams for help from inside…

But I had not needed to scream. Or to beg. Or even negotiate. There had been no demands, no innuendos. No flirting. He had not attempted to use his knowledge of my vulnerability against me. He had not tried to seduce or coerce me. He had treated me in every way exactly as before. The only difference was that faint hint of warmth – discreet, but unmistakable.

Wu Jiang had meant what he said. He wasn't going to take action against me. Nothing was to change. I was safe. Safe with him. I had become … attached … to one of the richest, most powerful and influential men in the empire, and from now on, he would protect me.

That night, for the first time since I was seven years old, I cried myself to sleep.

• • •

The battalion travelled for a further eight days before reaching the great river plain that was home to the City of Endless Serenity. In that time, General Wu made himself extremely busy – busy waging a subtle, clever and relentless campaign. Against me.

Oh, he was as good as his word. I continued with my work, and he with his. He made no improper advances. Indeed, no advances of any kind. Nor did he offer me any kind of favour or preferential treatment. When others were around, he acted exactly as one would expect towards a respected, junior colleague. When it was just the two of us – and never before had I realized quite how much time I spent alone with my senior officer – he was precisely the same.

He might as well have been my elder brother, or the impartial mentor that he appeared.

Except...

If, by chance, I should happen to mention within his hearing that pumpkin pancakes with toasted sesame seeds were a favourite dessert of mine, at the next meal I would be offered this exact treat.

If my brush were to begin to shed its hairs and cause me to mutter under my breath while working, the next day a new brush – far finer than any available from the army stores – would appear in my sack of supplies.

One morning I realized that the sword I had brought from home, chosen because it was of excellent quality but shabby-looking, and therefore unlikely to draw attention, had been stealthily removed from the scabbard in the night. It had been cleaned, sharpened, and the grip rewrapped with beautifully soft new leather. A few days later, Yulong's saddle received the same treatment.

And each night when I crawled into the small tent pitched in the shelter of General Wu's large one, there would be a flower waiting for me.

Even when we were miles from any town, village or farm that might sell flowers. Even if we were marching through a desolate bog where the only vegetation was reed-grass, lichen and slime. Even if I could have sworn that the man hadn't been out of my sight for as much as a minute. There the flower would be. Just a single bloom – often an orchid, my namesake – resting on my bedroll.

It didn't take many days of this for me to begin to suspect that the bullish, manly general was a secret and incurable dreamer. The type who had been addicted as a child to fairy tales, stories of derring-do, and noble heroism. Courtships such as this, chaste yet ardent, were the stuff of such stories. He saw me just as he had asserted: as that fantasy woman, the Virtuous Lady in Disguise. Such figures were common in folklore.

For girls, these stories were generally edited in order to change the traits of their heroines, or used as cautionary tales – easy enough since the Virtuous Lady in Disguise usually had a tragic if noble end. I had been taught that Dou Xianniang, for example, had flung herself from a cliff in order to avoid the advances of a cruel bandit king. Sad, but inevitable for a woman who ran around fighting men instead of staying home as was her real duty.

But for boys, who were expected to go out into the world adventuring, and glorify their houses with valiant service of the empire? It seemed there were none of those grim admonitions. Since joining the army I'd learned that most men, like Sigong, saw Dou Xianniang and others like her as immortal, legendary figures. Women to dream over and desire.

It made perfect sense that any sedate, proper young women whom Wu Jiang had been betrothed to since childhood would be unlikely to warm that small, fundamental ember of childish longing in his breast. The yearning for adventure, for burning glances, battlefield confessions of devotion, and epic, star-crossed love. But I, quite by accident, had set it ablaze.

It was strange. The first time I had ever seen the Young General I had felt an instinctive, almost overwhelming response. I had thought he was like a hero from a play or ballad. I had thought he was everything that a man should be.

I had never dreamed he would have a similar response to me.

But while I liked him, respected him, and found pride in his liking and respect for me… My heart was foolish and stubborn. And it still longed for someone else. Someone it simply could not have. Not in this world.

What is, is.

Anyway, my own feelings, much as I wished to linger on them, did not materially affect the situation. Marriage was about family, about responsibility and forming alliances that would protect and nurture the houses which arranged them. It was not up to me to decide whether Wu Jiang's suit was acceptable.

That decision would rest with my father … and with the emperor.

The thought of each of their possible reactions to General Wu's infatuation with me – if he really followed through – was enough to paralyse me with apprehension. Emperors had been known to dispose of their children's unsuitable lovers quite ruthlessly, and wipe out their whole houses if anyone protested. If Wu Fen decided that she did not like this match – and who, even knowing of her own humble origins, could blame her? – it might mean the destruction of my family.

Yet even if Wu Fen, by some extraordinary chance, was willing to consider the daughter of Hua Zhou as, perhaps, an honourable concubine for her foster son … what if my father objected?

He had removed our family from court influence once before, stubbornly walking away from power and riches even though it might have meant our lives. But that emperor had known him, and been his friend. This one was not.

How had I landed myself in such an impossible tangle?

Twenty

"Wu Jiang's occasional polite enquiries after my health took on a more serious tone as the days went by. He no longer joked that I was getting skinny, but stated it forthrightly. More sweet treats began to appear at our nightly meals. Annoyed with myself that I had apparently allowed my worry – and the slight hollowing of my face – to unconsciously leak through on to my mask, I stayed up late one night with a precious candle and my hand mirror, ensuring that the bloom of ruddy youth was restored to my illusion. I expected General Wu to be satisfied with this, and hoped that his suffocating concern would abate.

I hadn't given him enough credit.

"You're looking better this evening," the Young General commented as I was tidying my notes away for the night.

"Thank you, General. If that's all—"

"*Why* are you looking so much better?" he persisted.

"I've been following your advice, sir," I said, trying to keep my voice even. It was an effort not to let my resentment and frustration with what felt like constant scrutiny show. I had survived the brutality of the training camp and the early weeks of our journey without any help. Why did he now believe I needed him to guard and monitor me? "Eating better, attempting to sleep a little more."

"And it's agreed with you so well that in a single day you appear to have regained all the weight you lost, and healed up that bruise Sigong gave you in practice two days ago. If I didn't know you, I'd suspect you of a rather skilful application of cosmetics."

You don't know me!

I clasped my hands to prevent them from closing into fists, and looked Wu Jiang straight in the eyes. "The bruise was light. It faded. That's all."

The Young General squinted at me in the soft glow of the lamps. For a moment, I hoped that was the end of the matter. Then: "You're a banner-breaker, aren't you?"

I felt my body go still – a tiny, betraying stillness that I forced myself out of nearly instantly. It was already too late. General Wu's face lit up with a disarming, boyish grin.

"I've never – knowingly – met one in real life, although my aunt says she keeps several at court. I didn't even know women could possess the ability. Have you had much training?"

What freak of misfortune had placed me in the way of a man who twinned the straightforwardness of a charging bull with the subtle observational skills of an ancient sage? He stared at me expectantly. Clearly he wouldn't rest, or let me rest, until he had wrung some sort of confession from me, but the secret of my father's gift was inviolate. It was not mine to share.

"Obviously women do not normally manifest such traits. I have always been taught to keep it hidden, for the sake of future alliances and my family's reputation. Training…" I allowed my voice to trail off as I moved my shoulders in a faint shrug.

Wu Jiang nodded thoughtfully, apparently inferring, as I had intended, that I had little or no knowledge of my own gift. With the limited talent I had, it might as well be true anyway.

"That's a shame. So you can only use it – like this?" He gestured towards my face.

"Yes. To protect myself. To hide myself. It's an instinct."

"And the face I see now?"

"Is mine," I said quickly. "Merely a little … blurred."

"I suspected as much. It's very clever, how you use it." He paused, tongue passing over his bottom lip. "May I see it? Your true face?"

My jaw twinged with the force of teeth clenching together. Thoughts raced through my mind. How could I refuse when he held such leverage over me? What if he made it a direct order? Perhaps the sight of my plain old self would even cool his ardour a little, and win me some space from him.

But my rationality was at war with an overwhelming, instinctive need. I didn't want him to see me.

Need won.

"No," I said, firmly but gently. I realized that my voice had unconsciously lifted into a slightly more feminine register only when I added a belated: "I'm sorry."

I braced myself. This was the first – the only – personal thing he had ever asked of me, and I had denied him. How would he take it?

Wu Jiang ran his hand over his thick beard, half concealing the change in his expression from grin to a different sort of smile – small, pleased, private.

"Very well. I can wait." He cleared his throat and sat up straighter, pulling the mantle of command back over himself in much the same way that I spun my mask of illusion into place each morning. "Thank you for your hard work today. Good evening."

I returned the pleasantries and escaped, my chest still heavy with anxiety. If I were the mussel and he the fisherman, then my shell had well and truly been forced open, and my vulnerable innards exposed. That this man should have learned all my most closely guarded secrets while I had run away rather than confide anything in Yang Jie... Oh, that was bitter.

Yet. Wasn't Wu Jiang worthy of my trust? Hadn't he sought to earn it, painstakingly, day by day, through respect, courtesy and kindness? I wasn't sure what still held me back. Was it mere habit? I couldn't explain it, even to myself. Perhaps this secretiveness was a fatal flaw in me, that I could not bear to risk true vulnerability with anyone – not Yang Jie, not Wu Jiang – until, perhaps, it was too late to have any value.

The flower waiting for me on my bedroll that night was a blue hydrangea. The symbol of gratitude, enlightenment … and love.

We arrived at the city's yellow earth rampart two days later, at mid-morning. It was my first visit to the imperial seat where my father had lived for so long, and it was everything that I had imagined – and a few things I hadn't.

Rivers of people from all corners of the empire swarmed the roads to the city like colourful armies of ants. Merchants with carts full of fruit and sweets, herbal cures, lucky talismans and "tokens for your sweetheart!" hawked their wares cheerfully from the verges. Hooves and feet thundered as we crossed the bridge over the thirty-foot moat to the vast red-brick Gate of Shining Virtue: the entrance to the city. I gazed up in awe at its five individual gates – each one wide enough for a team of five oxen to drive through abreast. The central gate was the only one that was closed. It was never opened, the Young General told me, except for the emperor herself.

But I was more interested in the evidence of battle that scarred the city's gates. On the rampart above the gate openings there was a trio of great wooden watchtowers. One was hung with silk banners – the other two were under repair, with workman busily scurrying over them, and scaffolding in place. It gave the gate a strange, lopsided appearance.

"The Leopard himself attempted to assail the walls of the city at midsummer," Wu Jiang murmured as I rode beside him at the front of the column of men. "They drove him away in a single night, but he did a great deal of damage before he fled."

"I'd heard nothing of this," I said, trying to conceal my shock.

"My aunt has taken great pains that the story not spread beyond the city itself. We fear the knowledge that the rebel army has grown so confident might cause panic, especially in more remote regions." He nodded at me, then kicked his horse forward to greet a senior guard at the leftmost gate, leaving me blinking at the casual way he had imparted this confidence.

Men. All you have to do is save their lives once or twice and they think they can trust you.

My cynicism was feeble even in my own mind. In my saddlebags were a hydrangea blossom and an orchid, carefully pressed between the pages of one of my record books. They were the first of his flower offerings that I had bothered to preserve – and although I couldn't really articulate why, the thought that our path was scattered with the flowers he had given me, and I had cast away, cost me a faint pang.

After a few moments, Wu Jiang returned and signalled us forward on to the road that led through the second left gate. The scale of the city beyond made my breath catch in my throat. It seemed to cover more ground than any forest, lake or mountain range I had ever seen. The glint of three separate rivers wound through it – these, I knew, were tributaries of the Red, Gold Dust and Coiling Serpent Rivers – but they were dwarfed by the masses of buildings. My mouth kept dropping open of its own accord, and even though I knew I should preserve my dignity and adjust my shadow face to hide it, I simply couldn't spare the energy. There was too much to *see*.

Temples, public parks, grand palaces and government buildings, seething markets. Somewhere in there were also two universities and several army barracks. Wide roads of packed dirt – planted along the edges with magnificent elm, juniper and pagoda trees, and bordered with clean white sand – contained the traffic amid clouds of golden dust. Each road was aligned to the cardinal axes, and they – along with ten-foot walls – strictly divided the merchant wards from government enclaves, noble quarters from peasant ones, residential from public.

Somewhere ahead of us, at the very northern end of the city – its North Star – lay the Imperial Palace. A combination of dust, bright sunlight and distance hid it now, but Father had said that on clear days it was possible to see the very top of the highest, gold-tiled roof peeking out from among the lush trees that made up its vast parkland. It was the emperor's main residence, and its official name was the Centre of the Universe.

In a very real way, it was exactly that.

"Have you ever been to the city before?" Wu Jiang asked, leaning slightly towards me in his saddle.

I let out a long breath before shaking my head. "I never dreamed that I would have the chance to really see it." I saw the next question forming in his wrinkled brows and answered before he could voice it. "My father no longer cares to move in these circles. Our world is – quite deliberately – quiet. Retired from public life."

General Wu looked pleased. "Well, here you are, regardless. What do you think?"

I smiled. "It's going to be a long, dusty march, sir."

The Young General laughed, drawing stares from passers-by and the soldiers on the rampart. "Correct as always, Corporal."

Twenty-one

General Wu disappeared within moments of our arrival at the grand building where the barracks were housed. Since these same buildings housed the administrative offices for many of the army's senior officials, my guess was that he was now holed up in an official meeting somewhere with a group of scowling, grey-bearded men and reams and reams of paper.

Although generally an aide would have been expected to accompany Wu Jiang to any such meetings, he had given me the rest of the day as leave. And lest I imagine that this was preferential treatment, he'd also offered the entire battalion the same privilege, merely reminding Sigong to make sure that everyone knew about the city's curfew rules.

"Tell the privates that I want them all back here as soon as they hear the evening drums beginning, on pain of my extreme displeasure," he had said, hurriedly tucking his saddlebags under his arm. "Most of them won't have been to the city before – they need to understand that once the drums stop, the doors are locked and there's no excuse they can offer to get through. Even soldiers are subject to arrest or public punishment by the vagrant patrols when out of their proper ward. And Hua Zhi will have better things to do tomorrow morning than tour the city's jails bailing out hungover, bloody-nosed young fools."

Then he'd hastened away, leaving me with nothing to do but restlessly pace the confines of the small room I had been assigned. I'd already handed all General Wu's official reports in and had them logged by the department of military affairs – and I was grateful to be rid of them. As the days went on, the scribbled accounts had come to weigh rather more than their mere mass would have suggested. But now I had no idea what to do with myself.

My footsteps echoed hollowly on the bare, unpolished wooden boards of my tiny, yet private room. Sparsely furnished and utilitarian, with only a small, barred window through which I was unable to see unless I was willing to stand on tiptoe, it was still measures more comfort than the privates were afforded. Besides the bed and a small leather trunk, it contained only a desk well supplied with more paper, brushes, inks, stamps, seals and waxes than I'd ever seen in one place before.

The room was directly next to Wu Jiang's – also utilitarian, but far larger – apartment, in case he needed me in a hurry. For a ... note-taking emergency?

I'd joined up to be a soldier. Instead I had become a secretary.

I went back to the window and sacrificed my dignity by craning up to peer out. Not surprisingly in this maze of official buildings, the view was of a stone wall. Somewhere in the far distance a bird called. I thought of Bingbing with a lurch of sorrow.

More pacing. Why had Wu Jiang had to give me leave? What was I supposed to do with it? I'd got so used to scurrying around after him every waking moment that I felt rather lost without his presence. That was not a good realization.

Was I latching on to General Wu as a replacement for Yang Jie?

No, they were entirely different, and my feelings for them were, too.

So I was starting to get sincerely attached to Wu in his own right?

That was even worse!

Or was it? Was it so bad, when Wu Jiang had made it abundantly clear that any such feelings were already returned? My liking and respect for him grew with each day. I might have been given to a person I found far less personally attractive, if my father thought it best.

If Wu Jiang's promises came true, if he could win the emperor and my family around ... surely the match would be a brilliant one for my house, offering my entire family honour and opportunity. It would be a chance at an entirely different life from the quiet, country existence I had grown to dread returning to. I would almost certainly live here, in the capital itself, with access to a wider world that I had never dreamed I would have the chance to inhabit. I would be valued. Cherished.

Perhaps in time there would even be love.

But it would still be a life lived behind the carved wood and silk screens of the women's quarters. Bound by all the rules and events, and expectations – and yes, the joys and challenges – that made up a woman's life.

I whirled around and stubbed my toe.

A short, sharp scream tried to break from my throat. I bit my tongue to keep it inside.

Being planted in this snug, dry, low-roofed chamber was going to drive me mad after weeks under no roof but canvas and the sky. And I didn't want to roam the City of Endless Serenity for the first – and perhaps last – time alone. That felt worse than never being allowed to visit at all.

It had been over two weeks since I last caught so much as a glimpse of Yang Jie.

Perhaps … just perhaps … I could seek him out now. Not to unload any unwieldy confessions, but just to talk. Just to be friends again. He might be angry with me. He might turn away from me, as I had so cruelly from him. Yet if I could only talk to him for a while, tell him how sorry I was, then even if he were furious, contemptuous, it would be worth it.

But when I arrived at the barracks, I found the long, narrow room assigned to the east company empty. The privates were probably halfway to the markets by now. *Stupid.* I sighed.

"Hua Zhi?" One of the sergeant's voices – Sui. I turned to see him stepping into the corridor from the other wing of the barracks, his hair gleaming wet and his uniform replaced with a worn cotton robe: returning from the baths. "I thought you would be with General Wu at his meetings."

"No, sir – he gave me leave, with everyone else."

"Strange." Sui shrugged it off and asked, "Why aren't you with your friend, then – Yang Jie, isn't it?"

"I was looking for him just now, sir. I seem to have missed him."

"Well, you can find him easily enough," he said dryly. "I overheard him ten minutes ago talking about some special fancy woman in the northern quarter he'd saved up enough to visit. Apparently she's famous for a trick with ripe peaches? He wouldn't go with the others to the wine house I recommended."

I knew I was gawping at him, but I couldn't have controlled my expression, or kept it from affecting my mask, for all the gold in the Land of Clouds. "He *what*? Yang Jie said that?"

"I admit it seemed a little out of character. But apparently his older brother made a bet with him before he left, and he was determined to see this woman." The sergeant paused, eyebrows rising. "Are you all right?"

"He's never been out of his village before. And his older brothers *hate* him. It's probably some kind of awful joke. He's going to get himself fleeced. Or beaten. Or taken advantage of. Or all three, one after the other…" I said numbly.

"Surely not," Sui said, deadpan. "They could probably undertake at least the first two simultaneously."

"Sir!" I cried, horrified.

"Don't drown yourself in a bucket, young one," he said kindly. "I know he looks like an infant, but he's the same age as you, and he's surprisingly tough. I'm sure whatever he gets up to will only leave him wiser."

Not if it gets him killed! "I think I'd better go and check on him, sir."

"Well, if you think it best," he said with a suggestive smile. "It's your afternoon off, after all. But remember – never pay in advance. Half up front, half afterwards."

I bit back a sharp retort, obtained the name of the place Yang Jie had mentioned – the House of the Golden Moons – and headed out of the barracks into the city with a salute, fuming. What was Yang Jie thinking? It wasn't like him to let one of his brothers provoke him into acting like a fool. It was completely out of character! And he had never mentioned any such bet or any such woman to me.

And what if you stumble on him, not being robbed, but being deflowered? a sly voice asked in the back of my mind. *He is a soldier boy, after all. They do that sort of thing.*

Then I – I'll just apologize and – find something else to do, I told myself grimly. *But somehow I suspect that's not what's going to happen.*

My suspicions were confirmed when I entered the colourful northern quarter, official home to the city's dancing girls, courtesans and less salubrious prostitutes, and discovered that the address Yang Jie had been given was false. Not only had there never been any such house, but the quarter held no woman who did "a trick with ripe peaches", although it cost me some embarrassment to ask the giggling girls who did occupy the locality to make sure.

So where was Yang Jie?

"Forget your friend," the young woman I'd been speaking to said with a smile. She ran one finger down my arm, the bright silks of her robe whispering over the back of my hand, sending up a whirl of rather cloying, musky perfume. "I'm sure he's having a fine time. Let me give you a night to remember as well. Special rates for our brave fighting men."

"Thank you for the offer," I said gravely. "I'm sure it would be very memorable for both of us" – *what an understatement!* – "but I really must find Yang Jie."

She pouted for a second, then offered a surprisingly sweet smile. "Well, if you find him, bring him back here. Special rates for friends!"

I cleared my throat, feeling strangely overheated, and hurried away to check on another place the girl had mentioned, the House of the Golden Crescent. It was possible Sui had got the name muddled up.

After several fruitless – well, in terms of the right kind of fruit, anyway – hours, evening was beginning to draw in and the northern quarter's colourful lanterns were being lit, one by one, illuminating the growing shadows like glow-worms. The talkative ladies who had been draped artistically around their porches earlier to attract customers during the slow hours had either withdrawn with their company to their boudoirs, or were now busy preparing for their evening's work – dancing, singing, serving alcohol, and entertaining. The streets became strangely bare in the twilight and, despite the scarlet paper lanterns strung above the streets, the cheerful lights shining through window screens and door frames, and the muffled sounds of laughter, voices and music, it felt lonely and cheerless.

I finally admitted to myself that if Yang Jie had ever been here, he had either already concluded his business and left, or else was firmly ensconced in some house where he would be impossible for me to find. I had been wasting my time from the beginning. And the more I thought about it, the more it seemed likely to me that this bet with his brother – and the special girl with the peaches – was just a tale he'd spun to get the other privates to leave him in peace. Going on a drunken adventure would never have been his idea of fun.

He had probably been peacefully reading poetry under a cloud of late blooming flowers in a public park somewhere, or stuffing himself with dumplings in a quiet eatery.

I was a fool. I had wanted to believe that Yang Jie was in trouble because it would have given me the chance to sweep in and rescue him, proving I was still his friend. But even if he had got himself into a scrape, had I really thought it would be so easy to regain his trust and regard? He would have been unlikely to thank me for charging in to act as his hero. He was quite able to look out for himself.

I was the one who needed him, not the reverse.

If only I'd had the courage to admit that to him when it still meant something.

In several places in the near distance – on whichever of the six main thoroughfares of the city was running closest to me just then – drums began to pound in a stately yet unmistakable rhythm. I had never heard it before, but I knew it at once: the warning that curfew was about to be called. The drums would beat one thousand times, and when they fell silent, the doors between the wards would be shut. Anyone with sense would have noticed the deepening dark long before and already been on their way.

With a sigh, I turned and left the northern quarter at a brisk trot. It wasn't a long walk back to the ward where the barracks were situated, but I needed to make good time.

I nodded at the city guard stationed by the east gate as I passed, and hurried along the narrow road between walls. Ah, yes – to the left, and past the hulking shadow of this broken-down cart abandoned next to the wall. I remembered that from earlier. It couldn't have been there for long, or the city refuse collectors would have towed it away.

I swerved left to avoid a broken axle poking from the half-collapsed wreckage of the cart – then stopped as I heard a soft grunt from … above me? My head whipped up in time to see a dark shape – far too big to be a cat or any other city animal – slip over the top of the wall. It fell down into the shadows of the broken cart with an unmistakable flutter of fabric, and I heard a light impact that barely made the wood groan.

Someone was sneaking out of the northern ward.

Going over the walls instead of using the gates was punishable by fifty blows with a slim rod – and the gates weren't even closed yet. It made no sense to climb the wall instead of walking freely though the open exit. Which meant this person *couldn't* walk freely through the gate, couldn't risk going past the guard.

They had to be up to no good. A thief, a murderer. Maybe even an enemy spy.

Silently, I plastered myself flat against the wall and, with a reflexive shudder of discomfort, released my illusion mask. My face felt naked and vulnerable without it, but I ignored that and reached for my cloak of darkness, of not-here, of look-away, of half-seen shadows and textures that blended seamlessly into the deepening dusk. This simple illusion was the first I had ever made, as a child of seven, and I realized as it deepened into existence around me that I had missed wearing it.

There was no movement from the cart. If this escapee had seen me they would already have run – but they, too, were waiting, crouched so still and quiet among the jagged shapes of the broken vehicle that I couldn't make them out. If I hadn't known they were there, I'd have walked right by and never noticed them at all.

After several long moments there was a whispering sound – material slithering as a person shifted – and then the light tap of a foot hitting the packed dirt of the road. I made my breaths shallow and calm, centred my *qi*...

In a sudden burst of movement, a small shape flew out of the cart. My hands snapped out and caught them, fingers closing on handfuls of soft fabric. I used their momentum to swing them around, slamming them back against the wall where I had been hiding. The impact scraped my knuckles and forced a hoarse cough from their lungs.

I opened my mouth to shout for the guard – and paused.

A few incongruous facts were slowly bearing in on me. When I had thrown this person back, they had actually left their feet. Although I was strong, I was not Wu Jiang – thus, this person was very light. They were also not very tall. They smelled nice, too. They smelled of expensive perfume and something else, some enticing, familiar scent that gave me a strange urge to lean in closer and breathe deep.

And … they were crying. Soundless, painful hitches of breath that shook their narrow frame and reminded me irresistibly of my little sister Xiao Xia, who hardly ever cried and never wanted anyone to hear her when she did.

I had caught a girl.

My immediate instinct was to let go immediately, but I quashed it. Girls could still be up to no good, after all. She had broken the law right in front of me. But … if I summoned the guard, the penalty – the beating – would be carried out right now, in front of me, and … I couldn't quite bring myself to do it. Not without knowing more. I compromised by whispering, "Who are you? Why are you trying to evade the lawful authorities?"

"Let me go," she whispered back, voice choked and hoarse, but steady. "Please. I haven't harmed you, or anyone. Please just let me go home."

Involuntarily, my crushing grip on the girl's upper arms began to loosen. But I couldn't just release her, no matter how pathetic she sounded. "Tell me who you are and where you're going, or I'll call the guard."

"Back to my family," she said readily. "I know it's illegal to go over the wall, but it was the only way out I had."

"Are you a concubine?" I asked.

"No." She shook under my hands, then I felt her take a deep breath. "Yes. I – my family engaged me to a man – but after he took me away to get married he brought me here instead. He sold me to a madam in the House of Tumbling Blossoms to pay his gambling debts. I've been trapped here with no way to reach my parents, to let them know what happened. I – I won't let you take me back."

Her words were a stunning blow. It was illegal for any citizen of the Red Empire to be sold into slavery against their will, although sometimes people were forced to sign themselves into indentured servitude for a fixed term, to clear debts. But everyone knew that some people, especially young girls, were still vulnerable to this kind of unofficial slavery. There was often little the authorities could do to prevent it, and it was said that most of the victims killed themselves eventually. Their families all too often disowned them, and the shame was too much to bear. I had to help her, if I could.

I released her, but continued to loom over her in case she thought she could run away. "Put your hood down. I want to see your face."

She hesitated for a while, bowing her head. Then small, pale hands came up to push the folds of muffling fabric away from her head, exposing a delicate, heart-shaped face. In the darkness, her features were difficult to make out, but even beneath the layers of cosmetics that turned her skin as pale as moonlight and gave her cheeks and lips a deep flush, and the delicate lotus flower painted between her brows, it was obvious she was young. Younger than me. Maybe no more than fourteen or fifteen. Her eyes, though I could not see their particular colour, were huge and dark, pleading like a kitten's. A thin, livid red scar marred one side of her face, curving from just beneath her left eye to the corner of her upper lip.

It was a clean scar – the sort created not by some messy accident but with surgical precision, and a very sharp knife. It had been well cleaned and disinfected after it was made. And it had obviously been made very deliberately indeed. Whoever had put on the make-up had left it alone, making no attempt to disguise the mark.

"How did you get this scar?" I asked. I hadn't known I meant to ask it until I did, and I winced at my own rudeness.

She stared at me for a moment, brows crinkling. "The … the madam. After the first time I tried to run away. She said … a certain kind of customer wouldn't mind. She was right." She swallowed audibly.

I couldn't even bear to think about that. I nodded sharply. "Where are your family? Here in the city?"

"In the merchant quarter," she said. "But … I'm not really sure how to get there from here. Or if I can get there in time now…"

"I'll get you there," I said grimly. "Come on."

I took her by the arm again, gently this time, and began to tow her in the direction in which I had come. I'd passed through the bustling markets of the merchant quarter on my way from the barracks to the northern quarter – I was sure I could get her to the entrance in time.

"But what about you? Don't you have to be back at – your post – before—"

I cut her off, steering her into a run as we rounded a corner. "Don't worry about that. It's my fault you were delayed. Pull your hood up again." In the darkness, the too-large, too-heavy cloak could pass for a loose burnoose of the kind many women wore out of doors, both for modesty and to protect their skin from sun and dust.

How many drum beats left? More than half of the thousand must have passed now. We might only have five minutes remaining – not nearly enough for me to make it back to the barracks, even if I ran. But there was a chance for her. What was more, if I didn't get her to the right door in time she would almost certainly be rounded up as a vagrant, and from there who knew what would happen to her? She might end up being taken back to the madam for all I knew. Or worse.

My fingers slipped down her arm to clasp her hand as we broke on to the road leading to the east door of the merchant quarter. The guard stationed there tensed visibly as he heard running footsteps – then relaxed as he turned and caught sight of my uniform. I tugged a little on the girl's hand to slow her down as we approached.

"In a hurry, sir?" the guard asked when we were within earshot.

"Just need to get my sister home to our mother," I said casually. "She overstayed at her friend's house. I knew she would, the silly goose."

"Ah, very well. Don't let it happen again, young lady," the guard said sternly, allowing us past.

The girl let out a soft murmur that probably passed as "Yes, sir, sorry, sir". And then we were through the gate and into the broad streets of the wealthy part of the merchant quarter, surrounded by tall trees, their branches hung with lanterns, and large houses with clean white paths leading to their doorsteps.

"Where is your parents' house?" I asked under my breath, tucking her hand into my arm and slowing us to a seemingly casual stroll.

I sensed her head turning to and fro. "Much further down, on Six Coins Lane. We're not so rich as this."

Hence entrusting their daughter to the kind of man who'd turn around and sell her off, I thought. "Will they have worried about you, if you didn't visit or write?"

"I … don't know. I was supposed to be going away, out of the city. They might not have expected to hear from me for a while. My mother said she hoped she could visit next year, if Father's business took him that way again."

Hmmph. Well, that made me feel slightly better about the fact that I was going to hand her back over to them – and probably have to beg for a bed for the night, too. "Is Six Coins Lane this way?"

She shook her head. It struck me that she was rather quiet. Dazed by having actually succeeded in her escape? Apprehensive about facing her family after what she had experienced? Or … perhaps frightened of me?

"I won't let any harm come to you," I promised. I knew the words were rash, but I simply couldn't help myself. "If your family are – if they're angry, or difficult—"

"Oh *no*!" she cried, and her tone was so strong and impassioned that I stopped dead. Her hand wrenched away from my arm and she turned to face me. All I could see among the heavy muffling folds of her cloak was the liquid gleam of those large, sad eyes.

In the distance, the heavy repetitive noise of the drum beats suddenly cut off, leaving a quiet that seemed to thrum with tension.

"What is it?" I asked softly, all too aware that, to a girl who had suffered my ancestors only knew what at men's hands – a girl whom I myself had treated roughly – I probably made a less than reassuring figure.

"Nothing, but I can't…" Her voice wavered and she seemed to sag. I heard her take a deep breath. Then she darted forward and, to my astonishment, I felt a gentle press of soft lips against my cheek. A tingle like … like static in a thunderstorm buzzed through my insides, and I flinched.

"Thank you for your help," she whispered. "Goodbye."

"What? No, wait—"

But somehow she slipped through my fingers, twisting away from me with a supple, graceful movement that turned her into a wisp of smoke, dissipating among the shadows. The cloak flared out and came loose in my hands. I opened my mouth to call out – and remembered that she had never told me her name.

Just like that she was gone. Disappeared into the darkness under the trees. Between the houses? It had happened so quickly, I couldn't tell.

Cheeks still burning, the scent of rosewater rising from the cloth in my hands, it took me several minutes to realize that I was now stuck, after curfew, in a ward where I had no business, and no place to stay. I muttered a swear word that I had only heard out loud once in my life before. Now what was I going to do?

Did the merchant quarters have hotels or inns – or rooms for rent? Reflexively, I reached for the money-purse on my belt.

It was missing.

Twenty-two

I slipped back into the military compound only a little after curfew lifted at dawn. I was exhausted, sore and aching from head to toe, and still had bits of leaves and bark stuck in my hair and clothes. Although I was invoking the names of the last five generations of my ancestors that no one would notice my return, of course the instant I entered the large octagon-shaped courtyard that occupied the centre of the barracks building, I heard Sergeant Sui's voice call out to me from across the dusty, echoing space.

"My word, Hua Zhi! You've been out the whole night?"

I refused to let my shoulders slump, but it was a struggle. All sergeants had penetrating voices, and the empty courtyard seemed to amplify each word until they put last night's booming curfew drums to shame. After taking a moment to compose my illusion – the face underneath was a lost cause – I turned smartly and saluted.

"Only inadvertently, sir. I'm afraid I misjudged the time and ended up trapped in the merchant quarter."

I had an innocent-sounding explanation for that, but it was clear Sui wasn't listening. His eyes widened as they travelled over my dishevelled appearance. "I see you found that woman and her peaches."

"No, Sergeant, as I said, I—"

A door behind me opened, releasing a babble of voices and footsteps that fell abruptly silent.

"Hua Zhi?"

I let my eyes squeeze close for an instant, then turned my head to see a group of privates from east barracks … and Yang Jie. All staring at me with various expressions of awed respect, amusement, envy and, in Yang Jie's case, a coldness that I hoped hid shock rather than anger.

There was obviously no point in trying to explain this away – no one was going to believe a word I said. And technically the Young General's orders had only been for the privates, so I hadn't done anything wrong. I looked back at the sergeant with the blandest expression I could manage. "If you'll excuse me, sir, I think I should clean up before going on duty."

"By all means," he said, smirking.

I pivoted smartly on one heel and marched past the group of gawping men without looking at them. I didn't want to offer up any more grist for the gossip mill. And I didn't dare try to meet Yang Jie's eyes.

A half hour later, I was clean and so was my armour. I'd skipped today's use of the tincture – my supply was getting low, and I thought my voice would pass for another day – gulped down a hasty breakfast, and was back in my room, listlessly organizing papers and wishing with all my might that a nap was possible. But the Young General had given me no directions on when or if he would need me today – so it clearly behoved me to stay alert, and not curl up on the narrow bed, no matter how inviting it might look...

A sharp knock on the door brought me to my feet. Before I could call out, the door opened, revealing the errant general himself. As usual, his appearance was immaculate – but less usually when he was looking at me, his expression was stern. *Damn you and your big mouth, Sergeant.*

"Good morning, General," I ventured as I saluted, endeavouring not to let the words become a question.

"Is it, indeed?" he replied, voice giving away nothing.

I gulped. "Do you have orders for me, sir?"

"Yes, but first I want to know the truth of this tale about you, your harem of fancy women, and how you came stumbling in roaring drunk, waking up half the barracks singing bawdy songs about peaches at the crack of dawn."

I nearly fell over. "What?"

Wu Jiang closed the door firmly behind him, and instantly began to snort with laughter, stern expression dissolving. "Your face! You poor girl – don't worry, I don't believe a word of it, but I'm expected to come and read you a lecture, so here I am. What really happened?"

"I ... I'm afraid I *was* out all night, sir."

The laughter disappeared just as suddenly as it had arrived. "What? In this city? Alone?"

"Well, most of the time. There was this girl..."

His eyes bugged out. I couldn't help it – now it was my turn to start giggling. I swiped at my watering eyes and tried to calm down, but a glance at his slack jaw set me off again. My common sense was mortified. This was not the way to behave before a senior officer. Clearly the lack of sleep was doing odd things to my self-control. I had to put both hands over my face and take several deep breaths before I could look at him again.

Wu Jiang seemed to have relaxed a little at my laughter, but still looked uncharacteristically off balance. "Is this your idea of a joke?"

"No, sir – I'm sorry. Let me start again. I met a young girl in the city, barely older than my little sister. She had been taken advantage of and needed help. At least – well, I think she did. But she also robbed me of my money-purse, so perhaps I'm just a naive country boy, after all, who can't tell an innocent from a cunning thief."

I didn't really believe that. But General Wu had not met the girl. He couldn't possibly understand, and something in me resisted trying to express her intense vulnerability, grace and resilience in words. It was ... private. "In any case, I ended up trapped in the merchant quarter and spent the night hiding up a tree to avoid the vagrant patrols."

"No fancy women, then? No peaches?" he asked, smiling again.

"And no wine or bawdy songs," I confirmed.

"I am relieved," he said softly. Then his face changed, taking on its familiar look of official stoniness, and I fell quickly into parade rest, drawing my hands behind my back as I waited to hear my orders.

"Corporal, this morning I am summoned to a meeting with the emperor and the most senior generals of the war cabinet. As my aide you will accompany me, but neither of us will be permitted to make any written notes: what will be discussed is of the highest level of official secrecy. Instead you must commit the details of everything that is said and done to memory in order to help prompt my own memory later. Do you understand?"

"Yes, sir." I nodded sharply, although internally I quailed. My memory was good, but not perfect.

"Since you'll be required to stay at my side observing throughout the entire meeting, you will need a junior aide who can run any errands I'd normally ask you to do. Depending on what my aunt asks of me next, the position may become permanent, as yours is."

I blinked, my attention snagging on that last part. I was to be part of General Wu's staff *permanently*? I realized I hadn't given any real thought to what would happen to me once we arrived back here, but of course all the privates and officers I had trained with would be assigned to new posts in the army proper now. They would be split up, some of them sent away to other cities or military outposts. Wu Jiang had made it clear he wanted to keep me with him. Adding me to his entourage was the only way to ensure that.

My war, my fight for the future of the empire – in a very

real way, it was over. Over before it had even really begun.

And I might never see Yang Jie again.

I was so stricken by this knowledge that I almost failed to attend to what Wu said next – but my attention snapped back to him when he went on: "Is there someone among the men that you trust, someone you feel has the traits suitable for such an important post?"

I knew the answer immediately. Despair transformed into a rush of excitement and satisfaction. I trusted many of the men I had trained with, but there was only one who had the intelligence and discretion for this job. And this was a chance for me to help him, to use my own good fortune to elevate someone who truly deserved it. His family would have to respect him if he earned such a post. What was more, it meant he might be able to stay here, in the city, where we could see each other, instead of being sent potentially hundreds of miles away.

But… I hesitated. Was it what he would want? He had seemed pleased for me when I gained this position, and yet he had taken the trouble to warn me, too…

"If you can't think of a man of sufficient quality…" the Young General began.

I shook my head. "I have someone I believe would be eminently suitable, sir. Yang Jie, of east company. He's quick, resourceful and clever, and he knows how to keep a secret."

"Then I'll send a messenger to fetch him and explain what he'll be asked to do."

I frowned, puzzled. "Couldn't we collect him on the way, sir?"

"No time – you and I must go ahead, and he can meet us at the palace once he's briefed." He paused, cleared his throat. "My aunt wants to see me before the meeting in a personal capacity. I… Of course I haven't said anything to her yet. About you. Or your circumstances. But I – want you there."

I managed to hold the curse word behind my lips. But only just.

A visit to the sacred portals of the Imperial Palace was not for the weak.

Wu Jiang and I rode from the barracks through the first three ceremonial gates of the Centre of the Universe's grounds, but once we reached the terraces – endless layers of steps, each step faced with a different kind of glittering marble, red, gold, blue, green – we were forced to dismount. Reluctantly, I handed over Yulong to the palace grooms, resisting the urge to cling to him as if he were my childhood poppet. From there we went on foot.

General Wu walked the towering shadows of the halls of the Centre of the Universe at a rapid yet dignified march. I scurried in his wake. Servants, dignitaries and palace officials variously scattered out of his way, stared in interest, or nodded indifferently. The Young General didn't speak to me, and I was content to let the silence rest, trying, once again, not to gawp too obviously. My stomach churned with apprehension, but underneath the fear was a spark of exhilaration.

This was the Centre of the Universe. I had read about it, heard tales about it, listened to my father speak of it, but now I was seeing it *with my own eyes*. I never thought I would. The girl I had been wouldn't have. She would have died still dreaming of what I now beheld. I could hardly believe I was really here.

Heavy army boots thudding on the shining floors, we wove between massive pillars of ivory and precious scented wood inlaid with mother-of-pearl and gold, brushed by walls of tapestries worked so that the tales they told – a celestial dragon's blessing of the Red Emperor; a monkey stealing peaches from the gods; the Battle of the Field of Three Rivers – seemed to quiver with animation. Priceless artefacts glinted from every lacquered alcove. I had never seen so much ... so *much*.

These were the halls where the emperor received government ministers and entertained state visitors. They were designed to bewilder – to awe and intimidate. And it worked. My eyes began to swim and my head echo hollowly, as if I were in a fever dream.

My leg muscles were burning before, at last, we came to a halt at the edge of an enormous courtyard garden. It was at least a mile long, rectangular and filled with beautiful things – white sand paths edged with flowering plants, trees trimmed into fantastic shapes, ornamental ponds and half-moon bridges. The Young General's principle servant, Shu Yuen, awaited us there, resplendent in jade-green silk. He bowed as he came towards us. "My prince – you are awaited in the Pavilion of Luminous Beauty."

"Thank you, Shu Yuen. Please attend me," the general said. Then, to me: "Buck up. Nearly there."

I followed him, Shu Yuen at my heels, as he skirted the edge of this glorious garden until we reached a tiny white-and-gold pavilion entirely surrounded by a gently murmuring stream. Music echoed faintly from within. We crossed a white bridge that reminded me of a decoration for some elaborate dessert and then…

Then I laid eyes on the emperor for the first time.

I banged my knee in my haste to fall down into my deepest obeisance. That didn't stop me from ogling with all my might. After all, no one was looking at me.

Wu Fen. Daughter of Heaven. Emperor of the Land of Dragons. Just the memory of her still brings an ache to my breast – something like that exquisite, melancholy longing one experiences staring at distant mountains in the rising sun. For many years afterwards whenever I was asked to describe her, I simply refused. Even now, I feel that no words could possibly be adequate.

I can talk about what she wore. That's easy enough. It was with some surprise that I realized she was dressed in a very feminine and flattering version of male riding attire – slim trousers of scarlet, embroidered with gold, beneath a golden robe that fastened, not under the bust as women's clothes usually did, but at the waist, with a wide sash of vivid blues and greens, edged in gold thread. The sash was designed to match the exquisite headdress of iridescent kingfisher feathers and black pearls that was woven into her masses of bound-up hair.

I can tell you what she was doing. She knelt on a cushion, a zither before her. The air shivered with the last notes of her song, her deep, husky voice:

"Torn and tangled with my longing for you,
My lord, if you doubt my constancy, or my tears,
Open my chest and observe,
The pomegranate red of my heart…"

But what struck me most of all was the comfortable informality of the setting. Fat cushions and thick rugs were strewn about, scattered with piles of beautifully bound books and children's puzzles of carved ivory, coral and jade. A golden nightingale twittered fitfully in a silver cage hanging from the ceiling. Where were the servants, the attendants, the advisors, ministers, guards? This was no formal audience chamber. This was a family room – the emperor's family room. I could not believe I had been offered a glimpse of it.

Other than those things, the one significant feature of the emperor's that I can and will describe are her eyes. They were of no unusual colour, simply a deep, velvety brown. But they were large, and smiling, and full of light and power, and of such astounding loveliness that even though she did not look at me, I felt myself wobble and almost had to put a hand down on the cool tiled floor to support myself.

"Cousin! Cousin!" A slight, pale-faced little boy of around nine or ten sprang up from where he had been hiding under a mound of cushions – knocking over a large bowl of lychees with a clatter – and flung himself at the Young General. "You're back!"

Wu Jiang laughed, a carefree, boyish sound, and bent just in time to catch the child, lifting him up with an exaggerated grunt of effort.

"Li Xian? Can this be Li Xian? I almost didn't recognize you – you must have grown four inches at least!"

Li Xian? I gulped, unable to lower my eyes as I knew I ought to. This was the crown prince. The heir to the Dragon Throne. And he was giggling and play-wrestling my commanding officer.

"I'll soon be taller than you!" the boy cried eagerly, thin face alight.

"But then how will you ride on my shoulders?" Wu Jiang asked in mock dismay.

"Silly!" the little boy scolded. "You shall ride on mine!"

"Greetings, nephew," the emperor interrupted gently. "Welcome home. It's very good to see you. I trust you are well?"

The Young General carefully set the crown prince down, easing the boy's pout with a pat on the shoulder, and then went to his knee before the emperor, bowing his head. "Honoured and virtuous aunt, I am very well. It is my great pleasure to see you, too. I hope you and my little cousin are both in good health?"

"I am not little!" the crown prince protested, stamping his foot and causing his layers of silken robes to swirl in something perilously close to a flounce.

"We are, thank you. Your father visited recently – he asked me to send his regards as always, and to convey that your siblings and mother are all prospering. Wu Jun in particular is making everyone proud with his martial prowess. He promises one day to beat you, and says you must take care to come home soon and let him prove it."

The emperor's eyes crinkled with fine smile lines that

only made them more lovely – but I was distracted by the minute wince that General Wu could not quite suppress at the word "mother". I thought I understood. His father's wife might be a kind and virtuous lady, and a fine parent to his half-siblings, but she was not – would never be – his mother.

Then Li Xian interrupted again, noticing me on the step behind the general, and Shu Yuen to my left, apparently for the first time.

"Who are these persons? Why have you brought low-born grubs here? I don't like it!"

A grimace of fond exasperation crossed Wu Jiang's face, but before he could speak the emperor did. "My son, that man is a member of our Imperial Forces, who has no doubt fought bravely at your cousin's side." She reached out one hand, summoning Li Xian to her, where she smoothed his cheek tenderly. "He deserves our respect, does he not?"

"My prince, let me introduce Hua Zhi," General Wu said, sending me a sidelong look and a small smile. "He is my aide, and the son of the great Hua Zhou who served your own father with such distinction. Aside from acting as my aide, he has also saved my life at least three times. And he is my friend."

Wu Fen's smile turned on me fully for the first time. I felt a flush of immense warmth, as if I had suddenly plunged into a hot spring. "Indeed? Then you are truly welcome here, Hua Zhi."

I dipped my head lower, shaken and glad that no response seemed expected.

From the corner of my eye, I saw Shu Yuen's lips press tightly together, and realized General Wu had not spoken to defend him, and neither had the emperor – tacitly giving Li Xian's words validation. Given Shu Yuen's excellent and devoted service, that seemed harsh indeed. I caught his eye for a second, but he stared through me blankly. Perhaps, if he dealt with the Imperial Family frequently, he was used to such unthinking slights. Perhaps they no longer hurt him.

Perhaps.

There was a short pause as the emperor's eyes shifted back to General Wu – and, insensibly, I felt something change. The glowing, almost uncomfortable warmth which had permeated the pavilion slowly chilled. The air shifted, as with the rumble of an encroaching storm. It was the emperor's mood, I realized, as Wu Jiang tensed beside me, and Shu Yuen took a small, discreet step backwards. The songbird in the cage fell silent, and even the crown prince fixed his eyes on the ground, suddenly grave. Such was her power.

"And now, General. Perhaps you will explain how you came to allow the slaughter of Diao Tian Ning, one of my most valued and loyal commanders – one whom you knew was about to be elevated to a vital position in my court – when I specifically sent you to protect him?"

Her voice was like a sudden rain of snow high up in the mountains, cold and pure, glorious but terrifying. I wondered if she could kill a man with that alone. I trembled for a moment, then felt my body enter that paralysed stillness of a prey creature caught in the gaze of its predator.

Wu Jiang's position shifted to one of the very deepest obeisance.

"Your Imperial Majesty, I have failed you. No apology may encompass the depths of my shame over this loss, or the pain and inconvenience which I know it has caused you. I shall offer no excuses. I await your judgement with humble acceptance, and with gratitude in my heart for the privilege of having been allowed to serve you."

An icy sweat prickled up over the whole of my body. Great Dragon and Phoenix – was the Young General about to be sentenced to some horrible punishment? Was he about to be condemned – and perhaps me with him? The silence was crushing. I closed my eyes.

"Your service to me in the past has been exemplary, and I have loved you as nearly my own son. One mistake can be forgiven – if it is never repeated. On this occasion then, you shall receive the forgiveness of the throne. But you will not be so fortunate again. Is that understood?"

"It is, Imperial Majesty," Wu Jiang said fervently. "You are as merciful as you are kind. I am unworthy."

Just like that, the emperor's face relaxed into a smile once more. The ferocious chill fled the pavilion, as if her forgiveness was the blazing summer sun dissolving snow clouds into nothing. "You are entirely worthy. Rise, please, and let that be the end of it, my dear."

Wu Jiang rose smoothly to his feet, and gestured to me to do the same. I creaked into an upright position, feeling rather amazed that I hadn't turned to stone.

"Tell him, Mama, tell him!" Li Xian demanded, returned to his former self and clapping his hands furiously with excitement.

"In good time, my son. Wu Jiang, have you been keeping your skills sharp while you were travelling in the wilds?"

"I have attempted it, at least," General Wu said, smiling and relaxed again, as though that petrifying interlude had never occurred. "Why?"

"Because!" Li Xian cried, gambolling forward like a puppy. "We're going hunting!"

Twenty-three

Within five minutes, General Wu, Shu Yuen and I had been swept into a sea of confused activity in a stable-yard that was larger and more elaborately decorated than the entire house I had grown up in. Around me, servants bustled to and fro with loaded baskets and saddlebags, grooms led out horses of every possible type and colour, and a dozen middle-aged men in gilded armour or ornate riding attire appeared as if by magic, all of them looking flustered and annoyed, but not quite brave enough to express it.

"That is General Chi Xiu, commander of the Northern Mountain armies," Wu Jiang pointed out in a slightly harried undertone as he held his horse still, allowing Shu Yuen to adjust the stirrups. To my dismay, I had been offered a long-legged golden bay rather than Yulong, who presumably still waited for me on the other side of the palace. The mare was skittish, and the groom who should have been assisting Wu Jiang was having to hold her head while another adjusted the saddle for me. "The one with the very long beard is the Duke of Yang, commander of the Flying Red Horse division. To his left is Di Ren Jie, minister for military affairs. On the black stallion…"

My head swam with all the titles and details, but I did my best to memorize them as I allowed one of the grooms to give me a leg up into the saddle. "And what is this lady's name?" I asked the groom.

"Plum Blossom," he told me with a brief smile. "She's sweet-natured enough, once she gets used to you."

The golden bay snorted and sidled beneath me. I leaned over her neck and breathed into her ear, patting her shoulder with one hand. "Plum Blossom. Plum. Good girl. Good."

She quivered, shook her mane, and seemed to relax a little. I nodded my thanks to the groom, who trotted off to help an elderly man struggling to mount a horse that, to my eye, was far too fresh for him.

Beside me, Wu Jiang was having some difficulty with his own mount – a showy dappled grey. It reared, and then performed something frighteningly close to a battle movement known as a Hare's Leap, jumping from an upright position on its hind legs, with the forelegs tucked beneath it. Servants scattered in a panic, with only Shu Yuen holding his ground. The Young General fought the animal down – *dear ancestors, but his arms must be made of iron* – but the horse continued to jink and dance in place.

"The animals haven't been exercised yet," he told me

in a low voice, panting with effort. "My aunt sprung this expedition on everyone with no notice. The stables had no time to prepare the mounts. Even I had no idea the meeting would be taking this form."

"The better to keep it a secret?" I guessed.

He arched a brow, and I pressed my lips closed, taking that as a yes. I tallied the evidence: the emperor and her son both up just after dawn. The entire war cabinet summoned from their beds with no notice on a "hunting party" in the Forbidden Park. And everything done with the appearance of spontaneity, so that it seemed from the outside like no more than the emperor's sudden whim.

This was a very important meeting indeed.

"Cousin!" Li Xian called. I turned my head to see the boy on a tall grey pony that appeared the much smaller twin of Wu Jiang's massive mount. The crown prince's pale face was blotched red at the cheeks with excitement. "Come see what my royal mother has given me!"

Wu Jiang's dimple winked as he waved at the youngster. "Wait here, Hua Zhi – I'll return when I've quieted him down a little. Shu Yuen, make yourself useful."

The Young General muscled his horse into a turn and trotted off towards the crown prince. I patted Plum Blossom's side again, wishing I had thought to bring some dried apricots, or another treat suitable for a horse. Yulong had been given his before we left the barracks.

"Corporal?"

The distinctive voice made me stiffen in my saddle. Plum Blossom jerked her head uneasily – and I saw Shu Yuen, who was still standing near by, rear back in much the same manner as the horse. The eunuch grimaced and abruptly ducked away.

What was that about? What – or who – had he fled from?

Before I could try to manoeuvre my horse around, Yang Jie trotted into view on his own mount. He appeared well in control of the short-legged black gelding.

"Good morning," he said evenly. He was looking at me – he could hardly avoid it – but his eyes evaded mine. I thought he was tired, and upset. There were red rims to his eyelids and deep lines around his lips. "Private Yang Jie reporting for duty as commanded."

"Good morning, Private," I said formally. Then, in a rush. "I … it's good to see you, but – you don't look well. Are you ill?"

Now his eyes shot up to mine. I was shocked by the deep unhappiness there. *Did I cause that?* I had expected stiff, cold anger or furious contempt for my cowardice – not outright misery. As if he knew he had given himself away, his gaze darted down again. He patted his horse's neck, and it remained steady as a rock beneath him. "No, no. I'm just tired from my day off. I went to the wine shop with the others, you know – we were out late. Not as late as you, of course…"

His voice trailed off, sheepishly. Even if I hadn't already known, it would have been obvious from his drooping, guilty demeanour that he was lying. My curiosity about where he had really been last night flared up afresh, but it was secondary to my anxiety over him. He really looked … almost distraught. Had I made a mistake *again*?

"I hoped you would be happy about this appoint-ment," I said. "It's a chance to advance. If you do well, you might be promoted. I thought you wanted that – I'm sorry if I was wrong."

He shook his head, gaze now far off. "Not at all. This is a – a perfect opportunity. Better than I could ever have hoped for."

"Yang Jie," I insisted. "What's the matter?"

"Nothing." He swallowed audibly, then finally looked at me again. "Hua Zhi, I – I'm sorry."

Sorry? What in the world did he have to be sorry for? I was the one who had turned my back on him and ignored him for weeks. I opened my mouth to ask – and was promptly drowned out by the clarion call of a hunting horn. Wu Jiang cantered back towards me, his dark gaze taking in Yang Jie as well.

"Is this the private you recommended, Corporal? Good. We're ready to go. Where's Shu Yuen got to? Damn the man, why has he wandered off *now*? Remember, Hua Zhi, to stick close to me. You are to observe everything and commit it to memory. Thank the Great Dragon that the emperor at least gave *me* a little warning to prepare for this. I have a feeling that today is going to be significant."

I suppressed a desire to snort aloud at such an obvious statement and, as I turned my head, I saw Yang Jie allowing his own eyes to roll up slightly. I ventured a conspiratorial smile. His returning grin, though short-lived, eased my mind slightly.

I decided that once the general had dismissed me for the day, I was going to corner Yang Jie and squeeze whatever troubles he was having out of him, if I had to sit on him to do it.

After a few more moments of shuffling about, the emperor herself, seated on a glorious silver-grey stallion, led the huge cavalcade through the jade-and-gold lacquered gates into the Forbidden Park. Her son and Wu Jiang followed immediately after – I fell in with them dutifully, although I would have preferred to hang back a little. Behind me, the whole company wandered away in a disorganized trail. Despite the hasty nature of this expedition and its supposed secrecy, I counted at least eighteen servants laden down with extra baggage and five outriders carrying the personal banners of certain distinguished officials, all of whom could probably have been dispensed with if we were seeking speed, let alone discretion. The man with the hunting horn, although very skilled, had certainly been a mistake.

Beneath my cynicism, I felt another furtive thrill of excitement as we entered the lush green artificial wilderness. In general only the royal family and their closest intimates were invited to this private hunting preserve, which had been built by the crown prince's grandfather. To my knowledge, even my own father had never entered here.

We rode first through a menagerie full of strange beasts in tall, iron cages – tributes from foreign heads of state, Wu Jiang told me, pointing out a leathery grey creature with fantastic horns and an unpronounceable name. He said it had travelled over sea and land for six months to reach the empire. There were brilliantly coloured birds and things like goats, but with long necks and legs like horses. My favourite animals, glimpsed only for a moment as we passed, were a pair of large wild cats. Their lean figures, golden-and-white spotted coats and black, tufted ears were lovely, but what struck me were the eyes – enormous, round and a kind of glowing amber shade. I realized after a moment that their steady jewel-bright gaze reminded me of Yang Jie himself.

I looked back at him, wondering if he'd appreciate the observation. His downcast face made me bite my tongue. Some other time, then. But we were riding close together now – it seemed a waste not to speak at all.

"Where is Bingbing?" I asked him. "At the barracks?"

He shook his head absently, staring into the trees. "Here, somewhere. She flew off once I reached the stable-yard. Too noisy, I suppose. She'll be back."

A good thing, really. Wu Jiang was unlikely to appreciate such a note of whimsy just now. "I'll whistle her back for you when you want her," I promised.

Yang Jie nodded, gaze still refusing to cross with mine. Wu Jiang, ahead of me a little way, glanced around to see where I was. I gave up on Yang Jie for the moment and rode forward to be closer to the general, although Li Xian was occupying most of his attention.

We passed through an apple orchard, and were treated to the sight of a vermilion pagoda with a crescent-shaped lake at its foot. A herd of white deer grazing near by took fright and fled before us as we moved into a forest of strange foreign trees with slim, black-and-white trunks and round golden leaves like coins. When the wind blew, the coin-leaves spiralled around our company in a glittering cloud, provoking sighs of delight from several of the elderly men riding around me.

At the centre of this beautiful, alien forest was a great hall with blue, green and gold painted walls, and a peaked roof of interlocking logs. It was probably an emperor's idea of a modest little hunting lodge, though it had three wings, each with a covered porch, and a pretty courtyard with a circular fish pond and fountain. It was here that Wu Fen signalled the company to a stop.

"We shall rest and refresh ourselves," she called out, smiling, as a groom came forward from the lodge to take the reins of her horse. She dismounted with a supple grace that belonged to a girl half her age, and then went to help the crown prince herself.

By the time the more elderly members of the war cabinet had creaked off their horses, and the mounts had been led away to be tethered at the rail of the hunting hall or to the trees surrounding it, the servants had unpacked a lavish breakfast and spread it out over the courtyard, along with thick rugs, soft cushions and folding travel chairs for those who wanted them. The emperor seated herself cross-legged before the fountain, just as at ease as if this really were an impromptu pleasure trip, and urged her son to eat between bites of her own breakfast. Wu Jiang had taken a place next to her and was lounging comfortably. Everyone's eyes were on them but, among this seasoned group of soldiers and politicians, it was hard to read anyone's expression.

Birds trilled in the trees. A faint autumn breeze stirred

the golden leaves, and the fountain filled the courtyard with its serene music.

The tension was stifling.

I was glad for the corporal's stripes that made me nearly invisible in this august company, and tucked myself away, a little behind the curve of the fountain. Yang Jie seated himself next to me matter-of-factly enough, and attacked a fig. I nudged a bowl of preserved lemons close to him but otherwise left him alone. For me this was a very belated breakfast – by now I was starving, and I knew I needed to eat well if I was to avoid feeling sick and fatigued later on. I filled a bowl of my own and worked through it as quickly and efficiently as I could, hoping I could manage seconds before the meeting proper began.

Rather too soon for me, the emperor finished her repast, capturing everyone's attention by the simple movement of placing her ivory wine cup aside and sitting up a little straighter. I didn't need Wu Jiang's sharp look in my direction to stuff a last piece of tofu into my mouth and move closer.

"Gentlemen. Our thanks for indulging me in this rather precipitous meeting. You who are gathered here are the most trusted, honoured and decorated members of my court – my handpicked war cabinet, hardened and tested throughout my husband's reign and in some cases his father's, too. You have seen many enemies of the state come and go. So there is no need for me to dissemble." She blinked once, slowly. "We are losing this war."

There was an uneasy stirring among the gathered men – but no one looked surprised. My eyes shot to Wu

Jiang. His face was composed, unreadable, though a thin line of white ringed his lips. Was this really true? Had he known – or suspected?

The emperor went on. "Feng Shi Chong's campaign against us has been disastrously effective. Our grain and rice stores, military strongholds and gold reserves have been devastated, and it will not be long before our ability to fight back, or even to defend ourselves, is fundamentally compromised. Once that becomes obvious to the general population we shall have panic, riots, uprisings ... in short, the end of this dynasty. Perhaps even the end of the empire itself. For if in the chaos, the Leopard succeeds in seizing the Dragon Throne, I have no doubt that our country will be plunged into a dark age that may take our descendents a thousand years to escape – if they survive at all."

I felt a sick churning low in my stomach. My skin prickled with cold sweat – horror, disbelief and panic made my breath come more quickly. Wu Jiang's expression still gave nothing away. My eyes sought out Yang Jie's. I found him gazing back at me properly for the first time that morning, and his emotions were all too clear, the twin of my own.

How had things come to such a pass so swiftly? And how was it possible that we, our families, the people who thronged the city streets outside, had no idea? That life continued as normal while our country danced on the very edge of destruction?

"But Feng Shi Chong could not have accomplished this alone. His knowledge of precisely when and where to strike to do the greatest possible damage to our resources and infrastructure has simply been too acute. No one is that wise. No one is that lucky." The emperor paused, and then, as one who drops a heavy plate in expectation of a crash: "He has had help."

A long-bearded elder – the Duke of Yang, I remembered – leaned forward. "Imperial Majesty, surely..." He cleared his throat and began again. "The Leopard was once an imperial general. Before his attempt to steal the throne, he enjoyed the highest status and the greatest level of trust. It's only reasonable – if unfortunate – that a man with such a history would have inside knowledge of our weaknesses."

"No." Wu Jiang cut in before the emperor even opened her mouth. "Remember, Your Grace, since Feng Shi Chong's treason was discovered and he fled the capital, her Imperial Majesty has overhauled much of the administrative and military framework, for greater efficiency. The Leopard's knowledge is years out of date. Or it should be."

One of the cabinet ministers, a frail old man, hit his knee with his fist. "What are you implying?"

The emperor's gaze could have frozen an inland sea. "Very well, for those who are struggling to keep up, I shall make it plain. There is a traitor at court. Someone who has enjoyed the very highest levels of my trust, and has had access to the most highly protected military secrets. In short – either someone who is here now, or one of their intimates."

"Your Majesty!" the Duke of Yang protested. "Surely

the Leopard has placed spies among the servants and low merchants and grasping commoners who throng the palace – a dozen potential sources of information—"

Another man interrupted. "Yes! To accuse *us* is really—"

"After forty years of loyal service. After having laid down my sons' lives, and my grandsons' lives, in the defence of this nation…" one of the generals said sadly.

The emperor showed no reaction to her servants' indignation and outrage. She must have expected it. She leaned over and whispered in Wu Jiang's ear. He blanched visibly, and I saw his throat work as he swallowed, but he nodded.

"Gentlemen!" he shouted, his command voice rising over the discontented babble. "While you have been here, each of your houses, offices and properties, including properties belonging to your sons and other dependents, have been subjected to a thorough search."

Several of the more vigorous men leaped to their feet – and then froze as the servants and outriders whose presence I had wondered at earlier sprang into motion, weapons appearing in their hands as if by magic. I pressed myself warily back into the shelter of the fountain's edge, keeping my hand from the hilt of my sword with an effort.

Yang Jie cast me an inquiring, anxious look: *Did you know about this?*

I shook my head vigorously, trying to convey *Are you joking?* with my eyebrows.

It was suddenly very clear that the pleasant courtyard picnic had been a mere pretext to get all these powerful men here, off their guard and away from their supporters and staff. Now they were surrounded by servants loyal to the emperor only. A trembling silence fell over the courtyard.

"Are you listening now? Good." The emperor stood, majesty sweeping into place around her like an invisible robe. The dappled early morning light played over her, waves of light and shadow, applause from heaven. I drew in an awed breath, unable to take my eyes away even to see Yang Jie's reaction.

"Sit!" the emperor snapped at the two men who had remained on their feet. They collapsed back into their seats – puppets whose strings had been mercilessly severed. "Unless this treason is rooted out, the empire will fall. So let it end now. If you have a vestige of honour left, you will speak up. Who is the traitor?"

They were all trapped here. They knew it. Like a volatile mixture of elements poured into a bottle and placed in a fire, a reaction was now inevitable: one of them must reveal themselves. They might make a break for it, attack, or confess, but whoever it was must do something...

And yet the silence stretched on. And on.

Behind me there was a faint whistle – and a hollow thud. I turned in time to see one of the armed servants fall, an arrow in his back.

A black-and-gold arrow.

I screamed, "Ambush!"

Wu Jiang's hand blurred up and snatched another arrow from the air less than an inch from the emperor's face. She yelped, jerking back. Wu Jiang caught her shoulders and pushed her forcibly to the ground. I seized the crown prince, who was closest to me, and flung him down myself, covering his body with my own as a hail of the black-and-gold arrows turned the sky dark.

There were screams and yells all around me. Ageing voices took up the cry: "Protect the emperor! Hold the line! Protect the emperor!"

Beneath me the boy shrieked and squirmed, beating at my armour with tiny fists. I held on, my whole body cringing in anticipation of the impact of an arrow. My armour was light, made for riding. It would deflect a glancing blow from a sword or knife or a nearly spent arrow, but not a direct hit. And I was protecting the crown prince. At least half of the enemy arrows must be aiming for my charge – for me – right now.

But the piercing blow did not come.

There was a meaty thud, a choking sound of pain – cut off by a wet gurgle – and then a dead weight fell heavily across my back and shoulders. Li Xian's outraged struggling faded from my awareness.

Yang Jie.

Please. Anything but that. Anyone but him. Please, please—

Someone called my name. It was Wu Jiang. With one hand, he toppled Yang Jie's limp form carelessly from mine, then reached down to drag both me and the crown prince upright.

I caught a glimpse of Yang Jie's still face, the vivid red splashed across his white skin, the arrow that should have pierced me bristling from his armour, his back—

And I was screaming, screaming, screaming, wordless

cries torn from my throat, my own fingernails clawing at my face and hair, tears spilling down my cheeks, screaming, *No no NO,* and Yang Jie's name, but he didn't move, he didn't answer, *Yang Jie—*

"Hua Zhi!" Wu Jiang shouted in my face. "Look at me!"

I snapped back to find my hands hanging limp at my sides and my teeth closed so tightly over my own bottom lip that I had drawn blood. My eyes were dry. Wu was having to hold me upright as I sagged in his grasp. The moment of insanity had been in my head.

I felt myself turn numb and remote, distant, as I had once before, after killing Captain Lu during the ambush on the camp. Brushing the Young General's hands away, I made myself stand upright. Li Xian was sheltering, on his knees, against his mother's side. Black-and-gold clad men were flooding from the trees, dozens of them, quickly overwhelming both the armed servants and the elderly men of the war cabinet who had formed a square around the emperor and her son at the fountain.

General Wu spared one moment for a searching look at my face, nodded in apparent satisfaction, and turned to the emperor. He drew his sword. "We have to go."

"Inside?" The emperor's eyes burned in her face, but her hand, where it clutched at her little boy, was steady.

"It's not defensible. There are too many of them. We have to split up, try for the horses, and run for it."

I saw her bare her teeth, as if against a mortal blow. "Take him."

"Your Majesty—" Wu Jiang began.

The Duke of Yang, his long beard sodden red, fell back

into the small clear space around us. He staggered past me, caught at the edge of the fountain – leaving a bloody handprint – and crumpled, landing by the emperor. Li Xian let out a cry of shock. The line of men defending us contracted. We were running out of time.

The emperor grabbed the front of Wu Jiang's armour with her free hand, somehow managing to shake his massive frame. "You take him! Get him out of here alive, or I will flay the skin from your bones, do you understand me? Take him – now! And don't look back!"

Wu Jiang spared another look at me, this one boiling with fury and frustration. "Protect the emperor, Hua Zhi. Try to lose them in the trees – I'll get Li Xian out and bring help. Just stay alive until then!"

I nodded, wordless, as Wu Jiang reached for Li Xian with his spare arm. The boy screamed. "No, Mama! No!"

The emperor got to her feet, her head lifting proudly. The feathers glowed blue in her hair. "Hush, my son! Be brave. Go with your cousin and do whatever he says."

"Head for the hunting lodge but run past it – you'll throw them off," Wu Jiang said to me. He lifted the crown prince and held him against his side. The boy threw his arms around him, sobbing. "I'll go over the fountain. Three, two—"

One of the servants in the line of defence shrieked in agony as an enemy fighter slashed him. His voice drowned out Wu Jiang's – but I saw the movement of his lips as he formed the final number. And I saw him whisper, "My orchid."

Then we were breaking in separate directions with

our two precious charges. I hurdled Yang Jie's body – *Don't look, don't look, don't look* – helped the emperor over it, and then dragged her towards the house as the enemy fighters surged forward with battle screams, slaughtering the last of our defenders.

"Laying hands upon the Daughter of Heaven is a capital offence," the emperor panted matter-of-factly as I pushed her bodily up on to one of the covered porches and then heaved her down again on the other side.

"You may execute me later, Majesty." I let go of her, my knife leaping into my hand as I caught the reins of the nearest horse – a tall bay that snorted and bucked, reacting to my barely suppressed panic and the smell of blood on me. I didn't bother trying to untie the reins, just sliced them. It would make controlling the animal more difficult, but we had not a moment to spare.

I turned to help the emperor mount. She was already throwing her arm over the saddle, flinging herself up in an ungraceful, scrambling rush. I shoved my knife back into my belt sheath, grabbed for the other half of the reins, dangling free, and leaped into the saddle before her.

"Please hold on to me, and keep your head down," I said, as politely as possible, furiously denying the urge to turn in the saddle, to look back and see what was happening behind me.

To seek one last glimpse of Yang Jie.

What if I was wrong, what if – what if he still lived – what if—

No. He is gone.

I could not survive if I let myself cling to that false hope. And I could not, would not risk turning and unseating the emperor. Yang Jie was gone. He was gone and now, somehow, I must go on.

I felt the emperor's arms go around me in a bruising grip. Holding one half of the reins tightly in each fist, I wheeled the animal sharply about. Then I let the horse do exactly what it had wanted to do since the screaming and fighting began: gallop headlong into the trees.

Twenty-four

The thin branches of the white and black trees whipped at our heads as the horse careered wildly through the narrow avenues between the trunks. I dragged at my shadow face, desperately trying to find the focus and power to extend it, to force the threads of my *qi* to flare out and hide all of us.

My hands wavered and darkened before my eyes, disappearing against the horse's hide and then shimmering back into existence. But the horse's straining shoulders and flying mane remained stubbornly visible.

"You're a banner-breaker?" the emperor cried, a note of hope in her voice.

"Barely!" I replied, too preoccupied to feel either shame or anxiety at the admission. "I'm trying..."

I pushed again, a low grunt of effort punching out between my teeth as I tore the threads of energy away from my skin, mentally forcing them out around me in a crackling corona of colour and light. For an instant, I felt the emperor and the flying horse enveloped by the mantle of my gift.

The threads snapped back hard enough to make my vision blur and my head sag on my shoulders. I slid dangerously on the saddle – only the emperor's sudden fierce pinch on my arm kept me from fainting.

It wouldn't work. *It wouldn't work.*

I could hide myself. But not the emperor and not our mount.

Father could vanish this horse in mid-flight, turn the emperor's red-and-gold riding outfit into a mere shadow, and phase our pursuit without breaking into a sweat. If my father were here, the emperor would be safe already. But he wasn't here.

The emperor only had me.

"I can't hide us! I can't do it, I'm sorry!"

"We can't outrun them," the emperor shouted, despairing. "Not on a horse carrying two."

"I know," I shouted back. "We have to find a place to hide you."

"Veer left!" she screamed into the scale armour at my neck. "Past the lake!"

She knew the park – I didn't. I had no choice but to trust her judgement. I hauled on the left part of the rein, struggling to control the animal as the flat, grey mirror of a small lake came into view. More trees, thick, bushy green cone shapes that offered better cover, flashed by on either side.

"There!" the emperor shouted. "On the right!"

There was a small cluster of buildings by the edge of the lake – a brightly painted gate, towers, a little temple.

"What is it?"

"A play village, for my son! His favourite game is *The Ghost is Coming*."

A hiding game – so there would be potential places to conceal her, though many of them might be obvious, meant for a child. And the little village was so very bright and obvious, out in the open. It was the first place that they would look. I hesitated. What if there was a better hiding place further on?

I didn't know how close the enemy was. But I knew they would be following as fast as they could, and we probably didn't have much time before they sighted us. The horse was beginning to tire; we were slowing down. Even among all the trees, once they glimpsed us, all it would take was a lucky crossbow bolt to end this. We had to find cover before we were spotted.

I made the choice quickly, steering the horse towards the tiny fake village. Halfway there I drew the animal to a halt.

"What are you doing?" the emperor demanded.

"They'll be following the horse's tracks. If we can send it off in the other direction and make our way to the play village on foot, they may continue to follow the horse and not realize we're not on it for a while – or at least divide their forces to cover both possibilities."

Not that we have much more chance against thirty of the Leopard's soldiers than sixty... I could see she knew this from her expression as I helped her down from the panting horse. But instead of pointing it out, the emperor surprised me by quoting: *"Deceive the Heavens to cross the Ocean..."*

These were the teachings of a noted general from a generation ago. Girls and women were not allowed to read such books. But my father had allowed me to study them, and I supposed that an emperor would be another exception to the rule. I nodded. "Exactly."

She set off briskly, but with a slight stiffness to her gait. I turned the animal away, tied the reins up on its neck so that they would not tangle or trip it, and gave it a hearty slap on the rump. It let out an indignant whinny and broke into a tired trot. That was the best I could do. I hurried after the emperor, afraid of losing sight of her among the thick tree cover.

By the time we reached the eerie ghost-town quiet of the mock village, the stiffness of her walk had become a decided limp. Long strands of hair were unravelling from her elaborate coiffure, tangling with the precious pearls of her headdress, and the silk of her riding outfit was stained and torn in places. She leaned tiredly on the painted lintel of the fake temple for a breath, then straightened with a grimace.

"Do you know of any particularly good hiding places here?" I asked tentatively, made more uncomfortable by her obvious discomfort and dishevelment than I think I would have been if she had been stark naked.

She shook her head. "I've never visited this place with him. I only had it built."

Then it was up to me. I turned in a quick circle, assessing the buildings that clustered around a small village square, and finally picking the third largest house, on the reasoning that it would have more possible hiding places than one of the small ones, but would be less obvious than the temple or the miniature version of a local governor's house. I led the way, the emperor trailing wearily behind me. The small door, though unlatched, required both of us to duck to enter. Inside the house was mostly bare, thick with blown dirt and debris, and evidence of animal inhabitation. It smelled dry, but fusty. If Li Xian had ever played here, it had been a while ago.

The emperor made a small sound of disgust.

"The state of disarray is good," I reassured her. "It means our presence here will be harder to discern. One moment."

Quickly I began to sound the walls and floor. Two obvious hiding spots – a cupboard and a false wall next to a hearth – I discarded immediately. In the next room, though, I discovered a place in the floor that made a slightly hollow echo when I tapped it with my foot, as if one of the planks did not fit properly. Using the tip of my knife, I pried up the loose plank, and discovered a generous crawl-space under the boards. It had the same footprint as the room above, meaning there was enough room for both of us to hide. Best of all, if I could hold the plank firmly in place once we were beneath it, there would be no way to tell that any such hiding place existed at all.

The emperor made another noise of disgust at the

sight of the small hole in the floorboards. "Oh no – not in the dirt. Isn't there anywhere better?"

I ground my teeth together, then went to the window. The back of the house looked out over the woods we had just escaped from. I stared at them, wishing for Wu Jiang's spyglass. If there was no sign of pursuit then we could perhaps afford to move to another building and—

There was a glint of metal in the shade under the thick trees. Then another. I sucked in a sharp breath – then let it out as a foul swear word when I saw our horse, that *damned* horse, at the lakeside, leisurely bending its head to drink. It hadn't run at all, simply trotted out of my view and made itself comfortable. It would lead the Leopard's men straight to us.

I spun around to see the emperor staring at me, all traces of petulance wiped from her face. "What is it?"

"They're here, and they know we're here. Get in the floor now, Your Majesty. Hurry."

She scrambled down into the hole and I went after her. My boots hit moist earth with hardly any sound, and I reached back, caught the trick plank with one hand, and flicked it into place overhead with a thud.

In the stingy trickles of light that spilled through the gaps between the floorboards, I rifled through my belt and found the four delicate paperweights – smooth, white pebbles, oblong and only a little thicker than my fingernails, their tops engraved with the four opening lines of a famous poem – that the Young General had given me weeks ago. Hastily, I wedged the weights into the narrow spaces on each side of the loose plank, hoping they would help to prevent the betraying hollow noise I had observed if – when – someone else walked over the floor.

"There," I whispered, turning around cautiously on the uneven, crumbly dirt. The crawl-space was – barely – high enough for me to stand upright. The emperor was no larger than I, but with her hair in its tall binding and the headdress over the top of that adding height, she had simply chosen to sit down on the earth.

I expected more complaints about the conditions, and braced myself to bear them calmly and respond with respect and patience. She said nothing. Instead, silently, with deft fingers, she began undoing the crow-black swirls of her hair from the headdress, allowing them to fall down around her shoulders, and pulling the precious kingfisher crown off in sections. She piled them neatly by her feet with a sigh of relief.

Perhaps sensing my shock, she whispered calmly, "It weighs more than a newborn baby. My neck hurts. My head hurts. My back hurts. Everything hurts, in fact – but this, at least, I can do something about."

Before I could decide whether it was in any way my place to reply, I heard voices outside, and raised my finger to my lips. She nodded, her hands still moving as she quickly bound her waist-length tresses back in a simple plait. I turned away from her to stare up at the loose board again. She had instinctively chosen the far corner of the space, with her back to the earthen wall. I placed myself between that corner and the enemy's potential point of access.

The voices drew nearer. I tried to count them, but

there were too many: at least twenty, maybe more. One of them called out orders to search the place from top to bottom, while another agreed that "they" – we – must be here somewhere.

Shards of memory shattered through my mind, edged with the painfully sharp fear and panic of a child woken by assassins in the night. Cold sweat broke out over my back and upper lip. I felt my breathing begin to speed and I tilted my head back, closing my eyes, forcing my lungs to cooperate in an attempt to centre my *qi*.

You cannot fall apart now. You cannot fall apart now.

I blinked my eyes open and made myself focus on the sounds of the search instead. The men were shouting, hooting mockingly at each other, even laughing. Their accents were thick, regional, their vocabulary uneducated. They were both nervous and excited. Anyone attempting regicide should be nervous, but mercenaries or trained assassins would be quieter and more businesslike. These men were most likely criminals, like the bulk of the rebel army. That meant they had less skill as soldiers – which was good. But it also meant they were probably the lowest of the low: murderers, thieves, rapists.

Men who had no regard for honour, or the rules of war.

Men who ate women and children.

That ... was bad.

There was a bang – the door of the house flying open. The emperor and I both jolted. Now heavy footsteps in the other room. Shuffling sounds, a few more bangs. The footsteps came closer. They were in the room above us. I placed my hands lightly against the underside of the loose board, preparing to hold it steady against any telltale rattle of the stones if the searcher stepped on it. Another glance back over my shoulder showed the emperor's head bowed over her crossed legs, lips moving without a sound.

The footsteps crossed the floor in long strides. He was directly overhead now. He turned on the spot. One of his feet pressed down on the board.

It made no sound.

The man grunted. Then he walked away. The door banged again. Outside, a voice shouted, "All clear in there."

"No sign over here, either!" someone called back. "Maybe they're hiding in the woods, after all."

The emperor's head sagged a little. I allowed my hands to fall away from the floorboard, muffling my ragged gasp of relief behind one palm.

The sounds of the search ebbed and flowed around our hiding place for what felt like a long time, but was probably no more than ten minutes. Two more men roamed the house in turn, but none sensed our presence or the trick board.

Eventually all the footsteps and voices receded. I could still hear them outside, but none were close enough for me to make out their words. I began to feel a faint hope that they would be forced to abandon the fake village. Wu Jiang's men would surely arrive soon.

Then a booming voice rang out, "Your Imperial Majesty! I am Pei Yen, Lieutenant of the Free Army of General Feng Shi Chong. I know you're here! I know you're hiding. And I will not leave this place without you – or your corpse."

Crouching down, I stared at the emperor. A single, thin line of light fell across her face, and in it I could see perspiration standing out like seed pearls against the white of her make-up.

"You have five minutes to show yourself and surrender to me, Wu Fen. Or I will set fire to each and every building in this place and burn it to the ground, then rake the ashes for your bones. Do you hear me? Five minutes, or you die a fiery and agonizing death. And your brat, when we find him, will suffer the same."

A bead of moisture ran through the red crescent moon painted at the corner of the emperor's left eye. It made a trail of crimson down the side of her cheek. She lifted her eyes to meet mine. I saw the knowledge there. If we went out, we would be killed. If we stayed here, we would be killed. Each death would be equally horrible. Each death would mean the fall of Wu Fen's dynasty and victory for the Leopard.

We were trapped. There was nothing we could do to save ourselves, or the empire.

Despair sucked at my insides. If only, *if only* I could use my banner-breaking to hide her, to get her out. What a craven waste of skill and training – how *utterly pointless* it had all been – if my ability could do nothing for me, for the empire, now, at this most vital moment.

These men had killed women and children and eaten them. They had killed Diao and Yun and Ma Wen.

They had killed Yang Jie.

And now they were going to *win*.

I closed my eyes again, silently howling into the dark – howling at my ancestors, at the heavens. At my father. *Is this it? Is this my grand destiny? To watch, helplessly, as my emperor burns? To hide while the empire falls?*

Then, like a flash of divine light in that most terrible darkness, I saw it.

My ability allowed me to hide myself. As a shadow, or…

As someone else.

Behind someone else's face.

The emperor's face.

If they thought they had her, there would be no reason to search for anyone else. No reason to waste time setting fire to the village. They would leave, and the emperor could hide here and await Wu Jiang's reinforcements. She would be safe. The empire would be safe.

This. This was it. The reason my father had trained me. The reason a girl had been born with such a strong, yet narrow talent. This was the reason I had survived the assassins as a child.

The reason Yang Jie had given his life for mine.

This. At long last. My destiny.

"Your Imperial Majesty," I whispered. "I wonder if I could trouble you for your clothes."

Twenty-five

"You understand what they might do to you?" the emperor whispered, her slim fingers flying as they bound, pinned and knotted my hair. Our five minutes were almost up. "They probably have torments imagined for me, yes, but they apparently need me alive for the moment. Once they realize you're a man, a soldier, that you've tricked them – they'll make you wish for death. And you'll be given it."

I swallowed hard, staying still as she slid the last section of the kingfisher crown into my hair. "Your Majesty, I have no choice."

She turned me firmly to face her, scrutinizing my face. Her face.

I stared back at her boldly, still adding minute details to my illusion mask as I knelt there. Threads of *qi* sparked and glimmered, spinning out through my mental fingers and layering on to the basic likeness I had already created. The fine lines that were a fraction deeper on the left side of her mouth, the winglike shape and slight bronze tint of her brows, the smear in the white lead paint on one cheek from a careless swipe of her hand.

I was almost the same height as the emperor, but both nature and the musculature gained in all my training made my figure much broader, causing her silk riding outfit to strain over my shoulders and biceps, my hips and thighs. My voice was entirely different – ironically, far deeper and more manly, thanks to the tincture. And I smelled like a soldier, practically reeking of leather and horses and the faint tang of metal, nothing like the distinctive fragrance of her perfume – sweet basil, cloves, angelica, cassia and honey – which still clung to her body even though she was now wearing my linen shirt and leggings instead of her own things.

If any one of the rebels had ever been in her presence, had perhaps worked as a palace servant, been inspected by her as a soldier or as an imperial official in one of her offices – the differences would stand out like a shout. The mask itself had to be so good that it was beyond question or doubt. Without that, the deception would not, could not, work.

"You have a choice," she said.

I was so absorbed in my efforts that for a moment it seemed a random statement. Then I realized what she was saying. Asking.

"You are the empire. The empire must not fall to the Leopard and his men."

Her remarkable eyes were dry, but there was something almost vulnerable in them as they studied me now, something that was not the Daughter of Heaven, but purely Wu Fen. Her fingers tightened on my shoulders and her lips crimped up painfully at the corners. "It really is an astonishing talent. You look more like me than I do."

"Good. Imperial Majesty, please stay here, stay hidden. No matter what happens when I go out there, no matter what you might … hear. Stay and wait for the Young General. He will come soon."

She nodded and released me. Her eyes flicked away, and when they returned they were the eyes of an emperor again.

Outside, Pei Yen shouted, "Time's up, Imperial Majesty! Show yourself, or we start the fire!"

I had to go.

Fine tremors crawled up and down my limbs, making me clumsy as I pulled the paperweights from the plank and pushed it up, then clambered out. I leaned down and dropped the thin stones into the emperor's hands.

"Wedge them into the gaps after I'm gone," I said. Without waiting for acknowledgment or reply, I kicked the floorboard back into place, hiding her face from view.

When I straightened, alone and unobserved, it was no longer the soldier who stood there. It was the girl.

What am I doing here?

What have I done?

My breath came in short, panicked gasps, and my eyes prickled with tears that I would not allow to fall. I had to force myself into motion, to cross the musty, quiet room towards the world outside – the world where the enemy soldiers waited. But cross it I did.

It took an effort to walk, but no effort at all to shorten my strides to the small, dainty ones of a woman, to bring my hands up before me and tuck them modestly into my sleeves. The female aspects of myself were still there within me, as vital a part of myself as my quick reflexes and banner-breaking, as natural as blinking and swallowing. These men expected to see a woman. So it was a soft-spoken, graceful girl who would face them, as bravely as any man. Though I might tremble, I would endure.

I would finally make my mother and father proud.

I … I would make Yang Jie proud. If I could.

My mask thrummed with agitation, *qi* fluttering like moths' wings against my skin, but it held. It was the strongest illusion I had ever woven, and I had put everything I had into it. No matter what they did to me, while I was conscious, it would hold.

I pushed open the door of the little house, raising my hand to shelter my face from the brilliance of the midmorning sun.

A cry went up. Before I could dash the water from my eyes, footsteps thudded towards me and several pairs of rough hands seized my shoulders, my arms. I was yanked up on to my toes and towed forward. The dainty riding boots I had squeezed my feet into dragged on the ground, leaving dusty trails. All around me there were hoots and shouts and vile insults – a mob of faces distorted with furious triumph, mouths that gaped and eyes that glittered with febrile excitement.

What am I doing here?

What have I done?

I was dumped before a tall, commanding man. He was in his early thirties, unscarred and deeply tanned. His black armour featured the usual gold splotches, painted with slightly more skill than I had yet seen. This was Pei Yen. White teeth glinted under a long, thin moustache as he stared at me, and I read a trace of disbelief in his eyes. He hadn't known his gambit would work – not until he saw me.

"Your Imperial Majesty," he said mockingly as I straightened my back and lifted my chin. "Or should I call you the Imperial Whore?"

So it begins. A shudder worked down my spine, and my guts seemed to turn over inside me. What would the emperor say? How would she look at him? With dignity. With contempt. No fear. No fear.

My voice was still husky and low, but if I was careful to pitch it a little higher, it could pass for a woman's. I stared unblinkingly into his eyes. "Men always call women whores – when they are afraid of them."

The white teeth bared in a snarl. The man twisted away, his elbow coming up. I read the movement and braced myself. The hard, back-handed slap to my cheek made my eyes water again. My head snapped to the side and I rocked back on my heels. But I did not fall.

Inside the sleeves of the emperor's golden robe my hands knotted into fists.

When I looked at Pei Yen again, there was surprise in his face. He had expected to send me flying – a woman half his size, a civilian who may never have known the back of a man's hand, and would not be able to defend herself.

Coward.

This time I raised my voice so that everyone could hear. "Know this, Pei Yen. Know it – all of you. My son is safe. And one day he will seek you out, and flay the flesh from your bones, and your children's bones, and the bones of everyone you have ever known, until all that is left of all your houses is blood and dust, and rot, and your ancestors are as forgotten as you are. That is a promise from your emperor. Remember it."

Now it was his turn to rock back on his heels, eyes wide. Had he really expected the Daughter of Heaven to cringe from him? Then he was a fool, too. Around us some of the men surged forward with anger, while others shrunk back in sudden fear. I glanced sidelong at one of the ones who had dragged me, and had the satisfaction of seeing him flinch.

Pei Yen shook his head like a spooked horse and raised his hand. "Enough. The Leopard'll soon stop the bitch's mouth for her. Do it!"

One man caught the back of my robe, while another grabbed my jaw, holding me still as a wad of wet cloth was forced down over my nose and mouth. The stench was chemical. Ten times worse than the tincture, it burned my nostrils and made my head swim. They were trying to knock me out.

No! My mask – I have to stay awake!

Pressing my lips closed, I held my breath and struggled fiercely, jerking my face sideways to try to get clean air. Someone swore. The top part of the kingfisher crown tore loose, pulling my hair painfully before it fell away. A heavy hand clouted the side of my head and sent me reeling – but the stinking cloth stayed firmly clamped in place. There was no escape.

I mustn't breathe, I mustn't breathe...

It was no use. My lips opened on a desperate gasp. Fumes flooded into my lungs. I coughed, choked, still struggling, as my knees lost their stiffness and began to wobble. My attackers dropped me, and I folded slowly down, vision narrowing as though I was rushing away from the light into a long, black tunnel. I hit the ground, still clutching at the threads of *qi* that covered my face. The mask was shredding. *Not yet, not yet...*

The drugged cloth fell away as my cheek pressed into gritty dirt, but the curtain of my loose hair fell over my face, hiding me just the same. I blinked ... and was gone.

I was going to be sick.

Skull beating with agony, dizziness, and queasy cold shivers wracking my flesh, I heaved myself over on to my front just in time to vomit messily, retching until my throat was raw and my mouth tasted of blood. I didn't know where I was, couldn't remember how I had got there. It was dark, but everything was moving – creaking and shuddering. One of my shaking hands flailed out and found a cold, unmistakable shape. An iron bar.

I was in a cage.

Large animals of some kind – not horses – snorted and grunted ahead. A man swore at them, and there was the crack of a whip. The creaking and shuddering increased and the cage jerked violently. Still grasping the iron bar, I dragged myself across a rough floor away from the mess I had made, feeling clothes and skin snag on splinters. The effort squeezed my breath into short, painful wheezes – the bones of my head seemed to grind and flex against each other. I imagined the soft pulp of my brain bleeding under the pressure. *Am I dying?*

I curled into a ball. That was the last thing I knew for a while.

There were other awakenings, more or less miserable than the first. Sometimes I fell in and out of consciousness by myself, only aware for a few moments. At other times I was shaken roughly or had filthy water dumped over me, and food and liquid – mainly strong spirits – were forced past my dry, cracked lips, before the cloth with its awful burning chemical made its reappearance to send me to oblivion again.

They were transporting me somewhere. Doing what was required – only what was required – to keep me alive until I arrived. I tried to work out where we could be going. To keep track of passing days by the feedings, and by how many times the wooden pail in the corner of my cage – where I had no choice but to piss and void my bowels – was emptied. But the burning drug and the spirits made time contract and stretch out strangely, and some days I thought they did not bother to feed me, or empty the pail.

It was cold. So cold. And it was always dark. Somehow. Somehow, I never once saw daylight. It was as if I had been stolen out of the real world of sky, clouds, birds, wind, into a hellish, airless black grave that went on, deeper and deeper into the cold, dead earth…

As the pain in my head subsided a little, I regained the memory of why this was happening to me. This terrible end, in darkness and suffering, had been my choice.

That was what I told myself, at first.

The war cabinet had been slaughtered before my eyes, Yang Jie had been murdered before I ever had the chance to… But the emperor would survive. Together she and the Young General would root out the traitor and destroy the Leopard. He would pay. The Land of Dragons would heal.

Let that be my victory. My vengeance.

The thought sustained me for two, maybe three days.

It took me that long to realize my banner-breaking was gone. Maybe it was the drug, or maybe I was just too weak, too disoriented to locate the centre of my *qi* or manipulate it. It didn't matter. The thick tangles of my hair were everywhere – the remains of the priceless king-fisher crown and jewelled pins were unsurprisingly gone by the time I thought to feel for them – and my face was covered in swollen bruises and filth. And while the light of the lantern they used when they entered the cage was bright enough to make me flinch away and squeeze my eyes closed, none of them bothered to actually look at me. They thought their prize was firmly in their grasp.

Sometimes, as the journey stretched on, this knowledge made me laugh – unhinged, high-pitched cackles of laughter that caused the men transporting me to bang hard on the bars of the cage and shout curses at me. If I didn't stop quickly enough, they came in and gave me a few hard smacks with the handle of the whip they used on the animals. Apparently, despite everything, I unnerved them.

But my laughter was bitter. No matter how terrible their likely fate at the Leopard's hands – these fools who dared to bring him some nameless nobody when he had expected an emperor – what awaited me would be far, far worse.

Thoughts of triumph, honour and courage began to wither. No one knew where I was, no one was coming for me. I might as well be dead already. But I wasn't. My pain had only just begun.

If I could have induced my poor, drugged, starved brain to come up with a method, I would have tried to kill myself. To deprive the Leopard of a target for his rage, and the satisfaction of whatever tortures he had devised for the emperor, that would be one last worthy act. And – there was no use in denying it, not now – I was afraid. Terribly afraid.

But even if there had been anything other than splinters and a bucket of my own waste in the cage, I was too feeble and dazed to plan. Instead, I dreamed of death. Imagined a thousand ways of dying at my own and at the Leopard's hands. I saw my own blood pooling, heard my own last breaths, choked out my last words so many times and so vividly that it became a surprise, each time, to wake and discover the dark and the misery of my existence still dragged on. An unpleasant surprise.

I wished it was all over already. I wished I had never left my home. I wished I had given the emperor up and run away when I had the chance. I wished, I wished, I wished...

Eventually the poisoned cloth always appeared again – for the twentieth, hundredth, or perhaps one thousandth time – muffling all fear and thoughts and senses.

Then I woke up somewhere different.

The ground didn't rock beneath me. There were no animal noises, no breathing near by, no crank and clack of wheels. It was even colder than before, and I was very, very hungry and very, very thirsty. For the first time in ... however long it had been, my head felt ... clear. A little clearer, at least.

And there was *light*. A distant glow, yellow and faint and flickering, but enough for me to make out the pale, spiderweb fragility of my own hands, splayed against the darkness of the floor. *Light*. I lay still for a while and simply basked in the beauty of it, the relief of light that did not blind. I would have opened my mouth and drunk it like wine if I could.

That thought made me swallow dryly. How long had it been since I was fed or given liquid? How long had I been alone in this new prison?

Why ... why wasn't the Leopard here to torment me?

I focused on my surroundings, trying to keep panic at bay. What could I see? A floor of ... stone. Cold, rough stone. Smell? Damp. Hear? There was a dripping noise close by, intermittent rather than regular. *Water.*

I pushed myself up on to my hands and knees. Hanks of tangled, filthy hair fell over my face as, on shaky limbs, I crawled forward, towards the light and that tantalizing drip. The space I was in was narrow, and I shivered convulsively as my arms – clad only in rags of silk, now – brushed against chilly, damp stone walls. The stone scraped at my palms and bruised my knees. I crawled on.

The noise of water grew louder. I rounded an awkward, bulging corner of rock – and the light pierced my eyes. I recoiled as if I had been struck, burying my face against my shoulder. It took several long minutes before I could bear it enough to move forward again.

The narrow walls opened up ahead of me – enough that I could have spread my arms out if I wished. My stinging eyes fixed on a thin trickle of moisture that gleamed on a dark curve of rock and the small puddle on the floor.

I flung myself forward, cupping my hands in the tiny pool. The water was tooth-achingly cold, clean, fresh – the sweetest thing I had ever tasted in my whole life. I gulped at it greedily, only forcing myself to stop when my stomach let out an uneasy gurgle. I could feel my mind clearing still more, and some of the shakes easing from my muscles.

Thank you, ancestors, for this gift.

Another handful of water went to scrub my face. A cleanish rag, torn from the inside of the emperor's sash, dried it. Crusted blood and dirt came away until the silk was rusty-black. I scraped my hair out of my face laboriously, wincing as my clumsy fingers caught in knots and tangles. A single jewelled pin fell from a thick snarl, pinging on the stone. I tucked it into what was left of the robe's collar, and then I tied my hair back tightly at the nape of my neck with another scrap of rag.

A deep, slow breath. I closed my eyes and reached within, seeking the warm, bright comfort of my centre. It was there. Dampened and weakened by my experiences, more of a soft glow than the vibrant fire that I was used to, but it was there, and I could touch it once more. Use it once more.

I had my banner-breaking back.

With a sensation of returning home, I slowly, reverently, spun up my mask and drew it into place. I painted dirt and bruises, streaks of dried blood, as lovingly as a watercolour artist captures the feathers on an egret's back. My face was returned to me. My own imperfect, dirty, battered face. Perhaps it was a foolish use of my already depleted energy, but I didn't care. The relief was indescribable – almost the same feeling as those first, life-saving sips of fresh water. It was my own sanity that I tasted. I had nearly allowed it to drain away, in the black hell of that cage, but now I held it within my cupped palms once more, cool and clear.

Made thirsty by the thought, I carefully drank a little more. Then I reached for my pocket – the place where the familiar weight of my bronze mirror normally rested. My fingers froze in midair. There was no practical pocket in these ragged silk trousers. The mirror was not there.

Without realizing, I had left it behind in the leggings that I loaned to the emperor.

I bit my lip. The one thing my mother had given me. The one thing from my old life I might have kept. It would have been good to have it here with me...

I forced myself to look around again.

Before me there was a cell door. Wooden, clumsily hewn, fitted into a rounded doorway in the rock, and bound with iron. The top part was open, barred. It was from that opening that the light flowed. Outside I could hear nothing. Using the door handle to support shaky legs, I rose to my feet and peered outside. More stone walls. A single oil-lamp on a hook. Beyond that? Darkness, absolute. How long had it been since I saw the sun?

Will I ever see it again?

I leaned my face against the iron bars of the door and tried to cudgel my mind to more practical questions. That I had been brought all this way and then dumped in a cell instead of taken directly to Feng Shi Chong was ... unexpected. He had ordered the emperor taken alive. He must have plans for her. What were they? And how soon would they discover that their prize was worthless?

They had a spy in the capital – maybe more than one – and the news that the emperor had survived the attack and was still on her throne would warrant a very urgent message indeed. The intelligence could only be a day or two behind me at the most. Depending on how long it had taken the last of the drug and spirits to work their way out of my body and allow me to wake up here, I might only have hours before they came to check if it was true.

If I was to survive, I had to escape, and quickly.

And if I couldn't escape? Then I needed to discover that quickly, as well.

I could now remember several effective, if not pleasant, methods by which I might deprive the Leopard and his men of a target for their depravity. But now that I was myself again I did not want to use any of them. I needed to be sure that I had exhausted all other options first.

The lock on the cell door was heavy and the planks thick. Even if I were at full strength I couldn't have forced it open. But... I felt for the hairpin in the neck of the robe. They wouldn't expect the emperor to be able to pick locks. Or use banner-breaking.

If I could get out of this cell, I might see the sun once more.

Twenty-six

I expected the lock to confound me. This was a dungeon in the Leopard's lair, and I had been brought here by men who believed me to be the most powerful and valuable person in the world. A priceless hostage whom they had risked their lives to secure. Surely the prison they had chosen would be impenetrable to my feeble efforts.

No. The lock was simple and crude, the kind any random store cupboard or barn door might possess. The greatest difficulty was in holding the heavy tumblers down with the pin, which was gold, and inclined to bend under pressure. Even with a fierce headache and hands that still trembled a little, my count of seconds had only reached two hundred before I heard the telltale *click* that signalled the lock's surrender.

I pushed the handle down and the door swung outwards. I hesitated on the threshold, expecting …

something. Some further measures to keep the prisoner contained. But the glow of the lantern revealed no squadron of guards beyond and no pit lined with spikes. The Leopard was not a very good jailer.

Then again, he hadn't had much practice in taking prisoners, had he?

I moved to take the guttering lantern from its hook on the wall, but hesitated again. To carry a light with me would be to give away my presence, since the light must travel in advance of me wherever I went. I could whisk a cloak of shadow around myself if I heard someone approach, but the light would remain.

I swallowed hard as I realized I must bear still more darkness.

The ceiling of the corridor – tunnel? – was low enough for me to touch with my fingertips without standing on tiptoe. Two men travelling in opposite directions would each need to turn sideways to pass one another. The smell and feeling of damp was pervasive, prickling my skin with gooseflesh, and my fingers trailed through more tracks of water as I went. But the rock, though uneven, was smooth under my hands. This place, whatever it was, was old. Older than the rebellion, or the Leopard.

I turned a corner and left the diminishing glow of the lantern behind. The dark closed in on me, suffocating. I continued walking blindly forward, but my body began to quake and tremble with suppressed terror. How could any place under the sky contain such depthless, terrifying night? This was no castle keep, no mere dungeon.

It was no place on the surface of the world at all.

And then I knew. I was underground. A long way underground.

The realization made my shaking worse, but not with fear any more. My mind raced as I put the pieces together. We must have been travelling through tunnels like this one since the start of my captivity. It was the only explanation: the reason why I had never seen any light but lantern-light, and why my jailers made no efforts to be silent, didn't even bother to gag me. I had wondered if my endless journey into blackness had been a drug-induced hallucination, it seemed so impossible. But it wasn't impossible. Not if the Leopard had access to a network of tunnels, some kind of secret subterranean maze.

It must be massive. Miles of hidden caves and tunnels, some of them large enough to be used as roads, like the one I had travelled to get here.

And … there had to be an opening within the city. Maybe even within the grounds of the Imperial Palace itself. Close enough to the Forbidden Park that the men who caught me had been able to escape through it with me on the same day that they took me.

Great Dragon and Phoenix! I kept stumbling forward, the fear of darkness lessening its grip on me as I worked through the implications. This was vital information. The sort of fatal weakness in the empire's defences which was nothing less than disastrous. I thought back to what Wu Jiang had told me of the Leopard's abortive attempt to lay siege to the city walls. Feng Shi Chong might be evil and depraved – but he was also a genius. Who would believe that someone with a direct route *inside* the city's ramparts would bother wasting time, men and resources on assailing its walls? It was the perfect way to conceal his greatest advantage until he was ready to use it.

He must have been preparing, all this time, for a definitive final assault, gathering men and arms in anticipation. It would be an attack from a direction that the emperor would never see coming, and could not hope to defend against. And this would also explain how the traitor managed to correspond with the rebels in secret without his communications ever being discovered by the empire's agents. Through the hidden tunnel entrance.

The only surprise was that Feng Shi Chong and his men hadn't *already* laid waste to the city. Why this elaborate ambush on the war cabinet? Why bother to take the emperor alive? Why, indeed, this long, inconclusive campaign against the Imperial Army? A force of a few hundred could probably overwhelm the Centre of the Universe if they were able to gain access to the grounds in secret. There had to be a reason.

I could not guess at what it was.

But if I was right, capturing the emperor – as they thought they had – must bring that plan to its close. The rebel army would be preparing for their attack at this moment. I had to get out of this place. Get back to the city. Warn Wu Jiang and the emperor before the devastating invasion of the city began – before it was too late.

In the dank stillness of the tunnel, I made out a faint sound. Footsteps ahead. A faint, wavering glow of light, growing brighter. Someone was coming.

They weren't likely to be friendly.

A few breaths of frantic effort drew out my familiar cloak of *don't-notice-me*, tinged with the dark, damp gleam of rock. I squashed myself flat against the icy wall, hoping that the tunnel – which had gradually been broadening as I moved along it – was now wide enough to allow someone to pass me without touching.

The light rounded the faint curve in the tunnel ahead. I squeezed my eyes shut against it, then slitted them to observe. It was a young man. A boy, really. Not dressed in armour but in rags. He had a wooden yoke over his shoulders, a bucket swinging weightily on each end, and carried his lantern on a long pole ahead of him. The boy's face, in the flickering light, was dirty, hollow-cheeked and marked with lines far too deep for a youth of his age.

Around his neck ... a dark shape. A collar of iron.

A slave.

He was clearly not a threat to me, even in my weakened state. That didn't mean, however, that he would automatically be my ally. The collar could mark him as a lawful citizen of the empire, taken hostage by the Leopard. On the other hand, it could mean that he was a foreigner imported from the Land of Clouds, or the Joseon Peninsula. The Leopard had dealings with both nations. In that case the boy would certainly hate the Leopard – but he would probably loathe the entire Red Empire equally. I couldn't risk him giving me away.

What I could do was follow him. If I was right about the scale of this cave network, I could walk for days and never escape. The boy clearly knew his way through this labyrinth of caves and tunnels – maybe he also knew the way out.

I reinforced my illusion until it was as dense and impenetrable as I could make it, and stealthily dogged the slave's steps back the way I had come, placing my feet with the utmost caution. The tiniest sound might reveal me.

Almost immediately he diverged from what I had thought of as the main tunnel, manoeuvring awkwardly through an opening that branched off to the left. It proved to be far wider than the path I had explored. Within a minute of walking at the slave boy's heels, the tunnel brightened as lanterns, some guttering, others dark, began to show up on hooks hammered into the walls. The boy refilled the dark lanterns from one of the buckets on his yoke, and relit the wicks from his own light.

There were noises ahead, indistinct but growing. The echo of many voices, and a confusion of other sounds, including a low, regular creaking-and-grinding – perhaps a machine of some kind?

Suddenly enough to make me jolt, a group of seven or eight men burst from a side entrance into the tunnel before us. They were dressed in the loathsome black-and-gold painted armour, talking and laughing loudly and breathing clouds of ale fumes. They shoved the slave boy carelessly aside with a few cursory imprecations. I ducked back as quickly as I could, but one of them caught me with his elbow, hitting a heavy bruise on my ribs. A tiny whimper of pain forced itself from behind my lips.

The man ignored the sound and the contact completely. The slave himself seemed unsurprised, if somewhat ruffled, by the brutal encounter. He waited for the men to disappear out of sight before he straightened and picked up the long lantern pole he had dropped. One of his buckets had tipped, spilling a pool of oil. He stepped around the spill and moved on. Clearly, he was well used to such treatment.

The next corridor was short and wide, more like a cave in its own right. The sounds were almost deafening here, echoing from the rounded walls. I resisted the urge to put my hands over my ears.

I saw the reason for the level of noise with the next step, and stopped dead in shock.

The boy left me behind, his steps speeding slightly as he headed down a set of steps that had been crudely hacked out of a cave so massive, it dwarfed the halls of the Centre of the Universe.

The ceiling soared above, disappearing into darkness. The grey walls were streaked with lines of yellow, reddish and grey dirt. Below, a river – a true river, wide and crashing white, spanned here and there with makeshift bridges and rickety piers – flowed through the cave. Every other scrap of space was taken up with people.

It was practically a town – a town of slaves and soldiers. There were … dear ancestors, thousands of people, living down there in wooden huts in the orange-yellow light, crammed in among penned animals – pigs, oxen, geese, ducks and chickens, horses – and military tents.

In one corner, a water mill turned in the churning river. This was the source of the rhythmic creaking-and-grinding noises which shook the cave walls. Near by, also making use of the river, there was a smelter. It sent up clouds of toxic black smoke into the darkness of the cave's shadowy roof. In a smaller building alongside, an ironsmith was hard at work among flames and sparks, the ringing of his hammer lost in the cacophony. Swords, shields and other weapons were strung up against his walls on twine, like the prizes at a country festival.

Near one of the tents, a man in Leopard armour was beating a woman. He used a horse whip. Her back was already shredded, dark with blood. The woman lay prone, unresisting, either dead or unconscious. She wore an iron collar. No one looked twice.

Other armoured men drilled sloppily in sword-work. A second group were practising archery on crude targets painted on the cave walls.

Despite the flowing river and the cavernous roof, even up where I stood, the air positively boiled with the stench of effluent, unwashed bodies, animals, burning tallow, and metallic smelter fumes. It made the training camp's reek seem as sweet as the emperor's perfume. Anyone who spent more than a few days down there would probably begin to get sick – in their lungs, their heart, even their mind.

I took an involuntary step back. I did not want to go down there.

But ... there were multiple tunnel mouths, at varying levels, around the cave's walls. What if one led where I needed to go? Was it possible that I could discover which, before someone down there in that seething mass of people noticed the moving blot of shadow amongst them and caught me?

My father had always told me that banner-breakers needed to be wary of children and madmen. I couldn't see many children down in the cave – thank the heavens – but that there were madmen aplenty I had no doubt.

Grinding my teeth in thought, I scrutinized the rebel settlement. Along with the cave entrances peppering the walls, there were several other sets of steps hacked into the stone of the great cavern. A few of them met at different points. If I followed the steps down from here, I could reach one or two of those tunnels without having to descend to the great cavern's floor. There was as good a chance as any that one of those would lead me closer to the surface.

I looked again and squinted. Was that...? Yes. One of those staircases led not to an open tunnel mouth, like the one where I stood, but to a ledge. And above the ledge, halfway up the wall, was an iron-bound wooden door.

Where there was a door, there had to be something that needed to be protected. For instance, an entrance to the outside world. Locked and barred, to stop the slaves escaping. Or, if not, perhaps weapons ... something that might be useful to me in getting away from this place. Excitement made my head pound. I forced myself to be calm, to look more carefully. To try the door was a risk. There was no guarantee that I could pick the lock, and if my cloak of shadows was noticed, or failed me for a second, I would be trapped on the ledge in full view of the enemy soldiers below.

But I could not linger here in this entrance waiting for someone to trip over me all day, either.

Mind made up, I descended the uneven, crumbling steps to the level of the ledge and, hands grasping at the cold walls for support, scuttled down it towards the door.

It was identical to the one that had blocked the exit of my cell – except that there were two locks securing it. That must be a sign. Something important lurked beyond.

I picked the first lock quite easily, but the second proved more challenging. My back crawled with the awareness of thousands of eyes that might spot me at any moment. Clammy sweat trickled down my temples. My fingers shook and fumbled. The stink and deafening noise of the camp below affected my concentration – at a scream of pain from some nameless throat I jolted violently, nearly dropping the gold pin.

I was beginning to feel dizzy and faint. The scale and density of my cloak of illusion was burning up my already depleted *qi* dangerously fast.

Come on…

A soft click vibrated through the pin. I gasped with relief. A quick twist of the handle and I slipped through the door, shutting it hastily behind me.

I stared, astonished. I had expected to find another corridor, or a dank cave. Instead, I was in a medium-sized room. It was lit with hundreds of lanterns – metal, octagonal, decorated with intricate piercing and coloured glass – burning scented lamp oil. But the room was empty of inhabitants. Instead, it was filled with treasure.

Luxuriant rugs and animal pelts were piled on the floor three or four deep. The walls were hung with tapestries that rivalled those at the Imperial Palace for beauty. Grand but mismatched pieces of black, red and gold lacquered furniture jostled for space – a bed, chairs, a cabinet and a huge, ornate writing desk and stool. Bronze statues, carved jades, fine porcelain bowls and vases, boxes of jewellery, and sacks of precious metals in both coin and ingot form were piled against the walls. Next to the door there was a suit of gold armour on display, crusted with precious stones.

This was a gilded graveyard. I was looking at the remnants of thousands upon thousands of lives that had been destroyed and picked over for scraps.

And then I wasn't looking at any of it any more. On the desk there was food.

My illusion cloak puffed away like dandelion seeds in the wind. I pounced.

Roasted and spiced duck, stewed mutton with unleavened bread in sweet wine sauce, salted fish dumplings, soft buns filled with red bean paste or red pork, preserved plums, egg tarts... I tore into it all with my fingers, scattering half-eaten bites everywhere and barely tasting what I ate, at first, except to appreciate that it was not what I had been force-fed in the cage. There was a bowl of cold soup, and I spilled half of it down my front in my eagerness to drink.

A voice of caution rang faintly in my mind. I assumed it was telling me to slow down and ignored it.

It was only when my stomach started to swell out around the emperor's sash, forcing me to straighten up, that I realized my instincts had been trying to tell me something else. Something more important. My eyes had passed over the furniture, the bed, without really seeing it. Only now did I notice that it was made up with fine sheets. That the sheets were rumpled and trailing half on to the floor, along with a stunning silver snow leopard fur. A tray sat on the bed, with more plates of food, half-consumed. A toppled wine bottle had spilled dark drops over the cloth.

I looked down. The desk that I was leaning on ... there were papers. Scribbled notes. Brushes, paperweights, ink-stones and ink sticks. Official-looking documents: rosters of men, lists of resources and weapons. This was not here merely as a trophy room. Someone was using it.

That – that suit of armour I had noticed by the door...?

I turned slowly. There it stood, freshly polished, shining with gilt and gems. The round plate set into the chest guard was engraved with the imperial seal. The helm had a plume of snowy-white horsehair. It was the armour of a general of the armies of the Red Empire.

An ex-general, in this case.

I wasn't in Feng Shi Chong's treasure room. I was in his bedchamber.

Twenty-seven

RUN! *Get out, get out, now, go! Go!*

I forced the impulse down. I was a soldier of the Imperial Army. My first duty was not to preserve my own life. It was to protect my country. This was an opportunity that no loyal subject of the empire had ever been granted: access to the Leopard's private room and his most secret papers.

I dragged my eyes away from the door and turned back to the desk. The tally numbers, lying right there – they must be useful. I folded them up as small and thin as I could and tucked them beneath the bulky material of the emperor's sash. What else? Many of the notes were crumpled, blotted, barely legible. They seemed more like random, furious thoughts spilled out on to paper than military secrets. This one read: *The sun is black with my shame...* and trailed off there. Another: *Betrayal! No longer shall I steel myself to endure!* I grimaced and pushed them aside, searching for something that looked more substantial.

Here. The paper was a different size and quality – thick, curling from having been rolled, and with the broken remains of a jade-green wax seal attached. The penmanship was exquisite, like that of an official palace scribe.

> *Most respectable and honourable ally,*
>
> *I write to invite you cordially to a hunting party taking place shortly after dawn in the pleasant environs of the Forbidden Park. The party shall embark on the day after the return of He Upon Whom the Sun Rises, and will enter the park through the Glorious Dawn Gate. The fellows riding shall be composed of all your most particular friends, including the One We Have Often Praised. I am sure that She would be delighted to receive you at the Blue Jade Lodge. You shall be well looked after there, for She is planning to take at least twenty servants, who will be well equipped to protect Her and Her guests. It is advised that you should provide perhaps twice that number of your own servants, in order to seem well prepared. I rely upon your talents and wisdom as always.*
>
> *I End My Words*
> *With Deepest Respect,*
> *Your Friend*

This … this was the missive which had betrayed us. The letter that had brought me here, drugged and raving in an iron cage. These words had condemned Yang Jie to death.

My eyes prickled with tears of rage and anguish and my back heaved with a single, harsh sob. This – this flowery invitation, this obsequious little missive, the kind of letter that my own mother might write – it wasn't even in real code! The careless ruthlessness of it took my breath away. How could anyone write the death warrants of so many with so little ceremony?

Grasping the letter, I folded it up, tightly, tightly, tightly. Into my sash it went. I did not need to look at it any more: the contents were imprinted upon my mind now. There would be evidence in this. In the paper, the wax of the seal, the style of writing, even the ink. They all gave information away, information that I did not know how to read. But the emperor and Wu Jiang would.

This was the key to finding the traitor – and crushing him.

I shoved a final dumpling into my mouth, chewing defiantly as I stepped out from behind the desk and made for the door. I was halfway there when it began to open.

My mantle of shadows snapped out like great black wings, enfolding me in muffling darkness so dense that it made my vision cloud slightly, as if I looked out at the world through smoky glass.

A tall, bearded man with distinguished silver-grey hair entered the room. He was followed by two other younger men. One of them was Pei Yen, the man who had captured me. But my gaze glanced off them, drawn back to the first as a sliver of metal is drawn to a magnet.

Wiry and well-tanned, he had the tough look of one who spends most of his time on horseback under the sun. But … his eyes were strange. Wide and staring, the white showing all around the iris, as if he had just sustained a great shock. Yet his expression betrayed no such emotion. In fact, it betrayed no emotion at all. The black lacquered armour he wore was of fine quality, skilfully painted with a glittering pattern of gold spots down the arms and chest. From his shoulders hung a cloak not of cloth, but of leopard skin.

I had never seen Feng Shi Chong in my life, but I knew the Leopard when I saw him.

Rooted to the spot, I held my breath, not daring to so much as twitch, blink or shift my weight from one foot to the other. The Leopard stopped with his hand upon the handle of the door, his strange gaze travelling over the room. He stared at the plates of half-devoured food on the desk for only an instant.

And then his eyes found me.

The silver brows drew together as he squinted, then blinked, his head tilting slightly. His back straightened. The lips parted on a breath of surprise.

He knew something was there.

Beware madmen. They see the world as it is.

No. No. He couldn't possibly – he couldn't see *me*. He *couldn't* be sure what he was perceiving. Or even that anything was really there. I was just a shadow to him, a blot of darkness, a trick of the eyes. I – I still had a chance.

I just had to hold still. Stay quiet. Think. *Think.*

"General, what's the matter?" asked Pei Yen, stirring restlessly as his superior continued to block his entry into the room. "Did you forget something—"

"The door was unlocked," the Leopard said softly. His voice was surprisingly light in tenor, gentle and smooth. The sort of voice that would excel in reading poetry, or delivering bad news kindly.

"You think someone has been here?" the second young man demanded, hand flying to his sword belt. "A thief? A spy?"

"Perhaps." Feng Shi Chong let go of the door handle and took a step forward – a step towards me. "But also something … entirely more interesting. *SHOW YOURSELF!*"

The sudden bellow made me jolt like a startled horse. Behind the Leopard, Pei Yen and the other subordinate scanned the – to them, obviously empty – room, exchanged a tense look, and as one, took a hurried step back.

Pei Yen let go of his sword hilt to raise his hands in a placatory gesture. The other officer kept backing away until he was outside the entrance entirely. "Shall I go for the doctor?" he asked.

Pei Yen shook his head impatiently, waving the other to silence. "Sir, please, you mustn't begin to… Sir, please look at me. Remember what the surgeon said, about your humours."

"Fool," the Leopard whispered, eyes growing wider and wider as he stepped forward again. One of his hands lifted. Long, slim fingers grasped gently at the air like a maid servant pinching cobwebs from the corners of a ceiling. "Those who do not look cannot be expected to see…" In one more step he would be close enough to touch me with his outstretched hand.

But now there was a gap.

A gap between him and the doorway.

I felt the moment come, as if my gathered ancestors had leaned forward from the afterlife to speak in my ear. *Go.*

Pivoting on one foot, I dodged the Leopard's hand, and ran for the door. The Leopard let out a roar of rage, spinning on the spot, arms spread wide. Pei Yen, who still stood inside the room, flung himself back against the wall – away from the flailing arms of his unpredictable leader – but also out of my way. The doorway was clear.

I flew through it, dodging to avoid the second rebel officer who still hovered on the ledge outside. There was no way to pass him without touching. I turned in the other direction and made for that end of the ledge, where it intersected with another set of carved steps in the cavern wall. No choice but to head down now, into that mass of toiling, sweating, dying humans that blanketed the bottom of the cave.

My steps knocked loose tiny rocks on the steps, betraying my presence, but the sounds from below hid the noise of my footsteps. I didn't dare look back. I must, I *must* have left them at the top – none of them, not even the Leopard, could make me out in this dim and flickering light. I knew it. I could make it. I would make it—

Six steps from the bottom, a wildly swinging hand

came from behind and swiped a hard blow to the bruised side of my face. The impact spun me around. I tumbled head-first from the wall of the cave and landed like a lead weight, crashing through a crowd of milling people.

Two fell with me, one crumpling directly under my body. We hit the ground together in a tangle of limbs and rags. A bony shoulder drove right into my sternum with a sickening crunch. From me? Or the one who had broken my fall? I couldn't tell. I hurt so much. So much. I couldn't breathe. My eyes wouldn't open. Everything had seized up on impact, my muscles locking, limbs curling up and in helplessly, like a dying spider. I choked on air that my bruised lungs could not accept.

There was screaming all around me, a wall of noise.

My *qi* fluctuated wildly. The delicate threads of my cloak of shadows begin to dissipate, drifting back under my skin. I tried to grasp at them, to push them up, spin them back out. I was not fast enough. Not strong enough. The cloaking illusion flickered … and died.

There was a collective gasp – and then silence.

"Got you," breathed the Leopard's smooth, kind voice. A hand laid lightly on the top of my head for an instant, stroking my hair – then sank into the tangled mass, dragging me up on to my knees. I flopped back, head lolling as his grip momentarily loosened, unable to support my own weight. Water streamed from my eyes, turning my vision to a blur of darkness and piercing starbursts of light.

I heard the Leopard's harsh breath, felt his fingers tighten again until I whimpered.

"Pei Yen! *What is this?*" the Leopard screamed, shaking

me like a straw doll. He flung me away. I fell again, cheek bouncing off the stone floor as a heavy boot stamped on my spine between my shoulder blades. My ribs groaned. I whimpered again, animal and pleading.

"Sir – that is … that is the emperor." Pei Yen's voice drifted above me. "I don't know how she escaped from her cell—"

"This? *This* is what you brought me?" The boot pressed down, forcing the last breath from my chest. "*This is not Wu Fen!* You white-eyed idiot! This is … twenty years too young and two stone too heavy! And a banner-breaker! You've brought me her double, her decoy, you – you – useless, cringing worm! You think he will be satisfied with *this*? Lieutenant – take him! Wrap him in chains and throw him in the pit for the snakes!"

Above the noises of Pei Yen pleading uselessly as he was dragged away, I heard the musical ringing note of a sword leaving its scabbard.

I was going to die now. I knew it in my aching bones, in my bruises, in the blood that dripped from my nose and pooled, iron-thick, in the back of my throat. I was worthless to the Leopard, and he would rid himself of me with one or two quick chops of his blade.

It was a better death, a quicker, less degrading one than I had feared.

But I didn't want it.

There was no fight left in me, but I still wanted to fight. Despite all those dreams of death, I still wanted to live.

I forced my eyes open. Feet – bare feet, dirty, wrapped in rags. The slave who had fallen with me. Spatters of my own blood, red-black against the rough stone floor. A deep gouge in that same stone, in the shape of a cross. This was all, everything I had left. I must see every detail, absorb it all – live, live, live, in these few vital instants before he took my life away.

I imagined I could sense the air parting around the blade as it swung up, the point rising to its apex above me.

I am Hua Zhi. I am Zhou's daughter and his son, I am Jia Mei's eldest child, I am Da Xiong and Xiao Xia's sibling. I am a soldier, I am a banner-breaker. I am Yang Jie's friend. I am, I am, am am am—

The ground rocked beneath me. For an instant all the air seemed to have been sucked away. Then a hollow *BOOM* attacked my ears and the Leopard's heavy foot was suddenly gone from my back.

A great wind swept across my body, hot and stinging as though full of needles – and a wave of blackness followed, choking, billowing blackness. It burned my eyes. I squeezed them closed again.

Is this death?

A new pair of hands caught hold of me, and I tensed, crying out – I felt the cry leave my chest, though I could not hear it through the low featureless hum in my ears. But these hands did not seek to injure. They turned me deftly and cradled my face, brushing over the lines of my eyebrows and lips. One finger tapped on the tip of my nose – once, twice, three times, telling me: *It's all right.*

As I began to relax, the hands closed around my forearms and assisted me to my feet. My legs had no strength. They tried to go out from under me. I was clasped firmly against a shoulder that reached no higher than my own. Soft hair tickled my nose. I hid my face in it.

Coughing and gasping, I staggered forward blindly, following my faceless, silent saviour. There was heat at my back now, growing heat. When I dared to slit my eyes open, I saw flames lashing angrily behind a dark, distinctive shape. The smelting tower. It had blown up.

I sensed a new space ahead. A tunnel or another cave. Fresher air, respite from the throbbing and thundering in my ears. I felt one of my rescuer's hands squeeze gently around my shoulder – encouraging me. And so I struggled on. I didn't know where we were going, but I knew wherever it was, it was away from the Leopard, and that was where I wanted to be.

There was some fight left in me after all.

Hours or perhaps days later, I opened my eyes. I could hear water lapping lazily near by, and above me there were stars. But no stars that I knew. They clustered thickly against an opaque black sky, glowing with a blue-green light.

"Ah, you're awake. How do you feel? Can you move your arms and legs?"

If I'd had the energy or strength, I would have jumped to my feet. Instead, I rolled my head sideways on a surprisingly soft pillow, towards the whispering voice. I did not know it, but yet … it *was* familiar.

"Who—" I gasped the word. My ordeal had left my throat raw and my voice even more wrecked than normal. I wondered if I would ever need to use the tincture again.

A shape moved against the glow of the stars, and a woman knelt beside me. In the dim light I couldn't make out much. She was wearing armour. Some deep colour, maybe red, I thought, as my eyes travelled slowly over her, focusing with an effort. It was intricately lacquered, although the designs were a blur to me. The plates on the arms and stomach were diamond-shaped, like the ones in favour more than a century ago. Thick waves of hair cascaded wildly around a small, delicate face with … with a scar … that stretched from below one eye to the corner of her lip…

Helplessly, I began to laugh. The sound was harsh and broken, like the cawing of a crow. "You – you're my damsel in distress!"

The stars winked out. My laughter froze in my throat. *What in the world…?*

"Hush. The glow-worms like the quiet," she whispered.

Not a sky. A cave roof. Not stars, but worms. Not a trembling, frightened girl, but a warrior woman, a saviour.

"You were never a slave, were you?" I whispered. "You never needed my help at all. Who are you?"

"Some call me Dou Xianniang. And I was a slave, once. But not when you met me, no. Although your help was still much appreciated."

Gradually, the green-and-blue lights were beginning to glow again, filling the cave with their unearthly light, and bringing my saviour's face back into view. "Dou Xianniang," I breathed, squinting up at her. "You're real." One of my hands lifted to brush the scales on her forearm. The legendary scarlet armour of the lady warrior.

"She had eyes like a wild creature…" Sigong had said, laughing, yet still, underneath, serious. "Like a tigress at bay."

I had compared her eyes to those of a kitten, that night. By the Celestial Animals, I was a fool.

"As real as anyone can be," the lady warrior replied, a shade of amusement in her voice. "Now answer my questions. You've been through a lot – can you move your arms and legs? Does it hurt to breathe? I don't think anything's broken, but I'm not a surgeon."

Still dazed, I tried. My shoulder crunched and my ribs and back ached and my head throbbed and my left knee was hot and painful, but everything worked, even if it hurt like a dog bite to do it. "I think I'm all right. Why are you helping me? Where is this?"

"We're still underground, but this is a cave that the Leopard doesn't know about. We should be safe for now. And I'm here – helping you – because I do not allow myself to be beholden to men. You offered me assistance and kindness, and I was unable to repay you at the time. So I followed you, and took my chance to make us even when it came. I … did not realize you were a woman until it was too late to turn back. But now I am glad."

I swallowed dryly. "I am not a woman." The words hovered in the air, stark, nonsensical – and true. It was the first time I had ever said them to anyone. I couldn't believe I'd dared.

But I'd almost died today. Maybe I still would. Now at least I'd said it, said it aloud where some other creature than myself could hear.

There was a long pause. "Then what are you? A man after all?"

Cautiously, I answered, "Not entirely. I'm still – figuring it out. It's complicated."

There was a sound like a sigh. "There is nothing simple in the world that the world cannot make impossibly complicated."

Something in the response – perhaps the melancholy resignation in her voice – reminded me suddenly, unbearably, of Yang Jie. I turned my face away, jaw clamping as I breathed in sharply through my nose, blinking hard.

I should have told this to him. He told me he was sorry – sorry! For what? I was the coward! I should have said sorry back. Why didn't I say it back? Why didn't I tell him—

"Your name is Hua Zhi, is it not?" she asked me, either unaware of or politely ignoring my agitation.

"Yes." My voice was a dull monotone. I tried to force more animation into it. "Lady Dou. You've come halfway across the province, infiltrated the Leopard's lair and – I think – blown up his smelting tower. And you must have carried me most of the way here—"

"I'm stronger than I look," she interrupted dryly.

Yang Jie had been stronger than he looked. As strong and supple as a willow. Misery cramped my insides. The words wobbled as I said, "After all this trouble on my behalf, surely I am now beholden to *you*?"

I saw the scar move before I realized her dark-stained lips had curved up into a smile. "I have my own reasons for wishing the Leopard ill. So say only that you owe me a favour, Corporal. Perhaps I will choose to call it in one day. Perhaps not. But I shall regard you as my ally, either way. Misfits like us must take care of one another, if we can. No one else will."

She squeezed my shoulder, as Yang Jie sometimes had. Her hand was ungloved, and my robe was in tatters. The sensation of her warm, callused palm seemed to flare against my bare skin, brighter than the glow-worms above us. It was … comfort. Human connection. I craved it, more of it, suddenly, as a dying man would crave one last word from his beloved, one last look at the sun, one last breath. My misery disappeared beneath that desperation as she leaned closer, the smile slowly fading from her face. The dark wells of her eyes stared into mine – searching, searching. Tingles of nerves and excitement rippled up and down my spine.

A long coil of hair fell forward to brush my cheek. It didn't smell of perfume, but of the black, burning smoke of the smelting fire. I stared into those mysterious cat's eyes, rapt.

"Dou Xianniang…"

She stiffened, sitting up abruptly. Her hand fell away from my shoulder and she cleared her throat. "We mustn't linger here. The Leopard will have launched a search for you by now – and there's no telling if someone might eventually stumble across the entrance to this place."

Though my shoulder felt chilled without the weight of her touch, I nodded, struggling to sit up. Struggling through the despair as it rose again. "Where are we, then?"

"Directly beneath the Stone Forest," she said, voice

tinged with irony or humour. Some private joke, perhaps. It seemed best not to ask – not now, after that strange moment.

She made no attempt to assist me as I rolled away from her and got my knees under me. I found that my bed had been a standard army bedroll, and my pillow a folded cloak of warm cloth. Across from me, a large pool of water, black and green in the eerie cave-light, lapped at a shore of pale sand. It was beautiful. It felt wrong, awful, that something so beautiful was hidden in this place of suffering and death.

"Are you listening?" she asked, severe, and I realized only then that she had been talking to me.

My entire body ached fiercely, from the top of my skull to the soles of my feet, but I was mobile, and time was of the essence. "Sorry."

"I said, there's a passage there" – she indicated a bulge in the rock – "that leads up to the place where the Stone Forest meets the bamboo one. If you follow the road, you can return to the city in less than a week on horseback."

"Horseback?" I questioned, startled. I turned my head to look at her – and froze in shock as her small hands cupped my face again, as they had in the black smoke and chaos of the smelter explosion. "What are you—"

Her red lips pressed firmly against mine. They were dry, with a faint, faint taste of sweet citrus, and for a dizzying instant I could feel her breath in my mouth. Then she drew back.

"There are supplies at the entrance of the passage. Make use of them, and don't tarry."

She released me and stood in a quick, supple movement.

I gaped up at her. "But – where are you going?"

"I have business of my own to complete. Goodbye, Corporal."

She turned away. Without thinking, I cried out, "No, wait!"

Like a snuffed candle, the glow-worms winked out.

I shut my mouth, shivering, listening to the quiet that enveloped me as completely as the shadows did. When the light of the worms slowly filled the stone chamber again, I already knew what I would see. I was alone there. Dou Xianniang was gone.

I touched my lips ... and realized for the first time that I had forgotten about my mask. She had seen my bare face.

And I didn't mind.

My saviour had not mentioned the length of the passage that would carry me to the surface, or how steep and rough the climb would be. By the time I found the narrow slit in the rock that gave on to the upper world, the real world, I was in such discomfort and so exhausted that I was ready to curse her for it, however little sense that made.

But then... Light, real light, daylight, on my face. It dazzled me.

I could hear birdsong and wind moving among leaves.

I could breathe real, cold, fresh air.

Dropping the bedroll and cloak, I craned my neck

back, staring up as the grey-dappled sky slowly swam into view, stretching my hands out to let the fine drizzle bathe them. It felt like being born again.

"I'm alive, Yang Jie…" I whispered. "I'm alive."

There was a shrill whinny and a decided thump. I whirled around, steadying myself with one hand on the outcropping of rocks behind me. Among tall green bamboo trees, I saw a campsite – what must have been Dou Xianniang's campsite – with a tamped-out fire, saddlebags and a saddle piled next to it. Tied to a tree on the other side of the ashes… Yulong.

I let out a shriek. Yulong answered with another whinny of his own, stamping his front hoof twice, impatiently. I must have almost flown across the little clearing. In the next instant my arms were around his warm, quivering neck. I breathed in the horsey smell with a feeling of blissful homecoming. Even when I felt his teeth close over my bare shoulder in a painful bite, I didn't let go.

"I'm sorry I left you behind. I didn't mean to," I mumbled, leaking tears into his dark mane.

Apparently satisfied, he released my flesh and began whuffling at my head, letting out a snort of dissatisfaction at the smell. He nudged at me, and I reluctantly stepped away, running my hands down his neck to savour the familiar coarse-silk sensation of his hide.

"I know. I stink. But a bath is going to have to wait, dear friend. We have a long journey ahead of us – and a very important message to deliver."

Twenty-eight

The two city guardsmen stationed outside the room were talking in low voices. I couldn't hear precisely what they were saying, but the occasional snigger that punctuated their words enabled me to guess.

Their sergeant was not laughing.

"You expect us to *believe* all this?" he asked, for what must have been the fifth time since I had been stopped at the Gate of Shining Virtue, refused entrance to the city, and accused of being a thief.

"I don't expect you to believe anything without corroboration, Sergeant Lo," I said. My voice – despite the many days since I had dosed myself with the tincture – was gravelly and rough, deeper than his. I was by now fairly certain it was going to stay that way.

It was not easy to hold on to my patience and my facade of calm, when all I wanted to do was leap up and kick the man repeatedly in the face. Not that I had a hope of successfully executing such an attack right now, unless he laid on the floor and let me do it. I made myself go on calmly, "Which is why I have asked for a message to be sent to General Wu Jiang at the—"

"Who do you think you are, boy? I've told you that General Wu will not be disturbed on my orders for the likes of you!"

"Please address me by my rank, Sergeant," I said crisply. "Even if you have no respect for me, you should respect the Glorious Brotherhood."

He gawped at me, then narrowed his eyes. "Why you little—"

The sniggering guardsmen outside broke off their conversation. There was an indignant shout, and then the door to the interrogation room burst open, admitting Wu Jiang, a dull brown cloak thrown on over plain leather armour. His face was flushed and his hair dishevelled. The general's helm, with the horsehair crest, was tucked under one arm. He must have been sparring or doing an inspection of the troops when word reached him I was here.

I felt a starburst of emotion in my chest at the sight of him – so many emotions, so painfully sharp, I could scarcely pick out joy from relief from fondness. *He's all right.* In my mind, I had been sure that he must be. No mere rebel could hope to overcome his superlative skills, his sheer strength. But so many awful things had happened, it had been hard to allow hope, even justified hope, to remain alive.

I got to my feet as quickly as I could, secure that the

expression on my shadow face revealed nothing but the respect due to one's superior officer, but struggling to conceal the telltale stiffness that gave away my still healing injuries. A week, especially a week of hard riding and sleeping on the ground, was not enough time to repair all the damage my captivity had done.

"General, Corporal Hua Zhi reporting." The salute lacked some of the necessary sharpness – my shoulder was still too sore to permit it.

The words were almost lost in Sergeant Lo's flustered kowtowing. I winced as his forehead bumped loudly against the floor in his haste to make his subservience clear. Wu Jiang ignored both my official greeting and the sergeant's obeisance. He stalked across the room and dragged me into a crushing bear hug.

His breath was a hot, almost soundless exhalation against my cheek. "I thought you were dead. My orchid, I thought—" A brush of lips next to mine, and then he was stepping away, putting me from him. His eyes met mine directly for a second and, without really knowing why, I had to put out my hand to steady myself on the wall.

"The emperor, sir? The crown prince?"

"We got them both to safety. It worked, Hua Zhi. Your plan succeeded."

I closed my eyes in unspeakable relief. "Thank you."

He nodded. Then he turned away, and when he faced the guardsman, Wu Jiang was the Young General again, the mantle of command gathered around him so that his rough cloak and workaday armour seemed to shine as brightly as gold.

"Why have you detained this man here?" he demand-ed. "Did he not inform you that he was a corporal of the Imperial Forces, and my aide-de-camp?"

"Sir – I – we didn't..." the sergeant stammered. With what seemed to be a great effort, he sat up, squaring his shoulders. "Sir, we didn't believe him. He has no official papers, looks like a vagabond – and he had a horse worth at least a hundred gold coins. We thought him a thief."

"Unacceptable," the Young General snapped. "I shall speak with your superior officers. Later. This man has been on a mission of the most vital importance to the war effort, and you have already delayed his return too long. Come, Corporal!"

He swept from the room. I scurried after, thanking my ancestors that Wu Jiang had the sense to have spies among the guardsmen.

An hour later, I was tearing gratefully into my first decent meal since the one I had stolen from Feng Shi Chong, seated on a cushion on the floor of the Young General's large but rather bare quarters in the barracks. After a thor-ough scrubbing using the officers' facilities – cleared for me on Wu Jiang's orders – a generous application of sooth-ing bruise balm – supplied by the army surgeons, without question, also on Wu Jiang's orders – and a fresh uniform, I felt like an entirely different person from the ragged urchin who had slunk up to the city walls that morning.

"I can hardly believe it," Wu Jiang said. His fingers danced with uncharacteristic restlessness over the papers I had given him, spread out across his desk. "Do you realize that you are the first person ever to escape from Feng Shi Chong? That you're the only person who has ever seen his base and lived to tell of it?"

"Barely," I reminded him, around a mouthful of soup.

His face tightened. "Don't."

"Sir." I stopped, took a deep breath and began again. "Wu Jiang. I'm sorry. But it was my duty. You know that you would have done the same in my place."

He shook his head, brushing a hand over his beard. Then, with an obvious effort, he forced his lips to curve. "I don't think I could have played the role of the emperor quite so convincingly."

There was no sign at all of his elusive dimple. My heart squeezed. "You'd look rather fetching in a crown, I think."

The feeble joke did not lighten his soberness. He began to roll the papers up. "You did more than well. This intelligence is priceless. At long last we have the advantage over him."

"Not if we don't act fast," I said. "I imagine that he and his army are racing right behind me."

"Then I'll be ready for them, by the heavens," Wu Jiang swore. "I will be ready."

"We," I reminded him.

Wu Jiang paused in the act of tucking the papers into his scarlet sash. "We."

In an abrupt movement, he stood from behind his desk, crossed the room and knelt beside me. I hastily put down my bowl of soup, holding myself still as he reached out to lay one large, warm hand on the side of my neck. His thumb brushed slowly down the line of my throat.

When he spoke again, his voice was husky.

"Hua Zhilan – may I – will you do me the honour…"

He wants to kiss me. Do I want to kiss him? I don't know! What do I say?

"May I see your real face?" he finished.

No. The reaction was as instinctive and all-encompassing as it had ever been. *I don't want to.* But I didn't know how to express that without giving offence. How could I, when the reason for my resistance was a mystery even to myself?

The pause drew out awkwardly. His lips flattened, but he nodded, removing his hand from my neck. "Very well. Soon. When this is all over."

And without hesitation, he leaned forward and pressed a firm kiss – my second kiss – to my mouth. I gasped into the touch, and felt his lips curve again against mine. When he drew back his dimple was in evidence at last.

"Up!" he said, leaping to his feet in a blaze of energy. "We must see the emperor."

This time, Wu Fen received us in the splendour of the official halls of the Centre of the Universe, among priceless artefacts and the massed ranks of the foremost figures of court. Even in my own splendour – a hastily altered dress uniform with gilding on the chest guard and vambraces, and my very first crimson cloak, attached with bronze clasps at the shoulders – I felt small and insignificant, and glaringly out of place. The curious stares and barely muffled whispers of curiosity from the onlookers as Wu Jiang and I approached the seven steps leading to the Dragon Throne didn't help.

You have faced the Leopard. Are you really going to allow these people, who could no more harm you than a flock of butterflies, to intimidate you?

I raised my chin. Without the need to consult a mirror, I knew that the hollow cheeks, assorted cuts and slowly fading bruises that decorated my bare face were all in place on the shadow one. They had been from the moment I rewove it on approach to the city gates. That was more of a comfort to me than the borrowed finery. I must look like a soldier back from the wars – and that was what I was.

"Now, remember," the Young General muttered to me from one corner of his mouth, lips barely moving. "News of the ambush has been suppressed as much as possible to avoid panic. Too many prominent figures died for us to keep it entirely secret from the court but, officially, it never happened. You mustn't directly refer to it. Follow my lead."

I froze mid-step, then had to scurry to keep up. How on earth was I supposed to explain what had happened without referring to the attack on the emperor? And why hadn't he told me this before? I shrugged my shoulders restively in annoyance.

We were now close enough to watch the emperor as she watched us. I swallowed hard. No mere riding outfit today, and no informality. She wore a gown of glowing white, embroidered with scarlet, cut low on her snowy breast. Her hair was bound up in the cross style, with three great combs of coral and gold holding it in place. A delicate painted peony decorated the centre of her brow, red to match her lips. She sat so still, and her expression was so serene, that she seemed a part of the golden throne she occupied – a flawless image of an immortal, with thirteen imperial five-clawed dragons writhing around her, eager to do her biding.

It was almost impossible to reconcile her with the woman I had seen sweating, shaking and afraid, hiding in a hole in the ground.

"You may address her Imperial Majesty," a palace official intoned, bowing.

Wu Jiang went down to his knee at the base of the seven steps, and I followed suit, pressing my lips together to hide my grunt of pain as the still swollen joint protested. He recited the formal address to his aunt, and finally moved on to the reason for our visit.

"I present to you one whom has served the army and the empire with the greatest courage and honour, and whom we both had the sadness to believe had perished in his service until today. Most honourable aunt, Corporal Hua Zhi has returned."

There was a faint murmur of interest at my name. I didn't know if it was because of my father, or if some here knew the true tale of what I had done.

The emperor's hand made a slight sign.

"You may rise," the palace official told us.

As I struggled to my feet, the emperor looked in my direction. Her face was more of a mask than my own, and I wished I could properly see her eyes. "Hua Zhi, I am gladdened that you still live. If what General Wu says is true, then we shall soon enter the final battle with the would-be usurper and traitor called Feng Shi Chong. In reward for your service, I now promote you to the position of captain of the Imperial Forces, and give you command of a company of your own, whom you shall have leave to handpick. You shall be on the front lines in the defence of the City of Endless Serenity, and will no doubt bring your house and the empire much glory thereby."

I know that my face – both my faces – must have lit up like fireworks in the night sky. The emperor's scarlet lips twitched in response, and I thought it was as much of a smile as she would allow herself here. Wu Jiang sucked in a breath as though he had been punched in the gut, jaw clenching. His hands opened and closed. But he said nothing.

The emperor's gaze moved to him. She paused for a moment, as if perturbed by his obvious agitation, then went on. "Most honourable nephew. You too have earned great honour by your courage and loyalty, and deserve to be rewarded appropriately. In light of your extraordinary service, I hereby elevate you to the rank of Royal Duke of Wu, and confer upon you the responsibility of regent. You are now my son's foremost guardian. Should I be taken prematurely from the earthly realm to my place among the stars, you shall protect and guide him until he is old enough to ascend the Dragon Throne and take up his place as Son of Heaven. In recognition of this new role, you shall retire from the Imperial Forces immediately after the Leopard is defeated."

Wu Jiang stood like a stone beside me. His face had lost all colour and expression, and his fists were shaking.

I bit my lip. She was effectively sidelining him.

He would be forced to give up the role for which he had trained his entire life, in order to – what? Play politics here at court? Dance attendance on the spoiled little prince? He would hate it. He was a warrior, not a courtier.

Then he turned to me, and I was shaken by the look in his eyes. It was not anger, or devastation – but something fiercer, darker. "I'm sorry," he said quietly.

He turned back to the emperor, and in the split second before he opened his mouth again, I knew what he was going to do. But I couldn't stop it. I couldn't do a thing.

"I am honoured beyond any measure by the privilege you have conferred upon me, Imperial Majesty. I accept with joy and humility. But before the promotion of Hua Zhi is written into official record, I must make a confession. I have been guilty of a deception on this soldier's behalf. Hua Zhi has no right to the rank of captain, or to serve in the Glorious Brotherhood at all. Hua Zhi, in fact, does not exist. The one before you is Hua Zhilan. A girl."

A babble of surprise and outrage burst among the courtiers. The palace official at the foot of the steps visibly recoiled from me, almost falling. And for the first time since we had entered the halls of the Centre of the Universe, I saw a real expression on the emperor's face. It was blank astonishment. Total disbelief. Her lips formed a perfect circle as her eyes jumped from Wu Jiang to me.

I cringed, shrinking down into myself under a dark, crushing wave of shame. My armour was too tight and too heavy, my shadow face was strangling me, I could not breathe. *Dear ancestors, no. Take me away. Not this, anything but this.*

I wanted, for the second time in my life, to die.

The Young General did not flinch from the uproar. His eyes remained fixed on Wu Fen, face resolute.

"Is this ... some kind of jest?" the emperor demanded, and by the end of the sentence her voice had gone from unsure to icy, her hands clutching like claws at the arms of the throne.

My own hands rose, unthinking, to clasp at my waist. I bowed my head. My gaze fixed, insensibly, upon the polished, upturned tips of my boots against the marble inlaid floor. I didn't dare look up, couldn't bear to look up. It was a woman's posture.

"Imperial Majesty, I am entirely in earnest," Wu Jiang responded calmly. "Hua Zhilan is the oldest daughter of our great former general Hua Zhou – who was crippled in the Battle of the Thousand Steps in defence of Emperor Gao Zi. When the call to war came..." And without any sign of chagrin, without a hesitation or a stumble, Wu Jiang smoothly unfolded my story – every secret I had told him, that he had promised faithfully to keep – as if it were nothing more than a fireside tale recited for the amusement of the court.

He painted a fine picture of me as a chaste, virtuous and noble maiden, noted that a boy with my banner-breaking gifts would have felt called to serve the empire in its time of need as I had, reminded the emperor that I had saved his life at least three times, and compared me once again to Dou Xianniang.

The tale, the tale Wu Jiang had made of me, of my life, came to an end. Wu Jiang fell silent. But the halls themselves were anything but quiet. The walls rang with voices, raised in jeers, concern and confusion. Among the tangled tapestry of words I heard the amber-robed palace official speak, not overly loud, but with crystal clarity, "The girl must have been his whore, of course."

I squeezed my eyes closed.

"Enough!" The emperor's voice crackled like breaking ice, echoing through the vast vaults of the halls. The courtiers became instantly still. "Wu Jiang," she said into the silence. "You have been a party to this charade so far. What is your aim in exposing Hua Zhi – Zhilan, to me now?"

"I do not wish to cast any shadow upon this young woman's character," Wu Jiang said.

Too late, too late, too late…

"But although her service to Your Imperial Majesty has been remarkable so far, she is not fit to command a company in such a vital battle. My hope is that I may call upon your wisdom and mercy, and request that Hua Zhilan should be pardoned. Allow her to return home to her family as one who has fulfilled their military duty would. But if that is not your will, if you wish to punish her for her lie – then I ask that I should be punished, too, as an equal partner in the deception. She could not have succeeded without my connivance."

Oh, how kind, how very kind of him, I thought bitterly, staring down at my shoes again. *To attempt to shield me by taking credit even for my perfidy.*

"Hua Zhilan."

I started at the emperor's sharp snap of my name. My neck seemed to fight me, muscles twanging, bones grinding, as I forced myself at last to look up. What would I see? Condemnation? Contempt? Hatred?

But the emperor's eyes rested on me without visible expression. Her hands had returned to her lap. I waited.

"Have you anything to say in your defence?"

A million things. As many excuses as there were stars in the sky. A desperate plea for understanding. A passionate cry for forgiveness. *I only wanted to serve you. I only wanted to prove that I could do it. I love you. I love my empire. I wanted to be valuable to you.*

I wanted others to see me for who I really was.

Don't you see that?

Can't you, of all people, see me?

Wordlessly, I shook my head.

I thought something in her eyes hardened. She stared at me for another endless breath, then inclined her head. "Very well. In light of the exemplary service you have rendered, and my nephew's words on the purity of your character and intentions, I will pardon you. Return home to your father, Hua Zhilan, if that is where you are needed."

Her tone implied that she doubted very much Hua Zhilan was needed anywhere at all. She made another sign at the palace official, who shook himself, averted his eyes pointedly, and announced: "This audience is over! Please leave at once!"

Twenty-nine

The emperor was gone. The officials were gone. The courtiers and noblemen were gone. Only Wu Jiang and I remained in the great halls now, and the vast space felt as cold and silent as a long-abandoned tomb, peopled only by the dry bones of my ambitions and hopes.

I stood, frozen, still gazing down at my own feet. My feet in the soldier's boots that they no longer needed – that they no longer had the right to wear.

Hua Zhi has no right to the rank of captain.

Hua Zhi does not exist.

The one before you is a girl.

"I'm sorry," the Young General said.

It was the second time he had said that. I had no answer. There was nothing to be said. It was all over. Everything I had gone through, everything I had achieved. All for nothing. Nothing. A hollow, white void yawned inside me. Once that emptiness had been filled with fear. Now the thing that I feared above all else had come to pass. There was nothing left. Nothing to feel but emptiness. Emptiness, shame and sorrow.

"I had to do it," he said. There was no pleading in his tone. A hint of sadness, yes, but mostly firm certainty. "The battlefield – a real battlefield – is no place for you. This had gone on long enough. If I had let you fight without me, your secret would have been exposed, and you would have been shamed, Hua Zhilan, and dishonoured. And all your men with you. This was my only choice."

Did he want an argument? A debate? Something he could work with, twist and push and manipulate until he made me see it his way? Once again, I shook my head wordlessly, and made to turn away.

His hand caught at my wrist. Gently but inexorably, he forced me to face him. "Look at me. Speak to me."

I did neither.

"Rage and shout if you must, but at least do me the courtesy of acknowledging my existence!" Temper was rising in his voice now. "Can't you see how much I risked for you today? I was willing to die with you, if that was what she decreed."

"You knew she would never order that," I said wearily. I made no attempt to break free of his hold. What did it matter now? There was no one to see him handling me so familiarly, and even if there had been, how could they think less of me than they already did? The tale of the Young General's mistress – *a girl! Pretending to be a soldier! Can you believe it!* – would be all over court before the marble terraces outside had finished ringing with the courtiers' footsteps, and all over the city before curfew was called.

My family would probably receive word of it before they saw me again.

I had wanted to save them, to protect them and do them honour. Now everything would be ruined. Our name would be destroyed. My mother would never recover from the shame and my father... *Oh, Father. I failed you. Father, I am so sorry.*

Wu Jiang twitched my reply away like a restive horse flicking off a fly. "You don't know her as well as you think."

I looked away, unable to stand the sight of his face. *I trusted you.* "I never asked you to risk anything. I never asked for anything at all."

"What is that supposed to mean?"

"You were the one who made all the promises. And broke them."

My voice was dead and flat, emotionless. My words didn't even tremble. I wondered if my face was doing that thing Yang Jie had hated so much, the blank thing, my illusions simply unable to convey the depth of my feelings.

How I wanted Yang Jie now. How I wished...

"Is that what's the matter?" Wu Jiang asked, suddenly softening. His hand slid down my armoured wrist, attempting to entwine our fingers. I let my hand hang limp, still unwilling – unable – to find the energy to struggle. After a moment he gave up and clasped my hand between both of his instead. Cradling it as if it was ... fragile. Breakable. "I'm not trying to get rid of you. This doesn't change anything between us. I will keep my promises to you. After the war is over and the empire is safe, I will come for you, and I will meet your father and mother. And then I will bring you back here, to my home, and you and I shall be together."

He gazed at me ardently. It was clear, horribly clear, that he did not have any idea what he had done. None at all. How could a man of such intelligence understand so little?

"No." The word was like a heavy rock dropped into the quiet.

His patience was straining again. "I've already apologized. I will again, if you wish, but you must see that I had no choice. You must see this was for your own good."

A shrill, sharp-edged sound – the fey laugh that I had discovered within myself while travelling through the endless dark in an iron cage – broke from my lips. Now Wu Jiang flinched. His hands tightened on mine, but I had experience against attackers bigger and stronger than I: a twist and a jerk brought me free.

I stepped back when he tried to touch me again. "What you did was nothing to do with my good at all." Now rage was beginning to bubble up, prickling my skin and pounding in my ears. "You did this because you were afraid. You betrayed me because you are a *coward*."

His face flushed, eyes flashing with anger. "Take care how you speak."

"Why? What more can you possibly do to me now, Wu Jiang?" I asked, spreading my arms. "You have done what the Leopard himself could not do. You have destroyed me."

He baulked. "No, that's not—"

I raised one hand to silence him, and it shook, not with fear or upset, but with a fury that could gladly have torn him to pieces, and painted curses in his blood. I wanted to spit in his face, to scream at him. The effort of holding myself back made my voice emerge as a kind of low growl that echoed strangely from the jewelled pillars of the palace.

"If you had turned me in when you first discovered me, that would have been one thing. An officer doing his duty. But you didn't. You promised me that you would keep my secret, that I could serve my country. I was fit for the rank of corporal, fit to serve you in the Glorious Brotherhood, to fetch and carry and scribble for you. I was fit to save your life, and to defend the emperor, and sacrifice myself in her place if necessary—"

"But that's what made me see that this must end now!" he burst out. "It was sheer luck that you survived your ordeal – Hua Zhilan, I thought you were dead! I believed it! I wished I had died with you! How could you expect me to go through that again?"

I bared my teeth at him. "Women all over this empire must bear such a burden every day. If I were your wife or your concubine, you would expect me to wave you off to battle with love and encouraging words, and to wait patiently for your return. You would never stop to think of the courage that takes. The will that a woman must have, to live without knowing if her husband, the one who is her only protection from poverty, degradation and despair, is alive or dead. You *selfish*, spoiled prince. You were too afraid to let me go. And you had the nerve to call me unfit?"

I jerked around and began to walk away.

"Hua Zhilan!" he shouted, voice stony. "Return to the barracks. I will arrange for an escort to take you home. It's too dangerous now for a woman to travel the country alone."

The final cruelty. Without looking back at him, I replied, "I will never forgive you for what you have done today. You are the one who is unfit, Young General. Not me."

I stalked through the glittering pillars, almost breaking into a run. But I wasn't fast enough. Before I had taken five steps, I felt the heat of my fury drain away, leaving me cold and empty again. I clenched my hands and gritted my teeth to keep tears at bay. I would not cry for him.

I would not let him see me break.

I ignored Wu Jiang's orders. I was already, in his eyes, a woman in a man's uniform. Already insubordinate and insolent. I might as well be absent without leave, too. If Wu Jiang decided to have me flogged to death, it would at least save me the trouble of returning to my family and seeing the shame on their faces. So, riding through the city streets on Yulong's back, I asked myself: what would a man – a real man like Wu Jiang – do in this situation?

There was only one answer.

Midway through the third cup of cheap, throat-burning wine, I realized that Wu Jiang hadn't even presented my papers – the vital papers for which I had nearly died – to the emperor. The most urgent transfer of intelligence, in the face of an imminent invasion of our capital, and it had been deferred because he was too worried about his potential concubine.

It was laughable. I would laugh at it.

How was he going to explain that one to his aunt, I wondered? Meanly, I decided that he would probably seek to ameliorate her wrath by claiming the discovery of the intelligence for himself. After all, it was very evident that his idea of honour and mine were rivers that had never flowed together.

I didn't allow myself to suffer any pangs of concern for the war effort. Not a single one. It was nothing to do with me any more.

Yes, at this instant my comrades must be scrambling to succeed at an impossible task, forming a viable defence against an attack that could come from within their own city walls at any time. Yes, the identity of the traitor and the location of the tunnel entrance were both still unknown. Yes, I had planned to be there with them, fighting alongside them and laying down my life for theirs, if necessary. But it wasn't my concern any longer. I had been cast out.

I was unfit.

A serving man approached the shadowy corner where I was working steadily through my bottle of wine and tentatively asked me to stop laughing. It was disturbing the other customers.

I snarled at him through my teeth.

No one came to bother me for the rest of the afternoon.

By the time the curfew drums began to beat, I was

so drunk that I had stopped wondering if and when the invasion would come. Didn't care at all. All I wanted was a bed that stayed still, since the chair and the floor of the room where I was drinking kept heaving up and down like a river boat. I complained to the owner about it. He apologized earnestly, and had the serving man help me up the stairs to a room for the night. I heard a cheer go up behind me as I left, but didn't waste any thought on it.

Several hours later, I woke to darkness and a headache that turned my own heartbeat against me, transforming each thump of my blood into a hammer blow that rattled my ear drums in my skull. My stomach churned with sickness, and my stupid eyes were already filling with tears.

I still remembered everything in excoriating detail, but now I was also ill. The man's solution had failed me.

This, I thought miserably, *should not have been a surprise.*

Flowers on my bedroll, sweets, a new sword and a few kind words… I had allowed myself to be wooed into trust by these foolish things, and now I was justly punished.

The Young General. The fairy-tale prince. Handsome, intelligent, charming and gallant. What maiden wouldn't fall all over herself to become his *woman*?

I didn't know him at all. And he didn't know me. We had never had a single real conversation, had we? He hadn't sought one – and neither had I. We had colluded to keep our interactions on the shallowest level in every respect. Me, because I hadn't really wanted a relationship with him, hadn't wanted to play the role of "girl" for anyone, but had been too cowardly to admit it to myself or him. And he? Because he hadn't believed there was any other way to interact with me.

He hadn't thought there was more to know.

I remembered a little rhyme that my mother had taught me when I was a child. She had often repeated it to me during our weaving lessons:

> *"To become a master of any art,*
> *One must possess the hand,*
> *The eye,*
> *And the heart.*
> *Only two,*
> *Will not do."*

Was love an art? Building a friendship and the foundation of a family? I thought perhaps it was. This was what had been missing from all of my interactions with the Young General. Heart. Mine and his. How could anyone really care for another person if they did not seek to know them?

Wu Jiang had treated me like a figure from a ballad or epic poem. Like a fantasy woman. That sounded wonderful. But in reality it was terrible. In his head, that was all I was. An exquisite paper doll that walked and talked and breathed. Not a real person. Not a human being, like him, with my own ambitions, fears, passions, dreams. He had seen me as … a thing. An object. Something to be won and owned. A representation of his ideal.

An honourable man, I thought suddenly, should not have spoken of his feelings while I was in his power as his direct subordinate. He would have taken steps to remove me from his chain of command, even if that removed me from his presence. Instead, the Young General, seeking to secure his possession, had ensured that I was under his hand and eye at nearly all times. He had thought that was the way to entrap my heart.

It had nearly worked. Not quite. No. Not quite. He just couldn't stop himself from pushing me, could he? Pushing me at all the wrong moments and in all the wrong ways. Whenever he tried to force me closer, instinctively I had drawn back. But I couldn't flatter myself that I had been entirely immune to him, to this seemingly perfect ideal of manhood, and with a little more time...

I had been so very stupid.

The only person who had known *me*, seen me for who I truly was and cared for me anyway, had been Yang Jie. But I had not been ready to accept that understanding when he offered it. I hadn't wanted to be known, to take the risk of laying myself open to his perceptive eyes. I had been sure that if even one person saw through me, subjected me to questions or doubts, then the new self – the true self – that I was busily discovering, would fall apart. And so *I* pushed *him*. Pushed him away.

I told myself that it was to protect my secret, to protect his safety. That the world was too dangerous for us to be together. But it was just cowardice. I had not been brave enough to trust him to love me, or to trust myself to love him back. In my own way, I had been as cruel in my fear as Wu Jiang in his.

If I had been honest with Yang Jie, things would have been entirely different between us. Perhaps it would have changed nothing that happened during the ambush. Or perhaps... But even if not, I would have had something. Something of him to remember and cherish, something that was real, before I lost him for ever.

I rolled over and buried my face in the sheets, letting tears leak out and pool, hot and uncomfortable, in the hollows on either side of my nose.

Close by in the narrow room, there was a soft, telltale click. The sound of the screen door unlocking.

My hands curled slowly into fists among the bed-clothes. I focused on my breathing, forcing away my awareness of headache and nausea so that I could find my *qi*. With an effort that made my muscles tremble like plucked wires, I thrust the energy out of my pores, cloaking myself in a new illusion. That of rumpled sheets. The flat plains of an unmistakably empty bed.

If they were here to rob me then my saddlebags, thrown carelessly down next to the bed, would be their target. If murder were their aim, they would search the room for me. Which would it be?

I heard a cautious step – and then a surprised breath. They had expected to find the room occupied. No movement towards the saddlebags. I tensed, readying to fling myself from the bed and fight.

"Corporal, are you here?" a familiar voice asked softly. "I'm calling in that favour you owe me."

Thirty

"You are aware the curfew is in effect?" I muttered grumpily, pulling the folds of my cloak up around my face as I slunk through the darkened alley.

"Astonishingly, yes," Dou Xianniang replied over her shoulder, sounding both exasperated and amused. "This way, to the left."

"We're going to be caught."

"I've never been caught before."

I choked with outrage. "That's how we met!"

"Shhh! Yes, but that's the only time it ever happened. Through here."

We turned right this time, and I saw that we had reached a dead end in the alley, an awkward, cramped little space hemmed in by walls on both sides. It stank of stale piss and rotting food. A small creature scurried over my foot and I tried to restrain my panicked jump.

Clearly no one, including the department of municipal maintenance, paid much attention to this area.

Dou Xianniang waded fearlessly through piles of rubbish, reached in among the layers of half-dead creepers that covered the wall dividing this ward from the next, and then pulled back, leaning on her heels to utilize her full body weight.

A section of the wall swung slowly away, trailing a fine net thickly decorated with dead leaves, vines and cobwebs.

"This is completely illegal," I protested, shocked. "The city statutes – anyone who knows about this could be arrested and flogged."

"The people who know about this are well able to keep a secret. And I don't believe for a moment that a person who has broken so many of the army's laws really cares about city statutes. Now stop spluttering and help." She ducked under the carefully constructed mess of vegetation. "We have to pull it shut from the other side and make sure it doesn't show."

I swallowed more protests and followed her, helping to push the camouflage net up and out of the narrow opening in the wall, and then drag that swinging section – cleverly built of wood that had been painted to blend in with the bricks – back into place. Once on the other side, in another narrow and less than fragrant alley, Dou Xianniang dragged heavy broken boxes and more rubbish into place to conceal the secret opening.

"Where are we going *now*?" I asked as she led me away from the unlit alley on to a main road. Brightly coloured lanterns – and brightly coloured ladies – decorated the street, and music and laughter flowed around us like water. This was the northern quarter.

Dou Xianniang, rearranging her own cloak so that her face was even more difficult to make out than usual, replied, "I told you. The place I usually stay here in the city."

"But where is that? And if you have a place in the northern quarter – and a secret exit – then why in the world were you climbing over the wall that night we met?"

"Because I had other places to be," she said. I noted her avoidance of the first question, but before I could point it out, she went on, "And the guards were patrolling this part of the city too closely that night for me to risk using that particular way out. I'm going to explain everything you need to know later, but for now, put your arm around my shoulder and act drunk. Drunker, I mean."

"I'm entirely sober just now," I said, obeying her and trying to hide my wince as the movement pulled at bruised ribs. "Unfortunately."

"Were you always this whiny?" She laughed suddenly, a low, husky sound that sent an odd shiver down my spine. "Actually, never mind. You were."

A pair of guardsmen walked by, faces alert but posture relaxed. I watched them pass with a frown. Where was the Leopard's invasion? Had it been foiled before it started, and the story suppressed again? But surely victory over the rebels ought to be celebrated for public morale. Had they worked out the location of that tunnel entrance somehow?

Or had the invasion come at all?

What if it was happening right now—

"I can hear your brain whirring," she whispered, her breath disturbing the fine hair next to my ear. I shivered again, fingers curling in the material at the shoulder of her cloak. I almost missed her next words. "Quick, in here."

She yanked me sideways into the gap between two buildings. One fine-boned hand darted out and tapped a complex pattern on a narrow door. It opened silently, light spilling out into the dark gap. Dou Xianniang slipped inside. I took a deep breath, reminded myself that I had little to lose any more, and stepped after her.

Inside was … not what I had expected. I shrugged the hood of my cloak back, looking around curiously. The shabby receiving hall was small and badly lit. An elderly woman sat by a glowing fire, rocking a baby and humming low in her throat. She didn't open her eyes, or acknowledge our presence in any way. Wooden toys were abandoned on the floor at her feet, over a thick rug where a toddler slept, snuffling out bubbles of drool.

The person who had let us in handed her lantern to Dou Xianniang, then closed and locked the door behind us. She, too, held a child – a girl of four or five, balanced on her hip. The little one regarded us with large, wary eyes, chewing on her small fist. There was a purple, spreading bruise on her lower arm. It was the shape of a man's hand.

The woman herself was young, well-dressed and remarkably pretty. An old brand puckered the flesh of her left cheek. I recognized the shape as one applied to the families of traitors, if they were lucky enough to escape execution. From the size and positioning, the paleness of the scar, it had been done when she was very small.

"This is him?" the woman asked Dou Xianniang in hushed tones, eyes darting shyly away from me.

"Yes. I'll take him through to my room in a moment. Is Li Li all right?"

"In her body, at least. You must speak to her when you have the chance."

"I will. Thank you, Sun Mei."

"Good luck." Sun Mei allowed her eyes to meet mine again for an instant. "And to you."

I followed Dou Xianniang and the soft glow of the lantern's light into a narrow, dark corridor. The lack of space and the shadows made my fists clench involuntarily. I breathed slowly, seeking calm. "What is this place?"

"I call it the safe house. It's for women and children who need somewhere to hide, a little piece of quiet, security and calm, before they gird themselves to start new lives. Women who've fled from ill-treatment, abuse, cruel husbands and families, forced prostitution. Some of the ladies of the northern quarter set it up many years ago. In recent years it has also become the centre of my operations."

"Your … operations?"

Dou Xianniang drew back a paper-and-wood screen and gestured me ahead of her. The room beyond was small and bare, holding only a narrow, neatly made bed, a low writing desk and stool, and, incongruously, a small potted bamboo plant in one corner. There wasn't even a window.

Dou Xianniang quickly lit the stubs of two candles from the lamp and placed them on the desk, then sat down on the stool, gesturing for me to take a seat on the bed. Her hands clasped around her knees, then unclasped, then knotted together in her lap. I perched tentatively, unsettled by the obvious display of nerves.

"Now that I have you here, I'm not entirely sure where to begin," she admitted after a moment. She hadn't taken off her cloak, and I couldn't see her face at all under the folds of cloth.

I wet my bottom lip. "You need me to do something for you."

"Yes."

"Then start by telling me what it is."

She laughed that low, beautiful laugh again. "It's not so simple. Let me … let me tell you a story first. If you can understand it, understand me, perhaps you will do what I ask. Do you agree? Will you stay and listen until I'm finished?"

I was tempted to point out that surely, if she had come to fetch me in the middle of the night, time was short, and stories could wait. But her head was bowed, and her shoulders rounded. She looked small again, as she had when I first saw her the night I "rescued" her. Aware that I was probably being manipulated, I nevertheless let out a sigh of assent. "Very well."

Her hands steepled in her lap, almost a position of prayer. Then she pushed back her hood, allowing the waves of dark hair to fall forward over her shoulders. The lamplight made it gleam with deep red-gold lights.

"I took the name Dou Xianniang three years ago. Whether the first Dou Xianniang truly existed, or was simply a story, I believed in her mission – to protect the innocent from those who would harm them. I used the identity as ... my armour. A larger than life figure, who would never give way to fear or doubt." I heard her next breath shudder before she went on. "But I was born under a different name.

"Our house was of middling wealth and influence, but great ambition. When I was thirteen, my father made a gift of me to Emperor Gao Zi. He hoped I would win him power by becoming a favoured concubine, but the emperor already had hundreds of them. My house was not prominent enough to propel me into their ranks automatically, and I had no remarkable beauty or talent of my own. I was pretty, of fair intelligence, and an above average dancer, so I became one of the dancing girls who entertained the emperor and his guests at banquets.

"In some ways it was a good life. Safety, warmth, good food. Friends. We were treated quite kindly, especially compared to what I had been used to in my father's house. But in other ways ... in others it was torment. I never caught the eye of the emperor himself, but his guests often – made use of me. That was why I was there, after all. Some of the girls didn't mind it, but I just ... I couldn't bear it. You see, I was – I was in love."

She paused, lifting her hands to her face. I held my breath behind my teeth, watching her warily, as if the slightest movement or sound might frighten her away, or cause her to attack.

After a moment she dropped her hands. "Her name was Zhang Jing. One of the emperor's lower ranking concubines."

A woman. My heart did something strange: a leap and then a sudden drop.

"The emperor was old by then. He mainly kept to a few favourites and his new empress. Zhang Jing never had the privilege of lying on the Dragon Bed. But because she was an official concubine, and belonged to the emperor alone, no one else could touch her. She tried to have me elevated but I was already seen as … used. It was intolerable for both of us. Then the old emperor died.

"The women of his household – the ones who had no rank of their own, and hadn't given him children – were to have their heads shaved and be sent away to nunneries. It was a dream come true for us, a way out. She had already been saving any jewellery she received, and her allowances. When the time came for all of us to begin travelling, we ran away in the dead of night. We found a small village in the middle of nowhere and claimed to be widowed sisters. No one cared about us, no one was looking for us – we were safe. It was a simple life, and it was good. We were happy together. We had *earned* that happiness."

She stopped, drawing her lower lip between her teeth. Her voice cracked as she whispered, "And then … the Leopard came."

I covered my mouth with one hand, as if I could shield myself from the horror her voice conjured in my imagination. I saw the burned village of the bamboo forest.

The brittle, gnawed bones. The bloody scene in that little house by the river. What could I possibly say?

She went on in short, jerky bursts, as if forcing herself to speak. "When it was over, everything was gone. But somehow I survived. It was one of the first attacks and – they didn't call him the Leopard then. No one knew who he was, except me. I had seen him once, at court. I knew he was Feng Shi Chong. I vowed to find him. To avenge Zhang Jing, and all of them. So I became Dou Xianniang and I learned what I needed to know. I fought. Stole. Lied. Saved people where I could. Nearly died a few times. I made allies, contacts among the women and eunuchs of a dozen cities and towns. I stalked him, lost him, found him again. It's been three years and he has only grown stronger. Gained more ground. Now I fear that he will take the throne, and escape justice for ever."

"They won't let that happen," I said softly, when the silence had gone on long enough that I was sure she wouldn't speak again. "I brought back valuable intelligence from Feng Shi Chong's lair. They know his plan now."

"Do they?" She made a clicking noise with her tongue, straightening up with a toss of her hair, as if she could slough the shadow of tragedy from her back. "I'm not so sure, Hua Zhi. I don't think he even knows his plan. That's what's so dangerous about him.

"He eats the flesh of women and children. Murders his own men, his best men, gruesomely, on a whim. Throws tantrums and falls down upon the floor screaming and rending his clothes. I've intercepted communications from him that were nothing but gibberish. I thought at first it was a code, but most of it was ranting, self-loathing, like the last sputters of thought from a dying mind. I've learned that some weeks he never leaves that treasure room where he has his bed. I believe, and have believed for some time, that he's simply not capable of what he has achieved. A short-lived and bloody reign of terror, yes. But the strategy behind this astonishing success? No. Someone else is commanding his army. He's just a figurehead."

"The emperor was convinced there was a traitor within the walls of the palace," I said slowly. "And I found evidence to prove it."

"More than a traitor. More than just a spy. Maybe Feng Shi Chong started the rebellion, but this person is in control of it, and him, now. My belief is that they've used the Leopard as their strong arm, to destabilize the empire and establish ideal conditions for them to seize control themselves. Or else the Leopard would have long since spent his men's lives and his own in some grand, gory spectacle."

This coincided so neatly with my own questions about the Leopard's strategy that I could not dismiss it. But still… "Say you're right. As long as this traitor remains at large the emperor and the empire itself are in terrible danger. But what do you intend to do about it? I'm a disgraced ex-soldier, absent without leave, who was lucky to get away without being flogged in public this morning. You're a famous outlaw who's actually an ex-dancing girl who also probably has a price on her head." I shrugged wearily. "We don't know the identity of the traitor, and no one is going to care about our theories anyway."

"We don't need anyone else to believe us." Her shoulders squared. "My contacts – my spies in the palace? Every single one of them went quiet after midday today. None of the scheduled evening reports arrived. I sent a friend to investigate – a young woman who sells fruit and other things to the gate guards sometimes – and an armed squad of men whom she'd never seen before beat her for daring to approach. She barely dragged herself back here. Someone has sealed the palace up. Someone with a lot of power. And there's only one reason for anyone to have done that."

"The traitor is making their move. They're going to make another attempt on the emperor," I whispered, a chill whispering over the back of my neck.

"Exactly. If we can get in there, get access to the emperor's chambers – we can catch them in the act and end this once and for all."

I felt my lower jaw drop, but was powerless to do anything about it. The silence dragged out as I stared at her in growing disbelief. "Are you … insane?" I finally managed to ask. "You – you think that we could break into the Centre of the Universe? Into the Dragon Chambers? You and me and whose army, Dou Xianniang? And even if we could manage it – which we can't – they'd just arrest us and execute us for daring to be there! I told you, no one is going to care about our theories!"

"I think they'll care if we catch someone as they're about to strangle the emperor in her sleep," she said with sudden dryness, folding her arms.

I shot up to my feet. She took a step back.

"If the traitor is as high up as you say, he or she would just tell the guards that *we* were the intruders, and stand by making convincing faces of shock while we were dragged away to our deaths! And that's if this all unfolded the way you think it will, which you have no way of knowing. We could get there too early, too late, or nothing could happen at all, and then what? I – this is what you wanted me to do? Be a part of your suicide mission? No." I shook my head feverishly. "All I have left is my life. I'm not going to throw it away for this."

She took another step back, blocking the door squarely. "I saved your life."

There was a sharp pang deep inside me – the last of my honour, perhaps, dying – but I shook my head again. "That doesn't mean you own it. We're strangers. I don't trust you. I won't do it."

Dou Xianniang stared at me, either speechless or calculating. The room was too dim for me to see the expression in her eyes, but something made me look down, discomforted.

"What did they do to you?" she asked softly. "How did you become so … broken? So afraid?"

I made a scornful sound, and when my voice emerged it was harsh and ugly. "You don't know me. But you do know what happened to me today, don't you? Or else you wouldn't have known to look for me in that inn. So your question is already answered. There's only one person in this whole city that I would trust now – and he's dead."

I stalked forward until we were face to face. "Get out of my way. I'm leaving."

She remained motionless. "Not yet. I haven't finished my story. You said you'd stay until it was finished."

I swore savagely, banging my hand on the screen next to her head. "Stop playacting and move."

She didn't flinch. "Earlier this year, I was given information that something was wrong at the training camp run by Commander Diao – that the Leopard might have a spy there. I thought it presented an opportunity to discover the identity of the architect of the rebellion.

"With certain tweaks to my appearance I can easily pass as a boy. So I found a family who wanted to avoid sending their sickly son to war and bought his call-up papers. I took his place, infiltrated the camp, and found that it was home to an old acquaintance. One of my older brothers. He didn't recognize me, of course – he thought his sister dead – although I apparently reminded him enough of her that he tried to beat me to death. I think you will remember him. He was our captain. Lu Buwei."

"Captain Lu was your brother? But he was the Leopard's spy!" Then I stopped. Took a breath. Stepped slowly away from where I had been looming over her at the door. "*Our* captain?"

"That's right. I was in your barracks. You did know me. You do know me."

"Who…?" I kept backing away.

"Come on, Hua Zhi!" Her voice rose in sudden anger. "You must see it! I've been waiting for you to recognize me since that first night when you made me take down my hood, but you won't. It's like you don't want to. *Look at me!*"

I shook my head, staggering as my calves hit the edge of the bed. "No. No. This is a dream. He's dead. He died because of me…" My voice broke.

Her shoulders heaved with a deep sigh. "All right then. I'll prove it. Whistle."

I licked dry, numb lips. Swallowed. Blinked. Then I pursed my mouth and let out three long, high whistles. And from the potted green plant in the corner, there was a brief flutter of wings, and a familiar sweet trill of song. The song of a laughing thrush.

"Bingbing…" I breathed.

Thirty-one

"The arrow … the blood…" My knees buckled. I slumped down on to the edge of the bed, afraid to look at her. At him? No, no, I wouldn't believe it. If I let myself believe, even for one heartbeat, and it wasn't true… *"He's dead."*

Dou Xianniang came towards me cautiously, on soft feet, and sank down next to me on the bed. Close enough to touch. I inched away from her, shaking. Filled with a kind of fear that held me in the room more surely than iron chains.

"He's *dead*," I repeated. I could hear the pleading in my own voice.

"The arrow lodged in my armour. It nicked me, but it wasn't deep enough to be fatal." She tilted her head to one side, trying to force me to meet her gaze. "Most of that blood wasn't mine – it was from someone I'd just killed."

"He wasn't moving!"

"I hit my head on the edge of the fountain when I threw myself over you." She turned her face away, no longer seeking my gaze, and immediately, helplessly, my gaze fixed on her.

With a lurch of shock, I recognized the shape of her jaw. That elegant jaw I had studied so often that I could trace the line of it in my sleep, even in my nightmares.

No. No. Coincidence. It couldn't be real.

"When I woke up it was over," she whispered. "All that was left there were bodies. Just like before, just like when Zhang Jing died. I nearly went out of my mind, Hua Zhi. I didn't know what had happened to you, if you were dead or alive. I forgot about being Yang Jie, and my cover, about trying to discover the traitor. I took a chance that the Leopard's men would have transported you to the base in the caves – I had found the hidden passage into that place last year. I grabbed Yulong and a cache of supplies and went. The relief when I saw you there in the caves, alive ... and then my terror when I realized what was about to happen to you... The Leopard is lucky I only blew up his smelting tower. I wanted to rip him and his army apart with my bare hands. If it wouldn't have put you in danger then I would have tried."

Amidst her story my mind slowly arrowed in on one thing. Her voice, that beautiful low voice, so deep and husky for a woman... The timbre was slightly different, the words shaped more crisply, but the rhythms of speech, the underlying music of it...

"Y–Yang Jie?"

She turned back to me, touching my shoulder

as he – she – had so often done before. The touch of a comrade. But then the small, strong hand slid down and grasped mine. Her fingers caressed my own, delicately, as one would trace the petals of a flower. A shudder of fear and delight rocked my body, and gave way to a sense of warmth and safety – and then – I knew – *knew* – it was real.

Dou Xianniang. Yang Jie. They were the same.

"I'm sorry." My spine became water. I crumpled over her hand, taking it in both of mine and raising it to my lips. I pressed kisses and tears against it, feeling her tremble as she wrapped her other arm around my shoulders, pulling me into the shelter of her body. "I'm so sorry, Yang Jie. I should never have left you. I didn't trust you. I'm sorry. I missed you so much. I'm sorry."

I didn't even know if I was referring to my stupid stubbornness in pushing my friend away, or in not checking to see during the ambush if he was alive or dead, or if I meant my harshness just now. Maybe I meant all of it. I breathed in the scent of her long, silky hair as she moved still closer, and pressed my forehead into the crook of her neck. Her cheek came to rest, warm and solid and alive, against the side of my face.

"It's all right. I didn't trust you either, did I? I should have. I should have."

"Are you like me? Are you … complicated?" I asked, the words muffled in that long, glorious hair. Immediately, I regretted such a strange, vague question, but before I could take it back she – he – answered, laughing a little.

"Very. But not in the same way as you, I think. I can

do many things that men do, and I am good at them. I can pass as a man or boy. But no matter what others see, I am still a woman, inside. Yet I … I desire men and women in the same way. I love them not for their gender but regardless of it. Does that make sense?"

"I think so. I'm not like that, though. Inside. I was born as a girl, lived as a girl … yet I was never fully female in my soul. I know that now. Know why I never felt … right. Sometimes it's as though I'm entirely male. But … at other times, aspects of my femininity seem entirely natural. I don't know what I am. I don't know if there's anyone else like me." I hesitated. "Knowing that, do you think you could still care for me?"

"Idiot," she said, on a fond, exasperated laugh. "What do you think? Haven't you noticed my heart trailing around after you all this time?"

I laughed, too, in sheer relief. "No! Of course not. I used to wonder why you bothered with me at all!"

"Oh, I wondered that a few times myself," she said. "But all the same, I was sure everyone who met us must think me a lovesick fool. Hua Zhi – about the Young General. You … the two of you seemed … very close." There was remembered pain in her voice.

"No," I said thoughtfully but with emphasis. "We were never close at all. Not in any way that mattered. I think we intrigued each other for a while. It was a kind of hero worship on my part, for the traits he had that I wished I could emulate. But then he discovered my secret, and decided that he wanted me and he – he gave me no choice. Not really. And I was so lonely. All I wanted was to be with you. You weren't a fool – that was me. I couldn't admit it to anyone, not even myself. I've made us both so needlessly unhappy..."

"Come here." She cupped my face in her hands, fingers gentle on my battered skin.

This was no hasty press of mouths. It was sweet, and slow. Her lips captured my lower one between them, and wet it with a soft swipe of her tongue that made thrills dance across my skin. The backs of my eyelids prickled with tears. These lips belonged to my best friend. That wonderful, hauntingly familiar smell was Yang Jie's. This lemon-peel-scented breath, and these hands, the warmth of this shape... I felt my cheeks flushing with heat as my breathing quickened.

I drew my fingers through the soft strands of hair that I had always admired, ran my thumb along that unmistakable jaw, traced the delicate shape of an ear that had struck me from the very beginning as perfectly formed – and laughed helplessly into her mouth when she twitched, ticklish.

"Forgive me," I said, laying my hand against the side of her cheek.

"If you will forgive me," she said, far too serious.

"You know that I will. Always, always, always. There is no me without you." I closed my eyes, realizing how close I had come to walking away, not only from her, but from ... everything. From who I was. "No. There is a me without you. But not one I like. You help me to remember the person I wish to be."

Roosting on the plant in the corner, Bingbing twittered.

A new question occurred to me.

"Was she Zhang Jing's?" I asked hesitantly.

"Yes. All I have left of her. She's getting old now. I don't suppose she'll be with me much longer."

"She will always be with you. Zhang Jing will always be with you."

She kissed me again, as if to silence me. As our lips parted, I whispered, "I will always be with you."

She shook her head. "Don't make promises like that. You can't know you'll keep them."

"I can. It doesn't matter what happens to me or you." With an all-consuming, exultant thrill, I knew it for truth. "I'll always be with you, my dearest friend. I won't abandon you again. Even when both our bodies are dust and ashes, mine will lie with yours. That I can promise. I do."

She closed her eyes as if stricken, and I saw the glint of moisture among the dark lashes. With curious fingers, I touched the scar that marked her white skin. As I had suspected, my fingertip came away red. "Make-up."

She blinked rapidly, defeating her tears, then looked at me and deliberately raised a brow. I shrugged, conceding that I should have seen through the disguise before. But in my defence, with lead paint whitening her complexion, dark lines painted around her eyes and her lips stained red, she really was almost unrecognizable.

Yet, I had always thought Yang Jie was distractingly pretty. And I had felt compelled to help that young woman that night, even though she appeared a stranger, and it was a risk to my own wellbeing. Speaking of which…

"You owe me one gold coin, two silver coins and four

coppers," I said, mock severe. "And a new money-purse."

She snorted, and the sound was all Yang Jie. "I have your money-purse – and all the coins are still in it. I only took it because I was so hurt and annoyed with you. Rescuing strange girls when you'd ignored me for weeks! I felt terrible afterwards. I was trying to figure out how to explain things to you that day, before the ambush."

"I understand why it was hard. But you could have told me who you were when you saved me from the Leopard – I promise, I would have been so happy. I would have welcomed you back with open arms."

"I should have," she admitted. "I was just … afraid."

I sighed. "Of all people, I can understand how that feels."

"Yes." She sat back, sliding her hands from my face to my shoulders, and with sorrow, I saw her expression change to one of grim resolution. "But you also know what it means to walk through the fear and do what needs to be done. Hua Zhi, you do know me, and you can trust me. Will you come with me to the palace? Fight beside me to avenge the woman I loved, and all the victims of this senseless war? Now, tonight, before it's too late?"

All my arguments, the protests born of resentment and fear, had fallen away. This, her mere existence, was … a gift. From fate, or the heavens. It was a sign. Perhaps the sign I had been searching for my whole life. My destiny was not to die in the emperor's place after all. It was not even to save the emperor. At last I knew what I should have realized the moment I first met Yang Jie and was fortunate enough to have him call me friend.

My great destiny was simply to be at this person's side.

"On one condition," I said.

"Name it."

A grin broke across my face. "Tell me what I should call you."

"You may call me your heart, if you wish," she said, smiling. "But Lu Wan Hua would also be acceptable."

I took her hand and squeezed it, wishing to see her smile in return. "We share a name, Lu Wan Hua."

The corner of her lips quirked up before she bowed her head, surprisingly shy. "I've wanted to tell you that for a long time, Hua Zhi. Almost since the moment I met you." She cleared her throat. "Now – enough sweet-talking. We have an empire to save."

Dressed in borrowed, close-fitting garments of plain black, we approached the northern wall of the palace, and scaled it. With our training, and Lu Wan Hua's inside knowledge of the guard's movements, it was a simple if time-consuming matter to avoid detection.

"Later, if we survive this, and the emperor doesn't have us both killed," I said in an undertone, "I shall have some suggestions for her about her security."

"Quiet," Lu Wan Hua said, but I could read the smile in her voice. Then she swore, turning back at the corner of the wall and signalling me to a stop. "They've put a guard on the kitchen door. One I don't know."

We couldn't afford the noise of a fight. I ground my teeth in thought, looked around at the garden, then nodded. "If we can lure him this way, I think I can knock him out without killing him. With your help."

"I'm not exactly dressed for allurement," she said, looking down at herself.

"Don't be so conceited," I teased. "There are other ways."

She gave me an unimpressed look – that same look I knew so well – and I restrained a warm yearning to grab her and... No, she would hit me right in the mouth, and I would deserve it.

Later, if we survive this and the emperor doesn't have us both killed, I repeated to myself like a mantra. I was filled with lightning-crackles of excitement and anxiety, and they were only partly caused by the deadly serious nature of this mission.

I leaned around the edge of the wall, located the guard standing rigidly outside a humble wooden door – illuminated by the nearly full moon – and let out a soft whistle. The sort of noise that might belong to a bird. Or, if one had a suspicious mind, a human.

The guard's head tilted. He was the suspicious type. Excellent.

A determined push on one of the wooden frames that supported a plum plant, espaliered on the wall, made the leaves rustle dryly. Again, the sound could be innocent or suspicious. But I was betting the guard wouldn't want to risk looking stupid by calling for anyone else's help before he had checked it out for himself.

The guard took a step forward.

I looked back at Lu Wan Hua. "Hide."

Then I put my foot on the wooden lattice and swiftly

scaled the wall, sending the plant shaking and rustling hard enough that I was sure the guard would break into a run. My side and knee throbbed with pain, my shoulder made unhappy grindings, and I was panting as I pulled myself up among the thick growth of fruit-bearing boughs that mantled the top of the wall. When I crouched low and peered down at the white stone path below, there was – as I had expected – no sign of Lu Wan Hua.

The guard was rounding the corner, his short spear at the ready.

I waited until he had passed just under my place of concealment to drop down out of the leaves on to his back. One arm I wrapped around his neck, cutting off his air. The other hand clamped over his mouth to deaden any sounds that might get out.

The man staggered, but didn't fall. His spear lifted and flailed, flying back towards my face…

In a shadowy flicker of movement, Lu Wan Hua reappeared. She wrenched the short spear from the guard's hands, whirled it around, underhand, and hit him squarely between the legs with the wooden end.

The guard's muffled scream vibrated through my hand. He crumpled to his knees. I went with him, tightening my grip around his neck even as I felt my own knee crunch ominously at the movement. "Come on. Give in. Give in."

His struggles weakened, and at long last his body went limp. Lu Wan Hua helped me lower him to lie on the path.

"He's still breathing," she said. "Good work. Let's hide him in the plants."

A moment later Lu Wan Hua knocked on the door.

There was no response. In the light of the moon, I saw her brows draw together. She knocked again.

"We – we're not supposed to let anyone in..." a young voice quavered through the wood.

"Su Yi? It's Dou Xianniang. Where's Mama Jin?"

There was some scuffling and murmuring behind the wood. I turned to place my back to the wall, eyes searching the dimly lit garden for signs of the next patrol of guards. Then the door flew open, letting out a spill of warm lamplight. A middle-aged woman with grey hair and her arm bundled up in a makeshift bandage waved us in. A crowd of frightened-looking servants scattered out of our way.

"Thank the Celestial Animals you're here, Lady Dou," the woman said. "Someone's gone mad. They're saying the palace is under siege, but there've been no official orders, and instead of readying the defences, they've locked everyone in their rooms. When I tried to leave the kitchen, one of the guards nearly broke my wrist! I looked for Shu Yuen, to warn the Young General what was happening, but the damn eunuch's nowhere to be found!"

"I knew it," Lu Wan Hua said, under her breath. "Mama Jin, we think someone's going to assassinate the emperor."

An audible gasp went up from the kitchen servants. Lu Wan Hua ignored it and went on urgently: "We must get to her chambers as quickly as possible. Can you help us?"

Mama Jin glanced at me uncertainly. "Well ... I..."

"You trust me, don't you? Well, you can trust him, too, with your life. I know the servants here have hidden ways to get about the palace in secret – ways that the guards won't know. Please. Help us."

Mama Jin bit her lip. "You've never done us a bad turn before. All right. Su Yi, come here. Take a lantern and lead them up the under stairs and down the south passage to where the Dragon Chambers are. And no dawdling, child – you come straight back and leave them to it."

"Thank you," I told the older woman fervently, as a young girl in primrose robes, yellow ribbons fluttering in her hair, ran forward. The other servants clustered around us, gently patting at our clothes and heads, murmuring, "Good luck, good luck."

I tried not to cringe away too obviously from their touch.

The yellow-gowned girl pressed the wall, low down, with her foot. A panel swung open, leading into a narrow, low-roofed corridor. "It's this way. You have to be quiet – sound carries through the walls." She picked up a lantern from a nearby table and darted ahead on silk-slippered feet.

We scurried after the glow of light shining through her yellow silks, skidding around narrow corners, pattering down a series of short, creaking staircases, and then up a long one – as steep in places as a ladder – before moving down a long, straight stretch.

Finally, Su Yi came to a halt, nearly causing Lu Wan Hua to run into her back. The servant girl held her finger to her lips and extinguished the lamp, plunging us into what seemed like total darkness. I sucked in a harsh breath, tensing, and felt Lu Wan Hua's hand on my shoulder.

Slowly, I began to perceive wavering, uneven lines of gold piercing the dark. It was the light from the rooms beyond the makeshift passages, shining through cracks and gaps in the thin walls. After a moment my eyes adjusted enough to be able to make out Su Yi's face.

When she could tell that both of us were able to see, she leaned in to whisper to us, her voice barely a breath in the quiet. "The Dragon Chambers are directly across from this opening. There should be four guards outside the door. One of them ... might be Jun Wei. He's nice. Good luck."

She turned and floated away. The shadows swallowed her pale golden glow greedily, and she disappeared like a ghost. A wistful look flickered across Lu Wan Hua's face. Perhaps the sweet girl reminded her of her own past here, of herself, or of the lost Zhang Jing. But when she turned her gaze to me, all traces of sorrow disappeared.

"If there are guards outside that door – even Su Yi's nice one – they will attack us on sight. They may be innocent, or they may be in on it, but either way, if we want to get past them and to the emperor, we'll need to fight. Are you ready?"

I drew my sword, carefully pointing the tip to the floor to avoid accidents in the small space. "I am."

She drew her own sword, then flashed me that enchanting smile – sunny and sly at the same time. Voice low and husky, she whispered:

"The moon is in the black heights of heaven,
And the autumn winds blow without cease.
Oh, let these far-off battles end, at last,
And bring my husband home, to my embrace."

I drew in a shaken breath. Another poem – a love poem, this time.

Without another word, she slid the door back and slipped out. I did the only thing I could. I followed, grip tightening on my sword hilt, ready to fight.

We both halted in the corridor, startled.

Before the great golden doors of the Dragon Chambers, there were no guards. No servants. I turned and looked back along the wide corridor that ran the length of this wing. This part of the palace had hundreds of rooms, and must normally house nearly a thousand people. Eunuchs, serving girls, musicians, courtiers, officials.

It was entirely deserted. Not a single person to be seen. A chill ran down my spine. "It's about to happen. Come on!"

We rushed to the golden doors. It was no shock to find them unlocked. They slid back as easily as silk curtains under Lu Wan Hua's hands. The glorious chambers beyond were dim and silent – just as deserted as the palace outside, although an emperor should normally be attended by dozens of guards and servants at all times.

"Your Majesty!" Lu Wan Hua called. Her voice echoed from the vast, vaulted ceilings. "Your Imperial Majesty, you are in danger!"

There was no answer.

"What if she's not here?" I asked. "What if she's in

another part of the palace entirely?"

"She must be here somewhere. They wouldn't go to the trouble of clearing this whole wing for nothing. Find her!"

We split up and raced through the shadowy rooms, searching for any hint of a human presence. I felt despair creeping over me – *too late, too late* – when Lu Wan Hua let out a cry. "Hua Zhi! Here!"

I found her in a vast bedchamber. Unlike the rest of the suite, it was warm and well lit with several braces of hanging lanterns, and the scarlet and jade colours dazzled my eyes. Lu Wan Hua was kneeling by the massive bed, over a messy heap of embroidered cloths tumbled on the floor. I recognized the pattern of the fabric – red peonies and dragons on snowy white.

It was the emperor.

Too late.

Thirty-two

"She's alive," Lu Wan Hua said hurriedly, seeing my face. "I think someone drugged her."

There was a wine flagon and a plate of tiny, flower-shaped pancakes on a tray beside the bed. I sheathed my sword to search the thick rug where the emperor lay and found a fallen cup. Drops of dark liquid still stained the rim.

I sniffed it, but could only smell the strong odour of grape wine. "Is it poison?"

"I don't think so. I've seen fast-acting poison at work before. Her Majesty's heartbeat and breathing are normal, and there's no bleeding. She's just sleepy and confused."

As if to confirm her words, the emperor let out a weak moan and shifted restively. I knelt beside her, but her glazed eyes passed over my face without recognition.

"Do you think we could carry her together? Get her out?" I asked.

"Out where?" Lu Wan Hua sat back on her heels. "Nowhere in the palace is safe for her now. Everyone loyal's been locked up, the servants are terrified, and the guards have been sent away. Anyone who's out there belongs to the traitor. Whoever they are, they must plan to confront her themselves – so we have to be here to stop them once and for all, or..."

I knew she was right. But, Great Dragon and Phoenix, the *risk*. This was the emperor's life. The future of our empire. If we made a mistake, if we failed, everything we knew would be finished, including our own lives.

Did we truly have the right to make that kind of decision, disreputable misfits that we were? What would my father have done? What would Wu Jiang have done? Surely either of those men would have had some sort of clever plan.

"Hua Zhi." Lu Wan Hua touched my arm. "What are you thinking?"

I closed my eyes for a second. What was the reality? There was no one else here. We were all the emperor had now. We had to make the decisions – and be prepared to live with the consequences. I swallowed hard, then opened my eyes.

"We should move her to the bed. That's what the traitor will expect to see when they come in. We'll hide, let them show themselves, then use the element of surprise to subdue them."

Lu Wan Hua's eyebrows went up for a moment as she

worked it through in her mind, then she nodded. "That makes sense. You get her legs. I apologize for this, Your Imperial Majesty."

"Me, too," I said through gritted teeth, bracing my knees as we hefted the emperor between us and lifted her up on to the silken counterpane. She was a slender woman, but her robes alone probably doubled her weight, and she was wearing several pounds' worth of jewellery, too. My injuries were already protesting all this exertion. The pain sapped my strength.

I slumped against the side of the bed to catch my breath, studying the emperor anxiously. One of her hands twitched, batting at the air, and I realized that her hair – loosened from the elaborate hairstyle I had seen earlier, perhaps in anticipation of going to bed – had fallen over her face and was annoying her. I dared to reach out and brush it back.

Her eyes seemed to sharpen suddenly. "Hua Zhi? Where… No. Wu Jiang?"

"He's not here, Your Majesty," I whispered. "I'll find him for you as soon as this is over."

"Warn … Wu Jiang … My son." But her gaze had already slipped away, head lolling sideways on the lush pillows.

"You take the curtain beside the bed," Lu Wan Hua said. "I'll hide behind the screen."

I gave her a grateful look. Concealing myself in the curtain would allow me to lean on the massive carved bedpost. She acknowledged my gratitude with a quick tap on my shoulder, and then we separated again, Lu Wan

Hua melting into the shadows behind the screen. She might almost be a banner-breaker herself, I thought as I drew my sword. I realized I'd never actually told her about my gift. I'd simply forgotten.

One last secret to share, then. *Later, if we survive this and the emperor doesn't have us both killed.*

In all our urgency to infiltrate the palace, a sense of time spinning away from us had enveloped me. I really expected the traitor to burst in at any moment. But the wait dragged on. And on. Minutes mounted into an hour. Sprawled on the bed behind me, the emperor seemed to slip into an uneasy sleep. Despite my awareness of the intense danger of the situation, the sound of her faint snores made my own lids become heavy.

I was so tired. My bones ached with it. I pressed my forehead into the cool, lacquered side of a carved dragon on the wooden bedpost, and tried to keep my mind alert by mentally running over each individual thread of my shadow face, tracing and manipulating the bruises and cuts I had transferred from my bare skin. When that wasn't enough to keep me awake, I began to seek patterns on the carved panels of the walls – a face, a dog, a lizard, no – a snake... My blurry gaze fixed insensibly on the tray by the bed. I blinked. Alongside the pancakes and flagon of drugged wine, there lay a spray of white flowers. White chrysanthemums. The flower that symbolized nobility and elegance.

The flower one left as an offering on the altars of dead relatives.

I almost missed the faint noise of a door sliding open.

It came from an entirely different direction than the one I had trained myself to listen for. Not several rooms away, at the great golden doors that guarded the entrance to the Dragon Chambers, but close by – in this room. From the wall beside the bed.

By the very bedpost where I stood.

I straightened, fingers tightening on my sword hilt as my eyes found a part of the intricately carved and gilded wall – a part that looked identical to any other – slowly, slowly inching back. A panicked rush of blood made my head pound and my skin tingle. It was a hidden entrance. A secret door.

The panel clicked fully open.

The Young General stepped into the emperor's bedroom.

Dressed in silk court robes in rich, seasonal colours of bronze and gold, hair smoothly drawn back into a topknot and secured with an intricate *ji* that glittered with garnets, he looked the picture of a noble scion making a dutiful visit to his aunt. Except for the bared sword held casually in his right hand … and the black-and-gold-painted dagger clutched in the left.

There was no time for shock. For disillusionment or disbelief or confusion. Nothing that had come before mattered. His intentions now could not have been clearer if he had carried a banner marked with them.

Wu Jiang was the traitor. I had to stop him.

I drew my sword and I stepped from behind the curtain. "Don't come any closer, General."

Just like that, Wu Jiang's calm, resolute expression

shattered into one of abject horror. He actually swayed where he stood. "What are – no, you can't be here, Hua Zhilan – you have to leave, now!"

It was not the reaction I had expected. All I could think to say was, "In case you hadn't noticed, I'm not taking your orders any more."

It was as if he hadn't heard me. Instead of backing away he came towards me, gesturing with the dagger as if it were an ink brush or a chopstick. "Quickly. You can leave through this exit – it leads back to my chambers. Wait for me there—"

"Stop!" I raised my sword in clear threat. "Do you honestly imagine I would walk away and allow you to slaughter an innocent woman?"

"She is not innocent!" The furious shout made my muscles tighten like iron wires.

The emperor stirred and let out a soft whimper.

Wu Jiang drew in a deep breath through his nostrils, staring at me. "Why are you here? Why didn't you go back to the barracks to collect your escort like I told you? You were never meant to be here."

"I don't care what you ordered or what you planned," I snapped. "You are a traitor. *The* traitor. Nothing you say means anything to me." My mind was slowly grinding into motion, working to put the pieces together. How could this be? Wu Jiang, the emperor's nephew, the hero of the army...

My memory went back to that morning and the dark look on his face when his aunt had declared him regent. Back further, to the betraying note that I had brought with me from the Leopard's desk – the same note that I had entrusted to Wu Jiang, which he had avoided handing over to the emperor by unmasking me. All his protestations of affection that morning – a mere cover.

He was the reason for the Leopard's elaborate strategy, and why none of it had ever seemed to make sense. Because the plan was not for Feng Shi Chong to ascend to the throne. It was for Wu Jiang to do so.

How had I ever flattered myself that I understood this man?

"Your plan won't work," I said. "You may have arranged to slaughter all her leading supporters in the war cabinet and have the emperor name you regent, and you may have pushed the blame for everything on to the Leopard so far, but I won't let you kill her. This ends now."

"Everything I have done has been for the good of the empire." He spoke slowly, as one might address an inattentive child.

"Giving that madman Feng Shi Chong the information and resources he needed to rampage through the empire? That was for our own good?"

"Yes," he said, eyes deadly earnest. "Of course I regret every single one of the citizens that have been lost – but Feng Shi Chong was already in full revolt when I stepped in. By controlling and manipulating him in the guise of an ally, I prevented dozens of senseless attacks and saved countless lives. And by using him to create this situation, I can ensure that my rise to power is as bloodless as possible. Once I've succeeded, he will be easily disposed of, and we will finally have a true and lasting peace."

Am I really hearing this? "We could have had peace all along if you hadn't aided him! If you hadn't been plotting to kill your own aunt and use her son to rise to power under a veil of legitimacy!"

"You don't understand. She is not innocent," he repeated, softly this time.

"And what has the rightful emperor done that could possibly justify your actions?" I demanded.

He swallowed, then nodded to himself as if reaching a decision. He placed the Leopard dagger down gently next to the spray of flowers he had sent to his aunt. I edged closer to the emperor, the small of my back pressing into the edge of the bed, but his free hand only came to rest against his chest, fingers spreading over the cloth as if to soothe an ache there.

"She murdered my mother."

Even after all that had happened, what I now knew about him, the pain in the simple words affected me. My sword point wavered, dropping out of guard position briefly before I forced it back up. "You said she was poisoned by her enemies at court."

"Her enemy was Wu Fen." His eyes stared beyond me, haunted. "My mother was a princess. The old emperor's favourite sister. When Wu Fen was a mere concubine, she pushed for my mother to marry her brother, my father, to secure the House of Wu's position. But my mother was too beloved and respected in court. She was too powerful. A rival. Once Wu Fen took the throne for herself, she served her own sister-in-law a cup of poison – and watched her drink it, and die.

"Then she took me. My father had to let me go. He warned me: 'Don't cross my sister. Don't speak up too loud. Don't try her patience. Don't be like your mother.' I always knew that my own life was being held at the knife-point of his compliance to Wu Fen's will – and his life, and my stepmother's and siblings', was being held at the knife-point of mine. I must serve her, and please her, and never give her the faintest doubt of my loyalty. Or the rest of my loved ones would be rotting beside my mother before I had the chance to regret it."

He looked at me again. His eyes were wet. "We are her family. And she made us hostages. My whole life, she used us against each other."

He was Wu Jiang, the hero of Black Gorge, the Young General. The golden storybook prince. But he spoke not of fairy tales – but a nightmare. A tortured existence, a half-life spent in constant watchfulness. Never free. Never safe. Always afraid. If it was true… If it was true, what then? My sword point, almost against my will, began to drop back towards the floor.

In that teetering, queasy moment of doubt, Lu Wan Hua struck.

She appeared from the Young General's left, barely disturbing the tapestry that she had crept behind. Her sword made a technically perfect strike towards his unprotected side – and I opened my mouth to scream a warning, because I could already see that it would not work. He was too fast. Before I could get out a single word, his sword was moving, his body whirling into motion.

Their blades met with an eye-watering shriek of metal,

and Lu Wan Hua's sword flew from her hand. She twisted to avoid the return cut of Wu Jiang's sword. The movement brought her into range of his left hand. She made a helpless grunt of pain as his fingers seized her flying hair and forced her head down into the upward drive of his knee.

There was a terrible *crunch* and a bright spurt of scarlet. Lu Wan Hua fell, trailing blood from her nose. The Young General's sword flicked out to touch the curve of her neck.

It had taken less than two seconds.

"No!" The words finally unclogged from my tongue. "Don't kill her!"

He tilted his head at me, unruffled. "You know this … this painted whore?"

"She is my friend," I pleaded.

Lu Wan Hua coughed, spitting out a mouthful of blood. Wu Jiang made a sound of disgust, and placed his foot on her ribs to keep her still. She froze beneath him. Her eyes sought mine, and I stared back helplessly. I remembered exactly how it felt to be in that position. How the Leopard's foot had ground upon my vulnerable ribs, and I had known I was going to die.

Lu Wan Hua had saved me then. I must save her now.

Think of something. Come on. You're supposed to be good at plans. Think of something!

"This is not a fitting friend for you," the Young General was lecturing. "Look at her! Where did you even meet such a creature?"

I wanted to say that she was the current incarnation

of his beloved Dou Xianniang, that it was his own ideal that he crushed beneath his foot. But it wouldn't matter. He wouldn't believe it.

He did not know how to tell what he imagined from what was real. He never had.

"She is a person, not a creature – a person who has suffered through your actions. Her home was destroyed and family were murdered by Feng Shi Chong. Just as the people of the bamboo forest were murdered. Do you think she, or they, find it a comfort to know that their lives were ruined in your mother's name? What about Diao, and Yun?"

I saw the twitch of his shoulders and the words I had been about to say died. I felt my eyes widen, and the change reflect on my shadow face. His jaw clenched in response.

"You. It was you who killed them. Not Lu."

"Don't judge too harshly!" he protested. "I simply took advantage of the situation Lu had created. The fool thought he would curry favour with the Leopard by killing me. He never realized I was the one who had been paying him for intelligence." He leaned forward a little, seeming suddenly eager to explain himself to me.

I flicked a quick glance downward. Lu Wan Hua's eyes met mine again, and she nodded minutely. *Keep him talking.*

"But why?" I asked. "Why kill Diao – why – why the attack on the camp—"

"Diao was too loyal to Wu Fen. And the emperor trusted him. She planned to make him the crown prince's guardian and regent. I couldn't allow that. But I needed the attack as cover. You saw Wu Fen's fury over my failure to protect Diao. Without the excuse of having had to fight for my own life, she would have punished me severely."

My mind simply did not have the capacity to encompass such pragmatic savagery. "So when you came to see me in the stockade … making me fight to convince you that I was innocent, your promise to talk to Diao and not trust Lu … that was all lies. You'd already killed Diao and you knew Lu was a traitor. Why did you even bother to talk to me at all? Why let me out?"

He smiled ruefully. "I liked you. I wanted to test you, see how you would answer me – and I didn't want you to die in there. From the moment our blades crossed, I could tell you were special. After you killed Lu for me, I admired your loyalty and bravery more than ever. I wanted them on my side, and I wanted to reward you. That was genuine. Everything we've felt for each other since then, everything I've said to you, has been genuine."

No, no, no. I couldn't bear to listen to his attempts to woo me while Lu Wan Hua lay there, bleeding, under his heel.

"How did you know about the hunting party in time to tip off the Leopard? You said the emperor kept everyone in the dark about it until that morning. But you had to have sent that note at least a week in advance."

"Oh, she'd been planning it for a month – and she doesn't keep Li Xian in the dark. I gave him a trained message hawk two years ago as a birthday present. He writes me messages constantly, and no one has ever bothered to check what he says."

There was an image in my mind – the first moment I had seen the Young General, a giant on a rearing horse, burning against the sky … and a tiny hawk diving above him. He must have had his bodyguards deal with the bird whenever it returned to him, knowing that those men would jealously guard the duty, and the knowledge that he was receiving messages, from me.

Wu Jiang went on. "The whole time that Wu Fen had me out there surveying our forces, Li Xian was unwittingly passing on information. I used that information to control Feng Shi Chong. Don't you see? I've tried to arrange everything so that there would be as little bloodshed as possible. And I know that it went wrong, that the Leopard took you and hurt you … and I will spend years apologizing for that if I have to, but I promise I never meant for it to happen. It *wouldn't* have happened, if Wu Fen hadn't been so stubborn that day – she was supposed to pick me to guard her, not send me off with the boy. I'm just relieved that I had given orders for the rebels to take Wu Fen alive or I could have lost you…" His voice actually broke.

"I don't care about that," I said, hurriedly trying to redirect him again. "Why—"

"We don't have time for more explanations," he said, falling back into that soothing, authoritative cadence. "I promise, later, I'll answer anything you want to know. I've kept so many secrets for so long, I believe I'll enjoy telling all of them to you – but for now, you have to leave."

I drew in a shuddering breath, my gaze flicking to Lu Wan Hua once more. "You know I can't."

Unbelievably, he smiled at me again, that boyish dimple winking. "You can. You can even take your friend with you, if you wish." He nudged Lu Wan Hua's side casually. She closed her eyes.

"Hua Zhilan, clear your head of emotion and think. Once Wu Fen is gone and I am emperor, there will be no one to stand in the way of our union. I know it's more than you probably hoped for, but I mean it. You are everything I had dreamed of in my first wife, my empress. Brave, virtuous, loyal and modest. Together we can bring a new golden age to the Land of Dragons, the rebirth of the Red Emperor and his empress." His eyes glowed. "Just think of it. All the good we can do – that you could do. Don't you want that?"

On the bed, the emperor thrashed suddenly, letting out a pained moan. I knew why.

"And what will happen to Li Xian in your golden future, Wu Jiang?" I asked softly. "The boy you have been appointed to guard, to guide on to the throne? That little boy who adores you, and trusts you? What are you planning to do with him?"

Wu Jiang lifted his chin. But he did not answer.

The emperor moaned again, breath catching on a sob. "No. No…"

"I was a little boy when my mother was murdered," Wu Jiang said evenly. "Almost the exact age that Li Xian is now. And since then I have worked for this day. For this outcome. This moment. For years on end, I have played the fool and the nursemaid, and the doting nephew. Schemed and lied, bribed, killed. All that I have done has been to avenge my mother, and to free this empire from the rule of an unnatural, corrupt woman who should never, ever have been allowed to seize power. My cause is right and just. I care for you more than I have ever cared for any woman, Hua Zhilan. I even admire the moral strength that makes you resist me now. But I will not allow you to stop me. You know that you cannot win against me. So leave. Take this girl here if you want, and go home as you were ordered to. And when I come for you again, all this blood and darkness will be behind us, and we shall begin again in the light."

His shoulders loosened, and he raised his sword so that it hung above Lu Wan Hua's neck. "Stay? Try to fight me? And you and she will both die."

He was right. My fingers clenched to the point of pain on my sword grip as I realized it, cold sweat springing up on my lip and brow. I had never reckoned on facing Wu Jiang in an open fight. His strength and skill were beyond my level even if I had been at peak fitness. And though duty told me I should, must, try anyway … Lu Wan Hua lay beneath his foot. He would kill her before I could even complete my first strike.

I couldn't win.

Are you a coward, daughter?

Slowly, shaking and clumsy, I bent and laid my sword down on the rug beside my feet.

Lu Wan Hua gasped. "No!"

"Quiet!" Wu Jiang jabbed her with his foot. She curled up around the kick, choking for breath.

"Let her up," I demanded.

He turned that same glowing look on me. "I will. I will. But first you must show me you mean it. Show me … your face. Your real face."

The emperor sobbed dryly.

No. No. No. Fine tremors of fear and revulsion rocked my body. *Are you a coward, daughter?*

I whispered, "All right."

Thread by thread, I unravelled the *qi* that made up the surface of Zhi's face. It felt like pulling away the fibres of my own skin, clawing away layers of vein and muscle to expose the vulnerable, beating flesh of my heart.

"Yes," he whispered. What did he see? Whatever it was, whoever it was – I knew it wasn't me. He had never seen me. "Yes. You are as beautiful as I had imagined."

His foot lifted from Lu Wan Hua's chest as he stepped towards me, his sword point moving away from her throat. I let him approach, lowering my eyes modestly and tucking my hands together at my waist, though the dark, borrowed clothes had nowhere to hide them. I didn't want to meet his eyes.

"Look at me," he said softly. "So lovely, my orchid, my Zhilan."

I lifted my face to his, but kept my eyes closed. "Wu Jiang…"

Fingers caressed the loose strands of hair that had escaped from my topknot to fall around my face. I felt his larger frame curving around mine as *yang* embraces *yin*, and then his parted lips pressed against mine. My hands went to his shoulders to steady myself. I felt the muscles beneath my palms relax, ever so slightly.

Are you a coward, daughter?

I brought the bony point of my knee up between his legs as hard as I could.

No, Father. I am of the House of Hua.

Wu Jiang's breath left him in an explosive huff as he doubled over. I clamped both my hands down on his right forearm – his sword hand – throwing my whole weight on to it, digging desperately into the tendons of his wrist, trying to make him release the sword.

Wu Jiang was too strong. His open left hand dealt me a stunning blow to the side of the head that jerked his sword hand free and sent me sprawling back on to the rug.

"Whore…" he said, gasping, face twisted with fury. Tears stood out in his eyes. "Lying, traitorous…" He raised his sword above me in a powerful two-handed grip.

I am of the House of Hua.

I flung up my hand, drawing up *qi* with every bit of training and strength I had, all my rage and desperation, fear and heartbreak. And then … I let it go.

A cloud of dense nothingness burst from my palm. It was the dark that had cloaked my father's house the night the assassins came, and the dark of the dried black blood in that little house in the bamboo forest. The blackness of my endless, soul-destroying journey into the Leopard's caves, and the choking toxic smoke of the smelting tower. It was the darkness of Wu Jiang's own eyes. All the darkness that filled my nightmares, now, and always would. The darkness that had formed me, again and again, and made me who I was. It was inside me.

The illusion expanded like a thundercloud born on a storm wind, and enveloped the Young General's upper body. It wrapped around his face like a mask – the dark mirror of my own.

He screamed, dropping his sword and clawing at the shadows. He was blind.

The blackness writhed and swarmed, reforming and growing around him. Darker, darker. I did not have to push it, or force it. There was no need to hide any more, no need to hold back as I had always done, ready to disappear. My enemy was before me, and Lu Wan Hua was here. The energy poured out of me in a river of shadows, endless. Wu Jiang turned, stumbling, trying to run. But there was no escape.

The flagon of drugged wine hit the floor with a shrill shattering sound, spilling scarlet droplets everywhere. White chrysanthemum petals scattered, flecked with red. Lu Wan Hua was on her feet. She lunged towards the column of shadows in a single, fluid movement – and buried the black-and-gold dagger deep.

I rolled out of the way as Wu Jiang let out a harsh grunt of pain and crumpled where he stood, falling to the rug. My fingers curled, drawing the dark tide of *qi* effortlessly away from him. It flowed back into my skin like smoke, and disappeared. I pulled the warm, living *qi* of my shadow face – no, my *real* face – back into position with relief, then swiftly looked down.

Wu Jiang was still alive, but no longer a danger to us. His face was grey, agonized, and he shuddered, hands clutching at his side, at the blood-smeared hilt of the dagger with which he had meant to murder his aunt. He grunted again, clearly holding a cry behind his teeth.

Lu Wan Hua made a move towards the sword that Wu Jiang had dropped. I could see her intention in her squared shoulders and clenched jaw. She was going to finish him off. Impulsively, I put out my hand to hold her back.

Her gaze met mine, questioning. I shook my head. Understanding flashed between us, that strange unspoken understanding the two of us had always shared, even with all our secrets and misunderstandings. Maybe it was pity. Maybe it was something that, in another life, could have grown into love. But I did not want to see Wu Jiang die at Lua Wan Ha's hand.

Her fingers found mine and clasped them tightly for a moment. Then she kicked the sword out of Wu Jiang's reach, swiped at her still bleeding nose, and stepped away. "I'll find some cords to tie him up, just in case, before I summon the city guard."

Beside me on the bed, the emperor dragged herself over into a slumped, half-sitting position. She supported her weight on the bedpost with shaking, clenched fingers, breathing heavily, her hair still hanging in her face as she stared at me. Her expression seemed mostly of disbelief. But there was something else in her face, too. Something that might have been … admiration. Something that might have been awe.

"Bring bandages, too," she ordered Lu Wan Hua, her voice hoarse. "He must live long enough to be properly punished for this."

A low groan escaped the Young General at the emperor's threat. But his twisted face was turned towards me, not her. "No ... Zhilan ... my orchid..."

Wu Fen let out a ragged laugh, one broken with something terribly close to tears. "That is no *flower*, you fool. It is a praying mantis."

"And my name," I said fiercely, "is Hua Zhi."

Epilogue

There. That is my tale, complete at last, told in all of its strange, misfit truth. Just as your parents – or was it your aunt? Your teacher? Well, no matter – requested me to relate it to you.

It isn't much like the ballads, is it, child? Oh, there was love, and there were great battles, and there was betrayal and friendship and nobility, just as you might expect – but … somehow in real life things are never quite as simple, as clean, as the songs and stories make them out to be. And the more songs and stories they make up about you, the less truth seems to end up in any of them. For all that they are my stories, they still have the power to surprise me.

What's that? No, of course things didn't end there; you see me before you, don't you? A wrinkled old warrior, scarred and tanned, long in years and grey of hair. Nearly fifty years have passed since we finally choked Feng Shi Chong's rebellion to death, Lu Wan Hua and I. A miserable campaign that was, fighting all through the winter, through battlefields where the fallen drowned in icy mud before their injuries could kill them, and frostbite and exposure stole more men than the enemy did.

But without the Young General to direct the rebel troops and feed them tactical information, the ill-disciplined, badly trained army of criminals stood little real chance. Though they did damage enough before the end.

I began the campaign, at the emperor's order, as a captain, with my own hand-picked company. Lu Wan Hua was my sergeant. By the time we dragged the Leopard back to the City of Endless Serenity for trial – in an iron cage of his own, which brought us some satisfaction, I can tell you – I was a colonel. Field promoted, of course, but still no mean achievement. No mean achievement for anyone, let alone a soldier who had been revealed – as they saw it – as "female" before the entire court. Even after saving the emperor and unmasking Wu Jiang, by rights a person who had lied about their legal identity as I had should have been, at the very least, sent home in disgrace.

But Wu Fen liked me. I think. As much as an emperor can like any mere mortal.

She decreed that if a female could be the Daughter of Heaven, there was no reason those with the talents possessed by Lu Wan Hua and me shouldn't be soldiers, too. And if part of me wanted to argue that I was not truly a daughter, Lu Wan Hua's warning look and my own common sense kept that objection between my teeth, at least in the emperor's presence. It wasn't a very popular move, at first. But she commissioned her court poets and musicians, and artists and weavers to create every kind of art from the story of what I, and Lu Wan Hua, had done. By the time the war was over, we were more than two oddities who had defied law and convention. We were legends.

The Noble Warrior Maiden, the Lady Banner-Breaker, the Shadow Soldieress... My, they did give me a lot of names. In time I learned to live with them, though they never truly felt right, felt like mine. I envied Lu Wan Hua. They just called her Dou Xianniang, since that name already had its own power.

But there's always another war. Another uprising. Another fight. First it was a short-lived but messy rebellion in the eastern provinces, and then the invasion attempt from the Land of Clouds. We were promoted again, and I was offered a seat in the war cabinet. I took it, of course. My father was so proud. Bewildered, but proud. My mother, when she brought my littlest brother to meet me at last, nearly fainted at the finery of the chambers where Lu Wan Hua and I lived. She was more impressed by the thickness of the carpets than by any of my official honours – and I can't really argue that she was wrong.

Why should comfort, and home, be less important than glory?

A few more years passed before I finally understood the choice my own father had made, to walk away from it all. I think it was after we put down the Plains Rebellion that I began to realize I wanted more than to be a soldier for the rest of my life. Even a general.

The emperor was not entirely happy. But the legend of Dou Xianniang and the Noble Lady Warrior was still powerful enough to offer us some protection and, as I said, I do think she liked me. Just a little. And so, to Mother and Father's joy, I returned home.

I had been at war for twelve years.

I never married, of course. Well, they wouldn't let me marry Lu Wan Hua, would they? There was some idea at one point that we might both marry our neighbour Wang's son, and live as sister-brides under his roof; it would have been an easy way to become a family legally, and to have children. He was a handsome young man, too. Unfortunately, young Wang was quite clearly more frightened of us than his parents were keen for such a prestigious match. His bugged-out eyes might have made Lu Wan Hua giggle charmingly, but it simply wouldn't do.

She always accused me of putting a stop to the plan because I was jealous. Well, maybe I was. Or maybe I just could not bear to be forced into that unambiguously female role – bride, daughter-in-law, wife – after I had come to accept myself as someone else entirely. The thought of donning a gown, a wedding gown, even for a single day, made me miserable. I am human, even if the stories dispute it.

Instead, we built a new wing in my family's home, and Lu Wan Hua was adopted by my father. Then we, in turn, adopted our daughters with the help of the women of Dou Xianniang's safe house. My little butterflies, those girls. How proud Lu Wan Hua was of them. How proud.

Wan'er was the child of a man executed for treason. Her family were exiled, and in their hurry to escape, they abandoned her as worthless. She is now the prime minister of our nation. And a very gifted poet. I put that down to Lu Wan Hua's influence, for she was ever the lover of poetry herself. Remind me to give you a volume of Wan'er's works. I have several lying around here somewhere...

Ai was left on the steps of a temple as a baby – probably because her family had too many children and did not want another girl. She is married, with three daughters and two sons of her own now, and very happy. When she brings her family to visit, and they mix with my nephews and nieces and great-nephews and -nieces, the old house feels like a zoo. My mother would have been very glad to see such a healthy, numerous family. It was what she wanted for me – what she had always wanted for herself. She saw it begin, at least.

How I miss her, these days.

Your face seems troubled, young one. Have I shocked you? Or do you have any questions left to ask?

You want to know about Wu Jiang?

Of course you do – though that part of the story brings me little satisfaction. He was executed, obviously, but not until the palace interrogators had made him spill all his secrets. I would say his death came as a kindness by that point, but the emperor did not grant him a kind death. He had to be made an example of.

I never dared ask the emperor about her nephew's story, that grim tale he confided in her bedchamber that night. I never dared say his name in her presence at all, after the grim spectacle of his death was finished. She may have liked me, but not that much.

Although your question does remind me… Thinking back, the emperor did mention the Young General, and his mother, to me once. Just once. As it happens, it was shortly after I had requested retirement. I was waiting on her in one of her more private receiving rooms, and some of her waiting women were playing a new piece for us – a ballad involving a recent though minor victory on the battlefield against some truly moronic bandits. Under cover of the music, she asked me:

"Do you truly believe that you can happily retire to some provincial town in the mountains, and spend the rest of your life … weaving and … and raising goats and brats? You will be driven to the edges of sanity in a month, and crawl back to the City of Endless Serenity begging for your sword and your men."

This was a stinging rebuke, made all the more so by the genuine annoyance – and perhaps even hurt – in her voice. She seldom allowed such emotions to surface. Not after Wu Jiang. So it was with him in mind that I replied, "My emperor, there may be times when I grow bored and restless, and regret my decision. But you no longer need me, or Lu Wan Hua, here. The empire is at peace. My great battles have been fought. Let younger, fresher soldiers take their place at your side. Give them the chance to glory in serving you, as I have."

"Your tongue grows as silver as your hair. Perhaps you *are* getting old," she murmured acidly, staring beyond me, with bleak eyes, at the young, pretty girls who laughed over their instruments on the other side of the room. Fine, powdery lines of white make-up gathered in the marks of age on her face. She was still beautiful, but she was no longer anything like a girl. And she was right. Though I was not yet thirty, bright silver already streaked my hair.

"Perhaps so," I said, unruffled. "Great generals should die young, lest they invest too much in fighting and death, and come to resent the peace that they have helped to build."

Her eyes flickered closed for a moment, and I was suddenly sure that she was thinking of Wu Jiang, and perhaps of Feng Shi Chong. "Then you are not a great general."

"No. But *good* generals may survive to retire – because they know when the time to leave the battlefield has come."

She opened her eyes with a sigh, and looked at me, really looked at me, for what was to be the last time. "I loved him, you know. No matter what he believed, I did love him." Staring into those unforgettable eyes, pinned by their humanity, I dared not respond. But I believed her. After a long pause, she whispered, "Just as I loved his mother."

Then she looked away again, at the dancing, singing, laughing children. "Very well. You are a fool, but you have my leave to go. Go … and remember me fondly."

And then she reached into her long, bell-shaped sleeve and withdrew a small object – an object I recognized with astonishment as the bronze hand mirror which I had inadvertently left in her keeping well over a decade before. She pressed it into my hands, stood, and walked from the room.

It was the last time I was ever alone with her. But the mirror is over there, see, in the cabinet next to the fire. It is still one of my most cherished possessions.

I puzzled over her words for a long time. They were not, by any means, a confession – but I was sure they contained an answer of some kind. The emperor loved Wu Jiang. That did not save him from a grisly death. The emperor said she had loved his mother, too. And she had also died.

Whatever the truth, I do know I made the right choice that night in the Dragon Chamber.

My, how the time has flown! Night is drawing in. I expect the servants will be in to light the lamps soon, and my granddaughter will come to chide me, bid me drink one of those vile cordials the doctor mixes up, and make me rest.

You know, when this little study belonged to my father, he liked to leave the screens open at night. He would sit here, in the dark and the quiet, and watch the stars wink to light in the deep well of blue above the mountains. I thought it a rather strange habit, at the time. But now I find I enjoy doing the same thing.

The stars change, but they remain the same. As do we all.

That is my story, child. Have you any more questions?

No?

Good.

If you – or someone you know – have been affected by any of the issues in this book, the following organizations offer support for people of all genders.

Childline
www.childline.org.uk
Call for free from the UK on 0800 1111.

Samaritans
www.samaritans.org
Call for free from the UK and ROI on 116 123.
Email: jo@samaritans.org

Mermaids: a helpline aimed at supporting transgender young people
www.mermaidsuk.org.uk
Call for free from the UK on 0808 801 0400.
(9 a.m. to 9 p.m., Monday to Friday.)
Email: info@mermaidsuk.org.uk

Switchboard: a LBGT+ helpline
www.switchboard.lgbt/help/
Call at your standard network rate from
the UK on 0300 330 0630.
(10 a.m. to 10 p.m., every day.)
Email: chris@switchboard.lgbt

If you live outside the UK, there are many international organizations that can help you.

ZOË MARRIOTT is the author of many critically acclaimed and beloved books, including *The Swan Kingdom*, which was longlisted for the Branford Boase award and was an USBBY Outstanding International Book. *Shadows on the Moon* won the prestigious Sasakawa Prize and was an American Junior Library Guild Selection. Zoë lives in North East Lincolnshire and is currently the Royal Literary Fellow at York St John University. Visit Zoë's blog at thezoe-trope.blogspot.co.uk or her website at ZoeMarriott.com. Follow her on Twitter (@ZMarriott).

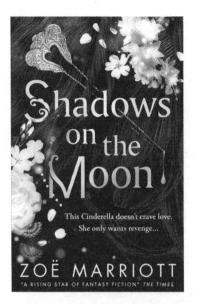

Winner of the Sasakawa Prize.

Suzume is a shadow weaver. Her illusions allow
her to be anyone she wants – a fabulous gift for
a girl desperate to escape her past. But who is
she really? A heartbroken girl of noble birth?
A drudge scraping by in a great house's kitchens?
Or Yue, the most beautiful courtesan in the
Moonlit Lands? Whatever her true identity, she is
determined to capture the heart of a prince – and
use his power to destroy those who murdered her
family. Nothing will stop her. Not even love.

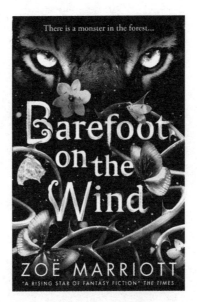

A companion title to Zoë Marriott's critically acclaimed *Shadows on the Moon*.

Everyone in Hana's remote village on the mountain knows that straying too far into the woods is a death sentence. When Hana's father goes missing, she is the only one who dares try to save him. Taking up her hunting gear, she goes in search of the beast, determined to kill it – or be killed herself. But the forest contains more secrets, more magic and more darkness than Hana could ever have imagined, and the beast is not at all what she expects...